PHOENIX

PATRICIA SIMPSON

LUCKY

Phoenix

Smashwords Edition

© 2020 Patricia Simpson

Lucky Publishing

United States of America

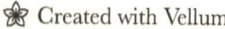 Created with Vellum

To love, you must first love yourself.

For Jessica, pool plotter.
And to Martha for her valuable input and enduring friendship.

1

EVA WILDER PAAR savored her rich chicken soup—happy to be eating without the suffocating presence of her husband Charles—when she heard an insistent knock on the door.

She paused, spoon in the air, and exchanged a quick glance with Hannah Alexander, her cook and servant. Visitors were nonexistent at the manor house in Port Pennwood. She and Charles had no social equals in the small village, and Charles conducted all his business in his office at the processing facility. She couldn't remember the last time a stranger had crossed the threshold of the house. Eva nodded at Hannah to answer the door, and then scooted back her chair to stand up.

The rap turned into an angry thumping. Alarmed, Eva walked toward the main hall, wondering what kind of visitor would knock so insistently. Something must have happened—an accident or cave in, perhaps. Caverns beneath the processing facility had collapsed a couple of times since her arrival and were a constant concern of her husband.

Hannah scurried ahead to pull open the heavy front door while Eva remained on the periphery of the main hall where she could duck back unseen into the dining room if the caller proved to be unimportant. She peeked around the corner.

On the doorstep stood two towering guards and a small man with a scar that ran from the corner of his mouth up to his cheekbone. Eva tried not to stare at the man and the ugly pink line that disfigured his face, but her gaze kept returning to the old wound.

"Out!" the small man barked, yanking Hannah by the elbow. The old woman stumbled over the threshold. "Your employment here is terminated." He set his cane in the small of her back and gave her a cruel shove. Hannah cried out and careened into the yard, flailing her arms to keep her balance.

"Citizen!" Outraged, Eva marched forward. No one barged into the house of a commissioner and treated the hired help that way. She faced the scarred man. "How dare you!"

"Out of my way!" the man snapped. He pushed past her, followed by the two larger men. They wore the uniforms and badges of the Enforcers, the elite security corps of the Overseers. Eva paled. Obviously, something *had* happened—something that concerned the top tier of the government. This could not be good.

Still, she was the wife of a commissioner. This was her house. Hannah was hers to command. She expected rules to be obeyed, even by top-level agents of the Overseers. She set her jaw.

"Citizen, this is my house. You can't just barge in and throw Hannah out."

"I can do anything I like."

"But there's a storm coming. She doesn't even have a wrap."

"Your servant's comfort is no concern of mine." The man looked around the main hall, as if evaluating it for cleanliness and style.

He was slender, smaller than average for Londo City. But he was dressed in the most elegant clothes Eva had ever seen—from his shining top hat and brocade vest to his trousers decorated with diamond-shaped studs from thigh to ankle. His boots were tooled from the finest leather, with a single seam at the back—the sign of high quality footwear. The heels of the shoes were the tallest Eva had ever seen a man wear. He probably thought the heels added to his height and therefore to his masculinity, but Eva thought the high heels produced quite the opposite effect.

He looked like the sculpins that darted in tide pools—fish with large heads, tiny bodies and bulging eyes. Bait-stealers, she'd heard them called by frustrated fishermen.

Eva took an instant dislike of the man's fastidious attire and the sneer on his lips. She stepped around him to look out the door. Hannah stood in the gravel yard, glancing from one potential master to the other—not knowing which person to obey—and grasping her apron with quaking hands. Eva's heart went out to the old woman.

"Hannah," she called. "Come back out of the cold. I am your mistress, not this person."

"Not any more," the man said.

"What do you mean?"

"You are Eva Wilder Paar, correct?"

She raised her chin. "Yes."

"Your husband, Charles Paar, was discovered committing an act of treason today."

"What?" Shocked, Eva stared at the small man, and for a moment was lost for words. She could not believe her cold, strict husband had broken the law. "My husband would never do such a thing."

"He would and he has. He entered an unauthorized zone this afternoon."

"He is the commissioner here. There are no areas prohibited to him."

"Oh, but there are. And he overstepped his authority. A fatal breach of the law."

"Fatal?"

Fatal breach of the law.

Black shadows from the past pressed in on her, playing tricks with her sight and respiration. Shapes blurred. She couldn't take a breath. The high collar of her shirtwaist was suddenly far too tight. She raised a hand to her throat while her thoughts swirled. She seemed to be stuck in a never-ending circle of treasonous partners—first her sister, then Aiden and now Charles. It couldn't be possible.

"Your husband was shot trying to free a prisoner."

"Shot? Is he all right?"

"What part of fatal don't you understand?"

"He's dead?"

"One clean shot to the head." The man smiled. "I never miss."

Eva stepped back, overcome by the news. If Charles were dead, then her life would change in ways she couldn't imagine. The concept of living the rest of her days as a widow was mind-boggling—even if she could think straight, which she couldn't. Not while this heartless man shocked her with every word he uttered.

"He tried to free a woman, but I stopped him."

The neckline of Eva's dress strangled her. She stared at the man, trying to make sense of the information that dropped from his lips.

"Charles would never break the law," she murmured. "Never."

"Perhaps you didn't know the *real* Charles," the man drawled, watching her. He seemed to derive pleasure from her distress. He appeared to be taking in her trauma as a form of sustenance—as if it were a delicious treat. She glanced at him. What kind of monster fed on the anguish of others?

"Does he have a sister?" the man continued. "A close cousin that he would break the law for?"

"No. Charles has no living relatives."

"Then a lover, perhaps?"

"Of course not! He's a married man. He's not like that."

"Does he know a woman named Margaret? What is his connection to her?"

"I've never heard him speak of a person named Margaret."

"Well, he gave his life for her. Stupid, stupid man."

He studied Eva, intently watching her reactions. She was aware that all color had drained from her face, and that couldn't be helped. But she kept a tight rein on her expression. During the months she had been married to Charles, she had mastered the art of hiding every emotion and reaction behind a placid façade. Charles had been critical and unbending. She had learned to avoid his censure by tamping down all facets of her personality and wearing a bland guise while in his presence.

Eva forced her gaze to remain steady and set her mouth in a straight line, even though her entire being reeled behind the mask.

Her composed façade frustrated the small man, as it had with Charles. Scowling, he broke off his glittering stare and swept the air with his cane. "So I am here to search the premises and gather information about your husband. For my report."

"There's nothing here. He never brings his work home."

"And what has he told you about his work?"

"Nothing. He never talks about it. *Talked* about it. I got the impression that he didn't like his work."

"But you know what he did."

"Processed prisoners for the Norsea work camps."

"And what do you understand such processing involves?"

"I don't really know."

He sniffed in derision.

"I'm telling you, I don't know."

"Surely your husband made comments. Pillow talk. That kind of thing."

There had been no pillow talk with Charles, but she would never admit that to a stranger—or anyone.

Thoughts of Charles brought frost to her stare. "No. We didn't talk much. He wasn't interested in what I had to say."

"And you didn't ask."

"I wasn't interested in what *he* had to say either."

"That's a strange attitude for a wife. You're supposed to be interested in a man's job, or at least feign interest."

"I didn't want to know about the people he is—*was*—in charge of. They are criminals. They have violated the law. Why should I care about them?"

"Really?" The man tilted his head. "I was under the impression that you and your sister had a real soft spot for criminals."

She studied the small man. She didn't recognize him, but he seemed to know her. He may have been at Aiden Bannister's execution, but she wasn't certain. That day was still a blur. He knew of her past, though. He must know about Aiden. But did he know everything? She fought to contain her alarm and stared at his short, thick neck and sloping shoulders while she tried to marshal her thoughts.

The only way forward with this man was to hide all traces of fear and take the offensive. She decided to invoke the right of any person living in the Anglo Territories.

"This interrogation has gone far enough," she said. "I would like to see your credentials, citizen."

"Of course." He smiled and pulled out an expensive leather wallet monogrammed with the initials "NM". He held out his ID card.

Eva took it and broke off her regal stare to look at his ID.

A year ago, she would have struggled to make sense of the letters and numbers on the card. But not any more. She hadn't sat around doing needless needlework, waiting for her husband to come home. She had practiced reading, using her sister's illegal book of medicinal plants, and had got all the way to the Rs. She could read proficiently now, except for some of the Latin names of the plants. But even they would come with time and effort.

"Neal Moray," she read out loud. "Provisions Director."

He smiled and reached for his card.

"That's me." He slipped the card into his wallet. "It's a newly created post. But before long, everyone will know about it *and* my name." He looked up at her. "While you, citizen, are now a nobody."

She kept her stare trained on his face.

His cruel smile cut through her. "That's right. As of

this moment, you are no longer mistress of anything, including that silly cow out in the yard."

At his glare, Hannah took off hobbling down the road.

Eva raised her chin. "You have no authority over this household."

"I have every authority. This port and everything in it is under my direction."

"Where is the paperwork to say so? I want to see a signature."

"I don't have to provide a signature. Your husband committed treason. Commissioners who commit treason lose their posts, if not their lives. And wives of commissioners likewise."

"What does this mean for me?"

"You lose this house, elite rations, your husband's salary, social standing and servants."

"But—"

"There are no buts, Citizen Paar. And now, I ask that you quit the premises. Immediately."

She stepped backward. "You'll have to throw me out."

"That can be arranged." Moray hooked the air with a finger. "Gentlemen?"

The burly guards shuffled toward her.

"What about my husband's body? Where is it? I demand to see it!"

"His body is no concern of yours. He was a traitor. He has forfeited his rights and yours."

"You can't do this!" Eva cried, moving backward toward the stairs.

"I can. And I will."

The guards dragged Eva from the house and shoved her out to the gravel yard. She nearly tripped on the hem of her dress. They slammed the doors and turned the lock.

She rushed forward and pounded on the tall wooden doors.

"Let me in!"

No one responded. She ran to the window and peered through the glass, and spotted the guards thundering up the staircase. Minutes later, they opened the windows on the upper floor and threw out her and Charles' belongings.

"No!" Eva shrieked. Petticoats and dresses sailed to the ground around her. She stood at the edge of the lawn watching her world dropping around her. Everything she had endured, all that she had given up for her position as a commissioner's wife, was being wiped out with each piece of clothing that fell at her feet.

She ran back to the door.

"Let me in!" She pounded with both fists. "*I* haven't done anything wrong!"

Moray swept open the door and stood on the threshold, his cane planted in one hand and a pistol in the other. He aimed the gun at her face.

"Get out," he said.

"I don't deserve this kind of treatment. I'm not a traitor!"

"I said get out. Or I'll shoot."

"You can't shoot an unarmed citizen."

"Really? What kind of fantasy world do *you* live in?"

Apparently she *had* been living in a fantasy world as far as her husband was concerned, but she would have to think about that later. "I have no place to go. What will I do?"

"I couldn't care less. Now get out!" He shot the ground near her feet. Gravel sprayed upward, stinging her face and hands. He cocked the gun again. She sprinted across the yard to the side of the house where shrubbery offered more protection. If she followed Hannah down the drive, she would be shot in the back. She was sure of it.

Eva ran to the rear of the property, choking on a torrent of indignation and shock. In the space of ten minutes, she had lost everything—and all because of a man. Again.

Behind the manor, the storm churned on the moor, gathering force. She could think of only one place to go.

2

EVA HURRIED along the cliff path, headed for a ramshackle shed on the beach, the only place she could think of to find shelter from the oncoming storm. Angry purple clouds rolled across the moor, dragging night over the land, pursuing her.

She increased her pace, intent on getting to her secret hideout before the rain drenched her. Wet clothes would mean a more miserable night than the one she already expected. Even now, raindrops collected in her brown hair and dripped down her forehead and onto her lashes. Underdressed for enduring the elements, she ran, half-sliding, half-falling down the sandy incline to the beach.

She was free of Charles and their oppressive marriage, and that was a relief. But she had no resources. Nothing.

Eva saw the truth of her situation as if the lightning streaking across the sky were a pen writing out words and the thunder a voice reading it back to her.

Loser. Failure. You are nobody again.

All the things she had sacrificed up to this point: Aiden, her child, her sister, her life in Londo—all those things had been sacrificed in vain. In the end, her marriage and future had come to nothing.

But she refused to cry. Instead, she grimaced at the irony in the world and pushed on.

Eva stumbled through the sand toward the shed. The structure had been built of weathered boards from wrecked ships and smooth pieces of driftwood. It was sited in a ring of rocks that protected it from wind as well as prying eyes. Before she discovered the hut, someone had added a pallet and chair. She'd never slept on the pallet, but tonight she would have to.

A roof had been fashioned of twisted tree limbs interwoven with kelp strands and gorse and covered with more planks. It was surprisingly weatherproof and cozy. She had no matches with which to build a fire, but at least she would be out of the rain.

Eva ducked through the low doorway of the shed, and for the first time that afternoon felt a modicum of relief. She had spent many an afternoon in this sheltered hut, improving her reading skills and learning to play a violin she had found stashed in the attic of the house she shared with Charles. The shed was her refuge, much like the tower garden had been her sister's special place. She would hunker down here for the night. Then in the morning, after she was sure Neal Moray was gone, she would find out what happened to Charles and retrieve some of her belongings from the house.

With both hands, she brushed the wet tendrils from her face and took a deep breath to steady her nerves. The old Eva would have run weeping from the tiny port where she and her husband had lived for the past year. She would have damned Charles and Fate for always working against her. But the new Eva didn't blubber or blame. She knew how useless that was. And more than anything, she refused to run back to Londo City with her tail between her legs. The one lesson she had learned the hard way was that running never solved a person's problems.

Damp and hungry, Eva sank upon the pallet and drew her knees up to her chin. As the hours passed, the storm turned into a gale, and then into a raging tempest that screamed across the beach and the sea beyond. Fortunately for her, she sat safe and sound inside the little hut tucked among the giant rocks. As the storm raged, she succumbed to the traumatic events of the day and fell into an exhausted sleep.

WHEN EVA AWOKE, she was surprised to find she had slept through the night and the storm had passed. She struggled to her feet on cold, cranky joints and brushed the wrinkles out of her skirt. Then she looked at the pocket watch she wore around her neck—her single piece of jewelry. It was 7 am. Just light enough to see her way to the house. She worried that the storm might have ruined the beautiful violin, even though she kept it safely locked in a case. The violin had become her most precious companion. She would go mad if one more thing was ripped out of her life.

The sooner she got back to the pile of belongings that the guards had thrown through the doors and windows, the sooner she would know if the violin was safe and what resources she had left to her. The Others might have come in the night and taken everything. The possibility worried her.

Charles had always claimed there were Others—wild Others, cannibals even—that lurked on the moor. He had never allowed her to go out alone, especially at night. He would have severely chastised her if he had ever discovered she spent hours and hours alone on the beach when he was at work.

But Charles would never chastise her again. She smiled.

All Eva needed was some kitchenware and warm clothing. With a few pots and pans, she could live on the beach if she had to—until she decided what to do. She could survive for a while on seaweed and the creatures that scuttled in the tide pools—even roots from the moor, if she recognized them as edible from Joanna's book.

Joanna would have known what local roots were edible without having to look them up, but Joanna was no longer part of her life. Eva turned away from the memory of her sister. Relegating her sister to the past had been the only way to keep her sanity. Their past must stay in the past forever.

Eva shut the door to the hut and hurried around the ring of rocks that had protected her during the storm. She couldn't believe what she saw. The beach looked like a war zone. Seaweed and driftwood littered the sand for as far as the eye could see. Trees had toppled off the cliff edge and fallen down the eroded bank. But more surprising was the sight of a ship that had run aground in the shallows and had been battered to splinters by the raging wind and waves, leaving its skeleton caught upon the reef. Wooden barrels, crates and rigging bobbed back and forth as the great sea breathed in and out.

Then she spotted a man lying face down near the water's edge, his legs twisted in kelp and his arms splayed out on either side of his body. He wore no jacket, and his white shirt glowed in the gray light of dawn. She could see no other bodies, and yet a good deal of clothing and empty shoes rolled in the surf.

Throwing off her usual reserve, Eva dashed toward the man, hoping he was still alive.

"Citizen!" she called.

He didn't move.

"Citizen!" She fell to her knees beside him. Freezing water soaked through her dress, slip and stockings.

She shook his left shoulder and tried to get a glimpse of his face, but his salt-encrusted hair hid his features. His limbs were covered with sand and seaweed. He was a dead weight beneath her hands. Maybe he had perished after all.

"Sir!" she said, trying again. She rocked his wide shoulders with both hands. His torso was as hard as stone, and shaped in straight lines that angled into a small waist and powerful arms, highlighted by the damp pleats of his shirt. He was much more muscular than Charles had ever dreamed of being, but not as massive as Aiden. As she rocked him, she could feel the man's hardness was made of flesh and blood and not of death. In a matter of seconds, his body heat thawed her frozen hands.

"Citizen, wake up!"

He didn't respond. Eva sighed, exasperated. If she were forced to administer mouth-to-mouth resuscitation, she wouldn't know what to do. She'd seen the lifesaving technique performed once long ago when a child had fallen into the Thames. But she doubted she could remember the steps. Still, she would try. She would have to roll this man onto his back, though, and that would be no small feat.

Eva moved to one side and threw her weight against his left shoulder.

He grunted, but settled right back onto his stomach.

Eva tried again.

"You big lug!" she exclaimed. "Roll over!"

He moaned.

At least he was alive.

She took a moment to assess him, and decided the best recourse was to check his eyes for signs of consciousness. If he were conscious and breathing, he wouldn't have to be resuscitated. That would suit her just fine. She brushed away the curtain of wavy hair that shielded his face and took a look at him.

Eva sucked in a breath.

Below the curve of her hand was the face of the most handsome man Eva had ever seen. His profile was perfectly formed, from his intelligent brow and strong sharp nose, all the way to his full, masculine lips and chin. His black hair, so uncommon in Londo, was wild with wind and sand, and his sideburns cut across his lean jaw, accentuating the tendons of his throat. He wasn't much older than she was, but even in his current condition, he possessed a simmering strength that put her on her guard. She was alone on a beach with a man who could easily overpower her—when and if he ever woke up.

Eva sat back on her heels, poised to jump to her feet. A snippet from her schooldays flitted through her mind.

Strangers bring dangers. Beware, call out, report.

She wasn't sure what to do: stay and help or run for her life. This man exuded danger, not only from a personal safety standpoint but also from the way his physical beauty struck her to her core. She knew how susceptible she could be to a handsome man—or any man that paid attention to her.

Eva would be asking for trouble if she remained on the beach. It would be best if she never set eyes upon this man again. She rose, just as his eyes blinked open.

Eva stared, caught up once again by the stranger's countenance. His eyes were blue. She'd never seen such eyes. They were as blue as the sea glass she collected—those rare jewels she found glowing upon the sand and then transformed into decorative pieces of art.

"Citizen?" she gasped.

The blue eyes searched for the source of the sound and landed on her face. His regard fused her in place. She couldn't have moved away if she'd wanted to. But she didn't want to. She wanted to stand there and stare at his unusual cerulean eyes.

The man glanced up at the sky and then back at her face.

"Is day," he murmured. His words were laced with an accent she had never heard.

"Yes."

"But you stand. In light."

"Yes."

What an odd thing to say. But she couldn't think about that now. "Are you all right?"

He rose on one sinewy forearm. She stepped back.

"Yes, I think," he said. His voice rumbled in a low baritone that reminded her of the sound a wave made when it crashed into a cavern.

"The rest of the crew?" she asked.

"Gone." He coughed and rolled onto his back.

For a moment, she stood there gaping at the plates of muscle showing through his wet, matted shirt. There was not an ounce of fat on the man's frame. Not a single sign of softness.

She realized she had quit breathing. She snapped out of her lapse.

"Citizen, I'm glad you survived, but I really must be going…" She indicated the path up the cliff face. The lighter it became, the greater the chance that someone would steal her belongings. She didn't want to leave the poor man on the beach, but she had to. She gathered up her skirt and took a step toward the cliff.

"Wait...where am I?"

"A small port. West of the city."

"Londo City?"

"Yes."

"Port Pennwood?"

"Yes."

"Then I make good landing." He closed his eyes and sighed. "Thanks God."

Eva shot a glance down the beach. "It seems you are the only one that did. I can see a lot of clothing strewn about. But I don't see any of your companions."

He followed her glance. "Bad storm. Very bad. They are dead."

"But where are the bodies?"

He shrugged.

"Well, the port is not far. Just up the path and to the left. There's a harbormaster who can help you."

"You leave me here?"

"I have to."

"Wait." He sat up. "I go with you."

Her heart skipped in her chest. "Really, citizen, you should rest a while. Recover your strength."

"No. I go." He rose to his feet, like a creature emerging from the deep, with the kelp falling away. He towered above her as he brushed sand and seaweed off his trousers and boots.

She stood rooted to the spot, mesmerized by the sight of his hands and fingers. Aiden's hands had been clumsy, beefy mitts. Charles' hands had been cold and frail. This man's hands, with their long, muscular fingers and sinewy wrists, seemed capable of anything, from brutal violence to exquisite tenderness.

"I go to factory. You take me? Or show me?"

"Factory?"

"Yes. Will you take me there?"

"There's no factory."

His dark brows drew together in confusion.

"There's only a prison," she put in. "A processing facility where people are held before they are shipped to the north."

"I understand there is factory. Warehouse. Wine."

"My husband is the commissioner here. I think I would know about a factory." Her scathing words echoed in her mind, mocking her. Apparently she had no idea what did go on at Port Pennwood.

Then a thought occurred to Eva. This powerful stranger could help her break into the commissioner's house—her house. She could have access to her secret hiding place, if she could only get back into the house—if someone could break down the door. She glanced at the man's powerful shoulders and legs with renewed interest.

"I tell you what. I'll take you to the harbormaster if you do something for me."

"Name this something."

"I'll show you when we get there."

"Do I trust?" His gaze seared over her, judging her. His mouth tipped up to the left when he talked, while his generous upper lip barely moved when he spoke. The unusual way he formed words captivated her. She found herself staring at his mouth, fascinated.

"Why would I lie?" she retorted. Again, her words came back in a mocking echo. She had lied so many times that she wasn't sure what was true or false any more. Her life had been built on lies. Everything she said or did was a ruse to conceal her private thoughts.

Then he smiled. "I decide. Yes."

The man had no idea who he was dealing with. Trust and Eva Wilder were mutually exclusive.

The man stuck out a hand, breaking into her thoughts. "Vinko Sunara."

"Eva P—" Now that her marriage had ended, she would return to her maiden name. *Eva Wilder.* She liked the sound of it. She liked the *independence* of it. She had always been proud to be a Wilder.

"Eva Wilder."

She raised her hand, but then paused. She wasn't wearing gloves. Good manners dictated that she not touch the hand of a strange man, especially with her bare hands. But good manners had done nothing to save her from her fall from grace.

Good manners be damned.

She shook his hand, knowing the gesture marked the end of an old life and the beginning of a new one.

3

THE STEAM CLOCK at the harbor tooted seven when Eva opened the back gate of the property. She gazed at the house beyond the walled garden as a wave of sadness washed over her. This ancient structure had been the crowning glory of her life. She would never live in a home as stately as this. And now she had to say good-bye.

The handsome sandstone house glowed in the pearly morning light, its slate roof dripping with moisture and fog rolling around the foundation all the way to the tall windows on the ground floor. No lights were on. That was a good sign.

Eva shot a glance around the grounds to make sure no agents were lurking in the shadows and then stepped out of the bushes and hurried across the rear garden. She studied the windows of the house, looking for evidence of a new inhabitant. She half-expected Charles to have been replaced overnight with another commissioner.

Vinko followed at a casual pace, taking everything in.

"Nice," he commented.

She assumed he referred to the back garden they

traversed. She had cleared and decorated the space with driftwood, pebble pathways and a magnificent sea glass wind chime—her best work yet. On any other day, she would have appreciated praise for the love and attention she had devoted to this place—as she had never received remarks about her accomplishments from Charles. But today was not the day.

"Can you please hurry?" Eva glared at him over her shoulder.

"What is hurry?" Vinko retorted. "Harbormaster is still in his bed, yes?"

"I'm in a hurry is all."

Vinko caught up with her and sized up the back door of the stone house. Then he glanced at her. "You are thief. Yes or no?"

"No thief." She frowned and glanced at him. Why was she copying his speech pattern? "Like I told you, this is my house."

"And I say, this?" He indicated the house with a sweep of his arm. "Suspicious." He crossed his arms over his chest and looked at her. "No key? You must be thief."

"I got locked out."

"Why are things in yard? Shoe, dress?"

Eva crossed her own arms. "Agents of the Overseers came last night."

"Yes?"

"And they threw them out."

"Why?" His piercing regard cut through her.

"It's a long story." She raised her chin. "And now is not the time to tell it." She nodded at the door. "Will you break down the door or not?"

"For price." He tilted his head. His eyes danced.

"Our bargain was that I would take you to the harbormaster."

"I am not sure I like job now."

"How can I convince you?"

"With kiss." He tapped his cheek and grinned.

Shocked, she stepped back.

"You are beautiful woman," he continued. The ice in his eyes melted into pools of warmth as his gaze flooded her face. "One kiss is price."

"That's never going to happen." She fought back a blush and planted her fists on her hips. "Put your shoulder to that door this instant or leave."

"So you are beautiful, yes. But fun? No." He raised an eyebrow. Even in his disheveled state, his warm smile and that angled mouth beguiled her. She turned away.

"Fun?" she retorted. "Life isn't fun."

"Is not?"

"Not here in the Anglo Territories." She jabbed a finger in the direction of the door. "Now break."

There she went again, mimicking the way he talked.

He sighed and his expressive mouth quirked to one side in a good-natured pout. "I do this. Only for you. One time."

"Thank you." She kept her voice frosty. His forward behavior rattled her, but she refused to let him know it. She'd been living a remote life for months, without the need to interact with anyone but her husband and Hannah Alexander. This brief interchange had made it obvious that the arsenal she had developed during her chilly marriage would be useless against the onslaught of this man's charm. She would have to sharpen her weapons if she wished to remain unaffected by the man.

From now on, men were off limits. She had given up too much of herself for the pampered life she had led with Charles. No more losing herself *and* her future to a man.

. . .

WITH TWO SLAMS of Vinko's powerful shoulder, the lock gave way. Eva walked into the conservatory with the stranger at her heels. He rubbed his right arm as he clomped across the stone floor, taking in the space.

"Nice," he commented.

"My husband was a commissioner."

"Was?"

"He was killed yesterday."

"I am sorry, Miss Eva."

"Don't be. My heart isn't broken."

He studied her for a moment with concern knitting his dark brows. "They throw you out same day?"

"I was told my husband committed treason."

"Ah."

"I had no idea."

"Wives and husbands? Secrets. Everywhere. All."

Eva nodded. But the truth still hurt.

She had longed for a partnership all her life. Someone to love her. Someone who would understand her and share his innermost thoughts with her. Perhaps it was never to be. Perhaps such a partnership was unattainable. Or maybe there was something about her that caused a disconnect with people. She suspected that was the case. She certainly hadn't been successful with relationships.

From here on out, she would have to forge her own path. Whatever she did and wherever she went, she would have to make her own decisions. And this time, she would be very, very careful. Especially when it came to men.

"Stay here," she said. "I'll be right back."

She hurried to the front of the house and out to the yard. The leather violin case glinted in the morning light on top of a mound of clothing. She snatched the instrument from the pile of dresses and scampered back.

Vinko blocked the front entry. He nodded at the case in her arms. "You choose music over this?"

He held up a woolen shawl. In his inarticulate way, he was criticizing her choices. She flushed and clutched the case to her chest. "This violin is very dear to me."

"Will save you? Keep you warm?"

"It keeps me sane."

He quirked his wide mouth again and gazed down at her. The skeptical expression annoyed her, but she could take it. A year of living with a critical husband had given her thick skin.

She tried to brush past him, but he stood his ground and blocked her forward progress to the house. Then his gaze turned to liquid as it had before.

"Music is good." His beautiful eyes shone down on her. He smiled and waved her in. "You are right to choose."

She raised her chin as she walked by him. She could feel his smile pouring over her and she hated him for it. His sunny humor burned her more than any criticism. She knew it was stupid and childish to choose a violin over a warm wrap, but she would never admit it to him.

Eva grabbed a kitchen towel and dried the case as best she could. Then, still carrying the violin, she headed for the servant's staircase off the butler's pantry. Vinko trailed after her.

"Please quit following me," she said.

"I help."

"I don't need your help." Her voice sounded curter than she intended, but she didn't have time to apologize. Soon curious villagers would learn about Charles and come looking for information and spoils of his misfortune. She didn't intend to stick around for that sad party.

Eva hurried up the narrow stairs, strode to her bedchamber and knelt upon the bedroom floor. She used a letter opener from the desk to pry up a plank near the wardrobe. She had discovered the loose plank months ago, and used the space beneath it as a hiding place for spare change hoarded from trips to the tiny market on the quay. Charles had never asked for the money back, and she had stuffed it in a stocking, in case of an emergency. She set aside the plank, looked down, and was surprised to see an ivory envelope lying on top of her secret stash. The envelope bore her name, scrawled in the unmistakable hand of her deceased husband.

Charles had known about her secret stash.

Violation streaked through her. She sat on her heels and choked back tears as her last illusion died. Charles had directed her every move in the house during their marriage. She had not had a single inch of her own space here. She had thought this one secret was hers and hers alone. But she had been wrong. Charles had known. He had known everything. He probably even knew about her seashore getaway. For the second time in the span of twenty-four hours, another facet of her life had been shattered.

Eva swallowed the lump burning in her throat, but it remained like a stone weighing down the noose within her neck.

"Miss?"

Vinko had not obeyed her command to stay downstairs and now stood in the doorway, still holding the shawl and blocking her exit. She stuffed the envelope alongside the credits in the stocking and thought of hiding them both in the folds of her skirt. The man behind her might steal the credits if he knew what the stocking contained. But there was no time for subterfuge. She stood up.

He nodded at the sock hanging from her hand.

"Same as music? Important?" he chided. "One sock only?"

"Yes," she answered. She was too busy swallowing her outrage and grief to think of anything clever to throw back at him. Besides, he probably wouldn't understand sarcasm when it was delivered in a foreign language.

He stepped aside to let her pass through the doorway and return to the main floor. Then he watched from a distance as she stuffed the credits and envelope into the violin case. She was relieved that he made no move to rob her. Afterward, she collected a skillet, small saucepan, plate, cup, matches and utensils and wrapped them in a cloak.

"Why take these things?" Vinko asked. "Where will you go?"

"Anywhere but here." She slung them over her shoulder.

"Friend? Family?"

"No."

"Ah." He frowned, as if he could sense her distress and was making it his own. He held out his hands. "I help you."

"Thank you. But I don't want any help."

He motioned toward the front of the house. "Do you want dress? Shoe?"

"I can get by with what I have. Less to carry."

He regarded her for a moment with eyes that darkened to violet. She thought she read genuine concern in those eyes. She could use genuine concern right about now. She could use a friend. But she knew that accepting kindness from a stranger—leaning on anyone—was the wrong direction to take. She would depend solely upon herself from now on. No leaning. She looked away from his kind, magnetic eyes.

"I have to go," she said. "You can find your way to the harbormaster's house on your own. He can assist you. It's just down the hill. The last building on the left."

He frowned. "Not bargain we make."

"I'm keeping the bargain as much as I care to keep it."

"So you are not to be trusted. You." He sliced the air with one hand. "Your word not good."

"I never said it was." She gave him a final hard glance and then strode out of the garden.

He trailed after her.

"Don't follow me," she snapped.

He stopped near the wind chime. It tinkled in the breeze, producing the only conversation that had ever been made in the garden—besides the chatter in her head.

Eva slipped through the gate and never looked back, even though she could feel Vinko's intense gaze tracking her. She increased her pace, trying to outdistance his regard as soon as she could. The gaze on her back burned as hot as the guilt she felt inside. She had treated him harshly and had not held up her part of the agreement.

"Good luck, Eva Wilder," he called after her, still generous with his care even though she had rebuffed him.

She would need all the luck she could get. The next few days would predict the course of the rest of her life.

4

As Eva lugged her meager belongings down the cliff path, she watched the light rise under a bank of gray clouds. To the east, where the light should have been brighter, she could see only purple. From her year of observing the weather at Port Pennwood, she could predict the sky would stay overcast and another storm would blow in from the east. This time, she would be prepared.

She carried the kitchenware and violin case to the hut and hurried back to the beach to gather driftwood for a fire. Even though she was curious about the letter Charles had left in her secret stash, she would have to read it later. She headed for the cliff.

After the previous night's downpour, it would be a challenge to find dry wood nearby. But there were piles and piles of driftwood at the base of the cliff where she sometimes went to relieve herself. Surely she could find something dry there.

A half hour later, as Eva finished building a fire in the primitive hearth, she heard someone approach the hut. She hid the violin case under the pallet and threw the shawl over the lump, just as a familiar voice called out from beyond the door.

"Eva Wilder? It is I, Vinko Sunara."

The shipwreck victim had found her. She had thought her hiding place was well hidden. But obviously it was not.

Frowning, she opened the door.

"I told you not to follow me," she said. Then she broke off when she saw Vinko standing there with a sack of supplies slung over his back.

"Harbormaster comes soon to help with cargo. I bring more for you." He swung the sack around and held it in front of her.

"How did you find this place?"

"Tracks." He waved at the sand behind him.

"Oh." She hadn't thought of that. She should have.

Without being asked inside, Vinko carried the makeshift sack to the hearth. He had filled a woolen shawl with food as well as a couple of her dresses and under-clothes. Eva watched him unpack the items and was touched by his thoughtfulness. His tall frame and wide shoulders filled the small confines of the shack, and his male energy permeated the air with a disturbing buzz.

She stood at the door, steeling herself against the waves of masculinity that rolled toward her while he moved about her rustic hideaway, making himself at home. She swallowed. His presence unnerved her so much, she couldn't think of a word to say.

"As for me, Vinko," he said over his shoulder, oblivious to her reaction to him, "I am hungry. You?"

She glanced at the bread, cheese and butter, and her mouth watered. But she could not eat with a man who invaded her privacy as well as her equanimity. She remained at the entrance of the hut, upset that Vinko had barged in on her like this. The hut was her domain. Hers alone. She liked it that way.

"I thank you, citizen, for bringing my things. Please, take the bread and cheese for yourself." Then she indicated the way out.

His brow furrowed. "You will not share meal with me?"

"I am not hungry," she lied. "And I have things to do."

He straightened and chafed his upper arms to get his point across. "Wait for harbormaster here? Me? Get warm?"

"You are not cold." She crossed her arms. "You're sweating. I can see it on your brow."

"From walk only."

She pointed at the door. "Take the bread and cheese, Citizen Sunara. And I thank you. But you can't stay. It isn't proper."

He shook his head, disappointed, and for a moment Eva thought he would argue with her. But he seemed to think better of it. He sighed and strode to the door.

"You aren't taking the food?" she asked.

He placed a hand on his flat stomach. "Not hungry now." He didn't look at her as he walked past her and into the wind. His black hair lifted in the breeze, and his generous shirt fluttered around his torso and elbows.

She had turned him out to face the coming storm. What a heartless thing to do.

But she *was* heartless. Everyone knew Eva Wilder had no heart, and that's just the way it was. She used people, abandoned them and went her way—always apart, always unloved. That had been the story of her life. It was better not to have a heart at all than to long for love and never get it. She had learned to turn off longing by closing off her heart and shutting people out. Being heartless kept her numb, and numbness was better than suffering.

Vinko Sunara could find his own shelter. She didn't have time to solve his problems. She had enough problems of her own.

Eva turned her attention to unpacking the items he had transported from the house, and was surprised to find the garden wind chime rolled in a towel. Vinko had somehow sensed the value of her best work of art and had rescued it. His thoughtfulness struck her again. But she turned away from the feeling. She must not soften toward him.

She held up the wind chime. The sea glass tinkled a musical whisper, encouraging her to be more whimsical—to go where the wind took her. She grabbed the glass to cut off the sound, and then lay the piece in the sand to mute its siren call. Never again would she allow whimsy to guide her life.

The noose in her throat tightened until she could barely take a breath.

The only cure was action. She threw herself into the task of stowing everything away and was just making tea when the storm hit. She wrapped her hands around the mug, grateful to be protected from the rain and wind and refusing to feel guilty for sending Vinko away. She ambled to the door of the hut, opened it a crack and looked out on the driving rain, just as the stranger came into view again, this time carrying a crate.

The man was back. Her spirits lifted and fell simultane-ously, leaving her dizzy. She grabbed the door latch to keep her balance.

Vinko's hair ran with rain and his clothing clung to his sinewy body as if it were a second layer of skin. Leaning into the wind, he fought to keep going in the storm.

Against her better judgment, she held open the door. Neither of them said a word as he hurried into the hut.

"Keep for me?" he said, adjusting his grip on the crate.

She nodded toward an empty space near the door. He lowered the box to the sandy floor.

"Thank you." He straightened.

She held out the cup of tea.

"Thank you." He sipped the steaming beverage. "Ah."

She watched his expressive lips as he savored the warmth of the beverage and was drawn to his vibrancy in spite of herself. He smiled.

The man had no filters. If he was happy, he emanated humor. If he was upset, his eyes darkened with storm clouds. If he teased her, his mouth quirked to the side. He displayed his feelings as soon as he felt them, without any reflection beforehand. She couldn't imagine behaving the way he did. Life had taught her to think twice about anything she said or did.

"We take cargo to factory soon. Cargo is safe."

"That's fortunate."

"I come back for box. Later?"

"I may not be here for long. I can't be responsible for it."

"Keep from fire and rain. Yes? Dangerous." He made an exploding gesture with his hands. "Poof. Understand, Miss Eva?"

She nodded and glanced at the crate. He was asking her to guard something that might explode. That was a lot to expect. And yet, she owed him for his help.

"You want me to keep that here?"

"Yes. Is important. For you. Londo City. All."

"What's in it?"

"Cannot tell." He shook his head and looked at her with sadness in his crystalline eyes. "You, I cannot trust."

She flushed. She had lost his trust. His sad gaze seared her from head to toe, and she fought hard to keep it from burning deeper. She couldn't allow his opinion to affect her on such a level.

She planted her fists on her hips. "Then I'll just see for myself. Later, when you're gone."

"You will not see much," he said. "You will not understand."

"What do you mean?"

"You will see only bags. Gray bags. Not shiny. Not worth money. Do not touch. Only gray bags, Eva."

Gray bags. Now she was curious as well as afraid. She didn't like the idea of a dangerous box, but he couldn't very well take it back out in the rain. She didn't want Vinko around her, but that didn't mean he deserved to die in an explosion.

"I really don't want it here," she said.

"You keep." He glared at her for the first time, cutting off her protest. Then, in the next second, his gaze softened. "You will see. Good."

He handed the cup back to her. "Thank you for tea."

She glanced up at his eyes, but only for an instant. "Thanks for saving my wind chime."

He nodded. Then, without another word, he ducked out of the hut and trotted into the rain.

Relieved that he had left her alone, Eva looked at the wooden crate and wondered what was inside. But according to Vinko, even if she looked, she wouldn't know what it was. She decided to ignore the crate and its mysterious contents. Besides, she had a letter to read.

Eva made a second cup of tea, using the same leaves as before, and opened the violin case. She picked up the ivory envelope and set her jaw against the berating words she knew would come from her dead husband, even post mortem. Then she tugged the only chair close to the fire and sat down.

Taking a deep breath, Eva studied the envelope. Her reading practice made it easy to interpret her husband's crabbed handwriting.

"In the case of my death," was scribbled on the back.

She stared at the words. He must have put the envelope in the hiding hole recently, as she had stashed credits in there a week ago, and hadn't seen the letter. Had Charles suspected that he might be killed?

She tore off the end and poured two keys onto her hand. One was an old-fashioned skeleton key. The other was a shinier gold key that looked like the ones used for government-issued door locks in Londo City. Her curiosity mounted.

Eva tucked the keys in the pocket of her vest and unfolded the letter.

Eva:

If you are reading this, you are either snooping unnecessarily or I have been killed. If you are snooping, read this letter as a revelation of the truth between us, and decide how to go forward with your life. If I am dead, read these words as a warning. Either way, in snooping or in death, our marriage is over.

It is unfortunate that our union has come to this. When we married, I had hopes that we could forge a warm, if not passionate, partnership. But the ghosts from your past stood between us like a wall, forever cutting you off from me and the rest of the world. I tried everything I knew—cajoling you, buying you gifts, giving you time to mend whatever had broken your heart, but you neither mended nor confided in me. I might have been able to help, had I known what tormented you. But you never allowed me into your private world.

I am weary of your tears and headaches. I have given up and,
if still living, will turn elsewhere for comfort.
        Thus, this letter.

Eva stopped reading and hung her head. Charles' words cut her. She deserved to be cut, but the pain was still difficult to bear. She shut her eyes, squeezing off tears she refused to cry and fighting the constriction in her throat. She thought back to the many times she had refused Charles and spent a stony night not sleeping, knowing he lay beside her, frustrated and angry. She had considered him heartless and pushy, and his coaxing out of place. She had thought it insensitive, even vulgar, that he could expect kisses and conjugal relations from a woman who was grieving so many losses. Each time he reached out to her, it had felt like an affront. Each time he went silent afterward, he shut her away in her grief, and she stayed there, not wishing to leave her mute space. She had never considered the notion that Charles might have been trying his best. Or that he cared what she was going through.

Eva stared at the fire, unseeing, with the letter on her knee. It was over, but she didn't care. She should care, but she didn't. The words of the letter rang in her ears, putting a new and even more painful spin on the past. She had been the insensitive one for not seeing her husband as a human being instead of a monster. The flames flared, as if stoked by the truth of her selfish behavior. She had been the heartless one. Not Charles.

Something unfurled inside her. A truth uncurled, coming into view just beyond the periphery of her consciousness. Had she misjudged Charles? Had he not been a monster after all? If she had talked to him instead of shutting him out, would their marriage have been better? Maybe. But Charles' touch had never affected her.

There had never been a single instant of desire or intimacy between them. Maybe their marriage would always have been a long, dreary flat line.

How else could she have acted? Enjoying the marriage bed had been impossible in her grief-stricken state. To give herself to Charles when she was grieving and unavailable would have been an act of the most heinous dishonesty— for her and to him. She grieved still. She suspected she might always grieve. And so, yes, she was heartless. She accepted the fact.

A tear dropped on her hand. She brushed it off and swallowed. She must regain control. Self-control was the only way to get through this letter and the rest of her life.

Their marriage was over. Good. She would focus on the positive. She would never have to refuse Charles' advances again. What a relief. She was free of his puny hands and recriminating glances. She was free of the way his small mouth turned into a tight line when he looked at her before turning down the lamp. She had hated that look and the days of silence that came after.

Eva took a deep breath and bent to the letter once more.

If I have perished from unnatural causes, I will have died at the hands of the Overseers. I have learned things about them in the past few days that are not meant for a commissioner to know. They may also come for you.

Beware of a man named Neal Moray. He is an Overseer and is often here for reasons I have yet to discover but suspect are not legal. He has something to do with a building to which I previously did not have access. I do now, as I have procured a key to it. The old key in this letter is a mate to one I recently discovered in a drawer. If I am dead, that means I used the key to gain entrance to the building and was caught.

I'm not sure you deserve my consideration, but I will give it anyway. I will provide housing in Londo and a small stipend to you, as long as you live discreetly and never speak of our dissolved marriage. In the case of my death, I ask that you see to the upbringing of my son.

Son? Eva flushed. Charles had a son? The revelation took her breath away. Apparently, she was not the only one with ghosts in the past. And what of the woman Charles had tried to save? Had the person named Margaret been his lover? What was that connection?

Her thoughts swirled, and she had to fight to clear her vision. Eva was almost too shell-shocked to keep reading, but she forced herself to continue. She held the letter to the light of the fire so she wouldn't miss a single word.

As soon as the authorities learn of my treason, they will hunt down my son. His only hope will be you. I beg of you, Eva, do one kind thing for me. Shelter my son.

Eva flushed again, this time with indignation. It was bad enough that Charles had produced an illegitimate son that he had never bothered to tell her about, as well as had carnal relations with another woman, but to expect her to take the boy in? That was too much, especially for a woman who had given up her own child in order to marry. But then, Charles hadn't known about the sacrifices she had made. She had never confided in him.

I have a townhouse in Londo that belonged to my father. If you care for my son—his name is Phineas and he is eleven years old— you can remain in the house and live out your life there or until the Overseers throw you out. I cannot predict what will happen in that regard.

Phineas lives with his mother at 13 Collins Lane. He will be wary of strangers, so be careful.

We did not have a successful marriage. But you were never cruel or unfaithful. For that, I am grateful. Therefore, I will provide for you in death or in separation. If you are reading this and I am not dead, I ask that you take the next available train back to Londo and remain in the townhouse at 21 Fairhaven. I will support you as long as you conduct yourself in a way that befits the wife of a commissioner. No scandals. No lovers. I will have agents watching you.

Charles

No lovers. As if she would ever open her heart again. Eva folded the letter and slipped it into the pocket of her vest. She might need it later if questioned by the authorities over ownership of the Paar townhouse.

She stood up. She would decide about the boy later. She owed Charles some consideration, but not as great as that of parenting a child. What of his mother? Was she dead? She must be. If that were the case, the boy would be hunted down as an orphan and imprisoned. Unfortunate for him—but why should she be forced to care for a bastard child? Once again, Fate was slapping her in the face.

How could Charles upend her life like this and expect her to pick up the pieces? She might have misjudged him, but he was just like Aiden after all, taking a risk and leaving her to clean up afterward. She burned. She was through with cleaning up after men. And that included taking care of a boy.

Especially the boy.

Eva planted her fists at her waist and looked around the hut, taking in her meager belongings and rustic surrounds. What to do? She would prefer to live in Port

Pennwood and stay near the sea. She loved the fresh air and occasional sunshine. But she couldn't survive here on her own. She had no way to earn money.

If she refused Charles' offer, she would have to return to Londo and a working class life. She had enough credits in the sock to buy a ticket back to the city. There, she could find a job and re-register for Distribution. But the prospect filled her with dread.

Or, she could take the easy way out and live the life of a commissioner's widow and not have to work or worry about food. She wouldn't even have to take care of the boy, not if she didn't choose to. No one would know about the boy. And Charles would never know if she fulfilled his last request or not. Charles was dead.

She had two days to make her decision. In two days, the train would arrive. She would decide how to move forward tomorrow, after she had more time to ponder her situation.

Eva poured a third cup of tea. While she sipped it, she gazed at the mysterious crate and heard Vinko's voice in her head.

"I do not trust you. So cannot tell."

She was untrustworthy and heartless. No use pretending to be something she was not. Eva set aside the empty cup and clenched her jaw. She knew exactly what she was going to do about Charles' love child.

5

———

THE NEXT AFTERNOON, hunger drove Eva to the Golden Hind pub. She had decided to use some of her precious money to buy a warm meal, and the pub was the only victualing house in Port Pennwood. Eva had never set foot in the tiny bar, or any bar for that matter. In fact, pubs were not allowed in Londo City and drinking was frowned upon. But Port Pennwood had occasional shipments arriving and departing by sea and rail, which involved men who needed food and lodging. The Golden Hind served as pub, inn and post office.

Even if she had possessed plenty of money, Eva would not have stayed at the Golden Hind. The place was for men only. A woman renting a room—especially a woman alone—would raise eyebrows as well as garner unwanted male interest. She intended to avoid both.

She prayed that Neal Moray would not be at the pub. She hoped he had ridden in, conducted his business and ridden out, and was not waiting for the train. A dandy like Neal Moray wouldn't suffer the indignation of riding in a shabby passenger train. He probably owned a fancy, well-sprung coach with a matched set of horses. At least she hoped so.

While the tide was out, Eva walked from her little cove, along the base of the high cliffs to the main harbor. A handful of cottages clustered around the quay, with only a couple of streets comprising the entire village. A lane to the left led up to the prison and another to the right curved up and around to the manor house at the top of the town. Eva glanced at the house she used to call home. She would miss living there. She would miss being the master of her own time. Going back to Londo and her old job would reduce her to a slave again.

She climbed the seaweed-laced steps from the sand to the harbor wall and then ducked into the nearest alley to make herself as presentable as possible. She had slept on a pallet all night and had washed herself in a spring near the cliff. She felt like a rumpled ragbag. Still, it couldn't be helped. She brushed back her light brown hair with her hands. Then she re-pinned the strands blown astray by the sea wind. She was the widow of a commissioner, and she would comport herself as one, even if her clothes were damp and wrinkled and her fine black boots were covered in sand.

Eva pinched her cheeks and moistened her lips, and then with head held high, walked to the pub. She opened the door. A bell tinkled, startling her and preventing her from slipping in unnoticed. The low murmur of male voices cut off as the patrons turned to look her way. They stared at her, branding her with their curiosity and hunger.

Her pretty face and well-proportioned figure had always produced such reactions in men. When she was younger, she had loved being the center of attention. She had craved it. But now, all she desired was to slip in and out of the world like a ghost, talking to no one and avoiding all connections. She steeled herself by putting on her bland mask. Then she headed for the bartender. At least he wasn't a complete stranger. She had met him on the street once or twice.

The bartender leaned over, holding a towel in his fist.

"Citizen Paar," he stammered, obviously as shocked as the rest of the men to see a woman come into the pub. "A good afternoon to you."

"Citizen Browne." She nodded regally at him while her knees trembled. Since her marriage to Charles, she had never had to speak for herself in public. She must learn new ways and learn them quickly.

"To what do I owe the pleasure?" he continued.

She glanced at the chalkboard behind him where menu items and prices were scrawled in yellow letters. She would purchase the cheapest thing on the list. "I would like to order supper."

"Citizen?" he stuttered in surprise.

"Citizen Alexander was dismissed yesterday."

"Hannah? Why? She's the hardest working woman I know."

"She is."

"Then why did you fire her?"

"I didn't."

"Who then?"

Eva could sense everyone listening to the conversation. She didn't like the idea of strangers knowing about her personal problems, so she didn't answer.

Instead, she pointed at the chalkboard. "May I order the cod, please?" She hoped the bartender would attribute Hannah's discharge to her stern taskmaster of a husband and not ask any more questions. Surely people were aware of Charles' hard nature.

"Of course. Of course." The barman indicated a booth near the door. "Please, have a seat and I will bring it to you when it's ready. Will you be taking it home?"

She raised her chin. "I will be eating it here."

"I see." His gaze raced over her face, searching for clues to explain this odd turn of events. Obviously he did not yet know about her fall from grace. "And…and something to drink, citizen?"

"Watered ale, please."

He paused, as if deciding something, and then leaned closer. "Is it true, then?" He lowered his voice. "About your husband?"

"That he is dead, yes."

"Shot for being a traitor?"

"That is what I have been told. But I can't believe Charles would have done anything against the law."

"Me neither. It's shocking."

"It is."

"I'm sorry for your loss, citizen."

Don't be, she wanted to say. Losing Charles, the person, had no effect on her one way or another, other than setting her free. Losing Charles, the social position, though, was another matter entirely. His death was a prison sentence. His death meant the end of any real life for her. She could never marry again. No children. No family. Nothing but meals alone, like the one she was going to have here at the pub.

"Thank you," she answered, and turned for her seat.

"Dinner is on me," Citizen Browne said.

Surprised by his kindness, Eva glanced at his wrinkled face.

"Thank you," she answered. "That is kind of you. Very kind."

"The least I can do."

She nodded and turned for the booth at the door. She swept her skirts around and plowed toward the seat, aware more than ever of the silence and the eyes of the men. Twenty feet felt like twenty miles. Once she sat down, she ignored the probing stares by gazing out the window. A sea bird hunted along the shoreline. She focused on the bird and dashed all other sensations away.

There hadn't been many birds in Londo City. There hadn't been many creatures at all. Just rats. But here in Port Pennwood, wildlife had begun to prosper. Life here, though quiet and lonely, was more real than in Londo where she had grown up. Here there was more sunshine, fresh air, plants and animals. She loved the optimism she could sometimes feel in Port Pennwood.

She dreaded the return to Londo, with the ever-present fog and curfews and ration lines. She dreaded going back to her menial job. She hated washing coal. Always cold. Always wet. But she would have to return. She would have to start over from where she left off or take Charles up on his offer with the strings attached. If the Overseers stripped her of the Londo townhouse as well, she would have no choice but to go back to supporting herself with menial labor. Thank Gottfried she and Charles had never produced any children.

When her supper arrived—a large filet of fish sitting on a mound of fried potatoes—Eva nearly drowned on her own saliva. She was starving, but she forced herself to eat slowly, as a lady would. No wolfing her food. But she hadn't been this hungry for years, and no meal had ever tasted as delicious.

Just as she had eaten the last potato, she heard the door burst open, sending the bell shuddering. Spurs rang on the plank floor as three men strode into the pub.

Neal Moray strutted by, followed by his two guards.

Her heart sank. She pressed into the corner of the booth. Maybe shadows would hide her. But when the small man's bulging eyes scanned the room, his gaze landed on her. Gaslight illuminated the side of his face, outlining his scar and making it look as if he were smiling at her.

He wasn't.

In the fading light of afternoon, Moray's eyes glinted an odd red color, probably due to the reflection of the gas lamps near the door. Still, his pale skin and strange eyes sent alarm coursing through her. She tried to look away from him, at anything but his disgusted, cruel expression, but for some reason, she could not avert her eyes.

"You," Neal Moray's lip curled. "I thought I told you to clear out."

"I can't, until the train comes."

"What's wrong with your legs?"

"You expect me to walk to Londo?"

He stared down at her, his anger mounting, until she thought he might explode. His face flushed as pink as his scar.

"Don't you ever," he poked her chest with his cane, "talk back to me." Then, in a sickening caress, he drew the tip of the cane up her throat and pressed it into the soft flesh under her jaw, gagging her. She sat, immobilized with fear but did not flinch.

"Don't let me see you anywhere in Port Pennwood again, citizen, or I will shoot you where you stand."

Eva's heart thundered in her ears, but she refused to budge until he removed his cane from her throat. She would not scuttle away like a frightened crab or let him see how terrified she was.

The pub fell silent. Out of the corner of her eye, she could see Citizen Browne polishing a glass and watching.

"Do you hear me, citizen?"

"Yes."

"Then get up!"

Eva remained where she was. She wasn't about to allow this small bully to order her around. He would have to shoot her where she sat. And she doubted he would shoot her in front of an audience.

"Did you hear me?" He struck the table with his cane. The sharp rap reverberated through the pub. "I said get up!"

"Citizen!" Citizen Browne exclaimed, coming around the end of the bar. "She's only—"

"Silence!" Moray snapped. He turned on the bartender. "Since when did you start allowing women into your pub?"

"I know, citizen, but she's—"

"I could have you banished for blatant disregard of the law."

The bartender stopped in his tracks, with his hands hanging at his sides and his expression slack with powerlessness.

"And you," Moray turned back to her. "You slut. One day after you lose your husband, and you're out hunting for a lover. You make me sick."

"That is not what I'm doing."

"Shut up and get up. Unaccompanied females are not allowed in public houses."

"Citizen Wilder is *not* alone," a man said from across the room. Eva glanced in the direction of the familiar voice and recognized the figure of the man ambling toward her.

She had never been more relieved to see someone. Not even Aiden.

6

VINKO SUNARA STROLLED across the floor and stood beside Eva. He put one hand on the back of her seat, framing her within the shelter of his presence. In the circle of protection, her fear subsided a few degrees, enough to allow her to take a breath.

"I asked Miss Wilder to meet me here. I apologize for not knowing law here in Anglo Territories. Where I am from, ladies welcome everywhere."

"*She* should have known better." Moray shook his cane in Eva's face.

"She is in shock, Citizen Moray. She has lost husband. Where is your heart?"

Moray didn't answer the question. He just sneered and narrowed his eyes.

Eva stared at the two men and wondered how Vinko had met Moray. It was obvious they knew each other. Maybe Moray had been involved in the shipwreck salvage operation.

Moray sniffed. "Still, she shouldn't be here. It's not allowed."

"I meet her here to thank her. Reward her for help on beach."

"What kind of help could she possibly have given you?" Moray puffed himself up, as if trying to compensate for his lack of height as well as his lack of humanity.

"She saved your wine, citizen. If not for Citizen Wilder, I would have died and all cargo of ship swept out to sea."

Moray glanced at Eva and then back at Vinko. He was losing ground, and he knew it. He looked Vinko up and down and then planted his cane on the floor. "So—I will let this slide, Mr. Sunara. Just this time, since you went above and beyond expectations."

"Yes. Is way of my family. We deliver. And we make good wine." Vinko winked at him.

Moray gave an exasperated puff at Vinko's irrepressible good humor. "All right. You may keep your assignation with this person. But I warn you. The Wilders are not to be trusted."

"I take my chances."

"Suit yourself."

"Buy you and men drink?" Vinko's expressive eyebrows lifted.

"Thanks, but no. We're working tonight."

"Tonight?" Vinko asked, surprised. "Is dangerous at night in Anglo Territories, no?"

"For some," Moray patted his top hat more firmly on his cropped hair, making sure it was tilted at just the right angle. "But I'm not afraid of the dark. Good evening."

Moray ordered a flask of something from the cowering bartender and then left without looking back.

When the bell tinkled, signaling Moray's departure, Eva finally took a breath.

"Thank you for that," she said.

Vinko slipped into the booth next to her. She felt his hard thigh next to hers and scooted away.

"The man is bully," he said.

"So far, nothing but." She clasped her hands in her lap. "And I'm surprised you know him."

"He took delivery of wine at warehouse. Signed papers."

"Ah."

Vinko's warm gaze swept over her. "You are oki doki?"

"Yes. For now."

"I buy you drink?"

Eva had never been asked such a question. She was fairly sure that wives of commissioners did not accept drinks from strangers and never in pubs.

Vinko chuckled. "Drink only, Eva. No more. To thank you."

"I should be going."

"Is raining. Wait until storm passes." He shrugged. "Little house on beach, cold."

She glanced at the sheets of rain hammering the windowpanes and then at his kind face.

"All right. A mint tea would be nice."

"I will get." Vinko stood up and then looked down at her. "No tricks. Stay. Moray outside, waiting for you."

She nodded. He was probably right. She should stay in the pub for a while. It made sense. Vinko smiled and walked to the bar.

Being in the pub with him was an entirely different experience than sitting in the tavern, eating alone. Rain splashed on the glass behind her, but it didn't sound like harsh splatters anymore. It was more of a musical tinkle. She was full and warm and no longer afraid. She couldn't remember the last time she felt as content as she did right now—since Joanna, if she were honest.

A lump of longing for her sister choked her. She had no idea where Joanna was or if she were even alive. She assumed she was dead. Eva forced her thoughts away from her sister's memory and distracted herself by studying Vinko as he stood at the bar, waiting for their drinks.

Yesterday when she'd seen the man, he had been a bedraggled mess, dressed only in a drenched shirt and trousers. This afternoon, he wore a black coat, white shirt and black vest, along with his breeches and boots. His long legs were lean but sheathed with muscle, and the cut of his coat accentuated his erect posture. She liked the proud angle of his head and shoulders, both of which spoke to his strength and intelligence. She liked the way his dark hair, now fully dry and soft with waves, curled behind his ears.

Eva had to be careful. She had no business admiring a man. She didn't need the distraction or disappointment that came with creatures of the opposite sex.

Vinko carried their beverages to the table. He had ordered a large glass of ale for himself. He sat down, too close for comfort again, and she scooted aside.

Eva lifted the teacup and appreciated its warmth in the curve of her palms.

"Did you locate your luggage?" she asked, nodding at him. "And find your things?"

"No." He touched a lapel of his coat. "Moray provided. There seems plenty clothes at factory. For shipping back to Londo. For something called Distribution?"

"Really? For the weekly distribution?" Eva took a sip of tea while she puzzled over the information. "Why would prisoners give up their clothes?"

Vinko shrugged. "Prisoners wear uniforms?" He shot her a hard glance. "You do not know of life of prisoners here?"

"Like I told Moray, I don't know anything about my husband's job. We never talked about it. We never talked at all, in fact."

Vinko took a swig of ale and didn't press her for details about her marriage. That was fine with her. The less Vinko knew about her on a personal level, the easier it would be to remain casual acquaintances.

"Moray is man who threw you out of house?"

"Yes."

"Bastard."

Eva gave him a grim smile of agreement, while inside she warmed to his comment. She appreciated having someone share her view of Neal Moray and sympathize with her predicament. It made her feel less alone in the world—and that was something she could use right now.

"May I ask where you are from?" she said.

"Croatia."

"I've never heard of it. Where is it?"

"Far away. In east. Must sail. Weeks on sea."

"Then you are a sailor? The captain, perhaps?"

"Me?" Vinko gave a small laugh. "I sail, but not captain of that ship."

"Then why are you here?"

"I am businessman. Protect family interest." A shadow flitted through his eyes that told Eva he was not divulging the real reason for his visit. So he was lying. She didn't care. She had no long-term interest in this man. Truth, lies —it was all just conversation. On both their parts.

"And the box you asked me to look after?"

"Yes. I pick up tomorrow."

"What makes it dangerous?"

"Chemicals inside."

"Chemicals?"

He squeezed her wrist. "No need to know, Miss Eva."

"It's Mrs. or Citizen to you, sir."

"You do not look like missus to me. So young."

"I'm a widow."

"You are far too young to play widow."

"I don't play at anything, especially that."

"I think you play."

His gaze locked with hers. "I see one Eva you show to Moray. To world." He swiped the air in front of his face, indicating the mask she wore, and let his expression go flat. "But another Eva lives here." He lightly tapped her left temple. "I see."

The touch of his hand and his intimate words knocked her off guard. She pulled away and sank back against the upholstered seat, struggling to think of a clever retort to make him see how wrong he was about her. But her mind had turned off.

All she could do was gallop like crazy to catch up to her façade. Desperate, she fought for control of herself as well as her growing attraction to him. She wanted to take his face in her hands and kiss him for understanding her so well in such a short amount of time. No man had been as perceptive or had even cared to notice who she was.

She plopped her clenched hands on the table top between them and stared at the far wall.

"Neither Eva should interest you, Citizen Sunara."

"Why do you say this?"

"I am better off alone. In fact I want to be alone. And if there was a way to earn a wage and live alone in Port Pennwood, I would."

"Not go back to Londo? Most powerful city in world?"

"Doesn't make it best." There she went again, copying his truncated speech pattern. She had to stop it.

Eva sipped her drink and thought of her previous life in Londo: the loss of her parents, the long hours working at the coal processing plant washing rocks, the Sunday Distribution lines and her run from the law. And here she was again, struggling to survive and running from Moray.

"Your eyes tell me Londo is not happy for you," Vinko said gently.

She looked down at her hands.

"Tell me of place," he urged.

Eva sighed. "It's a grim place. But I never knew how grim until I came here. Londo is always foggy. There is never any sunshine. There is never enough food. People take trains to the outskirts to work and then come back. Day after day. One gray day blends into the next."

"Then why go back? For family?"

"I have no family." She pressed her lips together to keep them from trembling. She never should have said the words out loud to a stranger. Her losses were still so close to the surface. Too personal and still too hard to talk about. She had no family. She had no one.

Eva changed the subject. "But there are jobs in Londo. And it is relatively safe."

"Safe? What about vampires?"

"What?" She glanced at him, certain she had heard him wrong.

"I come to Anglo Territories, land of vampires. Famous."

"Where did you ever hear that?"

"Travelers. And when I see you on beach, I think *you* are vampire."

That explained his odd comment about her being able to stand in the bright light.

"You think everyone in Londo City is a vampire?"

He nodded gravely.

"No, there are people there. Like you and me."

"This is surprise." He frowned, thinking about something. Then he looked up again. "But vampires also."

"No. That's just a rumor. I have never seen one. Or heard about anyone seeing one. So no. No vampires."

"Would you know vampire if you see with your eyes?"

"Of course." She shifted in her chair. "A vampire has white skin and big fangs and long, horrible fingernails. They look like the dead, supposedly, and they smell terrible."

"This is what you know."

"That's what I've heard. But I think it's just a tale children are told to scare them. To make them behave."

"Only story for you, then." Vinko looked thoughtful again. "I see."

"What about in Croatia?"

"Vampires?"

She nodded.

"More than story. We had them. Long ago."

"You did?"

Vinko nodded. "Long time. Before war. One or two I knew about after. But my father make sure they leave."

"So you actually had vampires in Croatia."

"Yes." Vinko took another swig. "No one knows where vampire comes from. Maybe creature lives always with human. But in Croatia, we say they come from mountains. In Romania."

"Romania?"

"Yes. Dark country. Full of fast, cold rivers, tall mountains, valleys so deep, no sun any time. Cold. Rocks. Darkness. Caves."

Eva shuddered.

"Vampires feed on shepherds. Pilgrims. Travelers. Then, want more. More house. More clothes. To be more like men. Less like animal. Now, hard to tell difference."

"They are still around?"

"Oh, yes, Eva. Old and clever and hungry."

"So they don't look like I said they did? With fangs and everything."

"No. Just like us." He put his hand over hers. "Just like us, Eva. Be careful."

Eva thought back to the red glint in Neal Moray's eyes and shuddered again. Surely, though, he couldn't be a vampire. He walked around during the day. He smelled fine. He was despicable and cruel, but a human being.

"It can't be true," she shook her head. "It's too far-fetched."

"Is not."

"We can't be living with vampires."

"Neal Moray is vampire."

She stared. Her heart seemed to stop beating.

"We want no more vampires come to Croatia with boats. Filling bellies, taking wine. It is like old days. People disappearing. Poof. People dead in beds."

His words chilled her. That was exactly what happened in Londo City. People disappeared all the time. It was an occurrence that everyone tolerated, no questions asked. To ask was to bring down punishment or banishment. No one ever questioned death or disappearance for fear the same thing would happen to them or their families.

"Your leader," Vinko put in, breaking into her thoughts. "King. Silas Stone. He is vampire."

"What?" She set her cup down with a rattle. Her hands shook. "You think the Anglo Territories are ruled by a vampire?"

"Yes." Vinko's sparkling eyes turned grave.

Eva stared at him.

7

Vinko squeezed her hand. "Is not impossible."

"But how could there be vampires? Londo has always been safe. The city walls have protected us for hundreds of years."

"No," he said.

She glanced at him in surprise. "What?"

"Like prison."

"No, it's not like that." Eva leaned forward and continued. "Sure, we have a lot of rules. And the Overseers are strict. But that's why Londo people have survived. We work hard and we are safe from the savage outside world."

Vinko rolled his eyes, unconvinced.

"We were taught a saying as children," she put in.

"And what is this saying?"

"No need to grumble or to chafe. Londo rules keep you safe. And it's true."

He lowered his voice, so that only she could hear. "Safe from all but greatest of predator." He stared at her with such intensity that she knew in her bones he spoke the truth.

"They keep you safe, but like cattle, Eva. Like cattle."

Eva's mouth went dry. Never in a million years would she have believed vampires ruled Londo, or that no one suspected such a thing. Had Charles known? Were the Others he warned her about really vampires? She couldn't believe he would have kept such essential information from her.

Vinko sat back. "I frighten you."

"Yes."

"Good." He finished his ale. "Where do you stay? In little house?"

Eva flushed, unwilling to admit that she was penniless and too proud to reveal that Charles had left her with nothing but the guardianship of a bastard child.

"In hut?" Vinko leaned forward again. "Not safe. Not safe at night on beach. Moray is here. Others."

"It will be fine." She curled her fingers around her empty cup and forced a confident smile. "It's only for one more night."

"Many things happen in night." His eyes searched her face. "You have no money?"

"I have money. But I'm not wasting it on a room. Especially here."

Vinko frowned and glared at the table. "Stay in the big house. Yes?"

"No. Moray has taken it over to await my husband's replacement."

He nodded.

"You are staying here?" Eva asked. "In the inn?"

"Until train tomorrow." He glanced at the window. "Rain still. More tea?"

She hesitated. So far, she had not had to pay for anything, but she didn't want to reciprocate by buying another round of drinks. Drinking was a frivolous waste of money.

"I buy," Vinko put in. "Payment for looking after box."

"Then thank you. Yes."

She watched him walk to the bar, so confident in his man's world, even though her country was foreign to him and full of strange idioms and restrictive laws. Nothing seemed to faze him, though. She admired that.

Eva eased back against the padded cushions of the bench seat. She had felt so uncomfortable when she had first entered the pub, but now it seemed cozy to her. The murmur of male voices had settled into a warm hum, the sight of Citizen Browne polishing glassware was strangely hypnotic, and the glow of lamplight in the darkening afternoon made the pub seem like a sanctuary instead of the den of debauchery she had always assumed it was.

She had never stepped foot in the illegal Londo pub where her lover Aiden Bannister had met his mates and fomented the riot. Her sister had gone there once, in blatant disregard of her reputation and personal safety. But then, Joanna had always been the brave one.

Joanna. Why had she been so nasty to Joanna the last time they'd spoken to each other? She had treated her sister so callously, after all that Joanna had done for her. Eva's guilt was like a broach pinned onto her heart, always hanging there, always heavy, and always a stabbing pain.

Eva distracted herself by focusing on the sight of Vinko carrying two goblets of wine to the table.

She flashed a wry smile at him to hide the painful memories churning inside her. "That doesn't look like tea."

"Is not. This?" He gave her a glass. "Wine from my country. Part of Moray shipment. Compliments of friend at bar."

Eva looked over at Citizen Browne and held up the

goblet. He gave her a salute and went back to his glass polishing.

"Barman does not like Neal Moray."

"Perhaps no one does."

"Often happens with vampire. They try. Be more like man, connect sometimes. But no real human connection." He wagged his finger between his chest and hers to illustrate his point. "Not learn this."

"Why not? I thought vampires lived forever. They have all the time in the world to learn."

"Of course. But not learn. In all time," he shrugged. "Stay same. Like some people, no?"

Even though his words were stilted and his speech patterns crude, she knew exactly what he was saying. But she also knew she was enjoying his company far too much.

Eva took a tentative sip of the wine. She'd never tasted wine before. The cold liquid passed over her lips and shocked her taste buds. She couldn't hide her reaction to the tart, musky beverage. She made a face.

Vinko grinned.

"I'm not sure I like wine." She shoved the goblet toward him. "Besides, ladies don't drink."

"In my country, ladies. Yes."

"Not here, citizen."

"First time for you then." He pushed the goblet back to her. "Be Croatia tonight."

She shook her head and fought back a smile.

"Enjoy, Eva," he urged. "Dead tomorrow maybe."

"Oh, that's a nice thought."

"Is true." He lifted his glass as he held her gaze. "To life, Eva Wilder."

She couldn't resist his sunny challenge. She raised her glass.

"Slow now," Vinko instructed. "Small drink. Not big."

He watched her lift the wine glass a second time. "Made from grapes near my home. You will like. Try."

She followed his gentle instruction. If Charles had wanted her to try something, he would have ridiculed her into acquiescing. Aiden would never have offered her anything to try. He had only taken from her. His physical needs and political cause had been all that he ever thought about. Vinko Sunara was different, and Eva had learned enough about men to recognize and appreciate his kind soul.

Careful, Eva, she reminded herself. Don't be fooled. There is always the talk, the period of false charm and promises, and then the disappointment.

She would never fall prey to a man's treachery again. She was a twenty-six-year-old widow and would remain in a chaste, solitary state for the rest of her days. She must embrace her new position and live a respectable and honest life, both for society and for herself.

But first, she must stop talking to herself.

"So, tell me of Croatia," she began, taking a hesitant sip. She swallowed and pulled back in surprise to stare at the wine. Vinko was right. The second sip was not tart at all. It was lush and velvety. It was as if she had just tasted sunshine, cake and firelight all at the same time.

"Ha!" he said, observing her every movement. "You like, no? What is taste now?"

She took a third sip and closed her eyes. "This wine is everything Londo is not. Warm. Lush. Sweet. Like a wonderful promise."

She opened her eyes to find his grin growing wider. His entire face lit up and his blue eyes danced with pleasure.

"You ask what is Croatia?" He nodded at her glass. "That is Croatia. Green mountain. Sun on sea. On lake. On grass. Croatia."

"It's warm there?"

"Sometime."

"And sunny?" She couldn't imagine a place bathed in sunshine.

"Sometime. More each year. Better than last."

"I would love to see the sun." She took another appreciative drink. "Sometimes I get a glimpse of it here. Before the clouds roll back in. Just enough to tease me."

"You go sometime. To Croatia."

"As if I could."

"What is prevention?"

"No one goes anywhere without a pass. I couldn't get a pass to leave the Anglo Territories. And even if I could get a pass, what would I do in Croatia? No one survives without a job and ID card."

He listened, but she could tell by his smile that he didn't put much stock in her excuses.

"In fact, Vinko, you aren't going to get anywhere without an ID. They won't even let you on the train."

"Oh, I have this card."

"You do?"

He winked and pulled a card out of his coat pocket. "I am Daniel Kane." He held the card next to his face. "Me."

He showed her the card. The black and white photograph on it was so faded that it could have represented any clean-shaven young man with lots of hair.

"And," Vinko added. "I am vampire."

"You stole that from a vampire? How?"

He winked again. "Special way."

She sobered. "Vinko, if you get caught, they will kill you."

"Not Vinko."

"Really?" She regarded him. "How can you be so optimistic?"

"What is this word, optimistic?"

"Sure. Not worried."

"Ah." He shrugged and smiled. "Optimistic, yes? Worried, no. As we say in my country, better to be bull for day than cow for year."

"But you are bound to get caught. People will notice you."

"Because handsome." He grinned.

"No, because you're so tall. And dark. And your eyes are really unusual."

He shrugged again, not convinced. "Like vampire, then. So good."

"And what about the way you talk? That will really give you away."

"You teach. On train." He tapped his right temple. "I learn. Not like vampire. I learn and remember. All."

She didn't doubt it for a moment.

"On that note," she said, finishing her drink. "I must go."

"Back to hut?"

"Yes." She stood up. "Thank you for the company and the wine."

He got to his feet. "I walk with you."

"No need." She waved him off and reached for her shawl. "I'll be fine. I'll hurry. It isn't quite dark yet."

"I go with you."

His eyes locked on hers. She paused, torn by the desire to spend more time with Vinko and take advantage of the protection he would provide, but worried that if she let him accompany her, once again she would be depending on a man.

"There is no need for both of us to walk all that way."

"Time I have."

"Really." She flung the shawl around her shoulders. "It isn't necessary. If I see a vampire, I'll hide my neck."

His expression turned dark and serious. "Is not for joke."

Vinko stepped to the door and held it open, all humor and charm gone. "Come. I get box from you."

Eva had no logical grounds to refuse him and a very good reason for having him return to the shack on the beach.

Get rid of the box. Get rid of the man. Exactly what she wanted.

She brushed past him and swept out to the street.

8

Londo City, The Anglo Territories

A SOFT RAP on the door broke Gabriel Stone's concentration. Frowning, he covered the Petrie dish and placed it onto the tray with the others. Specimen #10. Another failure. He had yet to find a substance to kill the fungus that was consuming his brother's skin. He pulled off his mask and sighed. He was running out of ideas. And Silas was running out of time. In the past few months, his brother had grown increasingly frail, as if his true age were catching up with him.

"Yes?" he called over his shoulder as he pulled off his gloves.

The door to the lab opened. His new secretary, Citizen Ritchie, stuck her head into the room. She was younger and more eager than Citizen Beach had been. Better yet, she didn't seem attracted to him. Within months of being hired, she had organized his office and inventoried everything in the lab. Patients came and went with efficiency and ease. The clinic never ran out of supplies and records were never misplaced. He should have sacked his former secretary long ago.

"There's someone here to see you." Citizen Ritchie rolled her big brown eyes meaningfully.

Gabriel gave her a half-smile. "And?"

"A Citizen Valentine? She says she knows you."

"Ruby?"

"You know such a woman?" Citizen Ritchie's eyes grew wider.

"We have a brief acquaintance, yes. Show her into the examination room, please."

Gabriel scribbled some notes in a lab book and then took off his white lab coat, all the while thinking of his older brother and what would happen to Londo—and to him—if his brother died. Complete chaos would ensue. Silas had ruled Londo for five hundred years, never letting up and never giving in. The survival of both vampires and humans had depended upon his strength. Once he died, however, infighting would destroy the infrastructure of the Anglo Territories, until a new leader emerged with a new vision.

If and when that happened, Gabriel would leave Londo. Somehow he would find Joanna Wilder, and if she were still alive, he would forge a new life with her. Somewhere. Anywhere. Once his loyalty to his brother had run its course, he would be free to live his own life. And it wouldn't be this one.

Enduring the past year without Joanna had revealed to Gabriel just how flat his life was. To be sure, he helped people. He saved children. He eased pain sometimes and set broken limbs. He had even talked Silas out of punishing the citizens of Londo for rising up against the Overseers. But his personal life was a dull expanse of ticking clocks and suffocating salons. His empty apartment at the Central Compound echoed with the footsteps of another life, making him all too aware of how hollow his world had become. For all intents and purposes, he had abandoned his apartment and stayed there only when visiting Silas.

He existed to work. That was all.

To escape the darkest hours, he played the piano at the lab townhouse, sometimes far into the night. He drank the newfangled "ELBI!" concoction so he didn't have to leave the townhouse to hunt. The only time he did quit the premises was to visit Silas. But even that he avoided as much as possible. He suspected that the fungus originated in the ancient buildings of the Central Compound, and the less time he spent at the compound, the better for his health.

Besides, he felt compelled to discover a cure for the fungus. The fate of his brother and the rest of the Overseers depended upon him. So he worked day and night, trying to come up with something that would cure Silas' affliction. He hadn't slept for months. He was exhausted and lonely. Gabriel sighed again and hung his lab coat on a peg by the door. Then he washed his hands and left the lab.

As he walked to the examination room, he tried to guess why Ruby Valentine had deigned to visit him. She'd never liked him. She had always been jealous of his relationship with Roman Brandt. But Roman must be the reason she was here. Unfortunately, Gabriel knew nothing about the fate of his best friend, other than he'd been banished to the north after the riot. Nothing Gabriel had said or done had changed Silas' mind about *that* particular punishment.

Maybe Ruby Valentine had some news for him for a change. Gabriel's heart lifted. He opened the door.

"Citizen Valentine," he greeted, holding out his hand.

"Doctor." With a derisive sniff, she allowed him to raise her hand to his lips. Her leather glove reeked of cigarette smoke.

"Please, have a seat." He indicated the chair by the examination table.

"I'm not here for an appointment." She swept her velvet skirts around in a dramatic swoosh. Another cloud of stale cigarette smoke enveloped him. He curled his newly washed hand under his nose to mask the odor and closed the door.

"No?" He faced her again and let his gaze wander over her.

Ruby Valentine dressed to fit her name in a riot of color that was prohibited to ordinary citizens of Londo. Every time he had encountered her, she had been attired in wine-colored velvet as she was now, with a crimson satin blouse and maroon feathers. She had a penchant for gaudy jewelry and complicated hats that overwhelmed her small face. He wondered if she were pretty under all the powder and lipstick. But who could tell, when she postured like a harlot, puffing hand-rolled cigarettes and enveloped in a cloud of fumes? At least she'd had enough manners not to smoke in the clinic.

"You know I've never liked you, Gabriel."

"I am aware of that."

"But I'm not a complete prick."

"I never said you were." He smiled at her use of the English swearword lexicon. No other woman he knew would refer to herself in such a way.

Ruby sniffed and looked down her nose at him. "You tried your best for Roman. I'll give you that."

"I did."

"That's why I'm here. Favor for favor."

"Favor? What are you talking about?"

"My boys told me something you might be interested in hearing."

"Oh?" Gabriel remembered the two young men who had helped carry Aiden Bannister to the boat—during a night that seemed lifetimes ago. That night had been one of the last times he'd seen Joanna. He crossed his arms, doubting that any information Ruby considered valuable would prove all that intriguing to him. But he let her enjoy the moment. "Do tell."

"It's about Joanna Wilder."

"What?" Gabriel came to complete attention. "What about her?"

"She's been captured."

"Where? When?" Gabriel grabbed the small woman's shoulders.

"What? Torn up about a common citizen?" She laughed at his sudden change in demeanor and ludicrous devotion to a human. "God, Gabriel. Listen to yourself."

"Tell me what you know. Everything!"

"I don't know all the details."

"What *do* you know?" He released her, desperate for information.

She drove him mad by taking the time to brush one shoulder, as if to sweep away his touch. "All I know is she was seen being put on a train."

"A train? To where? When?"

"Londo to Port Pennwood. At dawn."

"Good God." Gabriel turned for the door. There was no time to lose. The train had a good eight-hour start on him. His mind whirled. He would have to leave immediately. "Why didn't you come sooner?"

She shrugged and pursed her lips in an expression she probably thought was provocative, but the effect only accentuated the smudged line of her lipstick. "A girl has to get her beauty rest."

The delay could mean life or death for Joanna. He shook his head and yanked open the door.

"I'm coming with you, Gabriel."

"You'll never be able to keep up." He strode down the hall, told Citizen Ritchie that he'd be back in a week, grabbed his greatcoat, and headed for the mews, with Ruby Valentine clattering behind him. Damnation. Even in her heavy gown and high-heeled boots, she matched him stride for stride.

"You don't own a horse, do you?" Gabriel asked.

"Won't stop me."

Gabriel sprinted toward the gelding he owned but rarely rode. Horses never obeyed him, so he preferred to travel in carriages. But this afternoon, the gelding seemed to pick up on the seriousness of the situation. He stood still as Gabriel threw on the saddle and cinched it. He heard Ruby behind him, doing the same to a massive horse that belonged to Roman Brandt.

"You there!" a stable hand came running.

Gabriel guided his mount out of the stall as Ruby burst past him on the giant gray stallion, her breasts bouncing in the confines of her bustier.

"Citizen, that's not your horse!" the stable hand shouted. "Stop! Come back here!"

Ruby ignored him and thundered out of the building. Gabriel swung into the saddle and rode past the frustrated stable hand.

Amazingly, the horse followed his commands this time.

Gabriel leaned forward, urging the animal to run through the streets of Londo. He headed for the western gate. There was no time to spare. If he didn't get to Port Pennwood soon after the train arrived there, he might lose Joanna forever.

9

As Eva and Vinko walked along the quay, Eva evaluated the tide. If they were quick, they could use the shortcut along the foot of the cliff.

"This way." She grabbed her skirts and hurried down the slippery steps to the sand. Vinko followed. "If we walk fast, we can make it before the tide comes in."

"Is best path?" He scanned the narrow strip of sand ahead of them.

"In this light, yes. We can't take the cliff path at the top. The way down is too precipitous in the dark."

"Oki doki."

She strode down the beach, keeping up a pace that made her puff. Vinko walked beside her, not even winded.

"Teach me now," he suggested.

"Really?"

"No waiting."

"All right." She skirted a tide pool that she could barely see in the dark. Dusk merged everything into an expanse of gray. "First of all, you have to start using more words."

"More?"

"Yes. Especially the word '*the*.'"

"What is this word?"

"It goes in front of important words. Like 'This is *the* beach. I am *the* woman. You are *the* man.'"

"But same as 'I am man'. No difference. Same idea."

"Yes, but it's not the way we say things."

"Oki doki."

"And no one says that, either."

"Oki doki."

When she shot him an admonishing glance, he chuckled and gazed down at her with a smile full of merriment. She rolled her eyes, mostly at herself. She wasn't accustomed to being teased, only reprimanded and shamed. She must learn new ways of interacting, just as Vinko had to learn new ways of speaking. She could stop analyzing every word and gesture, especially hers. She could be herself. Be more natural.

But as if to prove her wrong, Fate put a rock in her path that she didn't notice. She stumbled.

Vinko took her elbow without stopping the lesson, as if the protective gesture had been offered on an unconscious level. "I am *the* man," Vinko said. "You, *the* pretty woman. Walk on *the* beach."

Eva did not pull back. She liked the way his long fingers clutched her elbow in a warm, firm grip that was all about assisting and not about possessing. There was a big difference.

She also liked the way his vigorous nature glowed next to her, bouncing and positive and eager to learn. His company seemed natural and full of unexplored nuances. She could sense in him a friend, lover or even family. Everything. It was as if he had always been part of her world—on the periphery—and she had simply discovered that he was there.

She longed to relax for once and enjoy the sound of his beautiful baritone voice and walk and walk and walk.

But then, with a gentle squeeze of her elbow, Vinko pulled her to a stop.

"Wait," his voice rumbled.

Surprised by the sudden change in his demeanor, she glanced at him. His entire body had gone rigid as he peered at something up the beach to the left. She followed his stare and studied the cliff, where it jutted out to separate the harbor from her little cove.

"Do you see?" he said, lowering his voice. She could barely hear him over the roll of the waves.

"No. What?"

"There is *the* man on *the* beach."

It wasn't the time to delve into the vagaries of the Anglo language, not when Vinko seemed so worried. She studied the boulders at the base of the cliff and finally spotted what he had seen moments before.

"The vampire." Vinko whispered.

"How do you know?"

"I see line."

"Line?"

"I see *the* line."

"No, I mean, what line?"

"The red line. Around the body."

She examined the figure ahead. All she saw was a vague silhouette of a man standing in the darkness ahead of them.

"I don't see it."

"In the night, I see the line around the vampire. Always."

Curious, she glanced at him. Maybe Croatian people had more acutely developed senses than those of Londo citizens.

He slipped something from the pocket of his coat and palmed it in his left hand.

"Walk now," he said. He pulled her forward.

She held back, not understanding the plan. "We're walking *toward* a vampire?"

"Time to start the work here." His voice had turned grim once more.

Vinko's reply puzzled her. Danger loomed in front of them, and they were walking straight into it. Fear grabbed her, but she kept silent. This was no time for explanations. She had to trust him.

Before she could stop herself, she clutched Vinko's bicep with her free hand and pulled closer to his tall frame.

"Vampire will ask for directions," Vinko continued. "Talk. Friendly. Not friendly, Eva. Never look in the eyes."

"Oki doki," she whispered.

They approached the figure. Eva could feel Vinko's muscles tighten as he prepared to confront a creature that could easily kill them.

The silhouette pulled away from the rock it had been propped against. The man blocked their forward progress. To get around him, they would have to wade through the roiling surf and risk getting bashed to death or drowned.

"Good evening," the man said. His voice carried over the plunging waves. The tone was pleasant and friendly— not at all what Eva expected from a monster. In the light of dusk, his face and hands looked as human as hers. She couldn't smell anything bad, either. He could have been a sailor from Port Pennwood, out for a stroll. Apparently, her education on vampires had been woefully lacking.

As her terror mounted, Eva kept her gaze focused on a piece of driftwood just beyond the stranger's shoulder. She prayed Vinko knew how to handle this encounter, or in a couple of minutes, they would be dead.

Then something dropped to the ground behind them and hissed. Shocked, Eva turned to look, breaking her hold on Vinko. A second man had leapt from the rocks behind them. He crouched and hissed and held up his hands like claws. This was the vampire she had always visualized.

In her shock, she looked straight at him.

"No!" Vinko yelled. He threw something at the crouching vampire and then grabbed Eva's head and pressed her face into the small of his shoulder. She struggled, hardly able to breathe, but his arms were like iron bands around her.

"Don't look!" he commanded.

Something fizzed and exploded behind her. Even with her nose stuck into Vinko's armpit, she sensed a bright light flare around them. The light was more brilliant than anything she had ever witnessed. And hot. Intense heat blazed across her back and shoulders. The air reeked of urine and sulfur.

The first vampire snarled behind her. To Eva's horror, he dragged her out of Vinko's grip and clutched her around her chest. A cold hand clamped over her mouth, hurting her jaw. The vampire's fetid breath blew past her ear.

Terrified, Eva stared at Vinko. She struggled to get away, but the vampire only clamped down harder, hurting her even more.

"Surrender your weapons," the vampire ordered. "Or I will snap her neck."

"And then where is supper?" Vinko countered. He slipped a hand in his trouser pocket, affecting a bizarre casual pose, considering the circumstances.

The vampire snorted, angry. "A jokester, are you?"

"No, the nightmare for you."

She stared at Vinko, pleading with her eyes for him to do something, not just stand there, teasing the monster.

In answer, Vinko passed his free hand in a quick pantomime across his eyes. She knew exactly what he was telling her to do. She shut her eyes. Tightly.

Again, she heard the hiss, the explosion and then was bathed in the hot light. As if by magic, the cold hand around her mouth disintegrated. It was as if the flesh and bone dissolved into thin air. It couldn't be possible. But Eva didn't dare open her eyes to see what was happening. She felt the same dissolving sensation behind her, as the pressure of the vampire's body eased and then fell away. She heard his clothes plop to the sand.

"Now open," Vinko said.

She opened her eyes and sucked in a breath when she saw the carnage around her.

All that was left of the vampires were coats, trousers and shoes and big white splotches fanning out on the sand, glowing in the faded light. The sea breathed behind her, unconcerned with the destruction that had just occurred.

"They're gone!" Eva sputtered.

"The big light kills the vampire," Vinko said. "Not just the sun."

"Good Gottfried." Eva stood staring at the white splotches, too shocked to move while Vinko emptied the wallets of the vampires. He folded the credits and handed them to Eva.

"Reward," he said.

"For what? You were the one that killed them."

"For not scream. For bravery."

Eva needed the money too much to argue. She stuffed the credits into the pocket of her vest. When she finished, she looked up to see Vinko studying her.

He took her by the shoulders. "You oki doki, Eva?"

She swallowed. "I will be. Maybe."

"We go." He took her hand and pulled her down the beach. She let him drag her. She was too much in shock to protest his forward behavior or the speed at which he walked.

"How did you do that?" she gasped.

"Special weapon. Family secret."

"Chemicals?"

"Yes."

"So that's what's in the box. Chemicals to kill vampires."

"Yes, Miss Eva."

She fell silent and struggled to keep up with his pace. It was almost too dark to see now. He squeezed her fingers.

"You are quick," he said. "I like this."

"What?"

"Quick. Not have to explain."

"Oh." She was still too deep in shock to refute the compliment. But it warmed her just the same.

"I stay at hut," Vinko said as they rounded the point to her little cove. "With you."

She couldn't think of anything more dangerous. Vinko and her alone in the small shack, sharing a tiny bed, could only mean trouble.

Then again, she *could* think of something more danger-ous: more vampires.

"It isn't something a lady would ordinarily say yes to," she replied. "But I'm saying yes."

"Always the lady." He shot her a quick smile. "And me? The gentleman."

Yes, he was. She could trust Vinko. But she wasn't so sure she could trust herself.

10

_____

Eva woke up the next morning to find Vinko dozing in the chair by the hearth. They had endured a long night, cold and uncomfortable, wary of building a fire that would attract attention. Eva had felt guilty not asking Vinko to share the narrow pallet with her, but she had been too afraid of what might happen between them when their defenses were down. Vinko probably would have refused the offer anyway. He had insisted on keeping watch. Now, the long night had caught up with him.

Eva rose and shook the kinks out of her shoulders and back and then padded to the tall man slouched in the chair.

"Vinko," she whispered, placing a palm on his shoulder. The touch of him galvanized her, fusing her to him far more deeply than the simple gesture should have. She stared at him, stunned by his effect on her.

He had touched her plenty of times—at the pub, on their walk and during their battle with the vampires. But she had never reached out to him since awakening him on the beach. It was entirely different to touch *him*. His strength and warmth sizzled under her palm and shot up her arm to dance in her chest. She longed to push her hand over the mound of muscle of his shoulder and caress his back. She could visualize running her hand up his neck and into his lustrous black hair. She could imagine dipping down to his lips.

Then his eyes opened, and she gasped. Her fantasy cut off as a much more powerful sensation washed over her. Being this close to Vinko, standing above him like this, and watching his generous spirit rise to animate his body was the most intimate moment she had ever shared with a man.

He blinked, and his eyes transformed from cloudy to crystalline in an instant.

"Eva?"

She struggled to regain her self-control. "Take the bed."

He glanced at the doorway. "Is morning...is *the* morning?"

"Yes."

"We made it." He patted her hand and sat up straight.

"Yes." Eva knew a dismissal when she received one. She slipped her hand off his shoulder and was sorry to break the connection. Then she stepped backward to allow him to get up. He stretched and looked down at her, smiling.

"Big man. Small chair."

"Yes." She smiled back. "And the pallet is not much bigger."

He glanced at the bed. "Still warm. Soft. I sleep."

"Good."

Eva could make a fire, now that morning had come and vampires weren't so apt to be walking about. *Vampires.* As if the idea were commonplace. She still found it difficult to accept the idea that such creatures walked among humans. Yet, she had seen it with her own eyes.

She bent to her task and later set water to boil for tea. Vinko slept soundly, his back to her and her shawls pulled over his shoulders. As she waited for the water to heat, she watched him sleep.

His presence calmed her in a peculiar way. Perhaps it was his slow, steady breathing that soothed her. Or his powerful frame that promised protection from danger. Maybe just having an amiable person around was the reason she felt so at peace. But deep in her heart, she knew that it was something more. There was something that glowed out of Vinko. His glow surrounded her, allowing him to hold her and understand her on a level that far surpassed any human encounter she had experienced.

She wondered if everyone felt his glow, or if she was the only one to notice it. She wanted to be the only one. She wanted to be special to Vinko.

Then again, she had *always* wanted to be special—to anyone and everyone—which was absolutely pathetic. Vinko was just another someone. As she was to him. She had to remember that.

Eva frowned at herself. She was done looking for recognition. Her job was to get on with life and maybe even do something with her time here on Earth. She turned back to the tea preparation and avoided looking at Vinko for the rest of the morning.

———

AT NOON, Eva and Vinko walked up the cliff and took the high path into Port Pennwood. Vinko carried his crate and a small leather case he had recovered from the beach. Eva carried her violin and some clothes wrapped in a shawl.

They could see the train just pulling into the tiny station on the quay and hurried down to the platform. But when they got to the station, Eva was surprised to see passengers were still sitting in the cars and men were running up and down the train, blowing whistles and yelling.

"Stowaway! No one leaves until we find the stowaway!"

Vinko looked down at her. "What is word, stowaway?"

"Someone is on the train without paying."

"Ah." He shifted the crate in his arms. "We pay where?"

"On the train."

"Ah." He studied the metal wheels and complicated undercarriage of the coach in front of them and bent down to inspect the mechanical apparatus. "Nice. No train in the Croatia."

"Then this will be a new experience for you." She would enjoy watching his reaction to the loud pistons, screaming rails and exhilarating speed of a train ride.

A conductor appeared at the top of the metal stairs. "Did you see a kid run past? A boy?"

"No," Eva replied, stepping closer. "We just got here."

The conductor popped back into the train car.

A woman hurried down the lane to the platform, lugging a large suitcase. When she saw Eva, she waved.

"Hannah," Eva greeted. "You're going back to Londo?"

"Yes." The woman plopped the case on the ground and straightened, rubbing the small of her back. "Aren't you?"

"Yes. I have no alternative."

"Me neither. I can't stay in Port Pennwood, not without a job. And being turned out without any pay has been really rough, I don't mind saying."

"I'm so sorry for that." Eva reached into her vest and

pulled out the wad of credits Vinko had taken from one of the vampires. She pressed it into Hannah's hand. "Here's something. It isn't much, but—"

Hannah looked down at the money and back up at Eva. "Are you sure? You were thrown out, too, weren't you?"

"Yes, but I expect Charles has something put away in Londo."

"He was that kind of man."

"Yes, he was."

"I'm sorry for your loss, citizen."

"Thank you."

"Will you need help in Londo? Cooking, cleaning?"

"I don't know yet. I don't know what my financial circumstances will be. I doubt I will be able to keep a house like the one here in Port Pennwood."

"Well, if you need me, you can find me at Distribution."

"All right."

"I'd rather work for you than sweeping the streets."

Eva nodded and held out her hand. "Thank you for all your hard work, Hannah. I hope to see you again."

"And you." Hannah shook Eva's hand and then shot a curious glance at Vinko. She must have assumed he was just another person waiting for the train and not connected to Eva, because she didn't ask about him. But Vinko noticed her regard. He stepped forward.

"I help you with the bag?" He pointed at the heavy case at her feet.

Hannah's wrinkled face broke into a smile. "Why, yes."

Vinko grabbed it and swung up the stairs of the coach. Hannah waved at Eva and followed him to a seat at a window. A moment later, Vinko hopped back to the ground, where Eva stood near bottom of the steps.

"My housekeeper," Eva explained. "Former housekeeper."

"You make me stranger to her?"

"Did you want to be introduced?" Eva flushed at being called out for bad manners. "Don't you want to travel incognito?"

"What is the word, *incognito*?"

"It means keeping your identity concealed. Hiding who you are."

"Sunaras do not hide. Soon, vampires know I am here."

"And that doesn't frighten you?"

"Is my job." He looked down at her, his mouth in a grim line. "In Croatia, all people know everyone. We stick together. We stay strong."

"In Londo, we can't stick together. The Overseers don't allow people to stand around and chat. They break up groups of three or more."

"Why is the reason?"

"So we don't plot uprisings." Eva thought back to the fateful day of the riot, when her life had fallen apart. She shut off the memory. "We work, we go home, and we lock our doors against the night. The only time we get together is during Distribution."

"What is this Distribution?"

"It's a time we get our rations and hear announcements. Every Sunday. But we don't have time to talk there, either. We have to stand in lines for each and every item of food."

"And you go back to this place?"

"I don't have a choice." The thought made her chest ache with dread. "But when we get back there, will you go by your real name, or the name on your ID?"

"Yes. Important." He slipped out the card and looked

at the name and number. "In Londo, I am Daniel Kane."

"Shall you be Daniel or Dan?"

"You choose."

She glanced at his tall, well-built frame and attractive face and smiled. "Daniel. You look like a Daniel."

"Then I am Daniel." He shrugged, winked at her and put the card away.

Before Eva could warn Vinko about his future in Londo City, she felt something drip on her hand. She glanced down and was shocked to see a red splotch on her skin. Blood. She looked up. Blood had dripped off the overhanging roof of the coach. She stepped back to get a better view of the car.

There on the roof, flattened against the metal slope, clung a boy, holding onto a bar for dear life, his face and hair covered with soot. All she could see were two white eyes staring at her—eyes glazed with pain and fear.

"Vinko." She grabbed his arm. "He's up there. The boy." She pointed at the roof. Vinko raised on tiptoe for a better look.

"He is hurt. I get the boy."

"If they see him, they will punish him. And us."

"Then not see."

He put down his crate and slipped off the small leather case he had slung over his back. The conductor pounded through the coach again, toward the back of the train, blowing his whistle. Vinko waited until the man had passed and then swung up the metal stairs. He disappeared into the coach and reappeared in the space between the cars, where he was tall enough to reach up and grab the boy's coat.

The boy cried out. Eva watched, dreading the next few minutes if anyone should catch Vinko in the act of rescuing a stowaway.

A moment later, Vinko appeared at the stairs, gripping the boy's arm. The boy didn't struggle as Vinko pulled him down the metal steps. Eva could see a red splotch on his arm where he'd been shot.

A movement caught her eye. Another conductor hurried through the coach in their direction.

"Quickly," Eva warned, stepping toward them. She pulled the boy into her arms, pivoted so that her body and dress shielded him and then surrounded his scrawny frame with her cloak, just as the conductor burst into view at the top of the stairs. Vinko planted himself in front of her and faced the train conductor.

"You sure you didn't see a boy?" The conductor peered at them. Eva clutched the boy more tightly. His strident breaths puffed on the small of her throat. He felt like a leafless shrub in her arms.

"Someone jump off. There," Vinko pointed at the end of the train. "He runs. Fast. Up hill."

Eva prayed the conductor wouldn't study her too closely and notice how lumpy she had become in the last few minutes.

"Jumped off?" the conductor studied the end of the train. He sighed. Then he added, "What's wrong with your wife?"

"She is sick. Baby time."

"Well, she better not be sick on my train."

"No, not sick on the train."

"There will be hell to pay if she is," the conductor grumbled, reaching for the corroded handrail. "No one makes a mess on my train. And no one rides for free, by Gottfried."

"We look for the boy."

"Obliged." The conductor swung up to the coach and

blew his whistle. "All aboard," he barked, his voice sharp with annoyance.

"He's shaking," Eva said, looking over her shoulder.

"He's hurt," Vinko replied. "I take him to the inn."

"They will look for him there."

"He is just the boy."

"He must be important for them to make such a fuss."

"My mother," the boy gasped, his voice muffled by the heavy cloak. "My mother."

"It's all right," Eva said into his hair. He smelled gamey, as if he hadn't bathed in days.

Vinko put a hand on her shoulder. "Bar man will hide."

"Really?"

Vinko nodded. "Not the friend of Neal Moray. Or Overseers." He put his arm around her shoulders. "Walk by station. Now. Boy, walk too, under the cloak. Boy?"

"I don't think he can."

"He has to."

"I will," the boy replied. He pulled back, and Eva loosened her grip enough to allow him to face forward.

Eva shuffled past the wall of the station and around the corner, trying hard not to draw attention to the awkward way she walked. She hoped that onlookers might think a husband was guiding his pregnant wife to the toilet.

As soon as they rounded the corner, Vinko held out his hands.

"Boy, come out." He glanced at Eva. "Go to crate. Watch. I come back."

She nodded, but before she could ask any more questions, Vinko swept the injured boy into his arms and trotted down an alley toward the back of the inn, a block away. Eva returned to the platform and stood next to the crate and her shawl-wrapped belongings.

For the first time since coming to Port Pennwood, she watched prisoners disembarking from the front of the train. One by one, men and women and children dropped from the last step of each coach and shuffled toward the processing facility. They were bound together by wide metal bands around their necks, linked to heavy chains. If one person fell, others would follow. If one person tried to bolt, the others would drag him back.

Eva raised her chin and tried not to stare, but she couldn't help herself. These were the lawbreakers of Londo City, the criminals and the unlucky. These were the murderers and thieves, as well as people who had done something as insignificant as swearing or not cooperating with an agent of the Overseers—just as she and Vinko had done moments before. The prisoners would be processed and shipped northward to the Norsea work camps, never to be heard from again.

Eva had ruined her life to avoid imprisonment on a train like this. But maybe a prison train had always been in her future. Maybe the specter of a train would keep haunting her just as self-centered men with agendas kept dominating her life.

Eva fought down a flush. Helping the boy might have been the most foolish thing she had done yet, but no sense drawing attention to herself now. There was nothing she could do but wait by Vinko's crate and hope he would make it back in time before the train pulled out.

Then a prisoner stepped off the nearest coach. Her chain dropped to the ground and clinked. For some reason the sound caught Eva's attention, and she looked at the prisoner's face.

In a single glance, in a single heartbeat, all thoughts of the boy and Vinko vanished.

11

JOANNA. Did she cry out her sister's name, or had the sound only blazed through her thoughts? Whatever had happened, the female prisoner turned to look her way. Their eyes locked and held. The prisoner's eyes were full of questions and confusion, but her glance raked over Eva's face like a brand.

"Joanna!" Eva mouthed. She took a step forward, but her sister cautioned her to stay back by holding two fingers away from her skirt. The gesture was a secret code they had used since childhood.

Eva stood rooted to the platform, drinking in the sight of her sister, until a guard shoved Joanna with the butt of a baton. Joanna stumbled forward and didn't look back as she clanked down the platform with the other prisoners. Her brown hair blew in the breeze and her skirts whipped around her slender, unbending frame. Even as a prisoner, Joanna was as proud as ever.

And she was still alive. Joanna was alive!

Eva stood in her boots, every particle of her being

suspended in the air, detonated by joy. The only things keeping her attached to the Earth were her boots.

So *what* if Joanna was a prisoner? So what if she walked in shackles? She was alive. *Joanna was alive.*

Eva thought of the keys she had stuffed in the pocket of her vest. Charles had died trying to use the keys to free a woman. She had to do better. She had to be more careful. She would free her sister or die trying, just like Charles.

For once, Joanna's life was in Eva's hands and not the other way around. She couldn't fail her sister. Not like all the other times when she'd been weak or lazy or just plain mean.

"Joanna," Eva whispered as she watched her sister march toward the processing plant. "I'm going to make it up to you. This time, I'm going to do right by you."

"All aboard!" the conductor called, hanging out of the middle car. "All aboard for Londo City."

No one but Eva lingered on the platform.

"Citizen?" the conductor asked, looking straight at her.

"Sorry, my husband is late coming back."

"I can't hold the train."

"I know, citizen."

The conductor shook his head in disgust. He probably was weary of dealing with passengers who were late, didn't have enough money or were desperate to get on with no credits at all, like the stowaway boy. But she didn't care about the trials and tribulations of a train conductor.

Her sister was alive. Joanna had come to Port Pennwood for deportation. She was a prisoner, but *alive*. To Eva, this day was better than every C-Day celebration combined.

The train signaled its departure in one long toot as the pistons and gears lurched into action.

"Last call for Londo City!" the conductor bellowed from the rear of the train. "Last call."

Then he swung a lantern, signaling to the engineer to leave the station. In a blast of steam and grinding gears, the train chugged to a start.

As the train pulled out of Port Pennwood, Vinko ran up behind her.

"Eva!" he said. "You missed the train. Sorry!"

"It's all right. I wasn't going to go anyway."

"Not to Londo City? Moray say to leave."

"I don't care." Eva grinned. "My sister was on the train."

Vinko glanced around, confused.

"Sister?"

"She was one of the prisoners that got off."

"Sister is the prisoner?"

"Yes, but I have a key to the processing plant. I'm going to get her out of there."

Vinko's eyes darkened as he studied her face. "This key? Key of husband?"

"Yes."

"Is dangerous, this?"

"Yes." She took in a resolute breath. "But it's something I have to do, Vinko. Or die trying."

He studied her, as serious as he had been during the vampire attack. "We talk first. We go to boy and talk."

"All right."

"Come."

Eva grabbed her bundle of belongings and followed him.

VINKO GUIDED her to the rear entrance of the Golden Hind and cautioned her to be quiet, even though they hadn't said a word since leaving the train platform. Eva could hear men talking in the public room beyond and could smell fish frying. Her stomach growled. But there was no time for eating. She trailed after Vinko, up the shadowy stairs to the rooms above the pub. Vinko opened the door with a key and motioned her inside.

Eva swept into the small room, no longer concerned about the rules governing the wife of a commissioner or the social conventions that prohibited her from entering the room of a strange man. Rules had lost their weight. Convention was a thing of the past. All that mattered now was Joanna.

Vinko's room faced the harbor and provided a view of the processing plant on the peninsula. Eva tried not to imagine what was going on there, and what Joanna must be enduring. Agents of the Overseers could be cruel, especially to those who had broken the law. Eva tore her thoughts away from her sister and glanced around the room instead.

There was a wardrobe near the door and a small table and chair and then a large bed with a metal frame. The boy from the train lay on it, propped up by two pillows, with his shirt off and a bandage around his left arm.

Eva guessed the boy to be about twelve years old, judging by his face, but his underfed frame made him seem much younger. His shoulders were bony and his ribs and breastbone poked out of pale skin that glowed white in the shadows of the rented room.

"Is he all right?" Eva stepped to the side of the bed.

"Shot in arm." Vinko surveyed the boy. "But the bullet goes in and out."

The boy stared at her with large, serious brown eyes.

"Please don't report me," he said. "Please, citizen."

"I won't. As long as you tell us what you were doing on that train."

"It's my mother. She was taken here. And it was all my fault." The boy flung his uninjured arm over his eyes and hunched forward, sobbing.

Eva stared. She knew first hand the anguish the boy was feeling. Seeing him was like looking through a window at her past. Before she could think twice, she sat down next to him.

"There now," she said, unsure of what to say or do. She had no experience with children. "It can't be your fault."

"It is. I took something. And they came."

"What did you take?"

"Food." He lowered his elbow and dashed his tears away with his fingertips. His nails were filthy. His tears forged tracks through the soot on his cheeks.

"Food?"

"I was so tired of being hungry, citizen. Me and my mum are always so hungry."

"What did you steal?"

"A wheel of cheese."

Eva shared a glance with Vinko. He ambled toward the bed.

"They take your mother for the cheese?" Vinko asked, incredulous.

The boy nodded, barely able to suppress more sobs.

"I found out she got sentenced for deportation. So I snuck on the next train."

"Your mother is already here?" Eva asked. "At Port Pennwood?"

The boy nodded again.

"Did you ride on top of the train the entire way here?"

"Just the last day, after they shot me."

"Good Gottfried."

Vinko walked to the door. "Stay, Eva. I get food."

She nodded. While Vinko left, Eva turned back to the boy.

The kid clutched her forearm. "Please don't report me, citizen." His eyes were hollow with hunger. "I'll do anything. I'll work, clean, fetch—anything you ask, but please don't turn me in."

She patted his hand. "Don't worry. I won't. I'm in a bit of trouble myself."

His worried eyes cleared somewhat. "You are?"

"I was supposed to leave town and go back to Londo."

"But you missed your train?"

She nodded.

"Because of me."

"No. It was my choice." She patted his hand again. "My choice entirely. What's your name?"

"Tam."

"Tam, I'm Eva."

The boy started to utter the usual words required of good manners, but he broke down sobbing instead and flung his arms around her. Eva had no recourse but to sit there and allow herself to be hugged. She put her hands on his ribcage and eased them around his back. The gesture felt wooden to her, but she forced herself to keep her arms linked around him. Holding him was like clutching a bag of bones.

Comforting the boy was awkward and unsettling, but she knew she had to do it. Comforting children was something adults did. And she was the only adult present. She shut her eyes and hoped Vinko would come back soon to take over the job.

The boy trembled against her. His thatch of brown hair tickled her skin and his tears soaked the neckline of her blouse. She turned her head to avoid smelling him. His hair was dry and reeked of unwashed hats. She wondered how long it had been since he'd had a bath.

Worse than that was the touch of his body. She'd cooked chickens that had more meat on them. This boy was like a walking skeleton—a smelly, walking skeleton. She could barely take a breath without gagging.

"Vinko is getting some lunch." She thought a pat on the back might cheer him, so she patted his back, all the while wanting more than anything to push him away. His ribcage sounded hollow. "And then you can talk to him."

He nodded against her neck.

"He'll have a plan, Tam. Don't worry."

He drew back. "He'll help me?"

"I'm sure he will." She gave him a confident smile, even though she had no idea how they would move forward. She leaned back and forced herself to push away Tam's dirty bangs in a gesture that showed she cared—even if he disgusted her. The boy released her and sank against the headboard behind him. At least she was free of his grip. She stood up, glad to get away from him, and walked to the window.

The sooner she could ditch this kid and leave him in Vinko's capable hands, the better. She had more pressing things to do—getting her sister out of the processing plant, for one. Babysitting a wounded boy would only drag her down.

12

As EVA CHEWED her last bit of fish, she looked over at the boy sitting in the bed. He had plowed through his huge plate of food before she had eaten half of hers. Poor kid. He had probably gone days without eating.

Even though he was not her responsibility, she hoped the food had eased the haunted hunger in his eyes. No child should go hungry in Londo City. But plenty of them did—including her when she had been his age.

Eva glanced at Tam's empty plate and then up at his face. He had fallen asleep sitting beside Vinko with his fingers still wrapped around the fork.

As Vinko eased off the bed, Eva set aside her plate. She slipped the fork from Tam's dirty fist. He murmured and stirred as she set aside the dish, but he was too exhausted to return to consciousness. He must feel safe enough with them to sleep. Struck by his trust, Eva pulled up the coverlet around his scrawny chest. Her hands shook.

The thought that the boy trusted her twisted something deep inside, enough to release a truth she tried never to think about. Why would a child ever trust her? She could turn her back on a child—on anyone for that matter—if it suited her needs. She was not a person to depend on.

His trust scalded her as much as the boiling water had scalded her arm months ago during the riot. She brushed the sleeve that covered her scarred forearm, as if his misplaced trust were crumbs she could wipe away.

"Boy is oki doki?" Vinko asked behind her.

She had to take a deep breath and get a handle on her churning emotions before she could look Vinko in the eye again. She struggled to come up with a subject that was easier to talk about than trust.

"All I know is he needs a bath." She could finally turn around now. "He reeks."

"Later for that. He sleeps. We talk." He motioned her toward the single chair and then sat on the end of the bed, facing her.

"We stay in Port Pennwood," he began.

"Yes. For now."

"You stay in room close to here," he held out a key. "Room 104."

"I can't allow you to pay for a room for me."

"Vampire money."

"Oh." Moray and his kind owed her. She had no qualms about accepting that kind of money from Vinko. She put the key in her vest, along with the other two keys from Charles.

"I stay with boy."

"All right."

"No leaving room when is dark or storm. Vampires about. Moray."

"Yes. I understand."

"No asking anyone to room. Vampire trick. Ask in? They come in. They must ask."

"You're saying that I can keep a vampire out of a room

by not letting them in? That seems odd."

Vinko shrugged. "It is one power you have against them. But," he held up a hand in warning. "They can look at you. Make you do things. Make you ask."

"So don't look in their eyes."

"Yes. Do not look. That is their great power over you."

"All right."

"If I say do not look, Eva, never look."

"I understand. If you see the red line."

"Yes." He held her stare. "When I say 'red,' you will know."

"Code word is 'red.'"

"Yes."

He took a swig of his ale and cradled the mug in his hand as he fell silent. She could tell from the way the sun went out of his expression that he was thinking about something serious. After a long silence, he looked up. His eyebrows rose.

"We help the boy?" He studied her.

Eva glanced at Tam and was struck again by the innocence and trust in his face as he slept.

"I want to help my sister," she said. "If Tam's mother is at the processing facility, then," Eva shrugged, "Why not save both of them?"

"And if mother is not in the plant?"

Eva glanced at Vinko's serious face. "I don't want to think about that right now."

"It is to be thought about."

"Maybe he has family back in Londo. We can take him back with us."

"A boy with family does not come alone on the train. Does not starve."

Vinko was right. She took a deep breath and let it out.

"Well, he's here," she said, thinking out loud. "We can't just abandon him. If his mother is here in Port Pennwood, we can help him find her. If not, we cross that bridge when we come to it. It's not like we are playing by the rules anymore. Are we?"

Vinko nodded and studied her. "Then we think the same, Eva."

His crystalline eyes held her stare for a long moment, and in his gaze she saw an embrace as well as a handshake. It was as if he were reaching out and taking her in his arms to share the sun of his heart and soul. Eva's spirit flowed toward him, aching for the connection he could so easily make with her.

Good Gottfried, his gaze was just as dangerous as a vampire's.

Eva broke off her stare and jumped up to collect the dishes. She stacked them on the tray Vinko had carried them up with. She could feel him watching her.

"I go to processing plant," Vinko finally said. "See how many men guard the prisoners. See the buildings. The doors."

"Or we could sneak in with the keys I have."

"Did not work for the husband."

"Yes, but maybe he didn't know about the vampires. Surely, if he had known the Overseers were vampires, wouldn't he have told me?"

"And risked all? His job? His money? He was director of plant, yes?"

"Yes."

"Much to lose then, with the truth."

"But how could he live like that—if he suspected vampires were herding us around like cattle?"

"He did not want to know, to see. Ruin all."

"But how could he go along with them?"

"Maybe he saw no choice." Vinko frowned. "But I do not understand this one thing."

"What?"

"Why use the key? Why disobey? Why did he do this?"

Eva crossed her arms over her chest. She might as well tell Vinko the truth even if it reflected badly on her relationship with Charles. "He did it because of a woman."

"Woman?" Vinko shot her a surprised stare.

"A lover."

"He would want another woman? Not you? Why would this be?"

Eva blushed at the compliment and then flushed at the prospect of telling Vinko why her marriage had foundered.

"I do not see this as possible," Vinko added. "You are young, beautiful. Smart. Why is not enough for him?"

His question burned through Eva. Why was it always about the man making the choice? Her cheeks grew so hot, she had to turn her back to Vinko, so he wouldn't see how his question had affected her. Anger choked her.

"Why does he need more?" Vinko added.

"Perhaps Charles wasn't enough for *me*," she said, her voice rough with the rage she had kept in far too long. She faced Vinko. "Does anyone ever think of that? Maybe it was Charles' shortcomings, not mine, that sent him to another woman's bed."

Daggers blazed from her eyes. She had kept her anguish tamped down too tight, and now it flared out to scorch a completely innocent person asking completely innocent questions.

"Why does it have to be my fault!"

Damn her lack of self-control. She tried to rein in her emotions, but they galloped off like a runaway horse. She had stuffed away the truth for so long, with no one to talk to, that now it roared out of her.

She had never been able to tell Charles the truth—that she didn't love him, that to make love to him would kill something precious inside her. If she ever told him the truth, she would put an end to their marriage and her future, without the hope of ever learning how to get along with each other. She had always thought they would find common ground after enough time had passed. So she had bottled up the truth, in hopes that her feelings would change. But in the months they'd been married, her feelings hadn't softened toward him, while the truth had become a stone in her gut.

"My mistake." Vinko stood up, flushing. "Bad question."

"Sorry, Vinko. I didn't mean to yell at you."

"You are passionate for this thinking."

"Yes." She lifted her chin. She knew now she would never back down on her requirement for the right kind of love from a man the next time she let one get close to her.

If that day ever came. Which it wouldn't.

She could finally take a breath. "So, to answer your question, Vinko, we didn't get along. It wasn't all his fault. It wasn't all mine. It was just a really bad fit."

Vinko nodded, watching her and waiting for more. She remained staring at him, her chin still lifted.

"I was not in a place to love someone," she continued. "And he didn't have the tools to help me love him, even if I could have. So he went elsewhere for love. I suspect he was in love with that woman all along anyway."

"You did not share the bed with him?"

"No." It felt good to let the truth out, even to someone who didn't understand the English language. But then,

Vinko seemed to understand the world on an intuitive level that required no translation.

"I was…I was sick when we got married. And grieving the loss of my sister. He let me be." She shrugged. "And then it just became easier and easier to say no."

"This is not a marriage for a man."

"Or a woman." She set her jaw.

Vinko studied her face and she let him. For once, she let the truth pour out of her eyes without tempering it first. For a moment, she felt like a genuine being, glowing and real—maybe the way Vinko felt every day.

"We don't marry for love here in the Anglo Territories, Vinko. The Overseers choose a husband for us. And only a lucky few are allowed to marry and produce children."

"Why is this?"

"Because there is only so much food to go around. And the Overseers want to control the quality of the offspring."

"Again. Like cattle." His eyes blazed, as hot as hers now. "What is this place? This Londo? What is a life there?"

"Not much, I guess. But until I met you, I thought it was all there was."

"Yes, life is hard. Everywhere, Eva. Even Croatia. But not all these rules like Londo."

"And that's why my sister was on that train and a prisoner. She decided she'd had enough."

"Your sister is right."

"She was always right." Eva crossed her arms and glared at the wall. "I should have listened to her. But I was a fool."

"You were too young."

Eva glanced at Vinko, wishing she could believe him, but she knew the truth. "No, I was a fool. I thought I could play by their rules and make something of my life. And that it would be enough."

"But here you are." A kind smile flitted over his generous mouth. He put a hand on her shoulder. His touch warmed her.

She didn't pull away. "I made a life all right. A bad one."

"Always time to change," he said softly. He squeezed her shoulder and released her. "Stay with boy. I go out to look at the plant in the daylight. Then we make plan."

She met his gaze, feeling more grounded than she had been since her parents died. Something dirty that had coated her entrails had been washed away by her confession to Vinko. She felt clean. How odd.

And how wonderful.

She fought back a smile. It seemed inappropriate to smile at a time like this. And yet...

He watched her as his own smile grew until it shone from his eyes as well as his mouth. "Eva thinking. I see it." He shook a finger at her. "Watch out."

"You can't possibly know what I'm thinking."

"So talk. Is better Eva, no? To talk to me. To say what is here." He touched his chest. "I listen."

She nodded. She couldn't speak. The glow inside her felt as if it might burst from her chest. Vinko had understood everything she had tried to say—even what she hadn't said.

Vinko stood up. "I go to the factory now."

"I don't understand why you are helping me. And the boy."

"If vampires rule this place, I have reason."

"So you expect to kill every vampire in the Anglo Territories?"

"Is not possible, Eva," he sighed. "But I kill enough to

make frightened. If I kill king, even better. Vampires never to come to Croatia where Vinko Sunara lives."

"What if they kill you first?"

"Hard job for them. Vampires do not hypnotize me."

"Why not?"

"Very much trained. Sunara family is master of this." He winked at her and smiled again, bathing her in the warmth of his confidence. Then he turned for the crate, unlocked it and slipped numerous gray and white packets into his pockets.

Eva walked up behind him. "Give me some of those. I'll come with you."

"No." He glanced at her and shook his head. "You stay with boy."

"But my sister is—"

He raised a hand to cut her off. "They will not question me. I am merchant. With the business question."

"But—"

"First time, I will go, Eva." He touched her shoulder again. "Is not safe for you. No sun in the sky."

"But—"

"I come back soon. You stay with boy." He stuck the long narrow case under his arm and grabbed the tray of dirty dishes. While Eva paced the room at the end of the bed, he walked to the door and turned to look down at her.

"Do not have anger for me," he said, searching her face to ensure she was in agreement with him.

"But my sister is in there. I can't hide away in this inn and do nothing."

"You will go soon."

"But what if it stays cloudy all week? I can't just sit here, babysitting that boy."

"I come back. Tonight we make a good plan. Oki doki?" He squeezed her shoulder.

Exasperated at being left behind, she heaved a heavy sigh and glared at the wall behind him.

"Good," he said, assuming she had agreed to stay behind. He stepped into the hall.

"Look for my sister," she said.

"How does she look?"

"She's taller than me, with darker hair. She sometimes wears glasses, but not so much the last couple of days I was with her." Eva broke off, trying to calculate how many months it had been since she'd seen Joanna. Almost a year. Where had she been all that time?

"What does she wear?"

"A black skirt and vest, with a white blouse."

"Like all the others."

"She wears our father's pocket watch. You'll notice it. It's blue."

"Blue?"

"He painted it, so the Overseers wouldn't think it was real jewelry and take it away."

Vinko rolled his eyes. "Overseers." He turned for the hall.

"Be careful," she called after him. He waved without looking back.

Eva stood in the doorway until Vinko disappeared down the stairs. Then she locked the door and moved to the window to watch him walk toward the processing plant. He had a straight, purposeful stride. She studied him, admiring his lean lines, until frustration with him burned away all physical appreciation of him. His plan kept her from Joanna.

Eva scanned the sky behind Vinko. She had hours until dusk. She could tell from having watched weather patterns at Port Pennwood for almost a year that the clouds would burn off in a few minutes.

She was done acquiescing to the agendas of men. Joanna was *her* sister, not his. She should be the one to investigate. Eva grabbed her cloak, made sure the boy was fast asleep, and then hurried down the back stairs of the inn.

13

AT THE DEPORTATION FACILITY, Joanna Wilder stood in stony silence as a guard unlocked the manacle around her throat. She welcomed the release, as the iron collar had chafed the back of her neck. Once free of her prisoner chains and able to walk unfettered, she was prodded into a small, windowless room.

Joanna glanced around, looking for escape options. A clerk sat at a desk with a gas lamp and a ledger, and another man stood in the shadows behind him. If they were ordinary men, she might have a chance of overpowering them and dashing through the door beyond. But then she recognized the silhouette of the second man's top hat and cane. Neal Moray was here. Dread spiked through her. He was *not* an ordinary man.

"Well, well, well." Moray peeled away from the wall. He stepped into the light of the gas lamp, which glowed along the side of his white face, illuminating the scar at his mouth. Joanna surveyed his ruined face. The wound she had inflicted a year ago had healed but had left him with a hideous smirk.

He caught her staring and tilted his head higher on his thick neck, which made his shoulders appear more sloped than they already were. "Look who's here. My favorite citizen. Joanna Wilder."

Joanna stared down her nose at the small man, hating his voice, his sneer and the way he always showed up at the most inopportune times.

"I am feeling so lucky right about now," Moray continued. "You?"

Joanna didn't answer.

Moray ambled closer and lifted the hem of her skirt with the tip of his cane.

"Tch. Tch. Looks like you've been wearing this dress past its sell date, citizen."

"It's my favorite," she replied, careful not to look in his eyes. She kept her stare fastened on his scar, knowing it would irritate him.

"I've been searching for you everywhere," Moray said. "Silas Stone will be thrilled to know I've found you. He'll be over the moon."

"You didn't find me. I was betrayed."

Moray ignored her rebuttal. He swept his cane away from the hem of her dress in a wide, angry arc. His pent up anger was not lost on her. "So where *have* you been?"

"Seeing the sights."

"I'll bet you have." His eyes narrowed. "And who's been helping you? That meddling traitor Gabriel Stone?"

"I don't need anyone's help."

"Oh, but you do. You've been a very bad girl." Moray glanced over his shoulder at the clerk. "Read the notes, so she knows we are onto her."

The clerk looked down at the ledger and ran his finger through the list of prisoner names.

Moray sighed. "It's Wilder. She'll be at the end."

The clerk nodded, turned the page and scanned the remaining names with his fingertip.

"Ah," he announced. "Wilder, Joanna. Age: Twenty-nine. Marital status: Spinster. Occupation: Gardener. Last day of work: December 20, 2506. Last criminal incident: Caught near the border attempting to bribe a citizen to take her to the forbidden Outer Islands. Additional crimes: Assault with a deadly weapon, violating curfew, leaving Londo City without a pass, aiding and abetting the leader of the C-Day Riot, practicing medicine without a license, suspected of homicide and false representation of another citizen."

"Impressive *cajoness*." The un-scarred side of Moray's mouth flitted upward in a cruel smile. "For a woman."

Joanna didn't know the unfamiliar word he had used, but she understood the gist of the comment.

She kept her expression flat.

"What makes you do it?" he asked.

"I get bored."

"So do I," Moray chuckled. "And here I was, thinking we had nothing in common." He crossed his arms and tilted his head to observe her. His small eyes took in every detail of her shabby clothing, making her feel twice as disheveled as she already was.

"To be honest," he continued. "I've been a little bored myself lately. Ever since you disappeared off the face of the earth."

"Maybe you need a real job." She shot him a glare.

He ignored the jab. "No one really chats with me the way you do." He ambled around her. "Or piques my interest quite the way you do."

She watched him out of the corner of her eye, never knowing what he would do next. She worried that he would strike her. Thank goodness a clerk was there to serve as a buffer. Then again, Moray would probably refrain from wreaking any major physical violence on her. He would want to deliver her to his boss, Silas Stone, so that Silas could make an example of her. It wouldn't be acceptable for her to be presented to the Londo public with cuts and bruises, as the Overseers' greatest claim was that no citizen was ever physically mistreated. So she figured she would be relatively safe until she was sent back to Londo to be executed.

Or until she found a way to escape.

Moray tapped his chin with the head of his cane. "What I'm really curious about is how you ended up here. Why did no one recognize the name of the most wanted criminal in Londo City?"

"No one cares as much as you, Moray."

"You have that right. I'm surprised Londo City is still standing, what with the way it's being governed these days."

"Bloodsuckers, the lot of them."

Moray ceased his nervous tapping to stare at her. "You know?"

"Of course I know."

"Gabriel Stone blabbed, didn't he?"

"Actually, it was you."

"Me?"

"The last time I saw you. When you bit me. I would think you would remember that incident. *Smiley*."

Moray's eyes blazed. His mouth dropped open. He raised a fist and almost struck her but caught himself in time. She watched him fight down his fury as it whirled inside his expensive velvet coat and shot down his stiff spindly legs. He pivoted away, stalking around the tiny room and battling the desire to retaliate.

She watched the cane. If he lost control of his

emotions, he might beat her with it. She shouldn't have riled him. But she hated the man so much she had failed to maintain her usual circumspect demeanor.

Flabbergasted by the conversation, the clerk watched them. Above the papers in front of him, ink dripped off the nib of his pen.

Moray whirled around. His glare landed on the gaping clerk. "What are you staring at?" Spittle flew between his clenched teeth. He flung his cane across the room.

"Nothing!" the clerk sputtered. "Nothing!" He shoved back his chair and scrambled to his feet.

Before the clerk could scuttle away, Moray seized him by the neck and threw him against the wall.

"Big ears cause big problems," Moray growled.

"I didn't hear anything, citizen! I swear."

"Liar." With a single sickening twist, Moray broke the clerk's neck, in the same way that he had killed Aiden Bannister.

Joanna stared, horrified. Her lack of control had resulted in an innocent man's death. She would have to be much more careful.

Moray turned. His eyes glowed red. He hunched over, glowering at her like an animal, with his hands curved into claws in front of him and his breath ragged with rage. Anger immolated the last scraps of his human appearance to reveal his true nature—that of a seething, slathering vampire. She stared, terrified by the sight of the hideous creature in front of her.

"See what you made me do," he hissed. "Now I have to get a new clerk."

Joanna was lost for words. Her mouth went dry. But she'd said enough anyway. Far too much.

"I'm not done with you." Moray straightened, pressed his lips together, and took a deep breath through his nose.

He seemed to be pulling his human costume back over his vampire form. Slowly, his head moved back over his tree-trunk neck, until his posture regained its usual haughtiness. A blue blur shimmered over his figure, and then he became the sartorially radiant Neal Moray once more.

"Your sister is here," he said. "I'd be careful, if I were you, citizen. She's not a freak like you. I'll bet she tastes like honey on the vine."

Eva was still at Port Pennwood? Hadn't she boarded the train? Joanna struggled to hide her alarm.

"And should you ever, *ever*, mention me or the Overseers like that again or annoy me in any way, I will take your sweet little sister. And it won't be pretty. Do you understand me?"

Joanna flushed.

Moray glared at her as he paced around her. "Well? Cat got your tongue?"

She clamped her lips together.

He planted himself directly in front of her and cocked his head to stare at her face. "Do you understand, citizen?"

She nodded.

"What?" His cupped an ear, mocking her. "I can't hear you."

Joanna took a breath and let it out, hating every moment that he lorded control over her. "I understand."

"Bitch." His lip curled as he raked her with a hate-filled glare. "Stupid cow. You're in for it. Believe you me, you're really in for it. And Gabriel Stone is not here to help you this time."

He grabbed her forearm and dragged her toward the second door.

She pulled back. "Where are you taking me?"

"To solitary confinement. You're returning to Londo on the next train. And then you're going to hang by the neck until you're dead. But until that happens, you're mine."

Moray shoved her through the door to the cells beyond, just as the first door opened behind them.

"Citizen Moray? You have a visitor."

"Christ." Moray glared over his shoulder. "Who?"

"A Mr. Sunara. Says it's urgent." The second clerk noticed the body on the floor and glanced up, shocked.

"He collapsed," Moray explained. "Heart attack, I think. Take care of it. I'll be out directly."

The workman turned to do Moray's bidding.

"Oh, and Smith?"

The worker looked up.

"Where are Lang and Brewster?"

"Don't know, citizen. They never showed up for work today."

"Unacceptable. The last thing I need is to be short-handed when a shipment comes in."

"I know, citizen. I'll do my best to locate them."

"Make sure that you do." Moray scowled.

Joanna guessed that Moray's displeasure would most certainly transfer to his treatment of her. She braced herself for the worst.

14

Moray motioned Vinko Sunara to a chair by the unlit hearth. He had summoned the visitor to Charles Paar's tiny office, which served as a workspace as well as reception room. A small fireplace and cluster of furniture sat at one end of the room, with Paar's desk and file cabinets on the other. Moray perched one hip on the edge of the desk and tapped his cane on one boot while he surveyed his guest. Sunara remained standing, his feet planted solidly on the floor and his alert gaze sweeping over the room. He carried a leather case that looked like it might hold a slender musical instrument or a collapsed pool cue.

Curious.

Moray felt unusually off-center in the presence of the stranger from Croatia. Maybe it was because Sunara's imposing stature created a natural physical advantage. But now that Moray had perched on the desk, he wasn't going to change position. To move would be to admit that the stranger made him feel lessened in some way—made him feel nervous and anxious about his status in the room. Even if he stood up, he would still be shorter than the Croatian. So what? Long legs and broad shoulders weren't the only measure of a man.

Sunara didn't realize whose lair he had come into. But he'd learn soon enough. Moray sniffed, both in derision and to catch the man's scent. Maybe Sunara, with all his male posturing, was just as nervous as he was.

But Moray couldn't detect Sunara's smell. How odd. Everything had a scent. Especially humans. But for some reason, he couldn't pick up this man's fragrance. It must be the sea breeze affecting his nose again. He wasn't accustomed to such wild country air. In fact, every time he came to this God-forsaken port, he suffered allergy attacks. He assumed his issues stemmed from the salt in the atmosphere and the God-awful reek of seaweed and muck. If he had his way, he would move this entire operation to Londo. But Silas insisted on keeping it at a remote location.

Silas still worried that humans would one day learn the truth and rise up against the Overseers. Moray curled his lip at the thought. Silas was afraid because he was old-fashioned. He had lived during a time when vampires were hunted down in their graves and killed with blunt stakes and wooden mallets. Thank God those days were over. The new world order had much to do with Moray's hard work and vision. But Silas didn't recognize his contributions or understand that times were changing.

With Moray's minions working the outskirts like wild animals, and the C-Day riot instigators dead, no human would dare make a fuss about anything. Not one little peep. Well, except for the Joanna Wilder bitch—and he suspected she wasn't entirely human. He didn't know what she was, exactly, and he intended to find out.

But he digressed.

He returned his attention to the visitor. "I am told there is something urgent?" he began.

Sunara's clear-eyed gaze landed on him. "I fear the sea is in the wine."

"What makes you say that?"

"Small cask I give to barman? When I taste, I taste sea."

"Surely your barrels are watertight."

"Storm very bad, Mr. Moray." Vinko held up the leather case. "I must test."

"How do you mean?"

"Test barrels here. Bad wine is bad for Sunara family. No more trade."

"This is highly irregular, Sunara."

"If bad, no bottles filled. No shipping to Londo City."

"Right. And no money." Moray stood up. "You got that? If the wine is bad, I want the money back."

"I understand."

"Where *is* the money?"

"In safe place."

"You don't have it on you?"

"I am the businessman, Mr. Moray. I do not carry the money around all the day."

"So what happens if the wine is bad? You'll be ruined. And I'll want my money back. Pronto."

"You trust me. I do the right thing." Sunara looked him in the eye, judging him, challenging him.

Moray could hardly hold the stare. Sunara's gaze contained a strange heat that burned a hole right through him. He hadn't met such a confident human since he'd been turned hundreds of years ago. Even before. The last cocky bastard he had encountered was the CEO of a startup company in Silicon Valley.

And what had happened to that swaggering sonofabitch? Turned to dust. The same thing could happen to this towering inferno from Croatia.

"I am here, yes?" Sunara added. "If I am bad business-man, I run yesterday."

"Fair enough. But I'd like to see where you *would* run. A ship isn't going back to your country for a good long while. And if your wine sucks, maybe never."

"We go across bridges then," Sunara motioned toward the door. His hand looked like it could swipe a man across a room. Moray tore his eyes off the Croatian's powerful palm and long fingers. "Oki doki, Mr. Moray?"

Oki doki. Some smooth operator this guy was.

Moray took his time getting to his feet, all the while thinking how satisfying it would be to pin this Adriatic Adonis to the ground and drain the life from him. Judging by the sheer virility of the guy, it would be quite a feast. A veritable Fountain of Youth. He didn't usually go for straight adult males, but—for nutrition's sake—he would make an exception. Although, it might take a couple of assistants to hold Sunara down. How would that make him look in the eyes of his underlings?

Maybe torture would be better. What a pleasure it would be to watch the bastard beg for his life. In fact, he could keep the guy around for a few days and then kill him. That would certainly liven up the evenings in this mind-numbing armpit of the world. With Sunara and Joanna Wilder at his disposal, he would have some decent entertainment for a change.

"Let me walk you over to the warehouse," Moray purred. "The foreman there can assist us."

"Good." Sunara nodded at him as he ambled to the door. "It is good that we do this."

"It is," Moray smiled to himself. "Indeed it is."

EVA LOOKED right and left as she walked up the lane to the prison, but didn't see any guards standing outside the compound. There was no need for sentries outside, as the high walls around the prison were topped with iron spikes, vertical shards of glass and loops of barbed wire. The only way her sister would get out of the compound was through a gate.

There had to be another way in and out of the prison. No one would design a place without an escape route. There must be a second gate in the back or on the far side.

Even though she had resided in Port Pennwood for a year, she had never ventured so near Charles' workplace. Her life here had been lived like a horse wearing blinders: keeping to the middle of the road, intent on her own path and not looking at the world around her. But now, if she wanted to help Joanna, she was forced to look at everything. The blinders had to come off.

Eva picked her way around the prison grounds, pushing through the dried weeds and thistles. The vegetation soon gave way to a narrow shelf of rock, no wider than a foot. Eva paused and looked down. Behind the prison was a small cove she had never known was there. The water ran deep and swift, surging up and underneath the rock on which the prison was built. The swells rushed in with a rasp of gravel and then retreated in a frothy rage. Dark shapes prowled back and forth in the blue-green water, just beyond the surf. She'd never seen such big, wicked-looking fish. They were longer than she was tall.

Eva glanced ahead. The trail narrowed in front of her. At the narrowest point, she thought she saw something protruding from the wall. It looked like the wooden sill of a door or window. Could it be the door Charles had been forbidden to enter?

To get a better look, she would have to pass across the wet, uneven rock of the cliff. The path looked slippery and sloped downward. One false step and she would plummet over the precipice and into the sea. There, she would either be pinned in the sea caves and drowned or devoured by the circling fish. Both prospects terrified her.

Eva stared down at the churning water far below. Knifepoints of fear streaked down the backs of her legs. She would be crazy to chance walking the narrow strip of stone. Yet if she didn't continue, she would have to retrace her steps and go back around the front of the compound. And that wouldn't be much of an advantage, as the same narrow path loomed on the other side of the building. Either way, she would have to face her dangerous rocky challenge or fail to discover what she hoped was a way into the prison.

As Eva stood at the wall and rallied her courage, she heard a scraping sound to her right. What she suspected was a door or window pushed open a crack. Then a solid wood portal swung out on screeching hinges. A door. But it led to nowhere and was built a good two feet off the ground. How odd.

Eva pressed against the stone wall and grabbed her skirts to keep them from whipping out in the wind and drawing attention. She thought for sure her pounding heart must be audible over the roaring surf.

She heard a man grunt. She quelled her breathing and watched. Something pale and unwieldy was shoved through the opening. Eva saw the shape roll down the rocks and drop through the air. She watched it fall, trying to make sense of what she was seeing as the object smacked the water. Then the large fish swirled into action. In a frenzy of fins and tails and teeth, the object vanished.

It couldn't be. Her eyes must have played tricks on her. The stress of the last few days must have been too much for her.

Eva sank against the wall, panting, overcome by what she'd just witnessed. She sucked in a breath and shut her eyes. But she knew that what she'd seen wasn't a figment of her imagination or the product of mental stress. And she knew she would never purge the image of what she'd just seen from her thoughts.

Someone had just thrown a naked human body into the sea. She prayed the person had already been dead.

Traumatized by the last few minutes, she let her grip loosen on her skirts. They flapped in the wind before she gathered them close again.

"You there!" a voice shouted.

The man in the doorway had spotted her.

Eva turned and ran, too afraid to look back.

15

VINKO FOLLOWED Neal Moray out of the office and across a gravel yard to a pair of tall double doors set in the side of a hill. To the right of the doors, was a fenced-in area where people shuffled around in the open air. The plot of land was fenced with barbed wire woven in a tight grid that prevented escape. Some prisoners hung at the fence, staring at him with eyes full of fear. One man stuck his arm through a hole.

"Please," he called. "I have done nothing. Nothing!" He waved his hand. "I have a wife and child. They'll starve!"

Moray ignored the man's plea and walked past him without a single glance. Vinko wasn't surprised. Moray's behavior was fitting for a vampire. Vampires had no sympathy for human beings. To a vampire, human beings were a food source and nothing more. In fact, from what Vinko knew of vampires, they had no emotions whatsoever, and made no lasting connections even between themselves. They existed only to kill.

"Prisoners," Moray commented with a sneer. "If you don't keep them out in the fresh air, they die like flies."

"There is no place for sitting."

"They don't need to sit. They need to exercise."

Vinko studied the inmates as they walked along the fence. "Why are children in this place?"

"Oh, criminals start young, believe me." Moray tucked his cane under his arm and unfastened the huge padlock hanging from the doors. "Some of the nastiest characters you'll ever meet are eight-year-old girls."

"Girls?"

Moray nodded and swung open the massive wooden doors of the warehouse. He motioned Vinko inside.

Vinko stepped into the shadowy vault. The change in temperature surprised him. He was accustomed to chilly warehouses, but this place was colder than any cellar in Croatia. This one had been hewn out of solid rock on the edge of the sea. Waves thundered far below. It was as if a dragon breathed beneath his feet.

Moray studied him. "You hear it."

"The sea is under here?"

"Yes. There are caves under us. One day the ocean will claim this entire operation."

"A bad spot for the prison."

"The caves below us were used as cells in the old days. Prisoners couldn't get out unless they swam out. Didn't need the barbed wire fence, that's for sure. But people tended to get sick a lot down there. Then we found this cave on the surface and used it for a while. Later, some fool built the rest of the place around it. I keep trying to move the prison closer to Londo, but the powers that be won't listen to sense."

The click of Moray's cane echoed in the cavern as the vampire ambled forward.

Vinko brushed past Moray, going deeper into the chilly darkness of the wine cellar. He shuddered. This was the perfect domain of a creature of the night: dank, bone-chilling shadows. Wooden wine barrels marked with the Sunara family crest were stacked in racks on the left. Still weeping from their time in the sea, the barrels dripped on the stone floor. Other, newer metal barrels were stacked on the right. Between the racks was an aisle that disappeared into the gloom. Mold fingered across the damp walls. In the distance, water dripped from the ceiling in a faint plop, plop, plop.

"Tell me," Vinko remarked, to get his mind off the dreary surrounds. "What is done with the prisoners at Port Pennwood. Why so many are here?"

"We collect them until there's enough to…transport."

"So the boat comes soon."

Moray shrugged. "In good time."

"How do you house and feed? There are so many people."

"Shipments come on the train. That was Charles Paar's job—provisions. He was your little friend's husband. Now I have to do his job until a replacement gets here. But no worries. I'll manage."

Moray swept the air with his cane. "So there are your barrels."

Vinko nodded. "I test."

Vinko felt Moray's penetrating stare as he set his leather case on the floor and opened it.

"So that's what's in that little case," Moray purred. "Tools of the trade."

"Yes." Years of labor as the son of a vineyard owner made opening a barrel second nature to Vinko. He grabbed the bung puller, tapped it into the plug and then pulled it out. Next, he took out the long glass wine thief and the small goblet used for tasting. He lowered the glass tube into the bunghole and lifted out a sample of dark red wine, which he released into the goblet without spilling a drop or overfilling the glass.

"You've done that once or twice," Moray drawled.

"Yes." Vinko held the glass up to the meager light of the doorway.

"Does it look compromised?" Moray asked.

"I taste." Vinko tipped the goblet to his lips while Moray watched him. The man's intense stare made the hair rise on the back of his neck. He tried not to shudder again, but he felt trapped with Moray standing between him and daylight. If he made the slightest misstep, Moray could destroy him here in the dark.

He had to take the offensive. He had to kill this vampire. If he killed Moray, he could cause enough chaos to shut down the entire operation at Port Pennwood. And this moment might be his only chance.

As Vinko considered his next moves, he swished the wine in his mouth. Then he slipped his free hand into the pocket of his trousers and affected a casual pose that Moray would not suspect as a ruse. He grasped a pod between two fingers.

"So is it compromised?" Moray asked again, stepping closer, too close now for Vinko to use his chemical weapon. "Can you detect any water damage?"

Sweat broke out on Vinko's forehead. He gulped down the mouthful of wine and eased backward, hoping to position himself far enough away for a kill, just as two workers shuffled into the cave. One carried a lantern and the other a billy club.

Vinko frowned. He couldn't kill Moray and then turn around and destroy the other two. To overcome the superhuman strength of a vampire required the element of surprise. To ensure success, Vinko either had to corner a vampire alone or throw a pod into a clump of vampires. He would not be able to attack on two different fronts like this. To make matters worse, he wasn't sure if the two workmen were humans or vampires. The light diffusing behind their bodies made it difficult to discern the telltale aura.

"You called?" the taller one said, tapping the end of the club on the palm of his hand.

Had he? Vinko hadn't seen Moray summon anyone. Yet here were men answering his call. Perhaps vampires possessed telepathic skills that the Sunara family didn't know about. In Croatia, vampires were solitary creatures, not prone to developing a social system like the one in the Anglo Territories. Maybe vampires were different here. That was worrisome.

"I want you to assist Mr. Sunara," Moray said. "He'll need help checking the lower barrels."

The workers nodded. Moray didn't bother to introduce them. Vinko was surprised. Such a breach of manners would never occur in Croatia. Someone was always related to someone, and discovering the connection made a job more pleasant. But when Vinko took a moment to shift his position and study the two workers against a darker background, he could see a red halo around each of them. They were vampires as well.

"When Mr. Sunara is done, bring him to Section B."

"Did you say section B?" The taller worker's voice rose in surprise. Vinko's unease deepened.

"That's what I said." Moray turned to Vinko. "You can give me your full report then."

Vinko nodded and put down the goblet.

"I have pressing things to attend to." Moray smiled, as

if at a private joke. Then he turned on his heel and marched out of the cave.

Vinko frowned. He'd lost his chance to immolate Neal Moray. Frustrated and buying time, he resumed his fake testing job while the two workers stood to the side with their arms folded, casually observing him. The taller vampire tapped the billy club on his shoulder. The constant movement reminded Vinko that time was of the essence. Soon the sun would go down, and he would be in real danger. A vampire's cunning and power increased tenfold when night crept over the earth.

Vinko pretended to concentrate on the third barrel. "Looks like the Sunara family has the rival," he commented.

The second vampire glanced at him. "What do you mean?"

"The barrels there." Vinko tipped his head in the direction of the silver vats on the other side of the cave. The vampires followed his line of sight. "Is more wine? Where is from?"

"Oh, that's not…"

The second vampire elbowed his companion in his ribcage, cutting him off.

"Oof!"

"That's supplies," the second vampire put in. "Nothing you need to worry about."

"So not wine."

"Like I said, none of your business, citizen."

Vinko shot a glance at the man, wondering why he was being so evasive. But it was not the time for solving mysteries. Moray was out of sight and earshot now. The vampires were standing next to each other. He could kill them with one pod. Slowly, he angled the left side of his body toward the wall where the shadows would hide his actions. He pulled a pod from his pocket, rotated, and flung the packet to the floor.

The pod exploded in a flash of light so bright that Vinko worried others might see. He should have lured the workers deeper into the cave. Too late now.

Vinko dropped his arm and assessed the damage. Nothing was left of the two workers except their shoes, garments and the billy club. No one was running toward the cave. Perhaps no one had seen the flare of light. Relieved, Vinko stuffed the vampire clothing behind the rack of wine barrels and kicked the billy club underneath.

Then he grabbed the lantern and his wine thief and strode over to the silver barrels. He had never seen wine barrels made of metal. Even the plugs were metal. There weren't many. He guessed a dozen containers were racked against the wall. He unscrewed one of them. Then he slipped the wine thief into the vat and withdrew a sample.

He tipped the wine thief toward the light of the lantern. The liquid in the glass tube was dark red and more opaque than any wine he had ever seen. Very strange. Even stranger was the fact that red wine was being stored in a container like this. Part of the reason red wine developed certain flavors was because it was aged in fine oak barrels. What winemaker would want their red wine to taste of steel?

Vinko's lip curled in disgust. He was not about to put a single drop of this concoction into his glass or his mouth. Instead, he released a few drops of the liquid onto the palm of his hand to inspect it. The consistency of the wine was not normal, but it was difficult to see much in the poor light. He moved closer to the lantern.

He dipped a finger into the red blob on his palm. The substance was more like syrup than grape juice. He rubbed the liquid between his finger and thumb and brought his fingers to his nose.

The liquid smelled metallic and was laced with an iron high note that was unmistakable. Blood.

These metal vats were full of blood.

Gagging, Vinko wiped his hand on his jacket, desperate to rid himself of the disgusting sample.

Whose blood was stored in these barrels? And why? Why keep a blood supply on hand? For food? What, exactly, was going on at Port Pennwood?

The light shifted as Vinko stood there with his thoughts churning. The winter sun, bleak and white here in the Anglo Territories, sank behind the horizon. The cave plunged into darkness, leaving him standing in a pool of meager lantern light.

He shivered. His work here was done for the day. If he intended to continue his investigation, he would have to come back tomorrow. And he would have to make up some kind of excuse to get back into the compound. For now, he would walk out the front gate, feigning confidence he didn't feel, and hope he wouldn't encounter any overly curious guards. Or Neal Moray.

He collected his equipment and slung his little kit over his shoulder, all the while wondering what he would tell Eva Wilder about his encounter. Or better yet what he wasn't going to tell her.

16

Eva paced the floor at the room in the inn, watching the sun going down and worrying about Vinko. If he didn't return in a few more minutes, she would be forced to go looking for him.

Then she heard footsteps coming down the hall. The footsteps paused at her door and a key turned in the lock. She grabbed the wooden chair, ready to defend herself, just as the door opened.

Vinko shouldered through the doorway, carrying a tray stacked with meat pies and a bottle of ale. Relief flooded through her.

"Vinko!" She put down the chair and reached for the tray, ecstatic to see that he had come back unharmed.

He glanced at her and smiled, but she could see lines of worry around his eyes.

"What's wrong?" She swept forward. "Did you see my sister? Is she all right?"

"We talk later."

Eva trailed close behind him, anxious for news of his foray. "But did you see her?"

"What about my mother?" Tam asked.

"There were lots of woman there. Plenty of woman. All in good shape. Nothing to worry."

Eva studied Vinko. His words rang false, but she had enough sense to hold her tongue until they could talk in private.

Vinko strode to the bed and ruffled the boy's hair.

"How are you, young Tam?"

"Pretty good." Tam scowled at Eva. "But she made me take a bath and wash my clothes."

"Good." Vinko sniffed the air. "I smell flowers now. Angels. So sweet. Only girls here now."

"What?" Tam sat up straight, indignant. "I'm no girl!"

"Show me. You get strong." Vinko chuckled. "Eat the pie and get strong." He patted the quilt that covered the boy's bare chest. "Grow flesh on the bones here."

"I'm ready for a pie right now." Tam grinned and held out a hand.

Eva gave a pie to him, relieved to see the boy smiling and glad to relinquish him into Vinko's care. Tam had been difficult to convince that he needed a bath. She had been forced to drag him out of bed and hold his head under a pitcher of water.

"I see you are much more amenable when Citizen Sunara tells you to do something," she commented.

"Because he doesn't make me do things I don't want to do."

"Do not be so sure," Vinko replied, crossing his arms. The movement accentuated the width of his shoulders. Eva was glad those shoulders were back in the inn with her.

"I am many more mean than Eva," Vinko added. He lifted an edge of the bandage around the boy's upper arm.

"Ow!" Tam exclaimed. He grimaced but didn't pull away as Vinko inspected the bullet hole.

"Wound has baby scab. Good."

Vinko released the boy's arm.

"See?" Eva cocked a brow as she gave the boy another pie and a cup of watered down ale. "I'm not the mean one after all."

"You're both pretty mean." Tam glared at her and snatched the food out of her grip. But she could see the barest hint of a smile tugging at his mouth.

"Scoundrel," she muttered.

Soon after the boy ate, he fell asleep. He obviously needed rest after spending three days on a train without food. Now, with a clean body and a full belly, he collapsed out of sheer exhaustion again.

Vinko finished his glass of ale and got to his feet. "We go to your room."

"Mine?"

"Across hall. To talk."

Eva nodded, even though she knew she should not invite a man into her room. If anyone saw them, they could be arrested for indecent liberties. But she'd take the chance. What she had to discuss with Vinko was not meant for a boy like Tam to hear—especially Tam, since his mother was an inmate in the prison.

"Have key?" Vinko asked.

"Yes." She held it up. "Is the hallway clear?"

Vinko looked right and left. "Yes."

She followed him out the door and unlocked room 104. She hadn't been in the chamber yet and was curious to see where she would sleep that night. She pushed open the door and swept into the room. It was an exact match to the one Tam slept in, with a small bathroom in the corner and a wardrobe and desk near the window. The only difference was this window faced the moor, not the sea.

"Sit," Vinko said, indicating the chair by the window.

She sank to the chair and looked up expectantly.

"You have gone out," he commented, pointing at her muddy boots.

Why did he always notice details she overlooked? She flushed.

"I couldn't stay here and do nothing. My sister—"

"Very dangerous, Eva. I tell you this before. And boy—"

"That boy isn't my responsibility."

"Not good. Both things, Eva."

Her flush deepened. Vinko had no right to chastise her. No one had that right.

"You can't expect me to stay here and babysit some stranger's kid while my sister is walking around in chains."

She expected a sharp retort. Charles would have thrown her words back at her, along with a comment about stunted logic or lack of upbringing. But Vinko stood there, looking down at her, and seemed to consider her words.

He heaved a frustrated sigh, ran a hand through his wavy hair and scowled at her. "Not enough sun, Eva."

"I don't care!" Eva jumped up, still angry. "My sister is in danger. Real danger. Moray knows about her. He knows that she helped during the riot."

"What riot?"

"A year ago. The C-Day riot. My boyfriend Aiden Bannister led a riot against the Overseers."

"You had boyfriend? And husband?"

"I've had a lot of boyfriends. Before my marriage."

Vinko's gaze raked over her. She raised her chin. She

didn't care what he thought of her. She was done with wanting to please everyone—especially men. She would say what was on her mind and own up to her actions, however misguided they might have been.

"Lots, Vinko."

"Yes." His gaze landed on her face. "Beautiful woman," he drawled. Sarcasm lent a gravelly edge to his voice that she had never heard before. "Hard to say no."

"Like you. I bet women fall all over themselves to get to you."

"Yes. Of course." He wasn't smiling. He seemed more upset by her boyfriend revelation than her escape from the inn. She could feel his anger turning to ice. But he held back, more reserved than she would have expected. He always seemed so sunny, so friendly. But he had turned cold, and his chilly behavior surprised her.

She wasn't accustomed to men holding back. She needed Vinko to make a move, so she could refuse his advance. It would make her feel more balanced. She needed to control something while everything else in her world was spinning off kilter. She needed a shift in power. And men had always been something she could control.

"So tall," Eva goaded him, mocking the way he talked. "Vinko Sunara. So dark. Handsome. Lady killer." She reached up to touch his lustrous hair.

He caught her wrist. "Do not say this word."

"Lady killer?"

"Not tonight." He squeezed the bones in her wrist, just enough to tell her to back off. He wanted none of her games.

She lowered her hand, shocked that this man was refusing her caress. She stood there, rubbing her wrist and struggling to make sense of his reaction. She wasn't sure how to interpret his words. He had said "not tonight." Did that mean he didn't want her advances tonight but might in the future, or he didn't like the phrase lady-killer tonight? She didn't know where she stood with him. Even worse, she didn't know where she stood with herself. The ground beneath her tipped precariously, threatening to send her falling over an edge into complete chaos.

Vinko sank onto the end of the bed and slumped over, his forearms on his knees. "We say words we do not mean," he said.

"Really?"

"You are frightened, Eva. Worried." He glanced up at her, his expressive eyebrows tilting upward. "I have the worry, too."

She frowned and crossed her arms, still stinging from his rebuke. She said nothing, while her thoughts churned with ways to strike back at him to regain control of the situation.

"Worry for you. Worry for me." Vinko sighed. "Worry for boy."

She stared at him, awash in self-doubt and anger. "Worry, or is something wrong with your libido?"

He raised his head. "This word, libido…"

"I think you know what it means."

He stood up. He towered over her. She was reminded anew how tall he was.

"When you touch me. Next time." He grabbed her wrist and held it between them. His navy eyes went dark as he looked down at her. "You touch with heart. Or never touch."

"As if I would ever really touch you."

"You want to." His gaze drilled into hers.

"You are so wrong." She flushed beneath his scalding stare but didn't break away. He seemed capable of looking into her and reading her thoughts. Could he see past her hateful words? Could he detect that she could barely take a breath when he was so close to her like this?

She was so weak. Despite all she had just said, she ached for his kiss. His kiss. Like that would solve anything. She had to put distance between them, or she would lose her mind.

Eva tried to pull away, but he grabbed her other wrist and drew her closer. Something akin to lightning crackled between their bodies. Her breath caught in her throat. If she took one tiny step, she could sink against the fire of his body and burrow her nose into the planes of his muscular chest. One step and she could be in his arms. She longed to be in his arms—to be held and protected and loved.

It was a step she could never make. She swallowed and tried to pull out of range, but he didn't release her.

"Both know truth, Eva. But you do not listen to heart. Not yet."

"Maybe I won't ever listen, Vinko. Maybe I don't have a heart." She tugged at her wrists, but he held her fast. "Ever think of that?"

"Everyone has heart. You?" He sighed, and his generous mouth pulled at one corner. "Yours is down. Buried deep."

She curled her lip. "You don't have the slightest notion about my heart or what I feel."

"No?" His gaze blazed over her lips, as hot as any kiss. The crackle between them flared, as potent as any embrace. She'd never felt so much on fire and yet so wary of a man, as if she were balancing on the head of a pin and trying everything in her power not to fall off.

All she knew for sure was that if she looked into his compelling eyes for a mere second more, she would lose her resolve. She closed her eyes.

"Look at me," he said.

"No."

"I say the truth."

"As you see it." She swallowed. "Just like any other man."

"I am not any man."

"You are to me." She had to break the spell they had fallen under. She had to get to his core belief about himself and give it a mean little twist. That was one thing she *was* good at.

Eva set her jaw, certain now of her path and sure of what would hurt him the most. "Don't kid yourself, Vinko. You *are* any man. Nothing special. Like all the others I have known."

She felt the fire between them go out as he released her. She stepped back, hating herself for saying such hurtful words, but knowing it was the only way forward.

No easy way out. No entanglements. No men.

"I go now," Vinko stated. He walked to the door.

"But we haven't talked."

"I am done with the talk." He reached for the doorknob.

"But what about Joanna?"

"I did not see blue watch."

"What did you see?"

"Evil." He glanced over his shoulder. He shrugged. "What else is here?"

His gaze locked with hers. She flushed again, branded by the accusation that streamed out of his eyes.

"I am not evil," she said.

"You are not kind. Same."

"I have my reasons."

"Not good enough." He pulled open the door. "For me."

"Vinko…"

"Good-bye, Eva Wilder."

He shut the door quietly behind him. He still possessed enough self-control not to slam it. How could he be so sure of himself—so contained—when she was falling apart? It was maddening.

She stared at the door as his words echoed in her head. He had said good-bye, not goodnight. This was probably the last time she would see him.

Fear laced with despair swept over her. She took a step toward the door, but then stopped herself.

"Get a grip, girl," she muttered. She had achieved her goal. She now had full control of her world. She was mistress of her own destiny.

She didn't need Vinko Sunara. She didn't need anyone.

17

"WAKE UP, MY PET."

Groggy at being roused in the middle of the night, Joanna lifted her head. For a moment she couldn't remember where she was, and panic swept through her. Then she recognized Neal Moray, and all disorientation fell away. She lay in a prison cell and this man was now her master.

Moray stood in a pool of light on the other side of the bars, studying her. He tilted his head.

"I can call you my pet, can't I? I think it's politically correct in this instance."

Joanna ignored the question. She brushed the tangle of hair away from her face and brought him into focus.

"What time is it?" She squinted at the light cast by the lantern he held at shoulder height.

"It's play time." He smiled.

Fear coursed through her. Her senses turned on full force. She sat up and planted both feet on the cold stone floor, ready to leap into action.

A guard turned the lock and pushed open the door so that Moray could enter her cell. She stood up.

"You know," Moray drawled. "I just couldn't sleep thinking about you."

"Pity," Joanna replied.

"I kept thinking to myself, 'What did Gabriel Stone see in you?'"

Joanna didn't respond. Wary, she watched Moray place the lantern on the end of the bed. He straightened to face her and smiled again. The guard stood on the other side of the bars, idly watching them.

"I'm curious. Because one, you aren't that beautiful. And two, you aren't entirely human. Are you?"

"Who's to say?" Joanna replied. She certainly had no answer, because she didn't know what she was, either. After Gabriel's experimental treatment to save her life, she now lived in limbo—not quite human and not quite vampire. Her strength and senses were heightened, far beyond that of a mortal woman, but she had no hunger for blood and could walk in daylight unaffected. Still, her newfound gifts were not enough to fight off Neal Moray. She had tried once and had only disfigured him.

"So," Moray said, interrupting her thoughts, "I believe a thorough inspection is required." Moray planted his cane to one side, his arm akimbo, while his gaze dropped to her chest.

Joanna's heart skipped a beat.

"Undress."

"What?" She stepped back.

"You heard me. Undress. Take off your clothes." His glance shot up to her face and back to her breasts. "Starting with those buttons." He pointed a pinky at the line of buttons that marched down her bodice from her Adam's apple to her bellybutton.

Joanna froze. She had never undressed in front of anyone. Only Gabriel had seen her naked.

"Did you hear me?" Moray demanded.

She glared at him. "I fail to see how my nakedness will reveal anything about my interior makeup."

"It's a good place to start." His scarred mouth raised on one side. "Plus, I'm curious. Maybe you have great boobs. Maybe that's what Gabriel saw in you."

"Gabriel is above such things."

"Humor me."

Joanna raised her chin in defiance.

He cracked his cane on the side of the bed. "I said, humor me!"

Moray's hot and cold temperament alarmed her. She fought to hide her terror. The only recourse she had at this point was to invoke the laws of Londo. She glanced at the guard.

"Will you not help me, citizen?" she called. "People are not supposed to be tortured in Londo. It's against the law."

"You aren't being tortured." He smiled. "And we're not in Londo, lady." His eyes glinted red. "Are we, now?"

Her hopes plummeted. She would get no assistance from a vampire guard. Joanna knew she would eventually have to obey Neal Moray's order. But she would stall as long as possible in hopes she would find a way to outwit him.

"I will not disrobe with that man watching."

"Never mind him." Moray shook his cane in her face. "And quit dragging your feet."

She fumbled with the tiny buttons. "My hands are too cold."

"Then hold them out."

She stared at him. He planned to strike her. A vision of her schoolgirl days passed through her thoughts: a teacher with a ruler demanding that she stand up and take the punishment she deserved. She hadn't deserved cruelty then. And she didn't now.

"I said, hold out your hands. Are you deaf?"

Joanna kept her gaze steady and her mind blank. She would not participate. She would not accept Moray's punishment. She had learned her lesson well as a child. Punishment involved partnership—one person to mete out the pain and the other to receive it like an offering. She wasn't about to play that game again.

She shifted her stare to the wall and refused to acknowledge Moray. Without blinking, she sat down on the edge of the bed.

"What are you doing?" he hissed. "Get up."

She ignored him.

"I said, get up."

She folded her hands in her lap.

Moray took a deep breath. His glare burned holes through her skin, but she didn't betray an ounce of fear. Instead, she focused her mind on Gabriel, calling to mind his boyish grin—the grin that could flash across his serious face and warm her all the way to her soul. How she missed that smile. How she missed the man.

"One last time, citizen."

In her peripheral vision, she saw him raise the cane.

She swallowed and brought back the memory of Gabriel's face, the freckles sprinkled over his pale skin, his burnished hair and the sound of his baritone voice. How she had loved the rich resonance of that voice...

When the first blow came, she let out a gasp and grabbed her upper arm. Moray had struck her with more force than she had expected from such a small man. When she didn't beg for mercy, he struck her again, enough to knock her off balance. She staggered to the side, choking back a howl of pain.

He followed her, striking her again and again. She took the punishment with her body while she forced her mind far away from the prison cell. Moray beat her mercilessly —on her arms and back and torso—until she collapsed to one side and knocked the lantern to the floor. The light sputtered and went out. Oil fanned out like the pain radiating through her body. The reek of kerosene filled her nose as blood filled her mouth.

"Jesus Good God Christ." Moray grabbed the lantern from the fuel spill. "All I need is a fire, you idiot."

In a blur, Joanna saw his boots standing near the bed as he surveyed her.

"Is she dead?" the guard asked in a hushed tone.

"She should be. The bitch."

"I don't think so. I think she's still breathing."

"Let her suffer." The boots turned for the door. "By morning she'll either be dead or cooperative. And I don't give a damn which."

The tumblers turned in the lock. The metallic clang echoed through her pain-addled mind. She tried to bring up Gabriel's face again, to take her far away from her broken body. But Gabriel failed to appear.

Everything went black.

———

IN A RAGE, Neal Moray plowed out of solitary confinement, through Charles Paar's office and across the yard of the compound, slamming doors and fuming. He marched down to the Golden Hind and flung open the door. The bell tinkled. Neal pivoted and—with a brutal whack of his cane—sent the tiny metal bell flying. It hit the adjacent wall and fell to the floor with a muffled clank, dead.

Citizen Browne, the bartender, stood behind the bar and didn't make a move, frozen by shock and fear.

"There," Neal said, yanking his jacket back into place. "That's the end of that annoying little nuisance."

He marched to the bar and dropped his stick onto the polished wood surface in front of him.

"Whiskey," he barked. "Make it a double."

"Your clothes, citizen…"

"What of them?"

"They're covered in blood. Are you hurt?"

Neal glanced down at himself. He hadn't realized Joanna Wilder had lost so much blood. Crimson splatters covered both sleeves and ruined the white cravat at his throat. In fact, his neck cloth was soaked with her body fluid. Now that he sat in one place, he could smell the fragrance of her blood surrounding him in a metallic cloud, marking him with a hideous winner's badge. He didn't know whether to gloat or gag.

He must have inflicted more damage on the woman than he thought. Good. He hoped she was suffering. One rebel bred more rebels. It was best to stop insurgency in its infancy. And as usual, it was up to him to take action. One more session with her, and she wouldn't trouble anyone ever again.

He noticed a long brown hair stuck to the front of his vest, picked it off and flung it away.

"Disgusting," he said. Then he glanced at the cowering bartender. The man didn't deserve an explanation about the state of his clothing, and he wasn't in the mood to give one either. "Where's my drink?"

"Coming. Right away, sir." The bartender broke off his stare and turned for the shelves of bottles behind the bar.

"Something from the north," Neal added.

In the old days, he would have called for his favorite Scottish single malt with one ice cube. But there wasn't such a thing these days. Single malts *or* ice. What a hellhole.

Neal Moray leaned on his forearms and seethed. He had thought to brighten his night with a little excitement from Joanna Wilder, but she had disappointed him by refusing to play. Deeply disappointed him. Frustrated him beyond all frustrations, as a matter of fact. Sometimes he hated his job. Sometimes he hated everything about everything.

One little change could change his mood. An ice cube. A cell phone. A latte. God, he would kill for a vanilla latte. His head sunk lower as he pondered the primitive state of his Anglo Territories world. Once Silas Stone was gone and he took over, he would introduce electricity. Semiconductors. Wi-Fi. He would bring everything back. He would make the world buzz again. He would be Edison, Marconi, Tesla and Einstein all rolled into one. A hero. He lived for that day.

For now, though, he sat in the bar of one of the most remote outposts of the Anglo Territories, soaked in blood. A true low point. Things could only go up from here. He had to cling to the thought.

Neal gritted his teeth and looked over his shoulder. Not another person sat in the pub.

"Where is everyone?" Neal growled.

"Went back to Londo on the train."

"Where is the Croatian?"

"Couldn't say, sir." Browne slid a tumbler across the bar.

Neal picked up the whiskey and downed it in one swallow. There wasn't any reason to savor whiskey these days. Better not to taste it. He slid the tumbler forward.

"Another?"

"Yeah." Neal wiped the corner of his mouth with one knuckle. The scar made it difficult to drink if he wasn't careful. The touch of his ruined flesh made him hate Joanna Wilder even more. Seething, he glared down at the polished wooden bar.

Browne set the second whiskey in front of him. After a few moments, Neal's rage cleared enough to allow him to bring the drink into focus. He knew he had to focus. He couldn't let anger get the better of him when everything else was falling apart.

"Is there anyone from Londo around?"

"Not that I know of, sir."

"What about the harbormaster?"

"He went to Londo on the train. With samples of the Croatian wine. Orders of Silas Stone."

"Then you." He took a sip of the drink and regarded the skittish bartender.

"Me, sir?"

"Yes. I have to get a message to the Central Compound."

"But the nearest pneumo station is two days away."

"I'm well aware of that."

"You want me to close down the pub?"

"Yes. Take a horse. And deliver a message."

"But, sir…"

"I'm down four men, Citizen Browne. Four men didn't show up for roll call tonight."

The bartender's eyebrows rose in surprise.

"Do you know what that means?" Neal shook his empty glass in the man's face. "It means we could be overrun by the Others. At any time."

"The Others?" The bartender's face went white.

"You know what I'm talking about. Something is killing my men. We need reinforcements. ASAP."

"But it's dangerous, sir."

"It's going to be equally dangerous here, if we don't get some help." Neal put down his glass with a loud clunk. "I want you to ride out. Now."

"In the dark?" The bartender stepped back.

"Yes."

"But I could be killed. The Others…"

"If you ride fast and don't stop, they won't molest you."

"Citizen, I beg you…"

"It's an order, Citizen Browne. Tell Central Compound to send troops. Sign my name. And then come back. Immediately."

———

WHEN DAWN BROKE, Gabriel decided the day was overcast enough to keep riding. He watered and fed the horses while Ruby stood at the edge of a clearing, puffing on a cigarette and watching him, one hand on her hip and her eyes narrowed to slits.

"So we aren't taking a break?" she said.

"If you need a break, take one. I'm not stopping you."

"But you're going to keep riding."

"I have to."

Ruby picked a fleck of tobacco from the tip of her tongue. "Are you sure she's worth the trouble?"

"She is to me."

Ruby's dark lashes fluttered, the only evidence of her reaction to his impassioned reply. She must be surprised at the depth of feeling he had for a human. Maybe she had never felt such an emotion or such a strong compulsion to act. But nothing on Earth mattered to Gabriel more than getting to Joanna Wilder.

"You're going to kill the horses," she said.

"They'll make it."

Gabriel patted the neck of his mount and pulled off the feedbag. The horse dropped his head to the sparse tufts of grass. Gabriel put away the fodder and reached into his left saddlebag. He pulled out two cans of ELBI.

"Here." He tossed one of the cans to Ruby. She caught it in one hand. "Sustenance."

"What the hell?" She turned the slender can in her gloved hand to inspect it.

"Someone at the Central Compound discovered it. I've been drinking it lately. It's not bad, and it saves a lot of time, not to have to hunt."

"ELBI?" Ruby's lip curled. "What kind of name is that?"

Gabriel shrugged. "I'm not sure. But it comes in a few grades of quality. Kind of like whiskey or wine."

"What's this one?"

"The middle one. Moderately priced, aged a year. It's best in a goblet, but the can will have to do tonight." He flipped open the lid and tipped the beverage to his lips. He drank the entire contents of the can and then crunched it down for storage in his saddlebag. In Londo, every scrap of metal was recycled.

"Drink up, Ruby. We have to get back on the road."

"Taskmaster," she grumbled. She popped open her can of ELBI and drank it as quickly as Gabriel had. Then she held the can in the air and stared at it, grimacing.

"God, that's awful."

"It grows on you."

"Maybe if it were warm."

"Maybe."

"It doesn't have the same effect. That zing. That rush you get from the surrender of a human being."

Gabriel swung back into the saddle. "I always thought that rush was wrong. Like being addicted to a drug."

"You would. And you sound like Roman." She stuck her pointed boot into the stirrup and hoisted her small figure onto the back of the massive horse. "When this is over, I am going to have a nice long bath. For hours. I'm growing blisters where a lady should never have them. I'm telling you, it's painful!"

Gabriel tuned out Ruby's constant chatter. He urged his horse onto the cobbled path that wound across the moor.

Ironically, the only highways to survive the centuries were those built by ancient invaders—the Romans. Mother Nature had long since reclaimed all other routes.

Some civilizations made indelible marks on the Earth. The Egyptians. The Chinese. The Romans. Gabriel wondered what would remain after the Overseers were gone. His brethren would not rule Londo forever. One day, the outside world would discover and decimate them, as they had destroyed vampires throughout history. And if that happened, what would be the legacy of the first vampire society—the preservation of the Celtic bloodline?

Perhaps that triumph would be enough. Perhaps the community he and his brother had built would count for something.

Gabriel smelled change in the air. He could sense a tipping point on the horizon. In fact, he hadn't felt settled since the night of the train wreck when he had first set eyes on Joanna.

Joanna.

He nudged his horse to a gallop. Another day, and they

might make it to Port Pennwood. Another day, and he would see Joanna.

AFTER A FITFUL NIGHT, Eva rose, took a quick sponge bath and dressed in the same clothes she had been wearing for the past few days. She hoped she didn't reek of fried fish, but there was nothing to be done about it.

As she locked the door behind her, she glanced at the room across the hall where Vinko and Tam still slept. A small stab of remorse pierced through her. Their argument the night before had been for the best. She was better off without the complications that came with the Croatian. She must not dwell on the way Vinko had walked out of her life. She must move on.

Eva hurried down the stairs and slipped out of the oddly quiet inn.

Port Pennwood was equally quiet during the morning hours. And now she could guess why: most of the inhabitants were asleep when she walked around town. A week ago she never would have dreamed that the work at Port Pennwood was most likely performed by vampires. That was why there had been no colleagues to befriend Charles and no visitors at the manor. Maybe Charles had actually known the nature of his workforce. And that was why he had warned her about the Others. The Others were probably vampires.

When she considered all the times she had spent alone on the beach, she shuddered. It would have been so easy to kill her. And yet, no one had ever accosted her. Perhaps because of Charles' position.

As Eva passed through the deserted streets, she wondered how many human beings even lived in Port

Pennwood. Probably only a handful. The thought sent a chill through her. Charles had been human. And there was Hannah. The barman at the pub, Mr. Browne. The harbormaster. But maybe no one else. She had been living in a den of vampires—and had been for almost a year. Panic constricted her throat. She fought the urge to run away as fast as she could and never look back.

But she couldn't run away. Joanna was here.

Eva clutched her cloak around her and forced herself to walk up the winding lane. She passed through the gate of the processing plant with her senses tuned to the slightest movement ahead, now that she knew danger lurked in every shadow. But no one challenged her.

Eva had never thought to visit her husband at work, and he had never volunteered to take her on a tour. But now she was curious. Perhaps he had been hiding more than his relationship with another woman. With any luck, Eva would soon discover the nature of her late husband's work.

Above the door of the main building was a sign that read "Office." This must be where Charles had worked. She reached for the latch.

The door to Charles' office was unlocked. She pushed open the heavy door and walked in, ready to make an excuse if she encountered a clerk. But Charles' office was empty.

For a moment, she glanced around the room where her husband had spent so much of his time. It was a pitiful place, dark and small, with a tiny fireplace at one end and a set of threadbare furniture. The room was ordinary, with nothing whatsoever to speak toward the man who had sat at the small desk. No paintings. No books. No knickknacks of any kind. Eva felt sorry for Charles and the sterility of his professional world, especially when compounded by the severity of his personal life. He had lived, eaten and dressed with serious efficiency. If not for Eva's insistence on a few colorful things, their home would have been just as cold and austere as this office.

The single window of the office looked out on the yard and gate. Perhaps Charles had been the sentry as well as the plant manager. And now that he was dead, there was no one to challenge visitors. But strangers had probably never been an issue. No one came to Port Pennwood of his own volition.

Eva breathed in and glanced around, reminding herself that she was here to find Joanna and not to reminisce on the life and times of a dead man. Now was her chance to explore while the vampires slept.

She had two avenues ahead of her. A door opposite the window or a door in the shadows behind the desk. The second door called out to her. But the thought of opening it sent fear spiking down her legs. Now was her moment of truth. She could either be a coward and run back to the inn or open that door and face whatever lurked on the other side.

Eva swept past the desk and reached for the knob, pushing herself to act before she had time to change her mind.

18

EVA PUSHED OPEN the door a few inches, enough to get a glimpse of what lay ahead. In the dim morning light, she could just make out a large, empty room. She couldn't see any guards or hear movement, so she opened the door all the way and stepped through. Trembling, she tested the latch to make sure she could get back the way she came, and then carefully closed the door.

While she allowed her eyes to adjust to the darkness of the large windowless space, she pressed against the wall. Images of a cafeteria slowly came into focus—long trestle tables, benches, serving window and a fireplace at one end. The faint stench of boiled cabbage hung in the air. This must be the place where the prisoners were fed. She could imagine Charles standing at the fireplace, with his hands behind his back, silently watching the prisoners eat, as he had watched her eat every night from his place at the far end of their dining table.

She spotted a set of double doors on the other side of the cafeteria and headed toward them.

The double doors were not locked either, at least from

her side. But they were designed to lock behind her. She pulled Charles' letter from the pocket of her vest and slipped it between the two doors to keep the bolt from engaging, and carefully eased the doors together. She turned around to face the room.

The first thing she noticed was an offensive combination of body odor, unwashed clothing and neglected chamber pots. A wide corridor stretched ahead of her with holding cells on both sides and a door at the end. Small high windows allowed light to filter across the space above, illuminating the high rafters and glinting off the bars of prison cells.

Male prisoners slept on one side and women and children on the other. She took a few soundless steps forward. A little girl sat up and stared. Eva held a finger to her lips to caution the child to stay quiet. The little girl watched her, but didn't cry out.

Eva scanned the cots, looking for her sister. There must be a hundred or so people here, still sleeping in the early morning hours.

One false move, and she would be thrown in with the rest of them.

With her heart pounding in her ears, Eva glanced at the doors behind her. She should leave. Right now. If she had any sense, she would run through those doors and never come back. She would run all the way to Londo City.

But she couldn't.

Instead, she forced herself to continue down the corridor, careful not to make a sound. Some of the women slept with their backs to her. One of them had hair that looked like her sister's. She moved closer to the sleeping woman and bent down.

"Joanna?" she whispered.

A couple of heads popped up. A young woman near her sat up and scrambled off her cot.

"Let us out," she entreated, wrapping her hands around the bars. "Please!"

"Quiet," a man hissed from the opposite cellblock. "You'll wake the guards."

"Please," the woman whispered. "Please help us."

"I can't. You people have broken the law."

"No, we haven't. We haven't done anything wrong."

"Why are you here, then?"

"I don't know!" Sincerity poured from the young woman's eyes. "They just dragged my brother and me off the street one night!"

Eva's gut told her the woman was telling the truth. Perhaps some of the prisoners were like Joanna, whose only crime was trying to help a loved one. Eva's mouth went dry. For once in her life, she had to make a decision that reached beyond her usual self-interested world. And she had to decide quickly.

"I may have a key." Eva slipped her fingers into her vest pocket for the key Charles had left for her. She tried it in the lock of the cell, but it was far too small.

"Doesn't fit," she replied. "Do you know where they keep the keys?"

"The guards always have them." The woman's knuckles went white around the bars. "Please, please help us."

"I'll try to get them. I promise."

"They took my brother yesterday."

"Where?"

"I don't know. They take us one by one."

"To the NorthSea camps?"

"We don't think so. Not one by one."

A man walked up to the bars across the corridor. "We think something else is going on."

"What?"

"No one knows. No one ever comes back. People are taken each night, and we never see them again."

The noose inside Eva's throat clenched tighter.

"Do you know of a prisoner named Joanna Wilder?"

"Yes. She came in yesterday."

"Do you know where she is?"

"They took her last night." The young woman put in. "Along with my brother."

"Where? Which way?"

The young woman pointed a finger at the door at the far end of the corridor. Then she turned back to Eva.

"Please help us. Please. I didn't do anything. I don't want to die."

"Who said anything about dying?"

"I think they kill us."

"But you don't know for sure."

"No," the man behind her said. "They keep us in the dark. Literally."

"Is there a woman named Margaret here?"

A brown-haired woman sat up. Eva strained to see her features in the dim light. From what she could discern, the woman had wavy hair and a frail figure. Her eyes were huge with fear. She was pretty but not beautiful. In fact, there wasn't much about her that drew the eye.

Margaret threw off her ragged blanket and walked toward the bars. In her plain black dress, with her braided hair coiled in a bun at the base of her skull, she looked like every other woman in Londo City.

"I'm Margaret," the brown-haired woman said. "Are you Commissioner Paar's wife?"

"Yes."

"Is he all right?"

"I'm afraid he's dead." Eva watched the woman's eyes. She saw heartbreak darken them.

So this woman was Charles' supposed lover, the woman for whom he had broken the law. She must have hidden talents, for she was an ordinary-looking person. Eva could see no reason why Charles would have given his life for her.

"Charles was executed for trying to save you," she added.

"Oh. No." Margaret clasped her hands together and cast her glance down, struggling to hide her emotions. "Oh, no, oh, no."

Eva could see the woman's hands shaking, but she didn't care. This drab person had destroyed her future. "His treason has left me with nothing, citizen. He ruined my life trying to save yours."

"I'm sorry," Margaret murmured. "So sorry for you."

"It was totally out of character for Charles to do something like that. I can't imagine why he would try to break you out of prison."

She wanted to punish this person. She wanted an apology. At the very least, she wanted to see remorse.

But instead of showing any sign of repentance, Margaret straightened her spine. She raised her glance, which was steady with sorrow. "Charles and I knew each other a long time. Long before his marriage to you."

Eva hadn't expected the woman to defend her illegal relationship, especially to the wife she had betrayed. Surprised, she raised her chin. All she could utter was a morbidly curious, "Oh?"

"He didn't want to go through with the marriage to you, but then again, he couldn't refuse and break the law, could he?" Margaret's unwavering gaze studied her, putting her in her place. "Charles prided himself on being a good citizen."

"Except when it came to you, apparently."

"Everyone has a breaking point. Because everyone has a heart."

Margaret's words stabbed through her like a dagger. Eva's mouth went dry a second time. If what this woman said was true, then Eva's plan to stay strong by staying heartless contained a flaw.

But no. She would not allow this woman's philosophy to alter her path or her sense of the world. Margaret had it all wrong. People *could* walk the earth bereft of hearts. People *could* be inured to Margaret's so-called breaking point.

Eva's silence allowed grief to overwhelm the other woman.

Margaret lowered her head and brought a fist to her mouth to hold back tears. "What did they do to him?"

"They shot him."

"Oh. Poor Charles." Her shoulders shook. The other young woman draped an arm around her.

"There's no sense crying now," Eva said, still put off by Margaret's lack of apology. "We don't have time. I'll try to locate the keys. I'll be back."

"Be careful," the man whispered. "The guards are nasty."

Eva nodded and headed for the doors at the end of the corridor.

A sign on the door read: "Authorized personnel only." This could have been the spot where Charles had been caught. Gently, she tried the door, but it was locked. She still held the skeleton key in her hand. With quaking fingers, she pushed the key into the lock. It slipped in easily. She rotated the key to the left, while her heart clanged in her chest. The tumblers turned, reverberating in her ears, and she prayed no one on the other side of the door had heard the noise.

One more step, and she would enter the inner sanctum of the Port Pennwood facility.

SOMETIME AFTER DAWN, Neal woke up, his head reeling. For a moment, he didn't know where he was. He lifted his pounding head and looked around. After numerous whiskies, he'd somehow made it up to the manor house where Charles Paar had lived and up the staircase to the master bedroom. But he hadn't managed to divest himself of the bloody clothing. He rolled onto his back and grimaced.

In the old days, he could drink all night and not feel bad the next day, especially if he kept to his single malts. But his vampire constitution didn't process alcohol well, and the crap available now was full of contaminants. He should have stopped drinking much earlier. But he'd been so down. So frustrated. Sometimes whiskey was all there was for him these days.

Now he felt wretched. Thirst burned in his throat. His belly roiled with nausea. His ears rang.

He rolled off the bed and staggered to the bathroom, divesting himself of his bloody jacket and ruined vest. He dropped them on the floor and stumbled to the sink. He took a long drink of water and then straightened to look in the mirror as he toweled his face.

Above the towel, dark eye sockets stared back at him. The whites of his eyes were tinged in pink. His skin looked gray. He was a haggard mess.

Then his glance fell on the reflection of his blood-soaked neck cloth and shirt. He sucked in a breath. He had to get rid of all traces of that bitch, Joanna Wilder. She had marked him enough with the knife. He couldn't abide her mark around his neck. The dried fabric choked him like a dog collar. Neal clenched his teeth. He was no one's dog. No one's lackey. And people were soon going to find that out.

He tore at the bloody shirt, unbuttoning it with fumbling fingers. But to his horror, the bitch's dried blood stuck to the rash on his neck. He gagged. The thought of their blood mingling at his throat made him want to vomit. Desperate to be rid of her, he ripped away the fabric stuck to his neck, not caring if he pulled off his own skin in the process.

Neal tossed the shirt in the corner and turned back to the mirror, expecting to see dark vampire blood trickling down his neck. But he saw no such thing. Panting, he turned his inflamed neck to the glass and stared at his reflection. No blood. No rash.

His hangover must be playing tricks on him. He turned to inspect the other side of his neck. No rash there, either. He touched his throat with his fingertips, all the way to his spine, searching for the telltale crust that he took great pains to conceal, especially since it had spread over the past year. Nothing. His throat was as smooth as a child's.

Confused, Neal turned up the gas lamp above the mirror, his thoughts racing. What had happened to his skin irritation? It couldn't have cleared up. He was sure the rash was some kind of cancer. So it must still be there. Cancer didn't resolve by itself. But the light that now poured over his throat revealed nothing but flawless, white vampire skin.

Dare he believe his cancer was gone? Neal stared at himself in the mirror.

"What the hell?" he muttered. He gazed at his neck until the truth dawned on him.

Call him crazy, but in his half-drunk state he could reach only one conclusion.

Joanna Wilder's blood had healed his cancerous lesions.

He blinked and forced his hangover to fade into the background as a new truth took shape. If Joanna Wilder's blood had special properties, he had to make sure she stayed alive. He sprang into action. He had to return to her cell immediately, get her medical care, food, anything to restore her health.

Neal picked up his bloody vest. He detached the pocket watch and clicked it open. Eight am. Far past dawn.

He should be asleep. He was tired and hung over and dirty. The last thing he wanted to do was get dressed and go out. But he had to attend to Joanna Wilder. He set his jaw.

Lately, it seemed his work was never done. The more he did, the more he had to manage. He was like one of those idiot developers from the old days—the Silicon Valley nerds who stayed up for forty-eight hours straight trying to solve a programming problem. He had always laughed at them for working harder, not smarter.

Well, now he knew what it was like. He sighed. It was the dues he had to pay to ensure his future. He had vowed to make a success of ELBI and earn Silas Stone's respect. But now he had something better. Spectacular, even.

If he could cure Silas' terrible illness, he would be The Golden Boy of all golden boys. Even Silas' own brother, Gabriel—a physician, for God's sake—hadn't been able to help him. If Neal could beat Gabriel Stone at his own game and show what a useless hanger-on he was? Well, that would be the maraschino cherry on top.

He loved maraschino cherries.

Neal yanked back a curtain to survey the weather. Gray clouds blocked the sun. He couldn't see a clear spot in the entire sky. Good.

Though he faced the possibility of exposing himself to sunlight, he would dress and go back to the processing plant.

WHEN A DECENT HOUR finally arrived that morning, Vinko rapped on the door of Eva's room. He had left her the previous night, determined to abandon her to her own devices. But morning light had recast that decision. He couldn't leave the young woman in danger and still call himself a Sunara.

"Eva," he called. He rapped again.

He couldn't detect a single sound from the room beyond the door. He tried the latch. It was locked. He frowned and planted his hands on his hips.

"Want to get in?" a voice behind him inquired.

Surprised, Vinko looked around to find Tam standing in the doorway of the room across the hall.

"I can't. She locked the door."

"Doesn't stop me," Tam said.

Vinko studied the boy more closely. "What do you mean?"

Tam pushed a hand into the pocket of his trousers and pulled out a metal pick. He raised his eyebrows, waiting for permission.

"You're a thief?" Vinko asked.

"I'm a supplier."

"Supplier?"

"My mother is sick a lot. If she doesn't work, she can't

get rations. So I have to get 'em." He shrugged one shoulder. "I get supplies."

"From where?"

Tam shrugged again. "Here and there."

"You know how to open the locks?"

"Yes."

Vinko motioned to the lock of Room 104. "I want to know if Citizen Paar is safe."

Tam nodded and strolled to the door. He inserted the tool and cocked his head to listen to the workings of the lock. Vinko stood aside, observing, while he worried about the boy's skill set. A bright boy should be learning how to work at something that would exalt him, not land him in prison. He would have to have a serious talk with the lad. But for now, he would take advantage of Tam's illegal talent.

Tam turned the knob and grinned. "Done!"

"Thank you," Vinko said. "I think."

The boy stepped aside to allow Vinko to enter the chamber.

"Eva?" he called softly.

He glanced around the room. The bed was made. No clothing was strewn about. He strode to the small toilet in the corner. She wasn't there. Eva was gone.

"Where is she?" Tam asked, trailing him.

"Good question."

"Do you think she went for breakfast?"

"I think she went for trouble."

"For trouble? What do you mean?"

Vinko didn't answer the boy. He headed for the door, held it open and waved Tam through.

"Go back to room and wait for me."

"Wait?"

"Yes. Wait for me."

"But my mother…"

"Your mother is in place not good for you." Vinko pointed at the room across the hall. "So you wait, Tam. I come back. You rest."

"Rest?" Tam heaved a frustrated sigh. "But I'm not tired."

"You do not go with me, boy. If Eva comes back, she is needing you."

"So I'm supposed to just wait around?"

"Yes. Village is dangerous." Vinko closed the door to Eva's room and stood in the hall until the boy acquiesced and marched back to their chamber.

"You stay." Vinko shook a finger at him and branded him with the same stern look his father used to employ with him.

Tam huffed into the room and plopped down on the bed. He pouted and crossed his arms.

Vinko shut the door and strode down the hall, knowing that a boy like Tam wouldn't stay put for long.

He had to discover where the vampires slept, kill the lot of them, and get Eva out of the factory before the boy got in the way or Neal Moray had a chance to interfere.

19

Eva pulled her cloak around her as she shuffled through the dark corridor. In this windowless place, there could be bats or vampires hanging upside down above her head. If she encountered either creature, she would lose her mind. Her heart thundered in her ears. Only the thought of rescuing Joanna kept her inching forward.

The passage was more like a tunnel chiseled through rock than a hallway. With each step she took, the warmer the air became. To help guide her through the darkness, she placed one hand on the rock. The wall was damp. With what? She grimaced while possibilities raced through her fertile imagination. But she didn't pull back. Water trickled in the distance.

Her hackles rose, but she continued her trek through the dark, with one hand on the wall and one hand outstretched in front of her. She listened for the slightest rustle or smell—the slightest hint—that something waited for her in the darkness. But all she could detect was the drip, drip of the water. She peered through the blackness, straining to see details of the path ahead. But without a light source, she could see nothing. Within minutes, her eyeballs started to ache.

Then her outstretched hand touched a wooden door. The surface felt warm. Curious, Eva paused to listen. Beyond the door, she could hear machines running, but she couldn't identify what kind they were. It sounded like a locomotive chugging in a station with its steam brakes puffing and its engine rumbling. Surely, a train spur didn't extend into this hillside.

Eva slid her fingers down the edge of the door, searching for the handle. She felt a latch and then the keyhole. With trembling hands, she reached for the old skeleton key. As she pulled it out of her vest, she dropped it.

"Dammit!" she whispered. She bent down and forced herself to run her hand along the dirty stone floor. She closed her eyes and tried not to visualize the spiders, beetles and slime she might encounter. Luckily, she located the key near her boot without meeting any of the denizens of this hoary hallway.

More careful this time, she concentrated on keeping her hand steady. She pushed in the key and turned it. The lock clicked open.

Once again, Eva cracked open the door and peered through the tiny slit. The chamber beyond was nothing more than a crude cave dimly lit by wall sconces. Gaslight flickered over the contents of the room, outlining humps of machines and equipment. At least she could make out some details.

The room contained a row of six-foot glass cylinders, hooked up to what Eva guessed were pneumatic hoses. Some cylinders stood upright. Others were oriented horizontally. Hoses attached to the ends of the cylinders curled through the darkness to a central machine with a flywheel that went round and round, pulling air through the hoses and exhaling great bursts of steam. A bellows rose and fell, creating a deafening wheezing din.

A figure with his back to Eva leaned on a shovel at the end of the room, staring at a gauge on the boiler that fired a massive engine beside it. Gears rotated, pistons marched up and down, steam valves shrieked. The noise in the room was so loud, Eva could have shouted at him, and he wouldn't have heard her.

All the better for her.

She slipped into the cave and darted into the shadows near the left-most cylinder. The air was hot. Stifling. She held her breath and waited, praying she hadn't been detected. No alarm sounded. No one shouted at her. Nothing happened. Sweat trickled down the sides of her face.

As she swiped away the trickle, Eva glanced at the cylinder beside her. Steamy air inside the glass created clouds of fog that made it difficult to see. But when details emerged through the mist, enough to allow Eva to make sense of what was inside, she sucked in a breath, shocked to her core. She clamped a hand over her mouth to muffle her cry.

There in the misty container was a naked man, his face ashen and his vacant eyes staring at the wall, hanging upside down with tubes attached to his neck. With every wheeze of the giant bellows, the tubes jolted and a red substance pulsed out of the man's body and down the tubing.

His blood. A ghastly machine pulled the blood out of the man's body.

Horror-stricken, Eva crumpled against the wall. People were drained of life here, just as the prisoners suspected. People weren't shipped to the Norsea camps. They were killed like cattle. Just as Vinko had said.

Eva closed her eyes. Her vision swam. She felt as if she would be sick. She panted, struggling to keep to her feet, and forced back tears of helplessness. What more horrors would she discover in this place? And what could one person do about them? She wasn't capable of dealing with this kind of situation. She was pretty little Eva Wilder. Fun-loving Eva Wilder—the girl who always looked her best and liked to laugh. She wasn't made for this ugliness. She wasn't made of the same tough stuff as her sister.

But what if she were the only living human who knew the dark secrets of Port Pennwood—that Londo citizens were being farmed and killed for food? Vampire food.

"Get a grip," she told herself, "You have to be tough. You can do this, Evie."

Quaking, she forced her breathing to deepen. She swallowed and straightened to her full height. She felt the rock at her spine—its hardness and invincibility. She took some of that hardness into her. Then she sucked in a deep, resolute breath. She wouldn't faint. She couldn't faint.

Once she gained control of her reeling senses, she opened her eyes. No matter what she saw here, she had to continue. She had to find Joanna.

Then the worst thought of all struck her. What if Joanna was in one of these glass cylinders, already dead?

VINKO TROTTED through the village and up the lane to the processing plant. As he ran, he scanned the wall surrounding the compound. No guards. Until now, there had been no need of guards. No one came to Port Pennwood voluntarily, and no one came to rescue loved ones. The law-abiding citizens of Londo wouldn't dream of mounting a rescue operation.

But he wasn't a Londo citizen.

Vinko strode through the open gate and hurried across the gravel yard to the commissioner's office where he had first met Neal Moray. He palmed a gray packet, just in case the vampire was up and about and working in the office. He'd missed his first chance to kill the bastard. He wouldn't fail a second time.

As a precaution, Vinko rapped on the door. He had every right to return to the compound. He had a tale prepared, in case he was challenged. He'd left his wine thief in the warehouse. Moray's henchmen had forced him to leave without it. He wanted it back.

When his rap went unanswered, Vinko pushed open the door and stepped into the office. He glanced around, saw the half-open door behind the desk and passed through it. He suspected Eva had been here before him.

He hurried across the cafeteria and down a dark hallway. He could see something stuck between a set of double doors. A paper. He pulled it out and took only enough time to see it was a letter addressed to Eva. She must have come this way and used the letter to keep the lock from closing. Clever woman. He opened the door and shoved the paper back into place.

Then he turned to see the two huge cells of the prisoners. They hung at the bars, calling out to him.

"Shh!" he cautioned. "You wake guards with noise."

The voices dropped immediately.

"Is Eva Paar here?" he asked. "Wife of commissioner?"

A man pointed at a door at the far end. "She went that way."

"Please, get us out of here," a woman whispered, desperate.

"I try." Vinko replied. "Where do they sleep?"

"Who?"

"The guards. Do you know? Anyone?"

Heads shook, mute.

"Oki doki." Vinko heaved a frustrated sigh. "I find guards. Get key. I come back. Promise."

He turned, only to see a short silhouette standing in the doorway of the cellblock. He must have been followed. Two guards stood behind the short man, their hats outlined by light filtering down from above.

"Promises, promises, promises," Moray drawled. "There's nothing more frustrating than empty promises."

Vinko paused. He could dash through the door behind him, lock it, and buy time to escape. But if he ran, he would arouse suspicion. He didn't move. He stayed and faced the vampires.

"I thought I heard voices," Moray said. "What do you think you're doing here, Sunara?"

"Looking for you. For wine thief."

"A likely story." Moray tapped his cane on the palm of his hand. "I don't like you, Sunara. And I certainly don't trust you."

"I am for trust." Vinko raised his chin, daring Moray's inspection.

"You were supposed to be going to Londo to arrange passage back to Croatia."

"Missed train. I get next one."

"In the meantime, allow me to provide accommodations." Moray leveled his cane at Vinko's chest. "Seize him!"

Vinko sprang into action, shoving a hand into his left pocket. But before he could pull out a pod, a vampire leapt onto his back. He turned, crushing the vampire against the bars of the cell. The other vampire flew through the air. Vinko roared and tried to fling him off, but he was no match for the creature's superhuman strength.

"Take him to solitary!" Neal ordered, pointing at the open door behind him.

As the guards dragged Vinko past Moray, the smaller vampire threw back his head and sneered at him, triumphant.

"I believe you have some secrets to tell me, Mr. Sunara."

Vinko glared at Moray as the two brutes grabbed his wrists and ankles and slung him between them as if he were a dead animal. The guards carried him back to the office. They jostled him through a door opposite the window and into a dark space that reeked of urine, not caring that his ribs and head hit corners of furniture and doorjambs. Then they flung him into a cell and slammed the door. Vinko landed with a thud on the hard stone floor and rolled onto a mildewed blanket. The lock turned with a resounding clank.

"There," Moray crowed. "Safe and sound until the choo-choo comes. Or you get a sudden fever and die. Wouldn't that be tragic."

Vinko didn't grace Moray with an answer. While Moray moved on, Vinko got to his feet and brushed himself off.

Then he heard Moray's voice say something surprising.

"Open Citizen Wilder's door."

Vinko rushed to the door of his cell and pressed his face against the bars, enough to see Moray standing aside at the next cell, as a guard fumbled with a large ring of keys.

Someone named Wilder was here in solitary? The prisoner next to him had to be Eva's sister. Joanna. He strained to hear what was said.

———

"Good morning, my pet. Rise and shine."

For the second time in less than a day, Joanna was awakened by the sound of Moray's voice. She opened her eyes but didn't sit up. After the beating last night, she didn't think she *could* sit up.

Gray sky glowed beyond the tiny windows near the roofline. Whoever had designed this space had been brilliant. The building was light enough so costly lamps weren't necessary during the day, and still dark enough to allow vampires to move about if they had to. No doubt a vampire architect had drafted such a plan. She wondered who had built this place and if he were still "alive." There was so much she didn't know about Londo. So much to learn.

Unfortunately, the clever design permitted Neal Moray to torment her day *and* night.

"I see you are still with us," he said as the guard unlocked the door.

She turned her head away, expecting the movement to cause excruciating pain, but it didn't. Her neck didn't hurt at all.

Moray walked into the cell and stood at the side of her cot. She could feel his hard gaze inspecting her.

"No worse for wear," he finally announced. "I don't even see a bruise. Fascinating."

He couldn't see bruises? It must be the poor light that

concealed her condition. She suspected he had broken her ribs and hands last night. Maybe her collarbone. But if that were the case, she wouldn't have been able to move her head so easily.

"I suspect you have an unusual ability, citizen."

"And that is?"

"Healing. Like a vampire." He crossed his arms. "A vampire can come back from almost any injury, after a certain amount of time has passed. And apparently, so can you. Only faster."

"Lucky me," she muttered. She didn't look at him. She hated the man. But his observation rang true. Thanks to Gabriel, she had healed overnight after she was trampled in Londo. But she had considered that a one-time occurrence, due to her blood exchange with a vampire. However, no blood exchange had taken place last night. Just blood loss. Hers.

Would she always be able to heal from serious injury? She glanced at her left hand.

After the beating last night, her hand had been as large as a man's thick woolen mitten. She hadn't been able to move her fingers enough to even pull the blanket over herself. Now, the swelling had abated, and she could bend every digit. Red lines branded her skin where Moray's cane had struck her, but even those marks were faint.

She blinked, astounded at the regenerative properties of her body.

"Yes," Moray said. "Interesting, isn't it?"

Joanna didn't answer. Some people didn't deserve a moment of her attention, and Moray was in that club.

Put off by her silence, Moray rapped his cane on the end of her tiny cot. "Get up."

He had to be joking. She had spent the night in agony, unable to turn onto her sides. Her face had swollen so tight that she had to struggle to breathe. Her right leg had throbbed all night like a giant heartbeat. Her hand might have healed overnight, but surely her torso and legs had not had time enough to mend.

"I said, get up!"

He struck her hip with his accursed cane.

Pain flashed through her, followed by red, hot rage. Somehow, someday, she would kill this man.

"Pick her up," Moray ordered.

The guards shouldered into the cell and grabbed her arms.

She cried out, unable to endure the spike of agony in her ribs without screaming. They held her in the air until she realized it would be better if she stood on her own.

"Let me go." She shook off their meaty fists. Her weight settled onto her shins and feet. The pain was so intense that she had to fight down the urge to vomit.

"Look at you," Moray purred. He tilted his large head as his gaze raked over her. "Ready for the ball almost. It's amazing. Truly amazing."

She clenched her jaw, panting through her teeth.

"One more day, and I suspect you'll be as good as new."

She hoped that meant he wasn't going to beat her again. Or maybe it meant he would wait a day, and then repeat his cruel treatment. She didn't know if Moray considered her a plaything, medical wonder or circus act. He was hard to figure out.

Moray padded around her, his cane propped on one shoulder. Then he stopped in front of her and smiled.

"I've decided to take care of you, Miss Wilder. Someone of your abilities will be very interesting to a colleague of mine."

So back to Londo. Maybe in one piece. Maybe if she

made it to Londo, she could get word to Gabriel, or he would find out about her capture. He would help her.

A rush of hope washed over her. She could feel her love for Gabriel fan through her ruined body in a healing wave. Gabriel had told her that the blood ritual had bound them together as mates. But now she wondered if the unconventional blood exchange connected them in more ways than he suspected.

Moray turned to one of the guards. "Wilson, get Citizen Wilder something to wash up with. And some clean clothes."

"Yes, sir."

"And make sure she eats the morning meal. You stay with her every minute. Make sure she eats."

"Yes, sir."

"I want you to be at her side at all times, like white on rice."

"Rice, sir?"

"Never mind." Moray sighed and rolled his eyes. "Just don't let her out of your sight. She'll be able to walk soon. And she can't be trusted. You understand? Stay alert."

The guard nodded.

Moray turned back to Joanna. "I want you fit and healthy, my dear." He tipped up her chin. "I want you fat and happy. Because you, Miss Wilder," he patted her cheek, "are going to make me a millionaire."

Refusing to cower, Joanna stared back at him, puzzled by his words. How she would make him a millionaire was a mystery. But she did know one thing. Somehow, she'd find a way to escape this hellish place. Somehow, she'd live to see the day that smirk was permanently wiped from Neal Moray's face.

"Now, I must get some rest. But I'll be back this evening to check in on you. Run some tests."

The guard locked her in and left with Moray. Joanna glanced around the cell, searching for something she could use as a weapon.

20

————

VINKO GRASPED the bars of his cell, trying to make sense of the one-sided conversation he'd just heard. Joanna Wilder hadn't spoken more than a handful of words, but he already knew that he admired her. There hadn't been any pleading from the cell next door. No sobbing. No begging. The few words she had uttered had been full of vigor and pluck. He liked that in a woman. In anyone.

From what he could gather, something physically debilitating had happened to Joanna Wilder, but she was on the mend. He hoped she could walk, because he already had a plan in mind.

"Ms. Wilder," he called.

"No talking!" the guard barked.

Vinko ignored the command. "My name is Vinko Sunara."

"I said no talking!" the guard tromped halfway to Vinko's cell and held up a fist. "This is solitary!"

"I know your sister," Vinko continued, without acknowledging the angry guard.

"Is she all right?"

"Shut up!" the guard shouted.

"She is good. Hide your eyes, Joanna. Now. Do not question."

"Silence, you!" the guard roared. He stomped the few remaining feet to Vinko's cell and pulled out his billy stick. "One more word out of you, Croatian, and I will make sure you won't speak again. Ever."

"Come and get me, fat man," Vinko growled.

The guard reached for his keys.

"Keep hiding!" Vinko yelled. Then he pulled out a packet and flung it in front of the guard's boots. The cell-block flared with light, and the guard disintegrated. His clothing, keys and stick fell to the stone floor, next to his smoking boots.

"You can look now," Vinko said. He bent for the keys, and within seconds had unlocked the door of his cell. He stuffed the guard's clothing and weapon under the mildewed blanket. The only trace left of the man was the white powdery splotch where he had stood making threats minutes before.

Vinko hurried to the next cell and inserted the key.

In shock, Joanna stood near the door, still gaping at the spot where the guard had disintegrated.

Vinko shot a glance at her. Joanna was taller than Eva, but not nearly as pretty. There was a directness in her eye, however, that made her looks inconsequential. She had a striking amount of gravitas about her. This was not a woman to kiss or tease. She was made for serious pursuits.

"Good Gottfried!" Joanna gasped. "How did you just do that?"

"I tell later." He opened the door and held out his hand. "Come. Can you walk?"

Joanna's eyes clouded. "I'm sorry. I don't think I can yet."

"Then I carry."

"What?"

He held out both hands. "I carry you from here. Safe. To Eva."

For an instant, she stared at him, judging him. He stared back. Then she seemed to decide she could trust him and nodded.

"All right."

She allowed him to sweep her into his arms. Under all her skirts and petticoats, she was as light as a feather. He wondered if she had been starving.

Vinko carried Joanna out to the office and set her down on the couch.

"Wait here." He held up the key. "If key work, I free others."

"Where will they go?"

"To inn."

"But Moray will see them."

"We are many. Moray is few. Food is there. We make stand. We draw out the vampire and kill."

"You know about them? That they are vampires?"

"Yes. I kill the vampire."

"Yes. I see that." Joanna studied him for a moment and then nodded. "All right. I agree with your plan."

"Stay." Vinko held up a hand. "I come back soon."

"All right."

He met her grave regard and then turned for the door to the cafeteria.

When the prisoners saw that he carried the ring of keys, they flocked to the bars of their cells, chattering excitedly.

"It is only try," Vinko said, holding up the largest key. "Wish luck to me."

He opened the cell of the men first, in case he needed physical backup. No alarm sounded.

"Listen," Vinko held up a hand. "Go to the inn. Food is there. When vampires come, we kill."

"Vampires?" a woman gasped.

"Yes. Vampire. All here in Port Pennwood?" Vinko swept the air with his free hand. "Vampire."

"Oh, my God," a man muttered.

"Not know?" Vinko turned for the lock of the other cell.

"Not in a million years, citizen."

"Vampire. They sleep now. I do not know where. If I knew, I kill them." He swung open the door, and a flood of women and children poured out, jabbering and squealing for joy. "They come to us at inn. Then I kill. Do you see?"

A cluster of men and women stood listening to him intently—the natural leaders of the prisoners.

"We don't have any guns," a small man said. "How do you expect to kill anyone, especially a vampire?"

"Yeah," a second man said. "Don't we need stakes to do that?"

"And sunlight?" a woman piped in.

Vinko calmed them down with a wave of his hand. "I have secret weapon. Do not worry. Go to inn. Now."

"But my brother!" a young woman said. "They took him. I can't leave him here!"

"Where?" Vinko asked.

"That way," the woman pointed to the door at the end of the cellblock.

Vinko glanced at the door. Could more people be imprisoned in this place? Had Eva gone in that direction? She may be trapped, hiding from Neal Moray. He couldn't leave if Eva was still here. She was unarmed and desperate to locate a sister that she would never find here now.

Vinko turned to the short man who had asked about guns.

"You," he said. "Take everyone to inn. There is woman in front office. Take her, too."

"Right," the man said, happy to be assigned an important task.

"I come back. Soon."

"I will go with you," the young woman put in.

"No," Vinko touched her arm. "Too dangerous. I go. You go to inn. I find brother. Go now." Gently, he squeezed her forearm.

Her lower lip trembled, but she turned and followed the others as they hurried out of their prison. Vinko watched them. There were at least twenty mouths to feed. He would have to come back to this compound and collect all the supplies, or the people would starve. The inn wouldn't have nearly enough food on hand to feed such a crowd. And where would they go? What would they do? Vampires likely ran the train. Vampires ran everything in this land. And could a prisoner even go back to Londo? Eva had mentioned ID cards. Surely the prisoners had been marked for death in some way by the authorities.

He couldn't think about the prisoners now. That wasn't his job. He had to focus on Eva. He had to find her and get her out of here. Now.

———

Eva crouched and scurried to the second cylinder. She peered inside and saw a woman hanging upside down this time, but also with vacant eyes. Her dismay mounted. Perhaps all the humans in this room were already dead, drained of life. Her heart thudded in her chest as she continued. If she came upon Joanna, and saw her hanging there with those awful, staring eyes, she would lose her mind. She wouldn't have the strength to go on.

When Eva got to the final cylinder and still didn't see her sister, she stood up, wondering what to do and where to go next. She felt shaky, having seen so many dreadful faces, so much death. But at least none of them had been Joanna.

Before she could decide what to do next, she heard a voice call out.

"You there!" The man at the boiler had spotted her. He grabbed his shovel and dashed toward her.

Eva looked right and left, searching for a place to hide. Darkness shrouded the right hand section of the cave. She clutched her skirts in one hand and ran for the shadows.

She couldn't see a thing and collided with a crate. She choked back a cry as the corner bit into her shin. She put her hand on the wooden box and limped around it. There were other crates here, stacked in rows. She hobbled through them, using their edges to guide her deeper and deeper into the gloom. She heard the boiler man swearing and puffing as he searched for her.

She crouched behind a crate, hoping he wouldn't be able to see her. If he were a vampire, he could probably see her in the dark. But if he were a human employee, like Charles, then he would be as blind in the darkness as she was. Since he was up and about in the daylight, he may just be a human.

It was so difficult to tell. Every time she thought about the real state of Londo and those who governed from the Central Compound, she still broke out in a cold sweat.

Then she felt a hand on her shoulder. She jumped, and almost shrieked in terror.

"It's Tam," someone whispered in a sound so soft, it sounded like a wisp of steam from the machine.

"Come out, you!" the boiler man shouted. He was only a few crates away now.

Tam was here? Why? How?

His warm hand tugged her wrist. She didn't know what else to do but let him lead her. She couldn't figure out how the boy knew where to go, but she didn't have a better alternative. She allowed him to pull her, on hands and knees, farther into the shadows.

The boiler man kept demanding that she show herself, but his voice became fainter with each foot they crawled. Soon, Tam urged her to her feet. They had come to a small tunnel, tall enough to allow them to stand. Still holding her wrist, he dragged her down the tunnel and flung open the door. Morning light poured over them, blinding her.

"Quick," he said, pointing at the opening. "He'll see the light. He'll know where we are."

Eva stumbled toward the narrow door and then pulled back. This was the door she had discovered at the side of the compound. This was the door at the top of the cliff where someone had disposed of a dead body—and where the rock face was a sheer drop to the sea. Her mouth went dry with abject fear. She collapsed against the stone wall.

"I can't," she gasped.

"You have to."

"I can't, Tam. I tell you, I can't."

"You have to." The boy glared at her. "He's coming. Get out there."

"I'll fall."

"No, you won't." He pushed her shoulder.

"You go first," she nodded at the door.

He glared at her again through the unruly fringe of his hair and then climbed onto the ledge.

"Come on," he urged.

Close to tears, Eva glanced at him and then back at the machine room. She could see movement at the far end of the tunnel. In seconds, the boiler man would get her.

She blinked back her tears and stepped out, refusing to look down, knowing she would see the giant fish cruising back and forth, waiting for their next meal. Waiting for *her*. She clutched the rock outcropping and pressed her breasts to the cliff, too afraid to move. The wind flattened her dress against her legs and whipped at her hair. If she didn't lose her footing and fall, her skirt would probably trip her. One misstep and she would plummet to a grisly death.

Tam scuttled to the right, his arms and legs akimbo, like a spider on a wall.

"Come on," he called. The wind swept his words away.

She took a tiny step in his direction, sliding her feet along the narrow border of weeds and rock and praying the ground would hold her weight.

The boiler man stuck his head out of the door. "Stop!" he called. "Come back here!"

She would be an idiot to obey him—even though she wanted more than anything to do exactly as he commanded.

"Come back here, you!" He struck at her with the shovel, almost hitting her hand.

Eva screamed and inched her way to the right, panting in terror.

"Right this minute!" the boiler man demanded. He struck at her again. But he didn't follow her. It took guts and desperation to shuffle along the face of the cliff. He obviously wasn't going to chance it.

"Fools!" he said. "I'll report you! You won't get away with this!"

Eva let his words roll off her back. She was too busy clinging for dear life to the face of a cliff. Sweat ran into her eyes, burning them. She could feel her armpits drenched by perspiration and fear.

"Almost there," Tam said.

"You did this before?" she gasped.

"That's how I got in." He winked at her. "Thieves never go in the front, don't you know."

"You're a thief?" she retorted, her cheek pressed against a rock.

"A good one."

"Does your mother know?" She kept inching to the right, clinging to Tam's confident young voice as much as she clung to the stone outcropping above. Stones fell out from under her boots and clattered down the rock face into the surf below.

"She knows," Tam continued. "But she never asks me about it."

"What about your father?"

"Don't have one." He gained solid ground and reached for her hand. "Come on, citizen. Almost there now. A couple more steps."

Eva closed her eyes, nearly fainting from sheer terror. She felt Tam's warm hand and clutched his fingers in a death grip. Then, suddenly, she felt the wind change as she gained the corner of the border wall. Blessed solid ground spread out beneath her feet.

Eva fell to her hands and knees and broke into sobs of relief.

"Citizen," Tam said, standing near her shoulder. "You made it. Why the tears?"

She peered up at him. "I've never done anything more frightening in my life."

When she felt her strength returning, she sat up on her heels and wiped her face with the small of her elbow. "And

I have never, ever seen anything more horrible than the things I've seen today!"

"Did you see my mother?" he asked. "Did you find your sister?"

"No." Eva swallowed and dashed her tears away with the tips of her fingers. "They must be in there somewhere, but I don't know where."

Tam urged her to her feet. "You need to rest, citizen. Go back to the room. I'll find Citizen Sunara."

"Where is he?"

Tam cocked his head toward the building behind him. "Still in there, I expect." He took her hand again. "Come on. We've got to get out of here. That guy probably went to sound the alarm."

In a state of utter numbness, Eva trailed after the boy, her fingers linked in his.

This was the boy she didn't want to be saddled with. This was the boy she didn't want to babysit, just as she didn't want to care for Charles' bastard son. But this boy had risked his life to save her.

She gazed at the back of his head, at his threadbare cap and thatch of brown hair, as he pulled her back to the inn.

Tam was taking care of her.

She flushed. Though she was exhausted, bruised and in a state of shock, she felt something turn on inside her. It was as if a switch flipped on in her chest, flooding her with a warm sensation she had never experienced.

"Look." Tam pointed at the sky above the Golden Hind. "Do you see it? There! It's the sun!"

Eva looked up, but tears flooded her tired eyes. She had glimpsed the sun once or twice here in Port Pennwood but only for a second before clouds obscured it again. But she had never seen anything like this. A stream of golden sunlight poured over the inn in gorgeous, heavenly shafts.

"Look at it!" Tam whispered, awestruck. "Just look!" He turned to grin at her. "Isn't it something?"

She nodded and squeezed his hand, too overcome to speak.

The same glorious kind of light flowed inside her, filling her all the way to her scalp, freeing her from the line around her neck. In wonder, she raised her shaking fingers to her throat. The noose that had strangled her for years had suddenly, inexplicably, fallen away.

21

EVA DARTED THROUGH PORT PENNWOOD, making sure to stay out of view from the manor at the top of the hill, in case Neal Moray was still up and about. She slipped into the back door of the Golden Hind and was surprised to hear a rumble of voices in the taproom, including the higher tones of women and children. Women were in the pub? Where had they come from? A train wasn't due for a week. Maybe a ship had arrived. But ships were scarce.

Shrugging off the unusual presence of women and children, Eva clambered up the back stairs of the inn. She would have to solve the taproom mystery later. Right now, she was filthy and frazzled by her ordeal at the processing plant. She would wash off the dirt and sweat and clean her clothing as best she could before Vinko and Tam got back.

Just as she had finished and was pinning her hair back into place, she heard a rap on her door.

"Eva?" Vinko called from the other side.

Her heart flip-flopped with joy. Though she tried hard to deny Vinko's effect on her, she couldn't suppress her relief at hearing his voice, not right now, not after what she had seen at the processing plant. She ran to the door, pulled it open and flung herself against his chest.

"Vinko!" She wrapped her arms around his neck and pressed her cheek against his vest. His warmth and strength poured over her. The thud of his heartbeat gave her more comfort than she ever would have dreamed. "You're safe!"

"Yes." He clasped both of her elbows in his warm hands, not quite letting her go, but not embracing her, either.

"You worry about me now?"

"Yes!"

"Change?" He tilted his head, perplexed.

The last time she'd seen him, she had pushed him away. She'd been heartless in her treatment of him. But that seemed lifetimes ago. Trauma had shown her the truth about her feelings for this man.

"I'm so glad!" She lifted her head to look up at his face. "So glad!" Before she could stop herself, she reached up to cradle his face in her hands.

Vinko gazed down at her with questions and concern swimming in his clear blue eyes. His eyes weren't vacant like those she had seen in the glass cylinders this morning. His eyes weren't hard like Charles' eyes had been. Vinko's were the kindest, most intelligent eyes she had ever seen.

He had a way of looking at her that made her feel as if every one of his senses was trained upon her and the outside world did not exist. She needed to be in such a cocoon with him right now. Safe and sound. Not alone.

"Eva?" he murmured.

She realized she couldn't say another word. In fact, she couldn't verbalize the most basic of thoughts. Shock had fried her ability to speak. She started to quake, and within seconds her entire body shook.

"Evie!" he murmured, his voice like a caress. No one but Joanna called her that pet name. How did he know to call her that? Tears sprang to her eyes.

Vinko urged her into the room and shut the door with his boot, all without releasing her.

She moved with Vinko through a graceful dance whose steps she instinctively knew how to take. She didn't have to think about tromping on his feet or going the wrong way or tripping. She simply moved in the direction he moved. Flowing through space with him was easy and natural, and something she had never experienced with a man.

A voice in the back of her mind told her that she should push away from him, but the rationale for that notion wouldn't coalesce. So she let it go. Besides, she didn't have the power to break the link of his arms. What she had seen and done that morning had sapped her mental and physical resolve.

"Evie!" Vinko curled his hands around hers and pulled her forearms against his torso. He rested his chin on the mound of their hands and looked down at her.

"Something is bad?" he asked, searching her face.

Sobs choked her. Her throat clenched, hard and painful. She shook her head, unable to reply. Instead, she lowered her head, skimming the side of her face against his cheekbone. His radiance blazed through her, like the light that flared from the pods he threw, purging her of the darkness she had seen at the processing plant.

Before she could consider the consequences, she turned her head toward him. And there was the side of his mouth —his expressive, masculine mouth.

In that instant, Vinko's mouth was all she wanted. All she could think about. All that mattered. He turned toward her, just enough to brush the corner of her lips and acknowledge the possibility of a deeper connection between them. She sighed. She couldn't help it. She wanted Vinko. She wanted to blot out the world and all that had happened, and Vinko could help her do that.

He seemed to sense the depth of her distress. "Evie," he murmured against her lips, all humor gone. She let her head ease back, and he released her hands to pull her against him. Eva sighed again, amazed at how the hardness of his body complemented the softness of her body. Everything tucked into place, safe and warm and right. She wrapped her arms around his neck, and let his mouth take command of hers.

A small cry of homecoming sighed through her parted lips. She let her body surrender into his. He pulled her into the kiss, until her feet nearly left the ground and their hips aligned. A hum shimmered down the front of her body, where his powerful chest rose and fell in time with hers and heat smoldered between them.

The kiss that blossomed between them was more complex than any kiss she had known. It began with a tenderness and communion that sent her reeling, then to a heated questing and recognition, and then burst into a ferocious hunger.

As desire roared between them, he backed her against the door and pressed into her, never releasing her mouth. His hands ran up and down her torso and hips, learning each curve of her body, as she learned his. He lifted her thighs, spreading her legs so he could step into her heat. She wrapped her legs around his waist, knowing what he wanted because she wanted it just as much.

It was Vinko's turn to sigh. He dropped his head to the small of her neck and ground against her. She raked her fingers through his glorious glossy hair and held him to her, closing her eyes as longing for him engulfed her.

She was aware of nothing but Vinko—his breath on

her neck, his hands under her thighs, and the press of his body in her most intimate places. His mouth tasted like she tasted, his skin felt as familiar as her own, and his body seemed to know just how she longed to be touched and held.

Eva wanted to feel everything with him, to take this glorious, aching embrace to completion, to never let him out of her arms until she had known every inch of him, inside and out. She pulled him closer, heart thudding, desperate for more.

Then someone rapped on the door.

"Mr. Sunara? Are you still in there?"

Tam.

Eva scrambled to attention. Vinko raised his head, as the fire drained out of him. He relaxed and looked down at her.

"One moment," he called to the boy.

Still holding her thighs, he smiled and winked, sharing a moment of silence with her that was more intimate and full of promise than anything she had ever known. The sight of him standing above her, smiling, his lips slightly apart, his cheeks still flushed with desire and his hair disheveled, flooded her with dew a second time.

Softly, he kissed her and eased her away from the door without making a sound. Then he set her down and gazed at her while they both took a moment to adjust their clothing. He smiled at her, his eyes twinkling at the delicious secret they had just shared. She shook her head and smiled back, blushing. They were still strangers to each other, and yet not strangers at all after what had just transpired.

Then again, Vinko had never felt like a stranger to her.

Vinko's smile tipped into a grin. He reached out a hand.

"Come," he said. "I have someone for you."

———————

THE DOOR OPENED, and Joanna looked up, ready to run from the room in the inn where Vinko Sunara had carried her. She wasn't sure she would be able to run far, but she would try. She swung her injured legs over the side of the bed and struggled to get up.

Then she saw Eva walk into the room. Relief and joy tore through her. Without considering how her sister might react, she held out her arms.

Eva ran into them and crushed her in an embrace so hard that Joanna knew something was terribly wrong. This wasn't an embrace of homecoming. It was an embrace of trauma. Eva hadn't held her so tightly since she had been a child.

"Evie," Joanna pulled back and held Eva's shoulders in her hands so she could get a glimpse of her face. "What's wrong?"

"Oh, Joanna!" Eva grabbed her again and clung to her neck. "You're alive!"

"Yes. Barely."

"What happened?"

"Moray beat me."

Eva drew back and exchanged a glance with Vinko, as if they knew what a bastard the man was. Maybe they did.

"But you are all right?"

"I'll mend. I mend really quickly."

Eva raked her with a concerned glance, and then her expression melted to guarded happiness.

"It's so good to see you, Jo. I thought all this time you were dead!"

"No, just on the run. I'm sorry, but I couldn't contact you."

In an uncharacteristic show of affection, Eva squeezed

her. Even though Joanna couldn't see her sister's face, she sensed the guarded happiness turning dark as Eva's breath fanned her skin with a heat born of grief.

"I'm so sorry, Joanna." Eva began to sob. "I'm so sorry for the things I said to you that day."

"It's all right," Joanna patted her back and glanced at Vinko, curious as to what had happened to her sister to change her so much. "It's all right, Evie."

"I know you didn't approve of what I did."

"It was your choice, Eva. Only you could make it."

"I thought I was doing the best thing."

"I know."

"So I could go through with the marriage."

"I know."

"Make it easier on everyone."

"It's all right."

"And get out of your hair."

The truth hurt. Joanna frowned, contrite. She *had* wanted free from her wayward sister. She had wanted a life of her own. And she had achieved just what she wanted. Freedom from everything in Londo. She had lived on the run for almost a year, without family or friends. Without Gabriel. Without Eva. And that year had taught her so much.

"I don't ever want you out of my hair, Evie." Joanna patted her back. "Never again. You're my sister. My blood."

"Oh, Joanna!" Eva released her and collapsed to a sitting position beside her. "Blood, oh, my God, Joanna. Blood!"

Joanna stared at her sister, shocked to see Eva's hands shaking. Her face had lost all color and her brown eyes looked haunted. Joanna touched her shoulder.

"Eva, what has happened to you?"

"I know."

"What do you know?"

"I know what's going on around here." Eva licked her pale lips. "I've seen…"

Eva broke off and covered her face with her hands.

"What have you seen?" Joanna urged gently.

Eva shook her head. Her shoulders shook.

Joanna glanced up at Vinko a second time, searching for answers, but the man only shrugged and looked worried. Apparently, he didn't know what was wrong with Eva either.

Joanna stroked Eva's back, making circles with her hand as she had always done since Eva was little. "Then tell me what you've been doing the past year."

Eva shuddered.

"Is Charles good to you?"

"He's dead."

"He is?" Joanna's hand paused.

"They killed him."

"They?"

"The vampires."

Joanna paused a second time. Eva knew about the vampires of Londo? She had to swallow back her shock. Still, she needed definite confirmation before she could confide in her sister. Gabriel had warned her that if she ever told anyone the truth, he was bound by an oath to kill her and whomever else she conspired with. "You think vampires are real?"

"I know they are." Eva finally looked into her eyes. "Vinko is here to kill them. I've seen him do it."

Joanna glanced at the tall, dark-haired man standing near the door. He certainly looked capable of violence, with his wide shoulders, lean legs and sinuous hands. Even the way he stood there, head high and back straight, gazing down at them, oozed authority and strength. He was nothing like the younger men who had littered Eva's life in Londo.

"But that's not all I've seen." Eva licked her lips again. Her eyes were so grave, so full of fear, that Joanna's heart went out to her. She'd never seen this side of her sister.

"What else?" Joanna urged.

"They have this room. This machine." Eva shook her head and covered her mouth with her hand. She shut her eyes.

"Go on, Eva. Tell us."

"Where they…" Eva blinked, her lashes thick with tears. "…Where they suck blood out of people."

"What?"

"Suck. The prisoners here?" Eva jumped to her feet. "They aren't sent to the NorthSea camps, Jo. Those camps probably don't even exist."

"So where do they go?"

"Nowhere. The prisoners are sucked dry and then thrown into the sea."

"My God." Vinko stepped forward. "You see this, Eva, with yourself? With eyes?"

"Yes. And I wish to Wanda I hadn't." Eva glanced from Vinko back to her sister. "They put prisoners in glass cylinders and attach tubes to their necks and drain them until they die."

The tall man scowled. "And then store the blood in the containers in warehouse."

Eva turned to stare at him. "How do you know?"

"In the metal barrels. I see this. I smell."

"So they are storing blood?" Joanna put in.

"Like wine." Vinko crossed his arms. "The vampire wine."

"And throwing people away like trash." Eva brought

her hands to her mouth again. "Fish eat them, Joanna. Fish!"

Joanna reached for Eva's hand. She had never seen her sister in such a state of outrage for someone else. Eva had always been self-involved. Boy crazy. Even a little lazy. Maybe the last year had changed her.

Eva flung herself into Joanna's arms again.

"I thought I'd find you in one of those cylinders, Jo!" she cried. "Each time I looked, I knew it was going to be you next. It was horrible."

"There now," Joanna patted her sister's back. "It's all right, Evie. We're safe now."

"If I had seen you like that, hanging upside down, with your eyes all milky, all vacant..." Eva burrowed into her. "I would have lost my mind."

"But you didn't. I'm here. We're together."

Joanna felt Eva break into wracking sobs. She clasped her even tighter.

"Don't ever leave again, Joanna. Don't ever, ever leave me again."

"I won't."

"I couldn't bear it."

Joanna stroked her sister's back and closed her eyes. "I couldn't either, Eva. I'm here to stay. Whatever happens, we're going to stick together."

"Yes," Eva murmured. Then she raised her head and glanced around until she located Vinko.

"We've got to decide what to do," Eva said.

"About tonight," he added.

"And tomorrow. And the day after that." Eva dashed the tears from her eyes and sat up. "All those people downstairs. Are they from the processing plant?"

Vinko nodded. "We must make the plan."

"As soon as possible." Eva heaved a steadying breath.

"I found my mother," Tam put in, grabbing Eva's hand.

"You did?" Eva squeezed his fingers and smiled at him through the tears that still hung in her lashes. "Oh, Tam!"

"Can I bring her up here, Eva? Can she stay in your room for a while? She's got one of her bad headaches. So she needs to be in the dark."

Joanna watched, amazed to see her little sister taking control of a situation for once. She leaned against the mound of pillows and let the conversation fade into the background. She would let them plot and plan while she concentrated on healing.

Maybe by the time evening arrived, she would be fit enough to take a stand against Neal Moray and his men. She had no doubt the vampires would attack when darkness fell.

She had to be ready.

22

Eva climbed the stairs of the inn, more exhausted than she had been in her life. She was grateful that Vinko had insisted that she rest for at least an hour. He suspected the night would be as traumatic as the day had been, and he was worried about her. His concern for her mental and physical wellbeing was as seductive as his kiss had been. She thought back to their kiss and smiled as a residual thrill fired her steps, enough to propel her to the top of the stairs.

She doubted she would be able to sleep. Her thoughts raced with the plans they had made that afternoon in Joanna's room. They would take a stand against the Overseers. But were they strong enough? Were they doing enough? How strong was a vampire? Did they have powers that humans weren't aware of? These were the questions that swirled in her head. Her brain felt hot.

Even now she could hear pounding and shouting as the prisoners barricaded the windows on the ground floor. While the vampires slumbered, a team had returned to the processing plant to gather provisions. They had come back with the boiler man who was, in fact, a human, but had been so indoctrinated by the Overseers that they had to tie him to a chair to keep him from running up to the manor to betray them. She could still hear him screaming.

"Let me go! They'll kill me! They'll kill all of us!"

Dread spiked through Eva as she remembered the terror in his voice. He could be right. They might all be killed. But there was no turning back now. Besides, they were many and the vampires were few. They had that advantage, at least. But would it be enough?

Eva unlocked the door of her chamber and quietly closed it behind her so as not to disturb Tam's mother sleeping on the bed. He had taken his sick mother upstairs early that afternoon, and she was still asleep. Or so Eva thought.

The lump moved and a head rose. "Hello?"

The woman shaded her eyes and face from the glare, even though the barest of light filtered through the lace curtains at the window.

"It's Citizen Wilder." Eva caught herself. How quickly she was purging Charles from her life. "Sorry, Eva. Eva Paar."

The woman scrambled to a sitting position. "Paar, did you say? This is your room?"

"Yes."

"You…you know about Tam?" The woman grimaced and shielded her eyes again. "Sorry, I have such a migraine."

"No worries." Still not seeing the woman's face, Eva walked toward the bathroom to freshen up. Then she planned to relax in the chair before she met Vinko and the leaders of the prisoners for a final meeting at dusk.

"Tam says you are his friend." The woman's voice carried across the room. "That you saved his life."

"As he saved mine." Eva splashed water on her face and toweled it dry. "He's quite the hero in my book."

"Mine, too." The woman's words warmed with pride, but not enough to dispel the weariness in her voice. "This is a lot to process, though. I never guessed you two would meet."

"He never should have come to Port Pennwood, that's for certain."

"It was his idea, not mine." The woman shook her head. "If I'm not better by tonight, Citizen Paar, would you watch out for Tam? He said the vampires will probably attack tonight."

"Of course I'll look after him." Eva pinned her hair and returned to the bedchamber.

"I don't want him taking any risks. He's just a boy."

"A very resourceful boy." Eva walked to the side of the bed and finally got a good look at the woman's face.

She sucked in a breath. The sight shocked her almost as much as the faces in the cylinders.

"Wait a minute," she sputtered, staring down at her. "You're Tam's mother?"

"Yes." Pale brown eyes gazed back at Eva.

"But you're Margaret."

"Yes." Her pale face flushed above the cheekbones.

"Charles'…friend." A chill trickled through Eva.

"Yes."

"So you have another son, then?"

"No, just Tam."

"I don't understand. I was told that Charles and you had produced a boy named Phineas."

"Yes. Phineas. That's Tam's real name. Phineas Thomas."

It was Eva's turn to flush. A spike of betrayal and disbelief shot through her. What were the chances that she would meet the bastard son of her husband—and befriend him? She turned away, hoping that Margaret hadn't read her expression of utter astonishment.

"He hates to be called Phineas," Margaret added, as if they were having an every day chat instead of a life-altering conversation. "Or even Phin. So I just call him Tam."

"I see." Eva clenched her jaw. Good Gottfried. She had met and befriended Charles' bastard son. How ironic.

Still, the boy could not be held responsible for the sins of his parents. And regardless of Tam's bloodline, she had already developed a soft spot for the lad.

But once again Fate had slapped her in the face. Her cheeks burned. She didn't know what to say or how to respond to Margaret's revelation.

"Do you want me to leave?" Margaret asked. "I didn't know this was your room."

And how fitting that you're ensconced in my bed, Eva wanted to retort. Instead, she sighed and turned for the door. "No. It's all right. I doubt I'll have a chance to sleep tonight anyway."

"I'm grateful," Margaret said. "Truly. For everything."

"Yes. Well…" Suddenly, Eva couldn't bear to spend another moment in the same room as this adulterous invalid with the magnanimous attitude. The woman's righteousness got under her hide. True love did not trump everything in life.

Eva reached for the doorknob. "I'll look after Tam," she said.

But as she pulled open the door, a thought struck her. She remembered something Tam had said. She paused, burning all over again, and turned back to the woman in her bed.

"One thing, though."

"Yes?"

"Tam told me he didn't have a father."

"That's right. We thought it best that he not know."

"Really." Eva's throat filled with bile. "And why is that."

"If the Overseers found out, he would be taken from me. I could be punished for having a child out of wedlock."

"And what about Charles?"

"Same with him. It would have ruined him."

"So you raised a boy who thinks he has no father." Eva slammed the door and marched back to the bed. "What kind of mother are you?"

"Please," Margaret's trembling hand rose to her forehead. "Please, my head—"

"I don't care about your head." Outraged, Eva balled her fists on her hips. "Do you have any idea what it's like to grow up without a father? Do you?"

Margaret stared at her, her mouth half-open.

"It's the worst thing you could have done to Tam!"

"We did it to protect him."

"You did not! You and Charles were protecting your own hides."

"Tam could have let something slip."

"He would never do such a thing. He's smart."

"But Charles…"

"Charles told you to do it, didn't he?"

"He gave us things. Helped us. I loved him."

"Charles was a self-centered bastard. Do you understand that?"

"But…"

"Your loyalty should have been to your son, not a man you never saw."

"But I loved him."

"More than Tam?" Eva could feel her eyes blazing. "More than your own son?"

"Please, my head!" Margaret wailed and fell back. "Please, I can't take any more of this."

"Maybe you can't take the truth, Margaret. Maybe you should rethink the life you created for poor Tam. Could he even go to school?"

"No. No one could know about him."

"Good Gottfried."

"Don't tell him!" Margaret covered her face with her hands. "Please, don't tell him. He'll hate me."

"Don't worry," Eva said through her gritted teeth. "I'm not going to do the dirty work for you." She plowed back to the door. "But he deserves to know the truth."

She paused again. She wasn't done with Margaret. She looked back.

"I grew up without a father. It's hell. The only reason I'm here today is because my sister Joanna stepped up. She became a father and a mother to me. That's what loving people do, Margaret. They step up!"

"Please! I've never had the strength. And Charles couldn't. His position…"

"All I'm hearing is excuses."

"You have to understand. I've always been sickly."

"Time for being sick is over." Eva shot her a glare and stormed out of the room.

Once in the hallway, she collapsed against the wall. She knew she had been overly harsh with Margaret, and she knew why. She could have been in the same situation as Margaret—struggling to raise a child outside the law. She, however, had benefited from knowing Gabriel Stone through her sister. She had been able to do something about her predicament.

But her decision would haunt her all the days of her life.

Eva tipped back her head and struggled to tamp down her galloping emotions. Had Gabriel not helped her, her child might have endured the same fate as Tam. But then again, he would still be alive.

Eva covered her face and wept for the shadow that lived beside her, no matter where she went or what she did. Had she made the right choice? She would never know.

She stood there, battling back grief and self-doubt, when she heard a step on the stairs.

Swiftly, Eva wiped away her tears and forced her chest to stop heaving. She pinched her cheeks, licked her lips, and pasted on a smile, ready to face whoever came up the stairs.

It was Vinko.

She swallowed.

His glance swept over her. "You are oki doki?"

"You should really stop saying that," she snapped, still upset at the world as well as herself. She intended to march past him, but he grasped her forearm in a gentle grip.

"How to say oki doki then?" His blue eyes glistened down at her, bathing her in the warmth of his good nature.

She rolled her eyes and sighed. "You say 'all right' or 'well'."

"Put 'the' in front, yes?"

"No. No 'the'." He was teasing her, trying to raise her spirits, and his methodology was working. Her equanimity reappeared on the horizon, enough to allow her to raise her glance to his face.

"So you are all right, then, Eva?"

"Why wouldn't I be?"

He tilted his head to study her more closely. "I thought you go to the room to rest."

"I changed my mind." She pulled at her arm. "Really, Vinko, why the questions? I'm fine."

"Me? I do not see fine in you."

He touched her cheek in a tender caress. She closed her eyes and savored the gesture, because she knew a simple touch was all she could ever share with this man.

Her conversation with Margaret had reminded her how dangerous desire could be. Why take such a chance again? She had never experienced the rapture that Aiden had achieved when he climbed on top of her to rut. All she had got out of rutting was a life-altering pregnancy.

She felt Vinko's breath feather her face and knew he was about to kiss her. Her heart raced. Even Vinko's simplest of strokes could set her on fire. She couldn't allow him to get close to her ever again.

"Please, Vinko." she stepped back, shaking her head. "No."

His brows drew together. "No?"

"I can't. I can't do this with you."

"Kiss only."

"Not even that. I can't."

She couldn't meet his gaze. Without giving him an explanation, she tore out of his grasp and clattered down the stairs.

23

LATE THAT AFTERNOON, Eva sat in a chair at the window of a room on the second floor with a pan on her lap and a spoon in her hand. She and Tam were assigned sentry duty. Tam watched the gate of the plant and the lane leading to the inn. Eva watched the hill behind the inn and the road up to the manor.

She gazed at the big stone house, amazed to see what it looked like in sunlight. She had never seen it outlined in gold like that, with the windows flashing silver and blue and the weathervane glinting as it moved in the breeze. She couldn't fathom how she had endured such dull, gray days all her life. The world could be so colorful. So vivid. The sunshine seemed to stream directly into her soul, lifting her spirits to a height she had never known.

Eva was still gaping at the manor house when she spotted two guards carrying a litter up the hill, most likely to retrieve Neal Moray. Moray wouldn't want to walk all the way down to the inn. He might get his shiny boots scuffed.

Eva frowned and rapped her pan twice. That was the

signal to those below who were armed with pods from Vinko's secret stash. Then she returned to her surveillance of the manor. The guards who had thrown her out of the house now carried the litter down the lane toward the inn. A handful of workers marched behind the box, comprising a paltry parade. Eva stared. Were these men the extent of the power that kept the Londo people prisoners? Surely, the taproom army could overcome so few vampires.

But then again, she had no idea what powers real vampires possessed. Only nightfall would tell.

Once she was sure no other workers joined Neal Moray's contingent, she boarded up the window and raced down the stairs to the taproom.

"There's only eight of them," Eva announced.

Tam ran up behind her. "And no one's coming from the plant," he added.

"Good." Vinko nodded at them and then looked at the twenty humans standing at the ready.

"Remember, if you throw the pod, you do not look. Burn eye."

The crowd nodded gravely.

"Say 'cover' before throw. So all know what you do." Vinko studied each and every face of the people in the room, forging a connection with them. Eva guessed they must feel the same bond she sensed when Vinko focused his full concentration on her. "We can kill them," he continued. "We kill all. Then free."

The crowd murmured.

"Stick together. Do not look at eye of vampire."

"They can hypnotize you," Eva added.

Vinko put his arm around her shoulder and drew her close. "Eva speak true. Very dangerous to look."

She allowed him to hold her against the side of his body. Nothing risky could happen in a crowd, and she appreciated the support. There was no telling how this night would end.

Vinko looked down at her. "You are well now, Eva?"

She gave him a brave smile. "Yes."

His gaze traveled over her face as if he were branding her into his memory. "We start something this night. Eva and Vinko."

"Yes. We do."

She held his gaze, knowing in her bones that his words echoed with a double meaning.

Ten minutes later, someone pounded on the door.

"Open up!" Moray demanded.

Eva jumped to her feet, not surprised that Moray had shown up after being transported to the inn.

Vinko held up his hand, making sure everyone stayed quiet. Then he pointed at the doors on the first floor. Squad leaders and their units raced into place, ready to defend their positions.

"I see you've boarded up the inn," Moray continued. "Laughable."

Eva exchanged a worried glance with Vinko. She had no idea if their fortifications would repel the vampires. Apparently Moray didn't think so. And since they had covered all the windows, they couldn't tell what transpired outside. The rest of the vampires could be standing there with Moray. Or they could have scattered to attack from all sides.

"I have no quarrel with any of you," Moray drawled. "You can all relax. No one will be punished. All I want is Joanna Wilder."

Eva reached for her sister's hand. Joanna's fingers grasped hers in a stranglehold.

"He's lying," Joanna said.

"Give Joanna Wilder up, and we can all go back to normal. No questions asked."

"Never!" Eva shouted.

"You'll be sorry," Moray warned. "I'm giving you one more chance."

Joanna stepped closer to the door. "Go to hell, Moray."

Moray did not respond. For a tense few moments, the crowd in the taproom stood mute and unmoving, wondering what would happen next.

Then someone screamed on the floor above.

"Mum!" Tam broke for the stairs, but Vinko grabbed his arm in time to stop him.

The scream broke off and footsteps pounded along the upper corridors.

"Let me go!" Tam writhed, desperate to protect his mother. "Let me go!"

"No, Tam." Vinko held up a hand. "I go."

"Cover!" A squad leader shouted, warning the others to shield their eyes.

Eva glimpsed a dark shape leaping out of the servant staircase near the toilets and heard a hair-raising snarl. But to watch what happened next would mean risking her sight. She couldn't chance keeping her eyes open. She pressed the crook of her arm across her eyes. Light flared and hissed.

"What *is* that?" Joanna whispered.

"Vinko's secret weapon. Some kind of chemical mixture."

"He used it in the jail." Joanna continued. "That's how he got me out."

"I think his family makes the pods. The burst of light kills the vampires."

"I know."

Eva and Joanna rushed to the center of the room where the rest of the humans formed a ring, armed with knives and pokers.

"Cover!" Another leader yelled. This time a vampire raced down the main staircase. A second flare engulfed the room. The stench of sulfur and burned clothing hung in the air as the vampire's clothing dropped, leaving his boots on the last two steps. A puff of vapor rose into the stair-well, the only evidence that a vampire had once stood there.

Silence fell over the crowd. Eva remained in the center of the room, listening for the slightest sound above. But all was quiet.

"They must have gotten to the upper floors somehow," Joanna said.

Vinko nodded grimly. "Vampires can jump. But that high?"

"Maybe they climbed."

"And went down the chimneys," Tam growled. "It's not hard to do." He pulled at his arm. "Let me go!"

"You stay," Vinko commanded. He shook his finger at Tam and glared at the boy. Then he looked at Eva for assistance. She wrapped both arms around the boy. Vinko clutched a pod in his hand and loped across the room to the back stairs.

As Vinko disappeared up the stairs, Tam kicked her shin.

"Ow!" Eva lost her hold on him.

Tam dashed away, frantic to help his mother. Eva ran after him.

"Tam, come back!"

He didn't listen. She pounded up the stairs after him, worried about what he might encounter. The last thing the boy needed was the vision of a dead parent forever branded in his thoughts. She knew that nightmare only too well.

"Tam, come back here!" she shouted.

But he ignored her and skittered into the room where Margaret had been resting.

"Tam!" Eva shrieked. She careened into the bedchamber, hoping and praying that Margaret had screamed because she was terrified and not because of anything more serious. But her hopes plummeted when she spotted Vinko kneeling beside Margaret's body.

It looked as if Margaret had been dragged out of the bed and thrown against the wall. She lay face down on the floor, with her arms and legs splayed and her back and neck contorted in unnatural angles.

"Tam, no!" Eva cried.

The boy ignored her command. He threw himself on his mother's broken body.

"Mum!" he wailed.

"Oh, Tam!" Eva fell to her knees beside him and draped her arm over his shoulder. His body shook with sobs.

Vinko's dark glance met Eva's. "Tam was right. Vampire came down the chimney." He pointed at the sooty footprints on the floor.

Eva looked, but her thoughts and heart were far away from vampire tracks. She had been unduly harsh with Margaret, and now the poor woman lay dead on the floor. She clenched her jaw.

She was not responsible for this. She was not responsible for Port Pennwood.

She was not responsible…

GABRIEL STONE PULLED up his mount and sniffed the air. "There's someone here," he said. He surveyed the moor on the right with his senses tuned to the smallest rustle, the slightest breath. Heather and crowberry stretched as far as he could see in the dark. A jumble of boulders sat at the base of a rise near the road. He trained his attention on the rocks.

Ruby Valentine stood in her stirrups and glanced across the moor.

"There," Gabriel pointed at the outcropping of rock.

"Not a human, surely," Ruby murmured.

"Then why hide?"

"They're probably rogue. Some of the rabble horde must have turned to thievery."

"Out here? In the wasteland?" Gabriel swung off his horse. "Not a very lucrative location."

"Don't assume the rabble are all that smart, Gabriel. Remember, Moray turned them indiscriminately."

"I am assuming the person is injured. I smell fear." Gabriel slipped the riding crop from his saddle and tromped across the moist grass at the side of the road.

"You there," he demanded. "Come out."

Silence.

"Are you injured? We mean you no harm. I'm a doctor. Dr. Stone."

A foot crunched on gravel.

"Doctor Stone?" a quavering voice called from behind a boulder.

"Yes. Gabriel Stone."

Ruby shifted in the saddle. "Looks like your reputation precedes you, Gabriel."

Gabriel ignored her acerbic remark as he watched a

slight man scurry out from behind the moss-covered rocks. His pale face glowed white in the dark. Ruby guided her mount to the rocks and looked down at the human, evaluating him with half-closed eyes.

"Thank Gottfried," the man said. "I thought you were one of them…"

"What are you doing out here, citizen?"

"I'm going for reinforcements."

"For Port Pennwood?"

"Yes. Something is attacking the village. We think it's the Others. We need more guards."

"The Others?"

"The things that live on the moor."

Gabriel exchanged a puzzled glance with Ruby. Then he looked back at the man. "What's your name?"

"Browne. Scott Browne."

"It isn't safe out here, Citizen Browne. You should not be out at night, especially on foot. That's why there is a curfew."

"I didn't have a choice. Citizen Moray made me go for help. We couldn't wait for the train."

"You'll never make it alive on foot."

"That's what I said."

"Come back with us. We aren't far from Port Pennwood. Then if we really need more guards, I will ride for them."

"I don't know…" Browne hugged his chest. "Citizen Moray won't be happy if I go back empty-handed."

"Let me deal with Moray. Come." Gabriel pointed the riding crop at Ruby's horse. "You can ride Citizen Valentine's horse, and she can ride behind you."

"Oh, no you don't," Ruby sputtered, backing away her mount.

Gabriel shot her a stern look. "It is only for a few more miles."

"Spent with my arms around him? No thanks."

"You will manage."

———

AFTER THE DEATH of Tam's mother, Vinko and a crew of men blocked every fireplace in the inn with beds and wardrobes. Vinko surmised that vampires would still be able to push away the furniture without too much effort, but at least the sound would warn the humans waiting below.

Eva wrapped Margaret in the bed sheets, and then Vinko carried the body to a storeroom in a far corner of the chilly cellar. The temperature would keep the corpse from decomposing until they could bury her. Tam didn't leave his mother's side the entire time. And he didn't say a single word.

Neither did Eva. She seemed uncommonly grim. Vinko kept glancing at her, trying to figure out what she was thinking, but she had become very hard to read since he had kissed her. Maybe he shouldn't have made his intentions so clear. Maybe he shouldn't have backed her against the door like he had. At the time, she had seemed to want what he wanted. And at that moment, pressed against the door with her, he had never wanted a woman more.

But she had changed after that passionate interlude.

Vinko turned to go back up to the taproom. He looked over his shoulder at the boy. "You come now, Tam?"

Tam shook his head.

Eva swept her skirts around the swathed body and

touched Tam's hair. "But soon, all right? I don't know how safe it is down here."

Tam nodded.

"Here." Vinko set the lantern near the boy's feet. "Keep her in light tonight."

Tam nodded but didn't look up.

Vinko paused. He put a hand on the boy's shoulder. Tam stiffened. Vinko wanted to hug the boy and tell him that he would get through all of this one day, but he let his hand slide off Tam's shoulder. He knew it was best to leave Tam be for now.

He shouldered out of his coat and draped it over Tam's thin frame. Tam had not accepted his support, but he accepted the warm garment.

Then Vinko followed Eva through the cellar to the foot of the stairs. Before she climbed back up to join the others, he reached for her hand. He could feel her trembling.

"Eva." He said softly. "Wait."

24

"What is not well with you?" Vinko asked.

"Nothing is *not well,*" Eva pulled her hand back, but he held her fast.

"You shake. Your eyes."

"It's been quite a day."

"You do not want this close. To me. Why?"

She shot a glance at him and then quickly looked away, but not quickly enough to mask the tenderness and regret in her expression.

"It doesn't matter what I wish," she said.

He blinked, confused, but didn't press her. He could tell she had something heavy on her mind, and she needed to talk.

"It's never been a matter of what I wish," she added. Then she sighed. "My whole life, Vinko. It's never been what I want." She set her jaw, as memories hardened her luminous eyes. "Don't do that, Eva. Don't go there. Don't expect so much. Don't think too much. Stand there. Wait. Don't complain."

Vinko regarded her. "Londo life," he said.

"Yes, Londo life." She yanked out of his grip. "Until I met you, I didn't know there could be anything else."

"So is good. Meeting me."

"No, not good. Not good at all." She turned to glare at him. "If we make it out of here, how do you expect me to go back to Londo, knowing what I know? And just take it?" She crossed her arms. "Now I understand why a friend of mine did what he did."

"What friend?"

"And old friend. Mine and Joanna's."

"What did she do?"

"It was a he. Aiden Bannister."

"Ah, the boyfriend." Vinko didn't care to hear about the men in Eva's life. But she seemed determined to talk about her past, so he humored her. "What did this Aiden do?"

"He and his supporters stormed the Central Compound. That's where the Overseers live. He hoped to take over the government. Or at least make them see the error of their ways."

"And?"

"The Overseers prevailed. As always."

"And your boyfriend?"

"He was caught."

"Sent to this place? Port Pennwood?"

"No, they were going to execute him, but Joanna got him out of prison."

"So he is alive? You wait for him?" He tapped his heart.

"No. He's dead. Neal Moray killed him."

"Ah. This sadness stays in the heart then?" Vinko dipped to look more closely at her face. "For the boyfriend?"

She sighed again and looked at the floor, trying to hide

the guilt and self-loathing she felt because of her dead rebel.

Her shoulders slumped. "One day I hope to think of Aiden and not feel like a complete bitch."

"You are not the bitch."

"You don't know me." She shot him a second hot glare. "And you should stay clear of me. I'm the most selfish, thoughtless person you will ever meet."

"I do not believe this."

"It's true." Eva sucked in a deep breath. "Do you know how cruel I was to Tam's mom? The last words I spoke to her were so self-righteous. I still cringe when I think of them. And now she's dead."

"I do not think you are this way."

"Well, I am." Eva grabbed the wooden stair rail. "I took one look at Margaret's plight, and all I could think of was my life could have been hers—full of secrets and fear and a child to hide. Tam could have been my fatherless son, Vinko. Mine. But did I try to understand her? No. I shouted at her."

"Not at her," he began. He thought he understood Eva pretty well, but she didn't allow him the opportunity to offer his view regarding the situation. When he began to speak, she interrupted him.

"I was so angry at her. She was Charles' mistress, Vinko. His mistress! I wanted to punish her for that. So I lashed out at her, using poor Tam as a weapon." She shook her head. "I am such a bitch. But I can't seem to help it." She leaned forward to plow up the stairs, but Vinko reached out for her. He couldn't let her return to the others in such an emotional state.

"Eva, wait."

Eva looked over her shoulder at him. He could tell that she wanted to talk to someone. He wanted to be that someone. But something held her back from confiding in him.

Her eyes glinted in the low light, full of self-reproach and anger. But then she turned around to face him. He could see in her expression that she hoped he might say something to make it all better. He had no idea what words would help her see herself in a new light. To express complex emotions in a language he was still learning made the task doubly difficult. But he had to try. If he could connect to the part of Eva that she hid from the world, maybe he could help her climb out of the darkness.

"Eva." He reached for her, and she allowed him to draw her off the step. He clutched the backs of her arms in a loose grip, just enough to keep her from running away. He wanted to draw her into his arms and give her a long, solid hug. That's what she needed. But after the kiss upstairs, he knew Eva was far too skittish for such closeness.

"You are not the bitch."

"You don't know that, Vinko."

"The words you say to Margaret?" He squeezed her gently. "You say them to yourself. No? Not to her."

"Oh, I said them to her all right."

"But the anger lives in you. Comes back to you."

Eva paused and blinked a few times as she stared at his chest. He could tell she recognized the truth in his words and was contemplating what he was saying.

"Why are you so angry at beautiful little Evie?"

She tried to pull away, but he held her tightly this time.

"Tell me."

"What good would it do?" Tears glinted in her beautiful eyes. His heart squeezed together. The last thing he wanted was to make this woman cry.

"I want to know."

"It's just dirty laundry. No one needs to look at my dirty laundry."

"Maybe I want to look. Then I know who you are."

"And what good would that do? We will always be strangers to each other, Vinko. That's how it works in Londo."

"I am not of Londo. I do not accept these rules."

"But I have to. That's the way it is. One of these days you'll go back to Croatia, and that will be that. So why bother to get to know each other?"

"Because I want to." He stepped closer to her, until his chest came in contact with her breasts. His body reacted to her immediately. He had to choke back his desire for her, so he could keep looking in her eyes and not ravish her on the spot.

She stared at him, white-eyed and weeping. Her eyes told him there was something between them, something that went far beyond friendship. But he could tell the connection tormented her.

Then she shook her head and looked down.

"No. It's a risk I cannot take, Vinko," she said. "Margaret's plight reminded me how dangerous it is to take chances."

"To follow your heart."

"It's pure stupidity on a woman's part."

"And you are not stupid."

"I can't afford to be." She raised her chin and stared down her nose at him. "I am a big girl now, Vinko. It's taken years, but I know what I have to do. I know how I must live my life. And I will do it."

"You will stay behind this wall." He waved a hand between their faces.

"Yes."

"And if I say there is the other way?"

"What other way?"

"My father send ship for me."

"Here? To Port Pennwood?"

Vinko nodded. "When work is done, I go back. To Croatia."

She regarded him with such force, he felt as if she were sucking in all his thoughts as she searched for the truth. Then again, she might not be searching for truth. Maybe she searched for hope, for a way out. He ached to give her that.

"You go with me, Eva."

She swallowed and swayed backward, as if she might faint. He gripped her arms tightly to hold her fast.

"Come to Croatia. Be free."

"I can't. My sister is here. My life is here."

"What life is it?"

"The only one I know." Her gaze met his, and he felt the heat of her conviction turning her backbone to stone. He could feel her drawing even farther away from him.

"We may not live tomorrow," Vinko said, hoping to soften her hard views. "Think of that, Evie."

"We may not. But I can't make decisions on maybes anymore."

"You are hard. Too hard, I think."

"I have to be." Her chin rose even higher. "Please, Vinko. It isn't wise for us to do this again."

"To talk?"

"To touch like this. To be close. To speak of things that can never be."

"Ah." He slipped his hands down to her elbows.

"If you are the friend you claim to be, you will give me space."

Space was the last thing he wished to grant her. But he

knew he had to accept her terms or risk losing her altogether.

"As you wish." He stepped backward and swept the air with a hand. "I am friend. Oki doki. Friend only."

Friendship. So utterly cold when compared to the kind of relationship he wanted to explore with her.

He hoped she would reconsider when she heard the friendship limitation spoken out loud. But she only pressed her lips together and nodded. Her brown eyes were still muddy with distress.

"Thanks," she said at last. Then she fled up the stairs, outrunning her desires and any chance he had to change her mind.

Vinko followed at a much slower pace, his footsteps as heavy as his thoughts.

As he had said to Eva, they might not survive the night. If he had to die, he wanted to die in Eva's arms, knowing that she cared about him. He wanted to know what it was like to share a real connection with her. But she had asked him to mute his voice and feelings and keep at a safe distance. He would never know how she felt about him now.

Perhaps he was becoming a Londo citizen after all.

"No," he growled under his breath. "Never."

He reached the top of the stairs and threw back his shoulders. "I am Sunara."

The night was not over yet.

NEAL MORAY STOOD next to the litter and scanned the inn. What was taking so long? He'd heard one scream and nothing else.

His guards shifted beside him, as anxious as he was, waiting for orders.

"Where are those two?" Moray said through his teeth.

"Something must have happened, boss," the taller guard replied.

"Like what? Are you telling me that two vampires can't dispense with twenty humans?"

"Looks like it."

"How? It's inconceivable."

"Something *has* been killing us."

"Or are we plagued with deserters?"

The guard shrugged.

"What could be killing a vampire? Or who?"

"Don't know, boss."

Neal heaved a frustrated sigh. "So it looks like it's up to me once again."

"Boss?"

"I always have to do the dirty work." Neal tucked his cane under his arm. "If something is ever done around Londo, it's always up to me."

"You're going into the inn?" The guard's eyebrows lifted in surprise. "Alone?"

"No, I'm moving on to Plan B."

"Plan B? What's that?"

"If in doubt, burn 'em out."

"You're going to set the inn on fire?"

"It worked in the Middle Ages. Can't see why it wouldn't work now."

Neal adjusted his hat with a smart tap. "Take me back to the manor. I'm sure Paar kept kerosene and matches somewhere in that dreadful house."

CLOSE TO MIDNIGHT, Vinko was startled out of a light doze by the sound of loud tapping outside the inn. Hammers. He looked down and caught Eva's eye. She had come instantly awake as well.

Vinko slipped out of the booth where they had been sitting and strode to the front of the inn. For a moment, he listened to the rap of hammers at every window in the taproom. Eva scrambled out of her seat to stand beside him while Joanna scooted back the chair she had been sitting in. Most of the others in the taproom stood up as well, on full alert.

"They nail boards to windows," Vinko announced. "From outside."

Joanna cocked her head. "To imprison us. Why?"

"To starve us?" Vinko glanced at Eva's older sister. She was taller than Eva and her mouth was much firmer. Her determination lent her features a fierce beauty that outclassed the looks of her younger sister. Yet he preferred Eva's softness and vulnerability. He loved the tentativeness in Eva's eyes and the tender curve of her cheeks. He loved the way she had melted into him before she remembered the restrictions of her society.

Joanna would never melt. Something had happened to her to make her as hard as stone. And Vinko knew if he didn't do something to intervene, Eva would follow in her sister's footsteps.

"Not starve us," a male prisoner added. "They're going to burn us."

A horrified murmur ran through the crowd. A woman with a child in her arms started to sob.

"I've seen it before," the man continued. "They round up troublemakers and just burn 'em."

"I've never heard of that," Joanna said.

"Oh, you'd never hear of it. But one day, your father

simply never comes home. Or you'll hear a train had wrecked. And the next thing you know, bodies show up at the door. It is always the Overseers culling the troublemakers, mark my words."

"Train wreck?" Eva's voice quavered so much that Vinko stared down at her, wondering why the remark had struck her to the core. Even stranger, Joanna wrapped an arm around her sister's shoulder and drew her close, as if to comfort her.

Eva's lips had gone white. "The Overseers would cause a train to wreck on purpose?"

"No, citizen. That was just the excuse they gave for killing a bunch of people. They'd never wreck one of their precious machines."

"And now, they're going to kill us," a woman wailed.

"No, they're not," Joanna countered. "Not as long as I am in this building. Moray wants me alive for some reason. He wouldn't dare burn this inn while I'm in it."

"Joanna is right," Vinko said. "We stand strong."

As if on cue, someone pounded on the door of the inn.

25

"Smell that?" Neal Moray shouted from the street outside. "That's kerosene. We've doused the whole place in it."

Joanna tipped her nose to the air and sniffed. The sharp reek of fuel burned her mucous membranes. Flickering light shot under the door of the inn. Moray must be holding a lantern or a torch, ready to set fire to the inn at the slightest provocation. Fear laced with adrenaline streaked down her back.

"Give yourself up, Joanna Wilder!" Moray shouted. "Or we set fire to the inn."

She had assumed Moray would return with a way to make her surrender, but not so soon. She had to decide what to do and decide quickly. She could feel the hard stares of the rest of the prisoners as they waited for her to react.

It had come down to her safety or the lives of all the people in the taproom. She couldn't expect them to protect her. They didn't even know her.

Eva grabbed her hand. "He's bluffing."

Joanna squeezed her fingers, grateful for her sister's support.

"He'd never burn the Golden Hind, Joanna. It's the only inn in Port Pennwood."

"I wouldn't count on it," Joanna replied.

"I'm giving you to ten," Moray said. "If Citizen Wilder doesn't come through the door by the count of ten, I will set fire to the building. And no one will get out alive."

"Please, no!" the woman with the child cried, stumbling forward. The little girl blubbered with terror. All Joanna could see was the same expression she'd witnessed on the face of her sister so long ago, and all she could feel was the compulsion to do something to alleviate that fear. Nothing had changed. She was still responsible for the fate of others. Still. Forever.

"I'll go." Joanna pulled out of Eva's grip and stepped toward the door.

"No!" Eva gasped.

"He won't hurt me. He needs me for something."

"Joanna, no!" Eva rushed forward and grabbed her arm. "No! Not when we've just got back together."

"We'll be together again." Joanna's heart broke as she gazed down at the stricken white face of her little sister. "Have faith, Eva."

"In what?" Eva's eyes filled with tears. "How can I believe *anything* now? It's all been lies."

"Not with us." She touched the side of Eva's face. "I'll think of something. I'll get away. I'll find you."

"Eva." Vinko reached for her. "Come."

Joanna glanced at the tall man. She was grateful that he was there for her sister. Leaving Eva was difficult, but not as difficult as it could have been, had he not been standing behind her, lending her his considerable strength and support. She waited until Eva's hands slid from her arm and then stepped closer to the door.

"Wait," Vinko clasped Joanna's upper arm. "Do not trust the vampire."

"I don't. But what else can I do?"

He drew her close to him and lowered his voice, so only the three of them could hear.

"We go out to Moray first, Joanna. You run."

"Where?"

"To cellar. To tunnel. Smuggler passage."

"Smuggler passage?"

"Inns on sea. All have the tunnel."

Joanna glanced at her sister, looking for a sign that she should trust the Croatian. Eva nodded, her face still white.

"Are you sure?" Joanna asked.

"If no tunnel, hide. Find the weapon."

"Find Tam," Eva added. "He'll help. And keep him safe."

"Tell Moray you come out last," Vinko added. "If you are first, we die."

"Okay." After a few moments, Joanna faced the vampire on the other side of the door and squared her shoulders.

"Okay, Moray. I will come out on one condition," she said.

"And what is that?"

"That you allow the prisoners to leave the inn. Unmolested."

"And go where?"

"Wherever they choose."

"Free them? That's against the law, citizen. They are criminals."

"Take it or leave it, Moray."

"Citizen Moray. It's Ketchum—from the boiler." The

boiler man writhed in his chair. "Help me! I didn't do anything wrong! And they've got me tied to a chair!"

One of the prisoners slapped the man in the face. Ketchum lunged forward, hobbling in his chair to get closer to the door.

"They are plotting something!" Ketchum yelled.

Beyond the door, Moray was silent. Joanna waited, staring at the planks of the floor as she listened for the slightest rustle beyond the door.

"All right," he finally said. "I'll let the prisoners disperse. But you come out first."

"No, I come out last."

"If you don't come out now, Wilder, there's no deal."

"Then we all burn."

"No!" Ketchum yelled. "Not me! I didn't do anything! Please, citizen!"

Before anyone else could protest, Joanna cautioned all to silence by holding up a hand. She could feel the prisoners holding their breath, just as she held hers. But she knew Moray. She knew what he had done with his bare hands to Aiden Bannister. She, herself, had been a victim of his wrath. The last thing she was going to do was trust him to keep a bargain. She had to remain firm.

Seconds ticked by. She strained to hear movement beyond the door, worried that Moray would decide to give up his pursuit of her and torch the inn. But her vampire hearing picked up nothing beyond the moan of sea wind.

Minutes went by. The light beneath the door disappeared. Joanna wondered if Moray had left to post men at every exit point to ensure that she couldn't get out of the building. Then she heard him tramp back to the door and the light reappeared at the threshold.

"All right, Wilder," he growled. "We'll do it your way."

Joanna clasped her hands together at her mouth, glad to have won the first skirmish.

"I will open the door. Prisoners will come out one by one, starting with your sister."

"My sister?"

"Yes. Your sister Eva."

"If you harm her, Moray—"

"No one will get hurt if you come out with your hands up."

Joanna turned and hugged Eva fiercely. Eva clung to her, her fingertips digging into her back.

"We'll get through this, Eva," Joanna said. "I promise."

Eva was too distraught to speak. She pulled away, fighting back tears.

"Go now, Joanna," Vinko said. He stuck his hand in the pocket of his trousers and slipped out a pod. He held it up and motioned toward his eyes. Eva nodded. Joanna watched them for a second, amazed at their silent communication and the newfound bravery of her little sister. A year ago her sister would have been sitting in the corner weeping with the woman and child, too afraid to make a move, or lashing out at having been put in such a dangerous position. Maybe even trading favors with the vampires to gain freedom, but only for herself.

She liked this new version of her sister. But there was no time to stand around gawking in admiration at her.

Joanna took off for the cellar stairs.

———

When Vinko was certain Joanna had gained enough of a head start, he motioned toward the door. Eva stepped up to it.

"Do not look in the eyes," he reminded her.

"I know. I know."

"I am behind you. Close."

She nodded and swallowed and gave him one last glance. Their serious gazes met and held, more potent than any kiss. Then she faced the door.

"I'm coming out, Moray," she announced

Vinko watched as Eva opened the door as wide as it could go. Smart woman. She was giving him a chance to see the lay of the land outside the inn so he could throw his pod. Then she marched across the threshold, head held high.

Moray allowed her to stride across the street, as if he were keeping his word and letting her go as agreed. Then he nodded his head at one of the guards. The brute broke away to pursue her.

"Cover!" Vinko shouted, bursting out of the inn. He paused in the street, took aim, and threw the pod at the guard's feet. As he covered his face with the crook of his arm, he felt the light of the explosion flare around him. His eyes burned. He had almost blinded himself in his haste to save Eva.

"Goddammit!" Moray swore at his left.

The sound of Moray's voice was a huge disappointment to Vinko. The vampire leader had survived the light. He must have been too far away to succumb to its effect.

Before Vinko could throw a second pod, he heard a strange swooping noise and felt a second flare of heat and light—but far different than the light from one of his pods. He uncovered his eyes and blinked until his vision cleared. To his horror, he saw the second guard had panicked and had thrown his torch at the kerosene-soaked inn. The entire side of the building was engulfed in flames.

"Shut it!" Moray yelled. "Shut the door!"

"Stop!" Vinko yelled. "You'll kill Joanna!"

The guard slammed the door shut and wedged his huge body against it as Moray reached for a board and a hammer. Moray planned to trap the prisoners inside and burn them to death. Screams and shrieks rose over the thunder of the rising flames.

"No!" Vinko shouted. He shoved his hand into his pocket. He had two pods left. One for Moray and one for the guard. The rest of the vampires, he would have to fight with his bare hands.

Moray didn't even look at him. Snarling, he pounded spikes into the board while the guard held back the mob trying to push through from the other side. If Vinko was lucky, he could kill both vampires with a single pod.

Vinko raised his hand, preparing to throw, but someone grabbed his wrist and yanked it back so hard, he lost his footing. The pod went flying. He crashed to the ground, slamming his back and head on the cobblestones. For a moment, all he could see were stars. He couldn't think. Couldn't move.

Then a vampire jumped on him, pinning him in place.

"Trying to be a hero, eh?" the vampire hissed. "Fool!"

Vinko blinked, struggling to get his eyes to focus. All he could see was a red mouth and pointed teeth heading for his neck. He flung his body to one side, using his large male frame to throw off the slight Londo vampire. But his human strength wouldn't last long against that of a vampire.

Like a cat, the vampire leapt upon him, knocking him flat to the ground again.

"Vinko!" Eva shrieked.

"Wind chime!" he yelled, praying that Eva would understand his meaning. He reached for the vampire's eyes, hoping to stave off the inevitable. He framed the vampire's skull with his hands and jabbed both thumbs into the creature's eye sockets. He might be fighting with a supernatural creature, but vampires had eyes as sensitive and vulnerable as a human.

The vampire howled in pain and reared up. Vinko pulled his knees to his chest and kicked the vampire in the solar plexus, knocking the wind out of him and vaulting him halfway across the street. The vampire landed with a thud as Vinko scrambled to his feet. Desperate, he glanced around, searching for the pod, but in the darkness, he couldn't locate it.

He looked up to see Moray glaring at him from his stance at the door of the inn, his red eyes glowing with hatred, as he considered his next move. For a split second, Vinko surveyed the vampire leader, careful not to look into his eyes.

Moray would probably not waste any more time here. He would go for Eva next, as she would make a valuable hostage. Behind the vampire, a wall of flames engulfed the inn, sending gray smoke billowing into the night sky. People screamed inside, suffocating in the smoke and heat, unaware of the possibility of a smuggler tunnel. The cries tore at his heart. But he could do nothing. And if he didn't find the pod within seconds, he would lose his own life.

His vampire assailant rose on one knee, shaking his stunned senses back to order and holding his abdomen. In moments, he would recover enough of his faculties to attack again.

With his heart thudding in his ears and the screams of the prisoners piercing his heart, Vinko strained to see in the darkness. He commanded his vision to sharpen. He blotted out every sensation but sight and focused with all his might. He had to find the pod. It had to be on the street somewhere. He had to find it.

JOANNA LOOKED over her shoulder as she and Tam pulled another set of shelves away from the wall, searching for the opening of the smuggler tunnel. She paused. The sounds from above made her stop what she was doing and consider running back upstairs. She could hear the thunder of fire and smell the smoke. But worse, she could hear the desperate prisoners screaming in terror.

"I have to go back!" Joanna cried. "Eva!"

"No," Tam grabbed her wrist. "You'll die."

"But my sister. The prisoners!" She yanked at her wrist, but the boy's wiry grip was strong. He did not release her.

"It's too late, Joanna. Too much smoke."

"But if they knew to come down here…"

"No time."

With his free hand, Tam yanked away the shelving unit, spilling jars and bottles onto the floor. Glass shattered around their feet, adding to the din from upstairs.

"Found it!" he crowed. "Come on!" Tam pulled open the old wooden door, just as the lantern went out, spent of fuel.

A blast of cold air rustled Joanna's clothing and blew through her hair. She tried not to breathe the fetid air, afraid of what ancient germs it might contain. She held her breath and scanned the void ahead. Her vampire vision allowed her to discern more details in the darkness than Tam could see. She could make out festoons of cobwebs and roots hanging down in the blackness beyond the door.

Every cell in her body warned her to stay out of the tunnel—that danger lurked in the darkness. But before she could protest, Tam dragged her forward. She crunched across the shards of glass to the opening of the passage and then stopped.

"It could be dangerous," she said. "We don't have a light."

"We'll feel our way out."

"What if there is a hole? What if the tunnel collapses on us?"

"It's better than burning to death." He kept hold of her wrist as he stepped into the passage. "Come on, Joanna. It's our only choice."

Tam was right. She had to plunge into the tunnel and hope for the best.

"Let me go first," she said. "I can see more than you."

"How do you know?"

"I just know."

His hand relaxed. Joanna shook out of his grip and swept past him. She took a deep breath, blotted out all thoughts of what was going on above her, and placed her hand on the earthen wall of the tunnel.

She would guide Tam to the beach or die trying. And if Eva were still alive, she would find her.

26

PANTING from her sprint up the hill, Eva crouched low and hurried around the far side of the manor to the back garden. She hadn't seen anyone return to the house, but she kept out of sight of the windows anyway. She had scrambled up the hill, through alleyways and scrub, over stone walls and brambles, desperate to keep off the road where she could be spotted but suffering the consequences of her nocturnal trailblazing. Her face and hands were scratched. Her hair was a tangled mess full of dried leaves and spider webs, and her left leg throbbed where she had turned her ankle. But she had made it to the manor. And she didn't think anyone had seen her.

Still, vampires had powers she knew nothing about. Maybe they had seen her and were just taking their time. She shuddered and hobbled across the back yard, hoping that Neal Moray would not think to look for her on his very own doorstep.

She had to sit down. She had to rest her injured ankle. The garden had always been her haven. She had always felt safe here. She would either survive until morning or die here, in her most favorite spot on Earth.

Eva ducked under a lilac bush and scooted behind the old stone bench where she used to sit out of view of Charles or Hannah. The spot could not be seen from the house and was close to the back gate if she were forced to flee. There was also a missing stone in the wall that afforded a view of the lane leading up to the manor. In the early days of her marriage, she used to look through the gap, waiting to spot Charles coming up the lane. If she saw him walking, she would have tea ready for him when he arrived, always anxious to hear news of his day. But after a few days of utter silence while he sipped his tea and stared at the fire, she had given up the practice.

Eva blocked out her memories of Charles and slumped one shoulder against the wall, hugging her knees to her chest to retain as much body heat as she could. Within minutes, the sweat from her strenuous journey had dried and the maritime air settled around her, chilling her to the bone. She could smell a sickening odor on the wind and knew it must be the burned prisoners. Her heart twisted in anguish.

She dropped her chin to her knees and gazed through the gap, praying that she would catch a glimpse of Joanna or Vinko or Tam. She wondered if they were still alive. She had to believe they were still alive, or her heart would break once and for all.

Eva swallowed back the lump in her throat. Joanna had urged her to have faith. It was difficult to have faith when everything in her life—everyone she cared about—was torn from her. But if she didn't have faith, what was the alternative? Blackness. Despair. Surrender. She hadn't come this far only to give up now. She set her jaw and concentrated on the road below.

Dawn glowed on the horizon. She prayed for another sunny day. If the sun shone like it had yesterday, Moray and his henchmen would have to take shelter. That would give the humans valuable time to come up with a new plan.

Unless she was the only one left.

CLOSE TO DAWN, Gabriel surveyed the sky. Already an orange glow lit up the edge of the moor. Yesterday had been a strange sunny day, forcing them to ride under the cover of trees and shrubs. It had been slow going. Today looked as if it would be a similar weather pattern. At this rate, they might never get to Port Pennwood in time.

He scanned the terrain ahead and saw a smaller path cutting off to the left. He could smell traces of human beings who had walked in that direction. He could also smell something else on the air. Something burnt. Something he couldn't identify. But the odor turned his stomach all the same.

He twisted in the saddle to address the man riding with Ruby. "Is that a shortcut?" He pointed at the track through the weeds.

"That's the beach path." Citizen Browne's voice cracked with weariness. His grizzled face was lined with fatigue. "But..."

"But what?"

"If the tide isn't right, the beach gets cut off."

"The tide looks to be well out to me."

"If you can see the beach, citizen, your eyes are much better than mine."

Gabriel ignored the human observation. "Is the beach path shorter?"

"Yes. You can cut across two coves. It's easy riding. But if the tide comes in, you'll get caught and will have to find your way up the cliff face. You'll also have to abandon your horse."

"I'll take my chances." Gabriel guided his mount off the main road.

"Hey!" Ruby shouted. "You can't just leave me with this guy."

"Then follow." Gabriel had no time for anything but getting to Port Pennwood.

The strange odor on the air worried him. Deeply.

JOANNA AND TAM huddled just outside the smuggler tunnel, ready to run back in if they had to. After hours of feeling their way through the ancient passage, they had finally made it to the sea. The tunnel opened behind a jumble of boulders onto a small cove, which was separated from Port Pennwood by a rocky spit. Before the Grave Mistake, skiffs could have come in on the high tide, unloaded their contraband, and rowed back out to an awaiting schooner with no one ever seeing them from the little village.

Joanna wondered what valuable goods had passed this way hundreds of years ago. She wondered what the world had been like back then, when people lived all over the globe, crammed into cities and driving those things they called automobiles. She had seen skeletons of such vehicles rusting away on weed-infested roads outside Londo.

But now only horses and carriages were allowed. The Reformation five hundred years ago had changed the way humans lived. The Overseers had turned back the hands of progress to a safer, simpler steam-based world, where never again would one person be able to destroy entire civilizations with the press of a button.

Here in Port Pennwood, Joanna could almost forget the Grave Mistake had ever occurred. With the sunshine of yesterday, she had caught a glimpse of life the way it used to be. The air had been clean and warm and fresh. The sky had been clearer. And blue. Gloriously blue. Even in her current dire straits, whenever she thought of the color of that sky, she couldn't help but smile. During her trek through the tunnel, she had often held that cerulean inspiration in her thoughts to give her hope.

In Port Pennwood, all evidence of the apocalypse had been swept away. Here, there were no abandoned vehicles sitting on weed-infested roads. Trash had been cleared and buildings were maintained in perfect condition. There were no ration lines, no men huddled on the corners, smoking and whining, no dour policemen trying to keep order. Port Pennwood was quaint, peaceful and in perfect order. At least on the outside.

On the inside, however, this picturesque village was nothing but an abattoir.

Another lie.

Joanna swallowed. All visions of the blue sky dissipated. Eva's words came back to her, haunting her. Apparently everything in the Anglo Territories was a lie. What *could* they believe in, now that they knew the truth about the Overseers? How *would* they live their lives from here on out?

All she knew was that running away was not the solution.

And no matter who or what governed them, they still had each other. They had to stick together.

She turned to glance at the boy sitting beside her. She put her arm around his scrawny shoulders. He stiffened under her touch, but he didn't pull away and she didn't release him.

"How are you holding up, Tam?"

"All right." He kept staring at the sea, his chin on his knees.

"It's tough to lose a parent."

He didn't say anything.

"I know. I lost both of my folks when I was young."

After a long moment he asked, "What happened to them?"

"We were told they were killed in a train wreck. But now I'm not so sure."

"Do you think the vampires killed them?"

"It's very likely. My father liked to talk. Tell stories. Everyone liked him, looked up to him. Leaders are always a prime target of the Overseers. Leaders have to be silenced."

Tam took a deep breath but said nothing.

"But things have to change, Tam. The truth about the Overseers has to come out. Too many of us know about them now."

"Unless they kill us all first."

"Yes." She hugged him and then slid her arm away from his shoulders. For a long while, they both stared out to sea as a pearly sheen grazed the tips of the promontory and gradually bathed the top in blessed morning light.

After a while, Tam spoke. "Do you think everyone in the inn is dead?"

"I hope not."

"That's why Moray burned down the inn, isn't it, Joanna? To make sure no one blabbed about their secret." He turned and squinted at her. "Do you think Eva is dead?"

"I hope and pray that she isn't." Joanna refused to give

in to the desperation she felt whenever she thought about Eva. "I think Moray would want to keep her alive to get to me."

Tam nodded and plopped his chin back down on one knee. "We've got to find her. As soon as it's light."

"Yes." She studied the side of the boy's face. His loyalty to Eva surprised her. But then again, males had always flocked to Eva. Tam was just a younger version of her typical admirer. He couldn't be much older than ten.

"So, I take it you were the boy on the train. The stowaway."

Tam nodded.

"Does your father know you hopped on a train, all by yourself?"

"Don't have one."

"What happened to him?"

"He died before I was born."

"Your mom raised you by herself?"

"Had to."

"She must have had relatives to help, surely."

"Nope. Just me."

"I don't see how she could have done it. How did she work with a baby?"

Tam shrugged. "I don't remember her leaving the house much. She was sick a lot. That's what sticks in my mind."

"And the Overseers never found out about you?"

"Nope. If you're smart and you know where to hide, you can survive on the streets of Londo. The secret is to keep moving. Never stay in one house too long. The bean counters of the Overseers never catch up that way. Neighbors don't have enough time to put two and two together. So no one turns you in."

"So you and your mom would move often?"

He nodded. "Every couple of months. You'd be surprised how many old apartments there are in Londo. Some still have running water. That's all you need."

Actually, she wasn't surprised. She and Eva had spent many hours in a hideaway of their own—an abandoned penthouse on the top of a skyscraper. But she would never tell anyone about it. Not even Tam. She may still have need of it one day.

Joanna gazed at Tam. The boy was so like her: determined, proud and not one to blubber when life turned dark. From what she knew of the boy, he had led the same kind of bleak existence she and Eva had endured—always outside the law. Living an unsanctioned life took a toll on a person's peace of mind, but it also gave independent souls a way to exist on their own terms. And now that she was back, she would rather live on her terms than accept one more crust of bread from the Overseers.

"We'll get through this, Tam." She shot him a brave smile. "You'll see."

"Right now, all I see are two horses coming this way."

He pointed at the strip of beach on the left where more rocks stuck up through the pounding waves. Two horses clopped toward them, with a single man in the lead and a man and woman on a large gray horse following him. They rode in the shadow of the cliff, but Joanna could still make out faint details, enough to see the color of the woman's clothing. She was attired in purple, from her hat to her boots.

"Good Gottfried," Joanna gasped. "It can't be."

"What?" Tam asked.

Joanna scrambled to her feet. "I think I know that person. The woman." She stared at the approaching figures until her eyes burned. "That has to be Ruby Valentine."

"Ruby Valentine?" Tam stood up beside her. "What kind of name is that?"

"It's a vampire name." Joanna turned to the boy and took his shoulders. "Tam, she's a vampire. But I know her. She won't hurt you. So don't take off. Just stay put."

"You know a *friendly* vampire?" Tam's voice rose with incredulity.

"A couple of them, actually." She let go of his shoulders to concentrate on the approaching horses.

Something about the rider in the front looked familiar. Those shoulders. The flash of reddish hair.

Could the rider be Gabriel? Her heart leapt into her throat. And before she thought twice, she broke into a run.

27

JOANNA RAN ACROSS THE SAND, her hair flying in the wind, her heart bursting with joy. She was certain Gabriel was the man on the approaching horse. When they had parted a year ago, she had thought she would never see him again. And now, like a miracle, he was here. Here in Port Pennwood. And now, he was galloping toward her on a horse, his coattails flapping against his thighs and his blazing eyes fixed on her.

When she was a few feet away, he swung out of the saddle and leapt to the ground. He spread wide his arms while his face beamed with happiness—from his kind blue eyes to his grinning boyish mouth.

"Gabriel!" Joanna cried. She flung herself into his arms.

He embraced her as she had longed to be embraced since the day she had left him on the riverbank. She buried her nose in his neck cloth and closed her eyes, savoring the touch of him, the smell of him, and the strength of him. He was here. He was real. He was not a dream. He smelled of horseflesh, sea air and leather laced with the unmistakable scent of his masculine musk and soap—a fragrance all his own. He smelled so good. So familiar.

His body felt familiar as well. He was muscular and fit, without an extra ounce of weight on his lean frame. So strong and yet so gentle. She wanted to burrow into the warmth and safety of his greatcoat, blot out the real world and never let go.

"Joanna!" he exclaimed. He pressed a cheek against hers and squeezed her tightly, telling her how much he longed to kiss her, but knowing they had to keep their romantic feelings hidden from the rest of the world. His chest rose and fell against hers, as he breathed as deeply of her as she did of him. His gloved hands swept across her back as if to prove to himself that she was truly in his arms —as if he had spent a lonely year dreaming of a phantom love as well. "Ah, Joanna!"

"I thought I would never see you again," she whispered in his ear.

"And I, you."

The jingle of a bridle interrupted their intimate words, as Ruby guided her mount to stand beside them.

"Really, Gabriel!" Ruby scoffed. "So you found your little pet. Good. But do we have to watch you making a fool of yourself like this?"

"Ruby." Joanna fought back a flush and gave a proud nod to the vampire.

"Citizen Wilder." Ruby touched her wine-colored hat. "Who knew a creature like you could torture a man like Gabriel? He's made me ride nonstop for days."

"It was your choice, Ruby," Gabriel countered.

"Well, I'm looking forward to a stiff drink and a hot bath. So wrap it up, folks."

Blushing, Joanna pulled back. Gabriel stood his ground and didn't release her or even look up at Ruby. His gaze remained on Joanna's face as his eyes sparkled with joy.

"Ride on to Port Pennwood if you prefer," Gabriel called over his shoulder. "I cannot vouch for what may happen in the next few minutes."

"Disgusting." Ruby urged the large gray horse to clomp past them.

"Find out what that smell is," Gabriel added. "We will meet you in the village shortly."

He had just said "we." How wonderful the word sounded. She had been an "I" for too long. She had spent so much time alone and had done everything for years without any help. The possibility of sharing life with someone—especially Gabriel—was like a wonderful dream. She kept her hands on the lapels of his vest, unwilling to break their connection now, no matter what Ruby thought of their behavior.

Joanna turned to watch Ruby and the other man depart for the promontory.

"Be careful," Joanna called. "Moray is out for blood. From all of us. And he's set fire to the inn."

Ruby waved her off, obviously not concerned.

Joanna meant to say more, but Gabriel reached up with a gloved finger and guided her chin back until she faced him.

"Ruby will be fine. Don't worry."

Joanna turned her attention back to Gabriel.

"Now where were we?" he murmured.

She gazed up at him, her heart brimming with love again. "Well, now that our audience is gone, I was hoping you might kiss your little pet."

"Gladly." He pulled her into his arms again and bent

to her mouth. She let her head fall backward into his hand as his fingers snaked into her hair and his mouth claimed hers. She had spent countless nights remembering the way Gabriel could kiss and had relived every second of their stolen moments together—over and over again. Those visions had kept him close to her heart and kept her sane. Now he was in her arms, kissing her with a tender passion that made the dream kisses pale in comparison.

"Gabriel," she said against his lips. "I've missed you so much."

"And I, you."

He pulled back and regarded her so seriously that she paused to meet his earnest gaze. His eyes told her far more than his hands and mouth, but she still wanted to hear what was in his heart. As if he could read her mind, he said, "Joanna, I love you." He crushed her against his chest again. "I love you so much."

She caressed his burnished hair and closed her eyes while his words filled her heart. Tears squeezed from the corners of her eyes, but she held him tightly, unwilling to let him go long enough to dry her cheeks. She had spent so many lonely nights, missing him and wondering what their life could have been like had they met under different circumstances—had they met as human beings.

But that kind of life could only happen in fairy tales.

Gabriel would never be a human being. Their relationship would never be conventional. They could never lead a normal life together. In order to be with Gabriel, she would have to recast her expectations and definitions.

From here on out, she would think of Gabriel as a *being*. Not just a human being. He was far more than a human being, and in some ways far less. But Gabriel in any form was more than enough for her.

"I should have told you months ago, Joanna. Before

you left. But I did not want to make your departure difficult."

"It was hard to leave even so. And harder still to be away from you."

"And I from you." He caressed her and sighed into her hair. "So many times I regretted not telling you. So many times. And when I thought of all the days and years and centuries that I would never see you again, it drove me mad. It's been a very difficult year."

"Yes." She hugged him. "For me, too."

After a long moment, he pulled away, enough to look at her face. "And you?"

"Me?"

"Do you love me, Joanna?"

"More than anything." She stared deep into his navy eyes. "With all my heart."

"I have longed to hear you say that." He hugged her again. "I thought you would never forgive me for what I did to you."

"You had no choice. I know that now. You did the only thing you could at the time. 'Do no harm,' right, Gabriel?"

"Yes." He pulled back a second time to study her. "Are you all right?" He brushed his thumbs across her cheekbones. "You seem thin."

"I've been living up north. Hand to mouth."

"But they caught you?"

"Someone betrayed me."

"Ah."

"How did you know I was sent to Port Pennwood?" she asked.

"Ruby told me."

"She did?" Joanna pulled back in surprise.

Gabriel nodded. "She doesn't like me all that much. So she must have done it for your sake."

"Then I am forever in her debt."

"Don't tell *her* that. She will hold you to it someday." He smiled and looked over her shoulder. "Who is the boy?"

"It's a long story." She took a breath and turned to see Tam walking toward them. "Come. Let's continue to Port Pennwood and I'll tell you about him. There's some work to be done today. And it isn't going to be pretty."

"What do you mean?"

"Moray set fire to the inn, Gabriel. It was full of prisoners. I think everyone is dead. But if there are survivors, we may need your services."

"Good God." Gabriel reached for the reins of his horse. "That's what I've been smelling on the air."

"Yes."

Eva had rested behind the bench for less than an hour when she spotted Moray and two guards dragging a man up the lane. The guards hauled the man by his arms, leaving his boots to bump along the cobbled road. Eva leaned closer to the breach in the wall, straining to see whom it was they carried and why the man was not conscious.

That black hair could only belong to one person.

"Vinko!" Eva gasped.

His skin glowed white against the dark sky behind him. What had they done to him? Killed him? But if they had killed him, why drag his body all the way to the manor?

Shafts of morning light chased the vampires into the old stone house. While they were busy unlocking the door, Eva hobbled to the side of the house, just below the parlor window. There, she could stand on tiptoe behind a shrub to see what transpired in the main hall.

Moray strutted into the hall and pointed his cane at the parlor. The remaining guard and a worker Eva didn't recognize dragged Vinko into the parlor and dropped him in front of the fireplace. Scowling, the guard plopped down in a nearby wingback chair. He reached into his vest and pulled out a pistol, which he cocked and rested on one thigh.

Moray yawned, said something she couldn't make out, and then turned for the stairs. She wondered if he were retiring for the day and leaving the guard to pull a double shift. By the sour expression on the guard's face, she assumed she was correct.

The other worker skittered back outside and down the lane, running for shelter before the sun rose any higher. The day promised to be bright. Maybe even warm. Good.

Once the worker had disappeared from sight, Eva turned back to inspect Vinko. He hadn't moved from the position in which he'd been thrown. He lay face down with his arms and legs splayed, his white shirt covered with soot and nothing to see of his head but his dark curls covered in ash.

"Vinko," Eva whispered in anguish. She couldn't see if he was still breathing. But if he were dead, there would be no reason for a guard. A small flame of hope flickered in her breast.

As she crouched at the window, she thought of her next steps. If Vinko didn't recover by the time the sun rose, she would run down to the inn to see who had survived. Then she would search the village and the beach for her sister. They hadn't thought to establish a meeting place. That had been a stupid oversight.

Surely, if the sun favored them, Joanna would chance

coming back to the village to locate her. Somehow, some way they would find each other.

She glanced at Vinko again, at his broad shoulders and outstretched hands. Such capable hands. She loved his hands. She loved how his hands had guided her, held her, and pulled her against him.

Heat and longing swept through her at the thought of Vinko's embrace. He had made her feel things no man had ever made her feel. He was a man who didn't just take from a woman. He offered himself and all that he could give. Even more to his credit, he had honored her request to step away. No complaints. No pressure. He seemed confident that one day she would change her mind.

Eva was certain that if she ever did change her mind and accept Vinko, she would come to know what real love between a man and a woman could be. He was a good man. A real man. The kind of man she wished she could have married.

Looking at him, so still and white, she realized that she loved him. She would do anything to save him, to ensure that he lived.

She loved him.

She realized now that she had never really loved anyone before. Not like this. Not even Joanna.

Eva swallowed back a lump of heart-wrenching self-awareness. Maybe it was too late. Maybe Vinko was too far gone to benefit from her love and devotion. But she would do everything in her power to rescue him. Perhaps there were pods left in his room at the inn. Maybe the entire place hadn't burned. She could arm herself with the rest of the pods, come back, and annihilate Neal Moray.

She had to hope for the best. Manifest success. But her first step was to return to the Golden Hind.

She ducked away from the window, hobbled back

through the garden and left through the rear gate. She still had to keep off the road and out of sight, so her return to the inn would be as treacherous as her journey up to the manor house. At least this time, she would be able to see where she was putting her feet.

Ignoring her throbbing ankle, Eva limped down the hill.

28

"Good God," Gabriel swore a second time. He handed the reins of his horse to Tam and strode to the front door of the inn, with Joanna at his heels.

Ruby stood near the door as the innkeeper kicked in the charred remnants of wood. The black boards splintered into shards of charcoal and ash and clanked to one side, still hanging off the corroded hinges. The half-burned sign above the door dropped through the air, almost hitting Ruby. She ducked out of the way, swearing.

The sign hit the ground in a puff of ash. Gabriel glanced at it.

"The Golden Hind," he muttered, too shocked to think of anything more to say. Joanna came up beside him and touched his arm.

"Gabriel, look." Her voice cracked.

He looked. Beyond the door, he saw utter carnage.

For a moment, no one moved, as they took in the effect of the fire.

"Oh, my God," Ruby gasped. She stepped back, fumbling with her reticule. She pulled out a cigarette case.

Gabriel stood at her elbow, assessing the scene, planning his next steps and searching for signs of life, even though he doubted anyone had survived the inferno. Still, he had to hope. The physician side of him demanded optimism.

Browne walked past him to stand just inside the doorway. In shock, he clasped his hands on top of his head and stared at his ruined workplace, thunderstruck by the devastation in the taproom.

Gabriel felt the morning sun already burning his back. He moved forward, into the shadow cast by the stone wall that still stood at the front of the inn. He looked over Browne's shoulder, surveying the carnage.

Remains of bodies provided clues as to the last minutes of the prisoners in the Golden Hind. Some still huddled in corners or lay on the stairs. Others had been trapped beneath fallen timbers. White splotches merged with ash where the intense heat had detonated something the prisoners had held in their hands and kept in their pockets. Not a living soul was left. All had been immolated in a fire so intense that it had burned through bone as well as flesh.

"Who would do this?" Gabriel demanded.

"The Others, I suspect," Browne answered.

"The Others? Who exactly are the Others?"

"We don't know. We just call them that around here. People have been disappearing. But more than usual lately."

"It wasn't the Others," Joanna put in. "It was Moray. Neal Moray. He and his guards did this."

"Moray is here?"

"In all his glory."

"What is he doing here?"

"Making some kind of beverage out of human blood."

ELBI. Gabriel scowled. The convenient canned beverage he had been drinking for the past few months

must be the brainchild of Neal Moray. He should have
known Moray was behind the innovation. Moray was
always proposing improvements and conveniences. He had
no patience for the slower, more careful pace of the
Overseers.

A sour taste flared in Gabriel's mouth. If Neal Moray
had anything to do with ELBI, he would avoid the drink
and go back to hunting. No more spending his days like a
human, as he preferred to live.

Gabriel shot a glance at Ruby, but she didn't seem to
care about the news of Moray. She was still reeling from
the sight in front of her. Highly agitated, she stood in the
shadows, puffing at her cigarette. She glared every so often
at the taproom, but mostly kept her gaze pinned to the
ground. Her hands and lips trembled. She tried hard to
show a tough façade to the world. But even a seasoned
veteran like Ruby could not stomach what had been done
to the people in the Golden Hind.

"I must check for signs of life," Gabriel said, releasing
Joanna's hand. "The rest of you stay back. It may not be
safe."

"I'm going with you." Joanna grabbed a hanky from
her vest and held it to her nose.

"No, Joanna."

"But Eva!"

"If Eva is here, I will find her."

"Gabe—"

"It isn't safe." He covered her forearm with his hand,
insisting that she stay back. "Stay with Ruby. Do as I say.
Please."

He shot a meaningful glance at Ruby.

Ruby swept forward and clutched Joanna's elbow. "Let
the doctor do his work. He's used to stuff like this."

"But my sister could be in there!"

"That's right. Do you want to see her if she's dead? It might not be a pretty sight. Do you want that in your head for all time?"

"Ruby," Gabriel admonished. "You are not helping."

"He's right," Browne clutched Joanna's other elbow. "You stay back, citizen. Stay with us."

"No!" Joanna cried, pulling at her captors.

Gabriel shut out her protests and plowed into the inn. He had work to do. His focus shifted entirely onto the taproom. He scanned the barren ruin, looking for survivors, using his vampire vision to detect the slightest glow of body heat and his vampire hearing to pick up the faintest heartbeat. Nothing. He moved deeper into the room, skirting the holes in the floor and the still-smoking timbers. Residual heat from the fire warmed his face and hands. The blaze must have been horrific.

He shut down the human part of him, the state he lived in most of his days now, and switched over to full vampire mode where mortal life was not held in such high regard. He had to switch off the human side of him so he would see only an alien world here—a world of ash and soot and charred wood. Nothing more.

As a vampire, he could move through the devastation in the inn and think of it as nothing more than ducking into a large fireplace to fix a flue. Messy. Dusty. But if he were careful, he wouldn't ruin his expensive clothes or get anything in his hair.

Gabriel stepped into his vampire self as if he were slipping into a second greatcoat. He could feel his heart turning to ice. His mind clicked on to a higher, sharper level of awareness. A buzz hummed through him, vibrating away the last vestiges of Gabriel, the doctor.

He was now Gabriel, brother of Silas Stone, leader of the vampires. In two beats of his vampire heart, all gray area thinking vanished. He could feel the undulating life of the humans behind him, calling to him. He hungered. He thirsted. He had to feed. But now was not the time. He could feel the prickle of sunlight driving him further and further into the darkness of the inn. It was kill or be killed now. It was survival of the fittest and smartest. There was no room for sentiment. There *was* no sentiment.

In this place of death, he had to become his vampire self or completely lose his mind.

"Joanna!"

Eva waved and hobbled as fast as she could go down the lane, ecstatic to spot her sister standing in front of the Golden Hind, alive. The sun bathed Joanna in light, turning her mousy hair to gold and casting a nimbus around her body. For a moment, Eva wondered if she had fallen asleep in the garden and were only dreaming. But then the figure extricated herself from two people that held her arms. Joanna broke into a run.

"Eva!" Joanna cried.

Eva was so glad to see her sister that she hugged her hard enough to break bones. But Joanna didn't seem to care. She hugged her right back.

"You're safe!" Eva gasped. "You made it!"

"Yes, we found the tunnel. And you made it out, too."

"Moray had me go out first." She glanced over Joanna's shoulder. "And Tam?"

"He's here. He took the horses to the stable. He'll be back."

"We have to stay together now."

"Yes."

Eva took a step toward the inn, but Joanna grasped her hand. "Eva, don't."

"Don't what?"

"Go over there."

"Why?"

"It's bad." Joanna's nimbus faded. "Everyone is dead. More than dead."

"What do you mean?"

"All the prisoners? They've been turned to ash."

"Good Gottfried." Eva's small moment of joy at seeing her sister deflated.

Joanna nodded. "Gabriel is in there now, searching for survivors, but I don't think he'll find any."

"Oh, no." Eva paused to stare at the ruins of the inn, trying not to imagine what Joanna had just described. Then the rest of her sister's words filtered into her consciousness. "Wait a minute. You're saying Dr. Stone is here?"

Joanna nodded. "He got word of my capture. He came as soon as he could."

"Really?" Eva pulled back to inspect her sister's face. "So he does care for you."

"Yes."

"And to go to the trouble of coming here? He must be in love with you."

"He actually said as much this morning."

"And you?"

Joanna nodded as a calm smile spread across her grave face. "I have loved him for a long time now."

"Oh, Joanna!" Eva hugged her again, bittersweet. "I am so happy for you. For both of you."

"But it is so complicated. We come from two different worlds."

"And you were not chosen to marry and have a family. You never got a silver envelope."

"And there is that. But…"

When Joanna's voice broke off, Eva pulled back a second time to search her sister's face. She could hear the seeds of protest in Joanna's words. She prayed that Joanna would come up with a way to get what she wanted, and in turn show Eva how she could achieve her heart's desire as well.

"What will you do, Jo?"

"I don't know yet. Get through this first. That's all I can think about."

The fatigue in Joanna's voice alarmed Eva. She squeezed her sister's fingers in reassurance. "Dr. Stone will help us. He always has. He'll think of something."

Joanna patted Eva's hand and pulled back. "But you must brace yourself, Eva, for what Gabriel discovers in the Golden Hind. Your friend Vinko might have perished with the others."

"Not in the inn."

"You know for sure?"

Eva nodded. "He got out. He saved me, in fact. But Moray got him."

"What do you mean, got him?"

"He's done something to Vinko. He's up at the house, unconscious."

"What house?"

Eva pointed up the hill to the large stone house with the shining weather vane.

"That one. Where I used to live."

Joanna gaped at the grand home and then glanced back at her sister. "You lived there?"

"Until Moray killed my husband."

"That bastard," Joanna said through her teeth.

"Moray or Charles?" Eva countered.

For a moment Joanna stared at her, as if struggling to understand what she had just said. Shock must be dulling Joanna's faculties.

But then Eva's dark humor settled over her and she shook her head with a grim smile. Eva was reminded of the old days, when they had each other and no one else, when she had not yet discovered men. Those days had been tough. But they had been a team then, inseparable, using irony and mimicry to keep up their spirits.

"So not a great marriage," Joanna commented, patting Eva's hand.

"A complete disaster."

"I'm so sorry to hear that."

"It was my choice." Eva met her sister's serious gaze.

Joanna nodded slowly. "Yes. And we will say no more of that."

Eva swallowed, grateful not to have to answer questions about her intimate life with Charles. Or lack thereof.

Joanna pulled Eva forward. "Come. When Gabriel is finished at the inn, I will ask him to go up to the house and get Vinko out of there."

"Will he do that?"

"Of course he will. Moray can refuse Gabriel nothing."

"Really? Why?"

"They have a...a history together. It goes way back."

Eva stared at her sister, confused. "But Moray is a vampire."

"I know." Joanna flushed and tugged at her hand again. "Come on."

"But—" Eva held back, her curiosity burning. "What do you mean, a history?"

"Apparently, they have known each other a long time.

That's what I've been told. Maybe Gabriel healed him in some way. I don't know. But come on. We have things to decide."

Eva allowed Joanna to drag her toward the inn, but her suspicions mounted with every step. For the first time in her life, she sensed that her sister had just lied to her.

29

"I DON'T KNOW about you three," Ruby Valentine said, grinding out a cigarette with the tip of her boot, "but I need some sleep."

Eva watched the woman in purple, amazed by her appearance—from her colorful dress and netted, feathered hat, to her white face and crimson lipstick. No one in Londo would dare to wear any color but black or use cosmetics, except on their wedding day. And no one smoked—least of all a woman. Apparently, she was a friend of Gabriel, so perhaps she was granted more liberties than a regular citizen.

The more Eva looked at Ruby, the more unlikely she seemed to be someone Gabriel would choose for his inner circle. Gabriel possessed an innate nobility and style. This woman dressed like a lady, but something was off. Eva couldn't put a finger on it, precisely, but Ruby seemed ill suited to the outrageous clothes she wore, as if she were playing dress-up.

Tam walked up, interrupting her thoughts. He brushed ash off his sleeves and squinted in the sunshine. He

stopped beside Eva, and—without thinking—she put an
arm around him. He looked up at her, his eyes far more
serious than they should be for a boy his age and full of
things he wanted to say—but not in front of strangers. He
looked so old and tired and beaten that Eva wanted to
wrap him in her arms and hug him. But he would never
allow that.

When no one said anything, Ruby looked over at them
and raised her penciled eyebrows. "So?"

"I'm turning in, too," the innkeeper said. "I've been
walking day and night."

"But what about Vinko?" Eva put in.

"Who?" Ruby's eyebrows arched even higher.

"Vinko Sunara," Tam said. "Our friend." He glanced
up at Eva. "Did he make it out? Or is he…"

"He made it out." She pulled him closer. "He made it
out, Tam."

"Good." The boy sighed. She felt his shoulders relax a
bit. "But where is he?"

"Moray has him up at the big house. On the hill. We
have to get him out of there."

Ruby scowled at the moor beyond the manor house,
where the sun climbed ever higher. She moved close to the
ruined wall of the inn, into a strip of shade that narrowed
by the minute. She must avoid sunlight to maintain her
snowy complexion.

"None of us are in any condition to rescue anyone,"
Citizen Browne said. "And who knows how long it will take
the doc to go through the inn."

"True," Ruby said. "We can't do anything without
Gabriel. Moray will listen to a fellow big shot."

Frustration spiked through Eva. "So you're saying we
just leave Vinko up there?"

Ruby's hard eyes surveyed Eva's face. "For now, yes."

"She has a point, Eva," Joanna put in. "Gabriel is the only one Moray will listen to."

"Who said anything about talking to Moray?"

"Yeah," Tam echoed, pulling away. "We can't just leave Vinko up there. He wouldn't leave us."

"Tam's right." Eva took a deep breath. "But we need ammunition."

"Some of those pods?" Joanna asked.

"Yes."

"But they burned in the fire," Tam brushed the bangs out of his eyes. "The whole chest is gone. I looked."

"You went upstairs? At the inn?"

"Of course I did. And downstairs, too. Where do you think I've been?"

Eva stared at him, amazed and horrified that the boy had put his life in danger by crawling through the charred remains of the Golden Hind. But it would do no good to chastise him about it now. She glanced at her sister.

"I think I know where I can get some more of the pods."

"Where?"

"In a hut on the beach."

"A hut? Where?"

"Not far from here." Eva pointed at the hidden cove.

"I came that way," Joanna said. "I didn't see a hut."

"You have to know where to look."

Joanna nodded, deep in thought.

"You could hide there, Jo. Moray would never think to look for you there."

"And there are pods there?" Tam asked.

"I think so."

"I certainly can't stay here in plain sight," Joanna mused. "If Moray comes back..."

"And we all need to eat. I'll make a pot of soup,"

Citizen Browne said. "For whenever any of you gets back. It's the white house there, up the lane."

"Wait." Joanna turned around to look at everyone. "Who is going to stay here and tell Gabriel where we are?"

"I suppose I can. I can hang around here for a bit more." Ruby waved them off with a gloved hand as she rolled her eyes. "You all go on. I'll wait for Dr. Stone."

Eva exchanged a worried glance with Joanna. She didn't know the woman in velvet, and she didn't trust her. Joanna dropped a hand in front of her skirt, with one finger extended. That meant GO in their childhood secret code.

Joanna trusted Ruby. So Eva would as well.

"Come on. It's already past noon." Eva took off for the stairs to the beach. "Every minute counts."

"You're telling me," Ruby grumbled, squinting up at the sky.

AT THE HUT, Joanna sank upon the chair, weary from the long night and the trek down the beach. She still wasn't fully recovered from the beating she'd sustained in the prison cell. And trudging through the sunshine had sapped what little energy she had in reserve. In fact, the sunshine had made her feel nauseated. She wondered if her vampire traits were steadily evolving inside her, making her more a creature of the night than of the day.

Worried and unable to tell anyone her troubles, Joanna watched Eva dig through a stack of clothing and wooden boxes. Her mind drifted far from the hut.

Thoughts of the future plagued her. Even if she survived Port Pennwood, she could not go back to Londo. As long as

Neal Moray was alive, she would be in danger. On the other hand, she didn't want to leave Gabriel again. And he would never leave Londo. His brother was there. More importantly, his patients were there. How could a future ever include him? And without Gabriel, why would she want to continue living?

Joanna chided herself for thinking such nonsense, but deep in her heart, she knew that for her to be happy, Gabriel had to be an integral part of her daily life, and not a person who existed hundreds of miles away from her. There had to be a way to be together. She would just have to come up with a solution.

Then there was Eva. Eva had picked up on the way Joanna had skirted the issue of Gabriel's connection to Neal Moray. Her sister could sense that Joanna was not telling the truth. But she had promised to keep Gabriel's secret, no matter what. Even from her own family. To live alongside Eva in a state of perpetual deceit would eat Joanna alive.

Eva had also made an enemy in Neal Moray. How could she ever live in Londo? She would have to avoid Moray as well. A dark wave fanned through Joanna's guts, as a stark truth descended upon her.

The only path forward was to get rid of Moray.

The apothecary/healer part of her rebelled against taking anyone's life. But in Moray's case, he was already dead. He was not a human. She had to believe that moral considerations did not apply in his case.

Joanna gazed at Eva, who had found what looked like a wind chime fashioned of sticks and colored glass and wrapped in a shawl. Stuffed all around it were Vinko's gray packets. She and Tam jammed the pods into their pockets and vests. Then Eva carried two hands full of the packets to Joanna and dumped them in her lap.

"Remember, don't allow them to get wet or hot," Eva instructed.

Joanna nodded and slipped the pods inside the pockets of her skirt.

Eva studied her face. "We're going to go up to the manor house."

Joanna rose.

"Not you," Eva said.

"I'm not staying here."

"Yes, you are. You're not fit. Stay here. Rest. There is some food in that chest." Eva pointed at the box under the window. At the thought of food, a wave of nausea swept over Joanna. "Make yourself a cup of tea, Joanna. Get some sleep."

"I'm going."

"No, you're not!" Eva bent to tie a knot in her skirt, which she tucked under her belt to hold up the hem of her dress. She didn't seem to care that she had just revealed a good portion of her shapely legs or that runs and holes marred her stockings or that her expensive boots were scuffed and dirty. The old Eva would have been mortified to go out in public with a single hair out of place. This new version of Eva couldn't care less how she appeared. Joanna stared at her, amazed once again by the transformation of her little sister.

Tam handed a large sharp knife to Eva, and she slipped it through her belt while he did the same with a second smaller knife. Neither of them spoke. It was as if they were part of a team that needed no words to communicate.

"Tam and I are going to run up the cliff path," Eva continued. "You'll never make it, Jo. You'll just drag us down."

"I can keep up," she lied.

"I don't think you can. Look at you. You are as white as a sheet."

Joanna raised her chin. "I'll be fine."

"We won't wait for you. We can't."

"Fine. But I'm going." Joanna threw back her stiff shoulders and took a resolute breath. She thought back to the times she had sprinted through Londo, so fast it was almost like flying, thanks to the vampire part of her. But right now, the prospect of even walking back along a flat beach seemed like a monumental task.

Still, she should be the one to deal with Neal Moray. Not Eva and the boy. She would make herself go back out. She would endure the afternoon sunshine, no matter how sick it made her feel. And somehow, she would get her aching body up the cliff.

30

"OPEN UP!" Gabriel pounded on the front door of the manor house where Neal Moray had slept the entire day. He was desperate to rescue Vinko Sunara himself, to save Joanna and Eva from placing themselves in mortal danger. They hadn't returned from their ammunition run, so he hoped he would be in time to thwart their rescue mission by getting up to the house before them. He'd run up the hill at the first sign of cloud cover.

As Gabriel waited at the door, he glanced over his shoulder at the threatening sun. It hung over the sea in the bank of clouds, about to burst free again. Gabriel had to find shelter within seconds or face being immolated.

If he had been able to sweat, he would be sweating now.

He pounded on the door, harder this time.

"Hold your horses!" a gruff voice called from the other side. The lock turned and the large door swung inward.

A beefy man in an Enforcer uniform and a gun in his hand blocked his path. The guard's surly gaze ran up and down Gabriel's figure.

"Yes?"

"I'm here to see Citizen Moray."

"He's not available."

"He will be for me. May I come in, please?"

"And you are?"

"Gabriel Stone."

The guard's small eyes narrowed as he evaluated his visitor. "Stone, you say?"

"Yes. Stone."

"The doctor."

"Yes." Gabriel felt his back starting to burn. "May I please come in?"

The guard grunted and stepped to one side, pulling the door ajar.

"Thank you."

Gabriel ducked into the house and out of the triangle of light cast by the sun. He shook his shoulders, allowing the shadows of the main hall to cool the heated air between his clothing and vampire flesh. A minute more in the sun, and he would have suffered enough damage to put him out of commission for a few days. He couldn't allow that to happen, not when Joanna was in dire need of him.

He glanced at the guard, who had shut and locked the door. "Can you summon Moray?"

"He won't be happy at being disturbed."

"His happiness is not my concern."

"It is mine, citizen." The guard balanced the pistol barrel in his hand and planted his feet on the slate floor. He wasn't about to budge.

"Is he sleeping?" Gabriel asked.

"Isn't my business to know what he does upstairs."

Clearly, the guard wasn't going to be much help. Gabriel glanced around, trying to come up with a good reason to rouse Moray. Then through the doorway of the parlor, he glimpsed the feet of someone lying on the floor. He stepped across the hall and peered into the austere room at the front of the house.

"Why is a man lying on the floor? Is he hurt?"

"That's none of your business, citizen."

Before the guard could stop him, Gabriel strode into the parlor.

"I said it's none of your business, citizen."

Gabriel ignored the guard's warning and knelt on the floor beside the injured human. The man was tall by Londo standards. His coloring was different, too, with his black hair and golden skin. This must be Vinko, the Croatian and friend of Eva. But Gabriel cared little about the man's provenance. He was far more concerned about the man's physical condition.

Even in vampire mode, Gabriel remained a physician at heart. He placed a palm on Vinko's back, spreading his fingers over his linen shirt and waiting for a lift of respiration. He couldn't detect a single breath.

"What happened to this person?" Gabriel demanded.

The guard shuffled up to stand next to the chair. "He killed two of Moray's men."

"And?"

"Moray punished him."

"By doing what?"

"You know what he's does." The guard blinked, struggling for words to express himself without criticizing his superior. "With that cane."

Gabriel's lip curled in disgust. He bent closer to Vinko and gently lifted one eyelid to assess his pupil. His eye reacted to light. Good. At least the Croatian was still alive. But barely. A red line, darkening to purple, marred the man's cheekbone where Moray had struck him. Another welt disfigured his neck. His left hand looked as if the metacarpals had been broken. Gabriel sat back with a growl of loathing for Moray, knowing that if he turned Vinko over and lifted his shirt, he would discover the man had been beaten, almost to death.

"This is not the way citizens of Londo should be treated."

"He's not from Londo. Look at him."

"Even strangers are to be afforded fair treatment." Gabriel rose, frowning. "You rouse your boss and tell him to come down. Immediately."

The guard's chin lifted, as if he were going to refuse Gabriel's command. Gabriel stood firm, glaring at him and thinking of the pain Moray had inflicted on so many people—on Aiden Bannister, Joanna and the people in the taproom, and now on Vinko. Moray was a monster. A monster that had to be stopped. Gabriel felt his eyes turning to ice.

Something in his hard expression must have made the guard reconsider.

"All right," the guard said. "But he's not going to be happy."

"Moray's happiness can go to hell."

The guard shot Gabriel a shocked look. Then he lumbered away toward the stairs in the main hall.

Gabriel turned back to the man on the floor. He could splint Vinko's hand with his handkerchief and a small flat object. He scanned the parlor, wondering why a commissioner would live in such bare surrounds. The only softness in the room was the tall velvet drapes, probably relics from the past. His gaze landed on a piece of kindling at the hearth. The kindling would span the distance between his fingers and wrist. Good. He grabbed it and knelt near Vinko's ruined hand.

Gently, he slipped the stick of wood next to the man's hand.

"Stay away from me," a deep voice rasped.

Gabriel glanced at his patient, amazed to see Vinko had opened his eyes to glare at him. The man's body was close to death, but his eyes were very much alive. The intensity of Vinko's blue eyes startled him.

"I can help you."

"Stay away."

The Croatian's blue eyes glittered, full of pain but still threatening.

Gabriel paused.

"Your kind has done enough," the Croatian added, tracking Gabriel's every movement with his chilly stare.

Gabriel had never sensed as much hatred from a human as he did from the half-dead man on the floor. Humans usually accepted his help gratefully, never guessing he was a vampire. And his fellow vampires respected him for keeping the peace in Londo. He wasn't accustomed to being reviled like this. But hate streamed from this human's eyes.

"Sir, I…"

"Get out."

Gabriel got to his feet, just as the guard tromped back into the parlor.

"Citizen Moray says he'll meet you in the study."

"Where is that?"

"This way."

Before Gabriel followed the guard deeper into the house, he took one last look at the Croatian. Vinko hadn't moved, and had fallen back into a stupor with his eyes half-closed. The sooner he received medical treatment, the better his chances for survival. After Gabriel talked with

Moray, he would return and try one more time to save the man's life. But he would have to be quick.

Gabriel padded down the hall to the small dark room in the center of the house. A set of windows looked out on the side yard, which was full of shrubbery blown sideways by the incessant wind. The plants afforded enough protection from sunlight to allow the drapes to remain open with no need for a lamp. Moray stood at one window, with his hands clasped behind his back and his thick neck accentuated by the high stiff cut of his collar. His coat, so out of place in a hamlet like Port Pennwood, was fashioned of black brocade stripes alternating with a black floral pattern. He turned, and the silver buttons of his double-breasted garment glinted in the dying light of afternoon.

Moray looked fit and well rested, unlike the rest of the inhabitants in Port Pennwood. Even Moray's own guard looked haggard and worried.

"Gabriel Stone," Moray drawled, sweeping him into the room with a grand wave. "What a surprise."

"Moray."

Moray ignored his chilly tone. He lifted a decanter half full with red liquid.

"Join me?"

"This is not a social call."

Moray ignored him again. "It's ELBI." Moray smiled and poured a glass. He lifted it toward Gabriel. "Here, try some."

"I already have."

"You have?" Moray brightened. "What did you think?"

"I'm not here to talk about a canned beverage."

"You drank the *canned* version?" Moray rolled his eyes and clucked his tongue. "My dear sir, the bottled version is the only way to go. It's the best thing since champagne.

Why did no one ever think of aging our favorite beverage?"

"Because it isn't a beverage."

"Right, Doctor Stone. It's our life's blood. Get it? L.B. Life's blood." He grinned. "ELBI."

Gabriel scowled, growing more and more impatient. This man could chatter on and on about a drink when people had perished in a fire for which he had been responsible. He couldn't have forgotten already. The stench still hung in the air as a grim reminder. Moray's insensitive cheerfulness sickened him.

"Back in the day," Moray placed a crystal stopper on the decanter. "There used to be a drink called Coke. Remember? They called it 'the real thing.' But this," Moray held up his goblet. "This is the *real* thing."

"As real as what happened at the Golden Hind? I think not."

Moray glanced at him, the goblet still in the air. For a moment, he looked as if he were at a loss for words. Then he took an agitated sip of his ELBI.

"An unfortunate turn of events," he replied.

"Turn of events." Gabriel crossed his arms. "Is that what you call it?"

"One of my men panicked."

"And started the fire?"

"Yes. I had no intention of burning those prisoners. I needed them!"

"For what?" Gabriel glanced at the decanter. Moray followed his stare.

"Yes, for the ELBI."

"You're using the blood of prisoners?"

Moray grinned. "Genius, isn't it?"

"There are no words for what I think." Gabriel stared at him, his disgust mounting.

"We were sending the prisoners north, where we had to clothe and feed them."

"They work in the mines. They earn their keep."

"But you have to admit, it's a huge expense for the Central Compound." Moray ticked off the items on his hand. "Travel. Shipping. Guards. Accountants. Managers. I've looked into it, Stone. It's a social program we can't keep funding."

"We've sent prisoners to the Norsea work camps for hundreds of years."

"Doesn't mean we have to continue the practice."

"So prisoners come here on the train, and, instead of being shipped out, you just kill them."

"I wouldn't say 'kill.'" Moray sipped his drink. "It's an enjoyable process. Kind of like being in a sensory deprivation tank."

"You kill them."

Moray sighed and frowned. "So? We're vampires. We kill. What's the big problem?"

"For one thing, you haven't brought this up with the council."

"I thoroughly intend to, once all the bugs are worked out."

"So this fire was a bug?"

"No, the fire was a result of a lot of things gone wrong. And I had nothing to do with them."

"Tell me." Gabriel leveled his coldest stare on the man.

With a clatter, Moray set down his glass. "It all started with the commissioner here. Charles Paar. I blame him."

"What did he do?"

"He was caught breaking into an authorized personnel only zone."

"Why?"

"Apparently a woman was involved."

"Eva Wilder?"

"No. One of the prisoners. A new one. Came in on the train."

Gabriel narrowed his eyes, trying to think of who that might be. He had looked into the background of Charles Paar. Charles had no relatives.

"Paar was okay with sending prisoners to the north. But when it came to someone he knew?" Moray chuckled and shook his head. "The man's true nature came out. Just another rebel."

"He tried to save the woman?"

"Yep. But I stopped him before he saw anything." Moray cocked his finger and shot an imaginary gun at the window. "One shot. Never miss."

"Paar is dead?"

"As they say, as a doornail." Moray glanced at the decanter. "Could be drinking him right now, as a matter of fact."

"But that doesn't explain why the prisoners were in the Golden Hind."

"That came next. When your little friend arrived on the train."

Gabriel kept his expression impassive. "My little friend?"

"Joanna   Wilder."   Moray   frowned.   "That troublemaker."

"And?"

"She and her sister and that big lug downstairs managed to set the prisoners free." Moray poured a second glass. "It was a freak of a day. The sun came out. After hundreds of years, the sun decides to come out. We couldn't pursue them."

"So they took shelter in the inn."

"Yes. And armed themselves."

"What do you mean?"

"They had something. Little bags of something. The Croatian killed two of my men with it."

"What was it?"

"I don't know. It exploded. It had the same effect as full sunlight on a vampire. There was nothing left. Just clothing."

Gabriel studied Moray as he gulped his drink, agitated.

"When he threw that sack, one of my men lost it. He dropped his torch, and poof, that was it."

"But the door to the inn was boarded up."

"I had to do something. If the prisoners escaped…"

"If word got out about your mishandling of the situation, you mean."

"I didn't mishandle anything." Moray turned, red with rage. "It was Paar that started it!"

"With you out here undertaking an unofficial and illegal activity."

"If Paar hadn't disobeyed the rules, it would have been business as usual. Everything was running smoothly. Product was flying out the door."

"So one slip, and this happens."

"Paar and those Wilder girls. They are at the root of this." Moray clenched his jaw. "If it's the last thing I do, I'm going to see that Joanna Wilder is punished."

Gabriel's blood ran cold. He didn't doubt that Moray would try his best to carry out his threat.

"I will have to report all this to my brother."

"So? I'm not worried."

"You should be."

"Well, I'm not. I have something up my sleeve."

"Oh?"

"Silas will be very interested in what I've discovered.

Very." Moray raked Gabriel with a nervous glance. "And so will you, if you have any of those spots."

"What spots?"

"The rash. You know, the red spots." Moray flushed. "That annoying rash that some vampires are getting."

"I wasn't aware that others besides Silas were afflicted."

Moray shrugged. "I've heard others have it as well."

Gabriel studied him. Moray was blushing and as nervous as a patient with a worrisome affliction he wished to keep secret. So Moray must have the same rash as Silas. It must be a virus. Gabriel's thoughts churned. A virus was much more difficult to eradicate than a bacterial or fungal infection. Perhaps that was why none of his treatments had been successful on Silas.

"What have you discovered?" Gabriel took a menacing step forward. "Tell me."

"Not until you promise to protect me."

"From what has gone on here? Never."

"Then the cure for the rash dies with me."

"You want me to keep silent on all this."

"For now. I was going to announce the project soon. I was almost ready!" He stepped closer. "And you can't blame me for the fire. Really, you can't."

"But you could have let the prisoners out."

"And had them overrun the place? Silas would never have condoned such a decision. He will applaud me for what I did here. Peace above all, isn't that what he always says?"

"I believe he means status quo above all."

"Okay, but Stone, really, give me a break. Don't tell Silas about this. I'll sweep things up around here, get production back on line, and then present everything to Central Compound."

"And the rash cure?"

"When I come back to Londo, I will tell you and Silas everything."

"When will that be?"

"A week? I have to wait for a new shipment and finish some processing."

Gabriel regarded the small man and his eager, overly taut body. The man must never relax—always plotting and planning in his thirst for power.

"On one condition, Moray."

"Name it."

"I take possession of the man downstairs."

"The Croatian?"

"Yes."

Moray sighed. "But he needs to tell us about those bags he has."

"Has he told you anything yet?"

"One more session with me," Moray pursed his lips, "And you can be sure that he'll tell me everything."

"One more session, and he'll be dead."

Moray turned on his heel and marched back to the window, as if to outdistance the truth in Gabriel's words.

Gabriel took a deep breath, determined to handle the situation with as little drama as possible. "I can find out more with kindness than you will ever discover with cruelty."

Moray pulled his head to the side, as if his neck cloth were choking him. He stared out the window, not speaking, as he considered Gabriel's words.

"There is nothing to consider, Moray. I'm taking the Croatian."

31

Moray finally turned from the window. "Supposing I do relinquish Vinko into your care, what will you do with him?"

"Ensure that he recovers, for one."

"And then what?"

"Find out what his secret weapon is. Determine if he is a threat."

"He's a threat all right. No question about it."

"And if I determine that he is a threat to the Overseers, I will take required steps."

"Such as?"

Gabriel raised his chin and stared at Moray, his gaze hard. He was unaccustomed to being questioned by an inferior and disliked the man's tone. Moray didn't have a choice in regard to Vinko. If Gabriel demanded his release, then Moray would have to comply. Gabriel had offered a bargain to Moray out of respect, not necessity. And still the man stepped over the boundaries. "That is for me and Silas to decide."

"I often wonder what side you're on, is all."

"Such musing is a waste of time, Moray."

"Really? I don't think so."

"My actions are no business of yours."

"Humor me, Stone. I'm curious."

"Very well." Gabriel crossed his arms again. "I take care of people. First and foremost. Whether they are vampire or human. Life first. Politics second."

"This isn't politics. This is out and out survival. If that Croatian has something that can kill us as easily as it appears, we need to do something about it."

"Killing him isn't the answer."

"Why not?"

"Do you actually think he is working alone?"

It was Moray's turn to raise his chin. He stared down his nose at Gabriel and blinked rapidly. It was clear that Moray hadn't considered the idea that there could be more Croatians, all with the ability to kill vampires.

Moray indicated the door with his glass. "Okay, then, take him. Do what you have to do."

EVA AND TAM skittered through the back garden of the mansion to the side of the house. There, Eva cautioned him with a finger to her lips. Then she rose on tiptoe to peek into the parlor of the house where she had last spotted Vinko. Her heart pounded in her chest, out of fear of discovery but also out of dread that Vinko might have succumbed to his injuries and she would see him dead on the floor.

Tam craned his neck, trying to make himself tall enough to see in, but he was still too short to get a good view. Joanna straggled behind them, somewhere on the hill below the rear gate.

"What do you see?" Tam whispered. "Do you see Vinko?"

"No." Eva peered around the parlor and strained to see across the main hall to the sitting room beyond. Shadows slanted across the floor, making it difficult to focus on details.

"He's not where he was," Eva added. She sank back against the sandstone blocks of the house and met Tam's worried eyes. Then she gestured for him to follow her. They eased behind the shrubbery and raced back to the garden to the stone bench. Eva collapsed on it, glad to sit down. Tam plopped down beside her.

"Now what?"

Tam shrugged. "I could sneak in."

"No, it's too dangerous."

"I'm fast."

"They have guns, Tam. They could shoot you again. So no."

He nodded and shoved his shaggy bangs out of his eyes. "Maybe they took Vinko down to the prison."

Eva glanced at the walled compound on the edge of Port Pennwood.

"That would make sense. They could lock him up there. They wouldn't need a guard to keep an eye on him." She paused, perplexed. "I still don't know why Moray didn't just kill him."

"Yeah." Tam frowned.

"Maybe he wants to use Vinko to get to Joanna."

"Yeah." Tam stood up. "Think we should go down to the prison?"

"Probably. But we need to wait for Joanna. Tell her what we are going to do."

A few minutes later, the back gate creaked open. Eva

turned, wanting to call out to her sister or wave, but she didn't dare take the chance of being detected.

Joanna slipped into the garden and stepped behind the nearest bush. Eva could hear her panting from the effort of climbing the steep path up the hill.

"Joanna," Eva whispered.

Joanna turned in her direction. "Eva, I just saw Gabriel."

"Where?"

"Leaving the front of the house. He and a guard put someone in a litter. It looked like Vinko."

"So they *are* taking him to the prison," Tam put in.

"Not necessarily." Eva leaned down to look through the break in the wall. Two guards carried the litter down the lane with Gabriel following on foot.

"Gabriel wouldn't agree to imprisoning Vinko." Joanna moved closer to peer through the hole as well. But she stopped to clutch a limb of a bush and then she bent over, heaving.

Eva stepped to her side. "Jo, are you sick?"

Joanna waved her off. "I'll be fine."

"You look awful."

"I said I'll be fine." Joanna stood up and wiped her mouth with the back of a hand. She cracked a weak, unconvincing smile. "See? I'm fine."

Eva had never seen her sister look so wan. Even her lips had lost all color. She could tell that Joanna didn't have the strength to go much farther.

"What about Moray, Jo? Did you see him?"

"No."

"Then he could still be in the house."

Joanna collapsed on the bench and closed her eyes. "I don't have the strength to deal with Moray right now."

"Do you think you could walk back down the hill?"

"In a little while."

"We can watch from here. See where Gabriel and that litter go."

"All right."

Eva studied her sister, worried about the state of her health. She squeezed Joanna's shoulder. "We'll stay here and watch. You can rest. Once it gets dark and no one can see us, we'll run back down the hill."

"But once it's dark, vampires will be able to attack us."

"Fine. Let them come."

"Yeah." Tam held up a pod. "Let them come. They'll be sorry."

32

AT DUSK, Eva ushered Joanna into the home of her former servant, Hannah Alexander. With any hope, Hannah had left behind sheets and blankets and her other household goods.

"Come on, Joanna," Eva said, shouldering the door open. "Sit down. I'll make a fire. Tam?"

The boy trotted to her side.

"You go to Citizen Browne's house. It's that white one down there." Eva pointed at the tall narrow terrace house that had once been part of the thriving Port Pennwood community centuries ago. "Bring back some soup."

"All right."

"And tell Gabriel to bring Vinko here. We need to stick together. He's probably there."

Tam nodded and turned on his heel. Eva swept into the house and turned on the gas lamps. Thank goodness the service still worked.

"There's no coal," Joanna commented, dropping into a chair.

"I'll find some." Eva picked up the empty coalscuttle.

As a safety precaution before building a fire, she pulled the pods from her pockets and deposited them in the parlor, hall and kitchen. Then she filled the metal scuttle with coal from the cellar and carried it to the parlor.

Joanna was already asleep in the chair. Poor thing. Eva found matches on the mantel and dropped to a knee to build a fire.

After she was sure she had a healthy blaze going, she hurried up the stairs to check on the bedrooms. She found three tiny chambers. Two of the beds were done up with sheets and coverlets. She found more sheets in a trunk and made the third bed. Vinko could recover in one chamber, she and Joanna could bunk together, and Gabriel could take the third. Tam could sleep on a pallet she'd found in the loft. She wasn't sure where Ruby Valentine would end up. Perhaps she could stay with Citizen Browne.

Just as she finished making the bed, she heard the door open and Tam's bright voice call her name. Eva hurried to the top of the stairs.

"Tam, bring him up here," she called back. Behind the boy, Gabriel stepped across the threshold with Vinko in his arms.

Vinko's head lolled back. He was either unconscious or deep in pain. His eyes were closed and his face was covered with red welts. His left hand looked misshapen and swollen. Streaks of blood slashed across his shirt and sleeves.

What had Moray done to him? Eva's throat constricted with worry. To see Vinko's sunny character dimmed like this pulled the noose around her neck, tighter than ever.

"This way, Gabriel," she called.

Gabriel shut the door with his foot and carried Vinko to the stairs. She watched, amazed that the slight doctor could manage a man as large as Vinko by himself. He must be stronger than he looked. Even more amazing was the ease with which Gabriel carried his patient up the stairs.

"In there."

Gabriel strode into the bedroom while Eva skittered in front of him to turn down the bed. She hovered at Gabriel's elbow, struggling to get a look at Vinko's face.

"How is he?" she asked.

"He will live." Gently Gabriel deposited Vinko onto the mattress. Eva reached for Vinko's boots to straighten out his legs. Then she pulled off his footwear to make him more comfortable. Vinko moaned.

"He's been badly beaten," Gabriel said, looking down at him. "Like your sister was."

"Moray. That monster." She clenched her jaw and surveyed Vinko. His breath was shallow and quick, as if he fought against pain. Red welts marked his handsome face and neck. His left hand was swollen and purple. Never once did he open his eyes.

"You're safe now, Vinko," Eva whispered, wanting to touch him but afraid she would hurt him again.

"I've got to splint that hand," Gabriel said. "He's got what is called a Boxer's fracture. Can you get cloths for a bandage? And something for a splint? A dish towel. Or some newspaper?"

"I'll look in the kitchen."

"Is there a toilet on this floor?"

"Yes, down the hall."

"Good." Gabriel straightened. "I'll have to clean that hand. It appears he might have a fight bite."

"What's that?"

"A scratch caused by the other person's tooth. In the case of a vampire tooth, it could be a serious problem."

"Oh, no."

"Tam brought my satchel. Can you fetch it as well? I

have an ointment that may keep the wound from becoming infected."

Eva headed for the door.

"And Eva?"

"Yes?"

"Where is Joanna?"

"Resting by the fire."

"Have her come upstairs. We can't be too careful, now that the sun has gone down. Tam as well. We have to stick together."

Eva nodded and headed down the stairs to do Gabriel's bidding. Her spirits lifted a bit, now that Vinko was safely in Gabriel's care. She flew down the stairs, happy to have something to do to help.

But, as she gathered supplies and located the doctor's bag, a thought struck her. Why had Moray allowed Gabriel to take Vinko out of the manor house? What trick was Moray playing now? She wondered if Gabriel had any idea how nasty Neal Moray was. They had to be on their guard. Her small patch of blue sky clouded and a shudder passed through her. Tonight could be the calm of the storm. Tomorrow might be as bad as the night of the fire. Moray could be planning a second, even viler attack.

Eva roused Joanna and urged her to follow her. Then she called out to Tam to bring the food upstairs. She would build a second fire in Vinko's room to keep him warm, and then they would eat their first meal in nearly two days. Her stomach growled.

An hour later, Eva finally sat down with a bowl of ham and bean soup. It lacked salt, but it warmed and sustained her. Gabriel declined the food, claiming that he felt ill from inhaling so much ash earlier that day. He did accept a glass of wine from a bottle Tam had found in the basement of the inn.

"So you didn't find any survivors," Joanna asked, her eyes tired.

"No. The fire was intense. I think the tunnel in the cellar caused a draft that created an inferno."

"That was the tunnel Tam and I used to escape."

"And your mom, Tam?" Eva asked softly, watching his expression.

"Gone. Completely."

"Ah, Tam."

"It's okay. I wouldn't have wanted her to be buried here anyway."

"You lost your mother?" Gabriel asked.

Tam nodded.

"I'm sorry, lad."

He shrugged, unwilling or unable to say more. Eva handed a plate to him. "More bread, Tam? Have some more."

He swallowed and took a second piece.

"A vampire killed her," Eva commented, glancing at Gabriel. "Not the fire."

"Ah."

"And that brings me to the subject of Neal Moray." Eva set down the plate.

"What subject?"

"Why did he let you take Vinko away?"

She surveyed the doctor carefully and saw a shadow pass through his eyes.

"I am his superior. He had to do as I say."

"I thought you were a doctor."

"I am. But I hold an important governmental position. Like a commissioner."

"So Moray just handed Vinko over to you." Eva narrowed her eyes. "That doesn't sound like him."

"He wants to keep what's happened here quiet."

Gabriel sipped his wine. "I used that as my bargaining chip."

"Lucky for Vinko," Joanna put in.

"In fact he agreed to let us all leave on the next train."

"Let us?" Joanna retorted. "*Let* us?"

Gabriel nodded. "He could make life very uncomfortable, as you well know, Joanna. I would lie low and get on the train, and count my lucky stars to get out of here alive."

"And go back to Londo?" Joanna shook her head. "I say we stay here and kill that bastard."

Gabriel touched her shoulder. "That will be no easy task, Joanna."

"I realize that."

"Perhaps even impossible," Gabriel continued.

"We have to try. We have to stand and fight." Joanna's troubled glance met Eva's. "Are you with me, Eva?"

"Yes. You know I am."

"Gabriel?"

Gabriel sighed and looked down. "I do not recommend this path, Joanna."

"As long as Moray lives, I will never be able to stay in Londo. You know that, don't you, Gabriel."

He nodded, his expression grim. "But to kill a vampire. That's serious business."

"We have the pods."

"Yes. Perhaps that will give us an advantage." He looked up. "Let us sleep on this idea and decide in the morning. All of us are tired, far beyond exhaustion."

"Yes," Eva said. "And I have a feeling there's something going on that you don't suspect, Gabriel. I don't trust Moray."

"None of us do, Eva." Gabriel held her gaze. "That is why we must be very careful. Especially tonight."

THE SOUND of murmuring female voices brought Vinko back to his senses. He opened his eyes, surprised to discover he was lying in a bed and not on the floor of the manor house. Darkness had fallen, and a single candle illuminated the room enough to discern basic shapes. He moved only his eyeballs, as he had done since the beating, to locate the source of the voices. Eva and Joanna Wilder stood across the room, talking quietly. Tam dozed in a chair by the fire, while a taller, darker figure came into the room, carrying a glass of water. A red line glowed around the man.

It was the vampire from the parlor.

Vinko tried to get up, but his beaten body wouldn't obey. Desperate and struggling to hide his alarm, he watched the vampire approach.

"Ah, you are awake," the vampire said.

"Stay away."

"Do not be afraid. I'm a doctor."

Vinko glanced at Eva and Joanna, standing aside and listening to the conversation, seemingly unconcerned about the creature in their midst. He had to tell them. He had to warn them.

"Eva," Vinko croaked. But a single word of warning was all he could manage. He sank back in the bed and had to close his eyes.

He heard the rustle of clothing. A warm hand clasped his.

"Vinko, don't exert yourself."

He could tell by the voice and the fragrance wafting off the clothing that it was Eva who had come to stand beside him. She seemed calm. The touch of her hand alleviated his panic, enough to think more clearly. Maybe she didn't know the dark figure was a vampire. Maybe he should play along until he could speak to her in private.

"Vinko, let Dr. Stone help you. He is a friend."

"Friend?" Vinko gasped without opening his eyes. His lips and tongue were swollen. His ribcage ached with every breath required to force out words. He couldn't keep talking. The pain it caused would make him faint.

All he could manage was to squeeze Eva's hand.

She brushed the hair off his forehead. "It's all right, Vinko. Don't worry."

Don't worry? There was a vampire in their midst. He had to think of a way to tell her the truth about the doctor without raising the man's suspicions.

"Moray's brother," he murmured.

"No," she brushed back his hair again. "No relation at all."

He had to warn her, but how? Pain and exhaustion prevented him from thinking straight, much less forming coherent sentences in a language he barely understood. But Eva was smart. She had the ability to comprehend things quickly, at least with him. In the past, they had communicated with only a glance, a touch. He had to have faith that she would understand him on the most basic level now.

"*Brethren.*" He squeezed her hand as hard as he could.

He felt her pause and go stiff, as the meaning of that single word sank in.

"No. He's a friend of Joanna's," Eva said. "A good friend."

A vampire was no one's friend. Or good. Vinko swallowed back his disgust and struggled to think of a way to convince Eva that a monster stood at her side. Why didn't she understand the gravity of the situation? Why was she disregarding his warning?

"Drink this," the vampire said, lifting his head and placing the glass on his lower lip. "It will ease the pain."

Vinko kept his lips closed. Why would a vampire help him? It didn't make sense. Why were Eva and Joanna allowing a vampire to do anything? The medicine the man tipped to his lips could be a drug that would render him unconscious or even kill him. But then why had the vampire gone to the trouble of bringing him back to the village, splinting his hand, and seeing to his cracked ribs?

Joanna joined the other two figures at the bed. "Vinko, do what Gabriel says. He's trying to help you."

Why, though? Vinko didn't understand. A vampire would never help a human being. Something was wrong with this scenario. He must be delirious. He must be dreaming.

"Please, Vinko," Eva put in, her voice tight with concern. "Drink the medicine. Please."

Eva had understood what he meant with the word "brethren." He was sure of it. And yet she stood by, not worried. Maybe she had a plan. Maybe she knew it was best to wait until he had more control of his faculties. He would have to trust her judgment, no matter how much he wanted to jump out of the bed and call out the vampire.

Besides, calling out the vampire now would destroy him. He had no packets on him. And he was no fool. In his condition, one more blow from a vampire, and he would be dead. He had to bide his time. He had to wait until Eva and he were alone to find out why she trusted this creature. He had to go along with whatever treatment the vampire administered and place his life in Eva's hands.

He drank the medicine. In moments, he felt darkness descend. But it was a sweet, painless darkness.

Like the kiss of a vampire.

33

"I will stay with Vinko and take first watch," Gabriel said. "You two get some rest."

Eva regarded Gabriel for the hundredth time. She was certain she had understood Vinko's warning that Gabriel Stone was a vampire. Ever since Vinko had uttered the word "brethren", she had searched Gabriel for telltale signs of a vampire. But she had found none.

She didn't really know what to look for. As she had learned at Port Pennwood, vampires existed. But they were not like the ones described in scary stories. They walked and talked like human beings and could mingle among the living, unnoticed. But Gabriel? It didn't seem possible that he was a vampire. Maybe she had misunderstood what Vinko had tried to tell to her.

She didn't want to suspect Gabriel of deceiving them all this time. He had done so much for them and for the people of Londo. But then again, she trusted Vinko's special vision. She trusted him completely, in fact. If he thought Gabriel Stone was a vampire, there must be a good reason for such a belief.

"Come on, Eva." Joanna headed for the door.

With her thoughts reeling, Eva took one last look at Vinko lying in the bed, flat on his back, his firm lips slightly open. His chest rose and fell in a deep, peaceful rhythm, thanks to the medicine. Surely, even if Gabriel were a vampire, he would not hurt Vinko while he slept. Gabriel had rescued him, after all.

Eva didn't want to leave Vinko's side, but she knew she needed to rest. For now, she would leave him in Gabriel's capable hands.

Eva tucked Tam into his pallet by the fire and then trudged down the hall after her sister. She followed Joanna into the master bedroom of Hannah's abandoned home and closed the door behind her.

Joanna turned to confront her. "What is troubling you, Eva? Your face is so long, I'm surprised you aren't tripping over your own chin."

Eva paused. She considered herself a master of the bland expression. She had thought she could hide all thought and emotion from the rest of the world—but maybe not from her sister. If Joanna could tell she was upset, she would badger her until she got to the root of the problem. But Eva didn't know how to broach the subject of Gabriel without alienating her sister.

"Just worried," she replied, reaching for the buttons of her blouse. "About Vinko."

"He'll be all right. He's a strong, healthy man."

Eva nodded and undressed, her mind racing, all the while avoiding the regard of her older sister.

They climbed into Hannah's small bed, and Joanna reached over to blow out the single candle.

"It's been years since we slept in the same bed," Joanna murmured.

"Since I was eight," Eva replied. "When Mother and Father died. Or were killed."

"Yes." Joanna's voice faded as they both thought of their parents' death in a new way.

Joanna fell silent beside her. Words burned in Eva's throat, but she didn't know how to start the conversation about Gabriel—the man her sister loved. Then again, she couldn't shake the notion that Joanna was hiding something.

Eva had always been the one to conceal things. Not Joanna. This turnaround between them was uncomfortable. Unbearable. Why would Joanna keep something from her? Didn't she think Eva was trustworthy enough to keep her secrets?

Eva flushed in the darkness, knowing the answer without hearing it said out loud. She was glad for the night. Darkness hid her shame at the thought of the person she once had been.

Minutes ticked by. Eva stared at the ceiling, tormented, while Joanna breathed softly beside her. Maybe Joanna would fall asleep, and Eva could wait until morning to confront her.

But then Joanna stirred. She rotated her head to peer at the side of Eva's face. "What in the world is troubling you?"

Eva swallowed. There was no stalling now. If they didn't talk, neither of them would get any rest. She decided to start with indirect questions. Maybe she could give Joanna enough clues to save Eva from coming right out and accusing Gabriel of being a vampire.

Eva looked at the ceiling. "What do you actually know of Gabriel?"

"Gabriel? For goodness sake, what do you mean?"

"Does he have family? Where does he live?"

"He lives above his clinic."

"Why don't we ever see him at Distribution?"

"He's a commissioner of sorts. Commissioners don't go to Distribution. You know that. You never saw Charles at Distribution, did you?"

"I wouldn't have noticed Charles. I would have noticed Gabriel."

"Why do you want to know about Gabriel? What are you getting at?"

"Don't take this wrong, Joann, but I don't think he's who he pretends to be."

"Pretends?" Joanna sat up. "Gabriel doesn't pretend anything."

"And I know he has been good to us, but…"

"But what?" Joanna's voice sliced through the darkness.

Eva faltered. She didn't want to disrespect her sister's choice of men, but if Joanna didn't know the truth about Gabriel, and Eva failed to tell her about him, Joanna would hate her for it. Either way, Joanna would hate her. Maybe it was best to keep silent.

Eva pressed her lips together and covered her eyes with the small of her elbow. The bed shivered as Joanna jerked around to stare down at her.

"Eva, what are you going on about?"

"I don't want to talk about it."

"I do."

"I don't."

Joanna reached out and touched her elbow. Eva jerked her arm away and flopped onto her side, facing the wall.

"Eva!" Joanna sputtered. Then she sighed heavily and sat back. "I'm not going to sleep until you tell me what is going on with you."

With her back turned, Eva found it easier to communicate. "It's just that…"

"What?"

"I got the feeling earlier today that you are hiding something from me."

"What would I ever hide from you?"

"I don't know. It's a feeling I got."

"When?"

"When you were talking about Gabriel and Neal Moray knowing each other."

"Oh."

"Why would Gabriel have a history with Neal Moray?"

"Gabriel knows everyone in Londo."

"But why? How?"

She could sense Joanna's shrug. "He just does. From being a doctor, I guess."

"I don't know, Joanna."

"So you distrust Gabriel. Is that what you're saying?"

"I don't think he's who he says he is."

"Is anyone?"

"Oh, come on, Jo, you know what I'm saying."

After a moment, Joanna sighed. "Are you jealous? I mean, what has brought this on? I thought you liked Gabriel."

"I do. He has been good to both of us."

"Then why question his character?"

"Because of Vinko."

"Vinko?"

"Vinko has a special gift. He can see red lines around vampires."

"He can?"

"His family shares his ability. They are vampire hunters."

"I see."

Eva flushed, struck by Joanna's condescending tone. But she had to press on.

"I think he can see a line around Gabriel."

Joanna let out a puff of disbelief. "Impossible."

"No, it isn't. I've seen him detect vampires." Eva turned back to face Joanna, eager to continue, now that the true subject of her torment had been broached. "He can see a line around them, especially at night."

"And how did he tell you this? The man can barely speak."

"Didn't you hear him, though? He told Gabriel to stay away."

"So, that doesn't mean Gabriel is a vampire."

"He squeezed my hand. He said Gabriel was a brother of Moray."

"Well, he's wrong about that. Gabriel and Moray have no substantial connection. None at all."

"He meant a brother *vampire*."

Joanna fell silent. Eva struggled to sit up. She pulled the blankets to her chest.

"I know you love him, Jo. That's why I didn't want to say anything."

"You think Gabriel is a vampire."

"Yes."

Joanna looked down at the quilt and fell oddly quiet.

"Joanna, don't lie to me. I can sense that you are lying to me about him. About something."

"Listen to you." Joanna shot her a hard glance. "After all the lies you told me when you wanted to be with a boy."

"I know, but—"

"How do you think I liked it?" Joanna glared at her again. "Being lied to my face all those years?"

"I know. I'm sorry, Joanna. It's just that…"

"No more talk." Joanna jumped out of bed. "I've heard enough."

"But what if Gabriel is a vampire? What if he doesn't have our best interests at heart? Yours?"

"I'll forget you said that."

Joanna grabbed a shawl and stormed out of the bedchamber.

Eva watched her go, her heart breaking and her thoughts swirling. She had thought the time they had spent apart and all they had been through had strengthened their bond. But she had been wrong. Nothing had changed between them. There would always be this friction. This schism. She didn't know if it was because of men, or if it was just the way they would always be with each other.

Eva slid back down in the bed and plopped her head on the pillow. She might have made Joanna angry. But that was all right. Joanna would go off and think. She always did. She would consider what they had just argued about.

At least Joanna had been warned. No matter how besotted she might be with her vampire doctor, she would be on her guard now.

JOANNA HURRIED down the chilly hall to the smaller bedroom where Vinko lay. Gabriel stood near the window, arms crossed, looking out at the night. For a moment, Joanna paused in the doorway to look at him.

His black jacket and breeches were rumpled from days of riding and his boots were dull with ash. Though his wide shoulders spoke of strength she knew she could count on, they were tipped to one side at a careworn angle, as if Gabriel carried a great weight on his shoulders. His head angled to the side as well, as if his thoughts were far from Port Pennwood. She wondered what a 600-year-old man thought about. He must have so many memories, both of joy and regret.

"Gabriel?" she called softly, not wishing to disturb the Croatian or Tam.

He turned, and his face transformed from dark absorption to awareness.

Joanna crooked her finger to indicate that he should follow her. She led him down the hall, far from the room where Eva slept.

"Can we talk?" she asked.

"Of course."

"In private?"

"Yes." He nodded at the stairs. "Shall we go down to the parlor? I will get the fire going again. We can have a cup of tea. You look cold."

"I am. I should have put on my boots."

He smiled at her and allowed her to scurry down the stairs in front of him.

Joanna put on the kettle while Gabriel started a fire with more of Hannah's coal. The old woman had no need of it. She might never return to Port Pennwood. Whenever a new commissioner arrived, she could be reinstated in her job, but there were no guarantees in Londo.

When Joanna carried the tray of tea into the parlor, she saw that Gabriel had dragged the settee close to the hearth and placed the ottoman from the wingback chair in front of it.

"Sit," he said, reaching for the tray. "Put your feet up. Get warm."

She obeyed without protest. She was exhausted from her stressful days at Port Pennwood, and all the months she had spent in the north, looking over her shoulder, worrying that today would be the day the Overseers caught up with her. And two weeks ago they had.

Gabriel handed her a cup of tea on a saucer.

"Thanks."

He remained standing in front of the fire, gazing down at her.

"We have never done this," he said, with a sad smile.

"Done what?"

"Sat together at a fire, drinking tea like an old married couple. It is nice."

"It is." Joanna nodded and raised the cup to her lips.

"Are you getting warm?"

"Yes." She chafed her feet together before the dancing fire. Then she sighed.

His brows came together in concern. "What is wrong, Joanna?"

"You have to let me tell Eva the truth." She glanced up at Gabriel, hoping he would see the determination in her eyes. "I know I promised not to tell her about you and the others, but she knows I am lying about something."

Gabriel gazed at the flames and said nothing.

"I have never lied to my sister, Gabriel. It goes against everything I believe in."

"You agreed to keep my secret."

"But she knows about the other Overseers. What difference will it make if she knows about you?"

"It will make a big difference." He swept the air with his arm. "Don't you see?"

"In what way?"

"I am a doctor. Being a doctor is the reason I am on this planet. Take that away, and you strip me of everything."

"Why would telling Eva the truth affect your work?"

"Think about it, Joanna. What human would come to my clinic if they suspected that I was a vampire?" Gabriel turned back to glare at the fire, his tea forgotten.

"You're implying that Eva would tell others about you."

"I can only assume she would." He shot a cold glance at her. "That's the way it would start. One little confidence."

"She's changed."

"Really?" Gabriel shook his head. "The Eva I know is self-involved and ambitious. Willing to walk over others."

"I think she's changed."

"Willing to walk over you, Joanna, to get what she wants. Do not be fooled."

"She's not like that anymore."

"I am glad you think of her in that way. But all I know of Eva is from my time with her in Londo. And I am sorry to say I cannot recommend her character."

Joanna jumped to her feet. "She's my *sister*, Gabriel."

"Blood is not strong enough to predicate such an important decision." He stared down at her, his color high. "Joanna, if I allow you to tell Eva about me, I break a vow."

"To whom?"

"To my brother."

"To *your* blood." Joanna glared at him. "What you are saying is that your blood ties are more important than mine."

"Careful, Joanna. Consider what side you are on. Consider well."

"There's nothing to consider. Eva is my sister!"

"You and she are so dissimilar that I venture to guess you are unrelated. Your natures, your looks, your smell—"

"What is *that* supposed to mean?" She turned on him, incensed. "That one of us is a bastard?"

Gabriel continued to stare down at her, silent and

unmoving and so sure of himself that she wanted to strike him.

"You're the bastard!" She flung the remains of her tea in his face and dashed away from the settee.

He caught her by the wrist.

"Let me go!" she cried.

"Listen, Joanna. Listen well." He wiped the drops of tea from his face. "You and Eva are no longer sisters. Regardless of genetics."

"You're wrong! We will always be sisters." She pulled at his iron grasp, desperate to get away from him and run far away from this dark little town.

"Since your healing a year ago, you no longer have both feet in the human world. You know that. Look at me."

Joanna clenched her jaw and stared at his chest, hating every word of truth that he uttered.

"Look at me, Joanna."

Her glare burned up his tea-splattered cravat and over his face until she stared into his smoldering eyes.

"I know it is difficult, but you must not cling to your old ways of thinking about Eva."

"Really? Because you say so?" she ground between her teeth. "What am I? A child you must instruct?" She yanked at his hand, but he held her fast. Then he dipped forward and grabbed her other wrist to keep her trapped in front of him.

"I do not know yet what you are, Joanna. Only that you are not the young lady I met a year ago. And you never will be."

"Thanks to you!"

"We are blood now." His eyes glinted down at her. "You and I. I am your family."

"No, you're not. I'm not part of any family!" Blurting

out the truth made the words sink in. A sob caught in her chest.

"Neither am I." He clenched her wrists even tighter, forcing her to look up at him again. "I am no more a vampire in my heart than you are. I don't belong at the Central Compound, and I don't belong with the people of Londo. But I goddamn well belong with you."

Shocked, she stopped struggling to stare into his eyes. He'd never spoken such vehement words before.

34

Gabriel stared down at her, waiting for a response. He had never been so certain of how he felt about a woman or so outspoken in regard to his feelings. He had expected a heartfelt response to his confession. But Joanna remained silent, standing there in her plain, worn shift, overcome by his words in a way that worried him. He could see in her eyes that she fought to fit her old life into the box with her new one. The two worlds simply could not coexist. But she didn't seem to be able to see that. Perhaps she never would.

"I see," he said, crestfallen.

"Gabriel, it's not that I—"

"Say no more."

Her silence told him everything. Sighing, he released her and turned his back, struggling to control his frustration and disappointment. Joanna didn't feel the same as he did. It was obvious now. And she didn't seem capable of accepting the truth or being the slightest bit logical.

But maybe there was hope. He had to believe there was hope.

Her behavior reminded him of the day he had shared

his secret with her. She had run away, aghast that she had just kissed a vampire. But she hadn't run far. She had remained in the doorway, trusting him enough to hear him out.

That memory gave him the only shred of hope he had at the moment. He was certain that if Joanna were given enough time and not pressed too hard, she would consider his view and try to come up with a compromise. It had worked before. He had to believe it would work again.

Even if she had just thrown tea in his face.

He heard her heave a big sigh. At least she hadn't walked off in a huff. She was still standing behind him, staring a hole in his coat.

"Gabriel, you are asking me to make a choice."

"You have to."

"Between my sister and you. That's what you're asking."

Gabriel shook his head. She still wasn't getting the point. "That is not what I said. I said you had to choose a side."

"I disagree, Gabriel."

He heard the rustle of her slip as she took a step toward him. Her scent wafted up, distracting him as much as her bare arms and feet. He could hear the blood surging through her chest and neck, hypnotizing him. He had to struggle to retain his human faculties.

"It's true," Joanna said softly behind him. "We are different from the rest. And we recognize that in each other. You aren't quite a vampire and I'm not quite a human. But we can't live in a bubble. I just tried doing that, living so far from everything I know and everyone I care about. And it is not something I ever want to repeat."

She placed a palm on his shoulder blade. Her touch sent a bolt of hunger through him, but he remained standing there, like a rock, his ears ringing as he listened to every word.

"We can't live in a bubble, Gabriel. Somehow we have to find a way to stitch together our befores and afters. And make something new."

The word "new" sent a whoosh of her breath fanning over the back of his neck, raising the hairs there. Her circulation system surged behind him, pulsing ever faster, giving cadence to his own heart. He would do anything to keep this woman safe, keep her happy and keep her in his world. Even if it meant stepping back to give her time and not crush her in his arms as he longed to do.

"Are you saying that you will accept a life with me?" he finally asked. The question dangled in the air for an eternity.

She sighed. Her hand swept down his back and away. "Yes. Somehow."

He turned part way around and glanced back at her. "And that you will keep my secret?"

"As far as I can. But I am not turning my back on my sister. Or telling her any more lies."

He slowly pivoted to look down at her. "You will not keep your vow to me, Joanna?"

"It's time to revisit it. That's what I'm trying to say." Joanna raised her grave glance to meet his. "She knows the truth anyway."

"And the truth about you?"

She flushed.

"Ah, that you cannot tell, can you?"

"I will someday. When I know who and what I am."

"And when do you think that will be?"

"I don't know. Do you?"

"No. We both travel new territory when it comes to your physical being." He grasped her shoulders in his hands to draw her closer and saw her wince. Surely, she wasn't so angry with him now. Surely.

"What is it, Joanna?"

"I don't know." She shrugged and pulled back. "It's my back."

"What about it?"

"Since the walk up the cliff."

"Let me look. Turn around." He urged her to rotate until the light of the fire danced over the back of her neck.

"Unbutton your shift," he instructed, modulating his voice in his best clinical tone, while the male part of him wanted to growl out the words at the prospect of seeing her undress. He felt his canine teeth transforming, turning his mouth to a weapon of destruction as well as seduction. He was so hungry and her flesh was so fragile, so fresh and so white. He could see the boundary of creamy, luscious skin where the sun hadn't ruined her. The white line glowed, beaconing him. He could see her warm, hypnotizing blood surging up her chest and down her slender arms. Ah, to taste her again...

But this was Joanna. He had to stop. He had to back off.

Gabriel struggled to control his animal hunger as he watched her unfasten the buttons of her slip. Then, ah—so innocently—she drew the feather light fabric from her shoulders until it slipped down to pool around her elbows. She grasped the linen between her breasts, just enough to cover her nipples.

"What is it?" she asked.

If she only knew. He was awash in an identity crisis, not knowing what part of him would gain the upper hand: vampire, human male or physician. To distract his darker self, he inspected the pink expanse of her upper shoulders and the back of her neck as a doctor and not a beast.

"It appears to be sunburn."

"Oh. I've never had sunburn before. I've never even seen it."

"It is not serious. It will be better tomorrow. Especially if I do this."

Gabriel bent down and lightly kissed the nape of her neck. He felt her tremble. He kissed her again. He couldn't help himself. He had to make contact with her flawless skin. His male body reacted immediately in a flood of heat. He stepped closer, aching to press her warm curves against him.

"Is that the usual treatment for sunburn?" she murmured.

"Yours is a special case."

She didn't step away. He could tell by her strident breathing that his kiss had affected her as much as it had affected him. She clutched the plackets of her slip at her chest, leaving the milky white mounds of her breasts exposed to view. He sucked in a breath at the sight of her, and slipped his hands around her torso to cup her small breasts in his palms.

"Ah, God," he murmured into her hair. He closed his eyes as a shaft of male hunger split away the vampire part of him—the part that lusted for blood instead of flesh. The human part of him had always been stronger, and raw male desire engulfed him now with unbearable need.

He felt her relax into him. Her head fell back to rest on his breast, just below his chin. He swept his hands down her torso and back up to her wrists, urging her to release her hold on her clothing. She let her hands fall, allowing him full access to her ivory skin.

"Ah," he murmured,

Joanna reached behind her to caress the side of his face. "I'm sorry about the tea, Gabriel."

"I have forgotten all about it."

He kissed the small of her shoulder and drew her even closer. "Am I hurting you? Your sunburn?"

"Sunburn? What sunburn?" Her voice was hoarse with desire.

He could hear a soft smile of surrender mingling with the hoarseness in her words, and his heart burst with joy. He reached down and caught her behind the knees to sweep her off her feet.

"Gabriel," she gasped.

"Do not speak," he whispered in her ear. "Until morning."

Then, with the sound of his own blood thundering in his ears and anticipation bursting in his chest, he carried her to the stairs.

Close to dawn, Joanna eased away from the hand draped over the small of her waist. At the movement, Gabriel sighed but did not wake up. He must be exhausted from his long journey and their hours of lovemaking.

She glanced at his boyish face, made even more boyish by the act of sleeping. His brows relaxed in an upward slope, giving him a quizzical expression, as if he were about to ask a question. That was Gabriel. Always inquiring after a person's well being. May I offer you a drink? Are you ill? What is troubling you? Her heart warmed as she gazed at him. She had never met a more caring man.

And now she knew the other side of him—his passionate, driving, but still—oh, so gentle—side. She had experienced the ecstasy and wonder of physically and mentally joining with his gentle spirit. She had never felt more connected, cherished or exalted in her life.

Love for Gabriel welled up in her. She knew she had just made love to a creature that was more shadow than man, and now that shadow dozed in his bed, sated and exhausted. She had given her body to him in defiance of all rules and good sense. But she was not afraid. And she was not sorry.

Joanna sat up. She felt as tired as Gabriel looked, but she hadn't slept a wink. She had to get up. She had to do something.

She slipped out of bed and snatched her slip and panties from the chair near the door, surprised by the way her legs and arms trembled with the effort. She stood still for a moment until she felt some strength flood back into her. She wanted nothing more than to sleep next to Gabriel until he woke up, and then to share more lingering kisses with him. But she had lain in bed for hours, her eyes wide open and her head buzzing with steps she should take here in Port Pennwood.

She would not be able to sleep until she took care of Neal Moray.

She tiptoed to the master bedroom and dressed, careful not to wake Eva, and then slipped down the stairs. In the parlor, she pulled back the curtain to look outside.

Once again, a cloudless lilac-colored dawn glowed above the rooftops of Port Pennwood, promising a third sunny day. All vampires would have to return to their lairs or chance immolation. Wherever Neal Moray was at this hour, he would be at his weakest.

She might be at her weakest, too, but she had to persevere.

Joanna filled the pocket in her skirt with pods she'd seen Eva hide in the parlor. Then, careful not to make a sound, she closed the door behind her and hurried up the street, scanning the village and the compound to the north as she walked. Light glowed from the window of the office at the processing plant. She hadn't noticed the lighted window before. Someone must be in Charles Paar's office. She would bet that someone was Moray.

SOMEONE PUSHED EVA'S SHOULDER, startling her awake. Alarmed and bleary, she rose on one elbow to see who had jostled her so roughly. She blinked her brain into consciousness. Tousled brown hair and a turned up nose came into focus.

"Hurry up," Tam whispered. "Get dressed."

"What?"

"Your sister just left."

"What are you talking about?"

"I've been watching the street. She just left the house."

Eva shot a worried glance at the place beside her in the bed where Joanna should be sleeping. The coverlet and pillow remained just as Joanna had left them hours before. It was obvious that she had not spent the night in the room. That meant she had slept somewhere else in the house or spent the night with Gabriel.

Eva couldn't believe Joanna would take such a risk. Even more, she couldn't believe her sister would take off without telling her. Then words of the previous night echoed in her ears, reminding her of how she had accused Gabriel of being a vampire. Maybe Joanna would never speak to her again.

Full of panic, Eva threw off the coverlet and jumped to her feet. The cold floorboards helped clear more fog from her brain. She glanced around for her discarded skirt and blouse. The knife she'd taken from the hut glinted next to her delicate boots, looking oddly out of place in a bedchamber. The entire scenario seemed like a dream.

Was she dreaming?

Still in a daze, she looked around and ran a hand over her tangled hair.

"Come on! Get dressed," Tam urged. "I'll meet you downstairs."

It was no dream. In fact, it was all too real.

JOANNA MADE sure no one was looking out the window of the commissioner's office and then slipped through the gate of the processing plant. No one seemed to be on guard duty. If Vinko's pods had killed enough vampires, Moray might be shorthanded. That would be in her favor. She dashed to the right, hoping no one would notice her running along the base of the high wall. Then she ducked at the waist, skittered across the yard to the commissioner's office and crouched below the lighted window. She knelt on one knee, listening intently and cupping a pod in one hand. She could hear someone pacing the floor and surmised that Moray was in the room beyond the window.

She would have to take him by surprise by bursting through the door, throwing the pod, and hoping for the best. Even if the person in the office were someone other than Moray, she would still kill a vampire and not waste a pod. If the person were human, the worst she would do would be to blind him for a few days.

She crawled to the door and reached for the knob, just as someone grabbed her from behind and dragged her off her feet. Snarling, she flailed her arms and legs, using her vampire strength to almost break out of the man's grip.

But then his arms locked around her torso, pinning her against him. If she had been able to use her arms and legs, she would have been able to break free. But he'd grabbed her from the back.

"Not so fast, citizen." He squeezed her so hard she couldn't take a breath.

Joanna threw the pod at the man's feet and shut her eyes against the flare of light. Nothing happened. The man behind her didn't dissolve. His stranglehold on her didn't let up. He was not a vampire. He must be a member of the elite corps of the Overseers, the Enforcers.

"Thanks for the light show," he scoffed. Then she felt his body shift as he turned to face the door. "Boss, I got her!"

The door to the commissioner's office opened, casting her in a triangle of light. She glanced up to see Neal Moray standing in the doorway, smirking as he surveyed the sight on his doorstep.

"Well, well, well," he drawled. "I was wondering when you were going to show up. I've been waiting all night for you." He waved her in. "Quickly, man!"

The guard jostled her into the office and shoved her forward. She stumbled, reeling, and caught herself against the back of a chair at the fireplace.

Moray shut the door. "Where *have* you been, Citizen Wilder? And what *have* you been doing?" He strutted toward her, his nose in the air. "You have a particular smell about you."

She glared at him.

"A very particular smell."

"Go to hell, Moray."

"I will have to report you, Joanna Wilder. Personal contact outside the bounds of marriage with a member of the opposite sex? Hmm. I should write you up. But that would involve a medical examination."

She clenched her jaw. He studied her, considering something.

"I'm not above doing Doctor Stone's work. But alas, there's no time for life's little pleasures today. As they say, we must make hay while the sun doesn't shine."

"And like I say, go to hell." She tried to sneak her hand into the pocket of her skirt.

He thwacked her wrist with his cane. "Not so fast, citizen."

Joanna blinked back tears of pain. Her wrist burned, but she didn't so much as flinch. She refused to give him the satisfaction of seeing her hurting.

"Now then," he purred. "You will keep your hands at your sides, won't you?"

She stared at his chest, refusing to acknowledge him.

"So I'm curious," he paced around her, his big head tilted on his thick neck. "As to those packets you people are throwing."

"I don't know what you're talking about."

"Oh, give me a break." His lip twitched with frustration. "Hold her arms!"

The guard grabbed her arms and twisted them behind her back, nearly yanking them from the sockets. Joanna bit back a cry of agony.

Moray plunged a hand into the pocket of her skirt and pulled out the last of her pods. He shook them in front of her face.

"I hate it when people lie to me." He leaned closer, until their noses almost touched. "Do you know how much I hate it?"

Joanna looked off to the side, full of fear and loathing, but refusing to carry on the slightest conversation with him.

"If you weren't so valuable to me, I'd kill you right now."

His words chilled her to the bone, but she kept staring at the wall.

"So instead, you and I are going to take a little trip."

Joanna didn't react physically, but her mind flashed on available transportation modes. The train wasn't due for a few days. Did Moray have a carriage? He would need one with blackout curtains if he planned to travel in the light that had come to the peninsula.

"Your friend Gabriel Stone thinks he has it all figured out," Moray continued, thinking she was paying close attention to his every word. "But he likes to do things the hard way. Neat and tidy. All kumbaya. But I prefer to—as they say—cut to the chase."

He dragged his cane down the front of her body, from her breasts to her knees. She fought back a shudder at the prospect of what he had in mind for her.

"Take her to the warehouse," Moray barked. "We leave with the tide."

Tide? He had a ship? A seagoing vessel must have arrived in Port Pennwood that she didn't know about.

The guard jostled her toward the door.

"I detest water. Especially the sea," Moray commented behind her as he shut the door and followed them across the gravel yard. "But to get the job done as it should be done, I'll just have to suck it up."

35

"WHERE DO you think they're going?" Tam whispered over his shoulder.

Eva stood behind him at the perimeter wall of the compound, peeking around the entry gate.

"I have no idea. An outbuilding of some kind."

"They're going to pay for killing my mum," he muttered through his teeth. "They are going to pay."

Eva put a hand on his shoulder. "Don't do anything rash, Tam."

"I'll do whatever it takes." He squinted up at her through the fringe of his shaggy hair. "I don't care what happens to me as long as Moray gets it."

"I care what happens to you. So don't take foolish risks."

Their glances met and held. She couldn't believe the words she had just heard herself say. She cared about the boy? How could she? Tam was the bastard son of her dead husband. And yet, her words echoed the truth that lay in her heart. She did care for Tam. She couldn't imagine a day without him in it.

His intense gaze burned into her. He was looking for certainty in her, judging her and wanting to know if he could rely on her. Almost unconsciously, she straightened her shoulders to assure him that she was worthy of his trust.

It was time she proved herself to everyone, starting with Tam. She *could* be trustworthy. She *could* be depended upon. She *could* face danger, the unknown, and vampires —*anything*—and keep her integrity. Even if it meant losing her life. A life lived without integrity and self-respect was a life only half-lived. Not worth living at all. She knew that now.

Buoyed by her new resolve, Eva watched Moray roll open a large wooden door of what appeared to be a warehouse. She could see the glint of silver barrels stacked inside, and recognized the shapes of the Sunara family wine casks that had floated to shore after the shipwreck. The guard shoved Joanna through the opening and tramped in after her.

"Come on, Tam." Eva took off across the yard, keeping close to the barbed wire fence of the exercise yard at the side of the warehouse, while Moray was preoccupied with closing the huge doors.

The boy soon outdistanced her, skittering ahead. He had no fear, which inspired Eva but also worried her. Still, she followed him along the tight barbed wire strands. His drive and her concern for Joanna gave wings to her feet.

VINKO SAT UP, every muscle in his body crying out at the movement. His left hand throbbed. He glanced down at it, and remembered how the vampire doctor had treated his injuries. He was still confused about that. A dull pain clouded his skull and his ribs hurt when he breathed. But he would live. He could defend himself now.

Light filtered through the lace curtain opposite the bed. He had slept all night, thanks to the medicine the vampire had made him drink. He dropped his legs over the side of the mattress and sat for a moment until his head stopped swimming. The medicine had left a metallic taste in his mouth. He swallowed and scowled as he surveyed the bedchamber.

No one was here with him. Not even Tam. The pallet near the fire was empty except for the blanket the boy had discarded in a lump. Not even the good doctor was in attendance. Bastard. He was probably sleeping upside down somewhere with his arms folded over his chest and his black coat draped over him like a cocoon.

Still, the monster had helped him.

Again, why? Maybe Eva knew the answer. He would find her and demand to be told what was going on.

Vinko slid to the ground and tested the strength of his legs. His left kneecap ached where Moray had slashed it. But the leg held. He could walk. He reached for his boots. It would be difficult to pull on his tall leather boots with his one good hand, but somehow he would have to do it.

A few minutes later, he padded down the hall. The nearest bedchamber door was open. He peeked inside. Someone had slept in the bed, but they were no longer there. He continued down the hall to the room farthest from the stairs. The door was closed.

Vinko curled his good hand around the knob and rotated it. Then he eased the door open, hoping the hinges wouldn't squeak. He peered through the crack. There was the vampire doctor, naked in the bed, with the sheets thrown over the lower half of his body. His white skin was almost as pale as the linen that covered him. Disgusting.

Vinko stared at the creature that had saved his life. The vampire looked strangely peaceful as he slept. Almost human. And so vulnerable. Vinko had never seen a vampire in such a state of repose. The vampires he'd encountered had been old-fashioned, clinging to their caskets and their caves. This doctor vampire, on the other hand, looked like an ordinary person lying there, with an arm flung out as if waiting to welcome a missing lover.

Vinko shook off the vision. He had to be extra careful. The vampire must have drugged him to make him think such thoughts. Vampires would never be human. At heart, they were cruel, self-serving animals. He would be a fool to entertain the notion that Gabriel Stone was anything but a savage beast.

Vinko slipped his right hand into his vest and pulled out a pod. Then he stepped into the bedchamber and raised his hand to throw.

"Sunara?" the doctor asked, blinking awake. "Is that you?"

The kindness in the doctor's voice and the normalcy of the question took Vinko by surprise. He paused, perplexed even more. Vampires hissed. They snarled. They never called humans by their names. They didn't bother to learn the names of their prey or adversaries. What kind of vampire was this?

Then in his confusion—even after years of training— Vinko made a fatal mistake. He looked directly into Gabriel Stone's eyes.

He froze. He could feel his mind turning to ice.

Gabriel nodded at his hand. "What is it you have there?"

"The pod."

"And what were you going to do with it?"

"Kill you."

"I see." Gabriel flung off the sheet and slipped out of bed. For a lean man, he was surprisingly well built. The muscles of his abdomen flexed as he reached for his shirt. "You plan to kill me with a bag of talcum powder."

"No powder. Special."

"I see. Croatian powder."

"Call what you will, devil."

"And why do you want to kill me?"

"You are the vampire."

"Really?" Gabriel buttoned his shirt. "And why would you think that?"

"I know. You do not fool the Sunara."

The monster studied him thoughtfully, with curiosity glinting in his gaze, not cruelty. Vinko blinked rapidly, assuring himself that he really could detect a red line around Gabriel's body. Yes, it was there. His sluggish mind churned with more confusion. Gabriel was unlike any night creature he had ever come across.

"Do me a favor, Sunara," Gabriel reached for his trousers without breaking eye contact. "Get to know me before you make judgments."

"You do not say no," Vinko blurted. "You are the vampire."

"I am a doctor." Gabriel faced him, his eyes blazing now. "I saved your life, man. So put away that packet."

Vinko blinked again, unable to move because of Gabriel's mental hold on him. He should kill the vampire now. Immediately. To hesitate meant death. But no matter how much he wanted to throw the pod at Gabriel, his arm remained frozen in place at his side.

"I have no interest in killing you," Gabriel added.

"But others."

"No. I drink only to feed. Never to kill."

Vinko studied the lean doctor, wondering if he could

believe a single word the vampire said. To even stand here like this, talking, was dangerous—pure madness. Then again, he was under hypnosis and not thinking straight. That was the way vampires tricked people. They muddled a person's mind with their cunning and their games.

"Put away your packet, Mr. Sunara." Gabriel's words hung with weariness and worry, bereft of cunning. "And help me find Joanna. I fear she may be gone."

Then the doctor broke off his stare, releasing Vinko, and baring himself to attack. The creature actually turned his back to put on his stockings and boots, giving Vinko the opportunity to throw his pod. How could the vampire be so confident of his powers of persuasion and turn his back like that? Or did the man value his worldly existence so little that he would play games of chance with death? Vinko was flabbergasted by the vampire's behavior.

Vinko raised his arm. Sweat dripped down the sides of his face as his warrior nature railed against the rational side of him that wanted to trust Gabriel Stone.

He dropped his arm. He couldn't do it. He couldn't throw the pod. God help him, he hesitated.

At the movement, Gabriel glanced over his shoulder. "Good," he said.

"If you hurt Eva or Tam. Even touch—"

"You have nothing to worry about on that count." Gabriel drew on his coat.

"I kill you, devil."

"Fair enough." Gabriel strode to the door. "But I have no more time to discuss this. It will be full daylight soon." He stepped into the hall and turned. "Come with me or stay, Sunara. It is your choice."

Eva paused at the end of the barbed wire fence and surveyed the warehouse ahead. "If we roll back those doors, Moray will see us. Or hear us. Those doors are loud."

"What if Moray isn't there? Why would he be just standing around?"

"He probably isn't. But we can't take the chance."

Tam stepped back to get a better look at the side of the building. Eva studied the warehouse, which was not much more than doors set over the opening of a very large cave. Behind the doors, the cliff rose up to the windswept moor above. A lone seagull sailed the morning breeze, watching them.

"Maybe there's another way in," Tam mused.

"What do you mean?"

"You know that kitchen in the main plant?"

Eva nodded.

"I bet there's a way to go from the kitchen to the warehouse. For supplies. There's always a back door to a kitchen."

Eva knew the boy was onto something before he had even finished his last sentence. But he might not be entirely right. The passage might not be from just the kitchen. There was that second door in Charles' office, the door she had never opened. It could lead to a toilet or closet, and not be of any use at all. But there was a chance it was the portal to somewhere important.

"Come on," she took off running for Charles' office.

The second door in Charles' office was locked. Eva tried both of Charles' keys, but neither of them turned the tumblers. She straightened and sighed, disappointed.

Tam glanced up at her and winked. He slipped his hand in his tattered vest and pulled out a slender metal tool, not much bigger than a toothpick. Without explaining himself, he knelt at the door and put the tool into the keyhole. He moved it around, listening intently and working the doorknob until Eva heard something click.

Tam shoved the door open and jumped to his feet. He waved her forward, grinning.

"I don't want to know where you learned how to do that," she said, sweeping past him. "Or why."

"It comes in handy. You'd be surprised."

Tam's words drifted away as she glanced around the corridor she had stepped into. Again, the space was comprised of rock walls and a flagstone floor, and from what she could see, might have been a natural cave at one time, adapted to house a handful of windowless prison cells. The flagstone path disappeared into the gloom beyond.

"This looks like a really old prison," Tam murmured, poking his nose through the bars of the nearest cell. "Look at those chains."

Eva glanced in the direction he pointed. Rusty manacles hung from chains bolted into the stone. The links were as thick as her fingers. A wooden bench hung from the wall with more chains. She could feel the presence of pain here. And death. Centuries of despair.

"Oh, Tam," Eva wrapped her arm around his shoulder. "I don't like this place."

"It's creepy. Maybe this is solitary confinement. Because, look, no windows."

"I noticed that." Eva released him to look for a switch to turn on the gas, if there was such a lighting system in the old prison. But all she found was a lantern and a tin of matches near the door. She lit the lamp and picked it up.

"I guess this will have to do," she said. "Let's see where the passage goes."

They walked past the handful of cells and then down a long passage that might have taken them under the exercise yard. She wasn't sure. It was difficult to judge distance when underground. After a few minutes, they came upon a door at the end of the long tunnel. Tam held up a hand and cocked his head.

"Hear that?" he asked.

Eva held her breath and listened.

"All I can hear is the sea."

"There's something else." Tam tilted his head to the side. "An engine or something. Hear it?"

Eva strained but could not make out anything but the roar of the waves below them. The sound unnerved her. She had not realized the processing plant had been built over the sea. She wondered how safe the building was, with waves constantly eroding the sandstone beneath it.

"I don't hear anything, Tam."

"It sounds like a train or something."

"Let's keep going." She tried the door handle and found it was locked. Tam looked up at her and raised an eyebrow, waiting for instruction.

She nodded, and he bent to the task of picking the lock again.

Once she opened the door, she could hear the sound Tam had referred to. A machine or an engine rumbled somewhere below them. Was there another room full of dying prisoners like the one with the glass cylinders? Eva paused, knowing her lips had gone white with terror. She couldn't face another room like that. She would not be able to keep her sanity.

But Eva had no alternative. She had to keep going.

36

EVA HELD THE LANTERN HIGH, throwing light over the steep narrow steps hewn from solid rock. The stairs descended into darkness before her. The way down was precipitous, with no handrail for support. She choked back fear and gave the lantern to Tam.

"Hold this for a minute." Grimacing, she pulled up her skirt and looped it under her belt. She couldn't take the chance of tripping on the hem of her dress during the descent. A fall could be fatal.

"I swear I am going to start wearing trousers."

Tam lifted his eyebrows at her outlandish idea and grinned. The lantern turned his face to a grotesque mask.

She pulled the wad of material through the belt at her waist and then held out her hand for the light.

"Let's go," she said, more to herself than Tam.

"Be careful," he answered behind her.

"I plan to be."

"You might have to turn off the light when we get to the bottom, depending on what we find."

"We won't be able to re-light it, though. I didn't bring any matches with me."

When would she ever learn to think ahead?

"Dammit," Eva added.

She had never sworn out loud before. It felt good. It felt right. And freeing. Heartened, she put a hand on the wall and took the first step downward.

JOANNA STOOD in the bowels of a giant cavern that had been carved by the sea over thousands, maybe millions, of years. Her arms were tied against the sides of her body with a length of damp rope the guard had found hanging from a hook. To the right was a series of dark humps of rocks surrounded by surging water that disappeared into the depths of the cavern. Water heaved in and out, racing along the rock ledge where she stood, but making little sound, which told her the sea ran deep here.

To the left was the western sky, still gray as dawn arrived on the other side of the world. Moray and his guard labored on board a boat that was moored to an ancient iron pole, trying to keep the vessel's engine running. Shading his eyes from the sunlight, Moray marched from the barrel and tubes at the rear of the craft to the hatch leading below decks, shouting commands to his guard. Then he marched back to the tank to fiddle with a valve.

Joanna had seen a few ships since her flight from Londo City. She had even traveled on a couple of vessels. But the ones she had seen or had taken passage on had been cutters, with cloth sails and rope rigging. This craft looked more like a fancy barge than a seagoing vessel. It sat close to the surface, with a long gold bowsprit decorated on the end with the statue of a crow with outspread wings. Near the rear of the boat were paddle wheels on either side, linked to the huge golden barrel and tubes of the steam-powered engine. In the middle of the craft, near the hatch, was an elegant tented seating pavilion, draped in heavy black cloth. A gold medallion had been painted in the center of the remaining deck space. It displayed a stylized letter M surrounded by birds and vines, boasting the owner's wealth and style.

Neal Moray owned a boat? Joanna couldn't believe it.

While she stood there, she saw two workers appear carrying silver barrels, which they stowed in the hold. They didn't look happy and argued heatedly with Moray before clattering off the barge. One glared at Joanna, his eyes glinting red in the dim light and his lip curled in anger. Vampires were being left behind, with nothing to feed on but the few remaining humans in Port Pennwood. She prayed that her sister would be careful.

The worker vampires left to return to the warehouse through the stairwell she had just come down.

The engine finally caught and held, chugging like thunder in the cavern and sending smoke and steam to the rock ceiling high above.

Moray minced across the gangplank, wary of the water below, and grabbed her upper arm. "Time to go, citizen."

He pulled her toward the rumbling barge. She dragged her feet, struggling against his grip until he glared at her and showed his pointed teeth.

"Stop stalling," he growled. "It won't get you anywhere."

"Gabriel will make you pay for this," she flung back at him.

"Gabriel Stone is a useless ass. A bleeding heart." He squeezed the upper muscles of her arm until she thought they would split apart. "And once Silas Stone hears what has gone on around here the past few days, he is going to see what a traitor the good doctor really is."

Moray stepped onto the narrow gangplank. Joanna looked down at the swirling water, wondering if she jumped in, if she could survive the current. But she couldn't go anywhere while she was bound by rope. She could barely even take a deep breath, let alone swim.

She balked at the edge of the stone ledge, doing everything she could to make Moray's job as difficult as possible. She could tell he was just as frightened of the water as she was. Maybe more. If she could knock him off balance, he might fall in. But then, again, he would probably take her with him.

"Bitch," Moray hissed. "Step on the plank."

"No!" With all her might, she lunged backward, jerking him forward. He had no choice but to release her or lose his center of gravity. She fell, landing on her rump and rolling to the side. It was alarming how difficult it was to keep her balance without the use of her arms. She glanced at Moray and wondered how much time she had to get back to her feet and run.

Moray's white face turned red with anger. "Guard!" he shouted. The engine drowned out his command. "Guard!" Moray yelled again, over his shoulder this time.

The guard stood at the gauges of the barrel, intent on keeping the contraption working and unable to hear his master.

Joanna rolled onto her back and got to one knee just as Moray pulled out a gun.

"Get back here, or I'll shoot you."

"No, you won't." She stood up and skittered back as fast as her lack of balance would allow. "You need me."

"Dammit, get back here!"

When he realized his pursuit would be useless because he would have to drag her across the narrow gangplank again, he turned and minced back to the boat, careful not to take a false step. Then he dashed to the guard and pointed at Joanna. The guard took off in her direction.

At the wall of the cave, Joanna glanced around, desperately looking for an escape route. She could probably outdistance a man if she ran up the stairs and back to the warehouse. But she would never be able to unlatch the door. The latch was far too high for her bound hands to reach. Her other choice was to run for the sunlight at the mouth of the cave. The guard might be able to follow her, but Moray could not. And that would increase her odds of escape.

She galloped for the end of the ledge. It led to nowhere. On each side of the mouth of the cave, the cliff plunged into the sea in a vertical wall. The ocean slid deep into the eroded slits and holes under the processing plant. One false step and she would be swept into the black labyrinth and drowned.

Desperate, Joanna turned, feeling the prick of morning light burning her neck and scalp. To escape Moray, she either had to jump into the sea or fight off the brute running toward her.

"Give it up, citizen," the guard said, reaching for her arm. She backed away, circling to avoid him as her thoughts raced. She had to get out of the sun but also position the guard so that he, not her, stood in the precarious position at the edge of the ledge.

Joanna glanced at the front of his body, looking for the most vulnerable spot. Private parts or knee? What would incapacitate him the most? She remembered how easily she had killed her field manager a year ago when he'd assaulted her. She was capable of fighting off a human

man. If sunlight had begun to affect her that meant her vampire traits were developing more and more as time went on. She had to believe that her superhuman strength was developing as well. It was her only chance.

Calling on every shred of her vampire prowess, she coiled her muscles, pivoted to the side, and kicked the guard in the knee.

He grunted in pain, but his tree trunk of a leg withstood the blow. She stared in disbelief. With a growl, he clutched her hair and dragged her back to the cave.

She was forced to stumble after him. If she didn't focus on keeping her balance, she would fall and tear her hair out by the roots. She clenched her jaw, stifling her cries of pain.

Just as they neared the gangplank, a second door opened and two shapes appeared, one short, one taller. Joanna stared. Somehow, Eva and Tam had found her. Disbelief and gratefulness swept over Joanna. Her little sister had found the courage to come looking for her. She gaped at Eva, amazed.

It took one second for Eva to assess the scene before her. Moray planned to abduct Joanna and flee Port Pennwood on a boat. She had to stop them before it was too late.

The guard dragging Joanna by the hair pulled up in surprise twenty feet from the gangplank. Moray stood on the far end of the narrow wooden walkway, holding a pistol.

Eva tightened her fingers around the pod she had at the ready and strode forward. She had to get close enough so she wouldn't miss. If she got close enough, she might be able to take down the guard and Moray at the same time.

"Hold it right there," Moray shouted. "Throw that thing, and I shoot."

"Throw it!" Joanna urged. "He won't shoot me." The guard punished her by wrenching her head around, so she couldn't see the others.

"Throw it," Moray continued, "and I shoot the boy. I'm not kidding."

"He won't be able to see me if you throw it," Tam said behind his hand.

Eva nodded, grateful for the boy's quick thinking.

Moray leveled his gun at Tam. "And don't think you can beat me at this game. A bullet is much faster than a sack of dirt. The boy will be dead before I am."

Eva paused, wondering if Moray was right and trying to think of a way out of the predicament.

"Put down that packet, or I will shoot."

Eva remembered Vinko's warning about the pods being too close to heat or exposed to rain. She used that as an excuse to gain time. "I can't. The ground is too wet. It will trigger an explosion."

"Then give it here." Moray wiggled the gun and glanced at the guard. "Citizen, get the packet. And any others they have stashed in their clothes."

Roughly, the guard pushed Joanna away. She staggered off kilter, almost falling over the edge into the racing water. Horrified, Eva lunged forward.

"Stop!" Moray barked.

"But he almost pushed my sister into the sea," Eva protested.

"Because of you, you meddler." Moray's lip curled. "Guard, search them." Moray turned to glance at Joanna. "And you, not one step or I kill the boy."

Joanna heaved a sigh and ceased her backward motion.

Eva watched the guard pull a pistol from his belt and limp toward them. "Empty your pockets," he ordered.

Reluctantly, Eva emptied her vest pocket and the pocket in her skirt. Tam handed over his pods as well. Then the guard patted them down from neck to knees. Satisfied that he had got all the pods, he tramped away, leaving them standing in the half-light, powerless to help Joanna. Eva was glad she had stopped to release her skirts from her belt before entering the cavern. The guard hadn't noticed the weapon she had slipped into the top of her boot.

"Good. Now run along," Moray said.

Eva burned with frustration. They could do nothing but stand there and watch Joanna be abducted by Neal Moray.

"Guard, bring the prisoner aboard," Moray commanded.

The guard grabbed the knot of rope at Joanna's back and shoved her toward the gangplank. As Joanna stumbled forward, she extended an index finger and pointed toward the ground, in their childhood sign language.

"She's going to try something," Eva whispered to Tam.

Joanna was pushed and prodded toward the gang-plank. But just as she got to the iron pole, she bunched her muscles and pivoted sharply to the right, heaving the guard's bulk to the left. She caught him by surprise, and he teetered on the rock ledge, his bad knee taking the weight of his body. Joanna grabbed the iron post and held on for dear life as the guard flailed one arm and tried to clutch at the rope knot. But his fingers slipped off the wet rope.

For a moment, Joanna thought he would fall into the water, but he fought hard for balance as he teetered on the edge. Grunting, he threw his weight forward, falling to his hands and knees on the ledge, narrowly escaping death.

"Bitch," he growled. "You're going to pay for that."

Eva could tell that one of his knees was injured by the way he winced and swore when he tried to get up. He paused, his weight on his good knee.

Just as he raised his head to try to get up again, a war cry flashed through the cavern and a blur streaked toward the guard. Eva stared in horror as Tam barreled toward the guard. He lowered one shoulder at the last minute and charged into the man's chest, knocking him back. With a bellow of disbelief and terror, the man plummeted over the edge. The water lit up a sickly yellow-green color, as the pods exploded around him like a halo.

Eva could see that Tam wouldn't be able to stop his forward progress. She lunged forward, but the boy sailed into the sea after the guard. He disappeared under the current.

"Tam!" Eva screamed. Her world exploded. All she could see was red—red-hot anger directed at Neal Moray. Still running, she grabbed the knife stuck in her boot and dashed across the gangplank, swiping blindly at Moray, who stood there in shock, distracted by the fireworks in the water.

At the last minute, he whirled around to fend her off. She swiped, snarling with hatred. Vengeance gave her strength and courage she never knew she possessed. She felt the weapon tear into his flesh. His face. His cheek.

"God damn you!" He stumbled backward, firing his weapon. He missed. The bullet ricocheted off the wooden deck. He staggered away, holding the side of his face as blood poured through his fingers. She'd cut him in the spot opposite to where the ugly scar marred his mouth and cheek.

"You bastard!" she screeched. "You killed Tam!" She rushed forward, knife held high, screaming like a banshee, planning to plunge the blade into his heart before he had time to take a second shot.

He reached for her throat. She stabbed his hand, snarling like a wild animal. A murderous frenzy blinded her to all but Moray. She would kill him for what he'd done to her sister, Vinko, Hannah and now Tam. She didn't care what happened to her. She would slash away until she killed him or he killed her.

37

MORAY TOSSED ASIDE his gun and grabbed Eva's wrist, his eyes blazing. She shifted her stare to his blood-splattered shirt, knowing she should never look in his eyes. She braced herself for an attack. No matter how terrified she was of the vampire, she had to stand her ground.

She thought of Tam. The memory of the boy's pluck and courage fired her own. She gripped the knife harder, intent on striking Moray in a vulnerable spot. She would aim for his heart. He was a vampire, after all.

"You think that puny knife is going to kill me?" He laughed, splattering blood down his brocade coat. "You are an idiot. Just like your sister."

Before she could react, he grabbed her other wrist. He squeezed so hard that she thought he would break the bones of her hand. Then he shook her arm roughly, until she was sure it would rattle out of its socket. Pain forced her to drop the knife. It clattered onto the deck.

Moray yanked her close to the front of his body. "Look at me!"

"No!"

"This is what happens when you forget your place!" Using both hands, he flung her away. She crashed against the tank at the rear of the barge. Heat burned through her clothing. She gasped and staggered to the side.

Moray marched up to her and caught her by the elbow. The stench of his oxidizing blood made her gag. So did her fear of what he was going to do to her.

"Get over here, Citizen Wilder!" he yelled over his shoulder to Joanna. "Or I kill your little sister. Right now."

"No!" Eva shouted.

But it was no use. Joanna wouldn't stand by and allow Eva to be killed. No matter what price she had to pay. To save Eva, she had placed herself in danger on numerous occasions or had taken punishment in her place. All those times when Eva had been selfish or headstrong or just plain thoughtless, Joanna had been there for her. Eva's throat clenched together as the impact of all that Joanna had sacrificed for her hit her like a blow.

Joanna walked across the gangplank, her eyes dark with hatred and her lip curled.

"Now then," Moray grabbed the gangplank and threw it aside. "Let's get this show on the road."

Eva reached for the knot to untie her sister, but Moray swung around and kicked her in the gut.

She fell to the deck, struggling to take a breath.

"Keep your hands off her," Moray growled.

His eyes were so cold and his wounded face so horrible-looking that Eva tore her stare off him. She struggled to her feet, retching.

Moray now looked like the monster he really was. All the expensive clothes and perfume couldn't disguise the ugliness and stench of his real being. Eva hung back, her thoughts racing. They had to get off the barge before Moray sailed out of Port Pennwood, but how?

Working swiftly, Moray unfastened the bowline and stern line and threw them aside. Then he rushed to the wheel. The vessel rocked in the water, as the gears shifted into place.

"Stop!" someone shouted.

Desperate, Eva glanced toward the sound of a familiar male voice. Gabriel had come down the warehouse staircase with a taller man behind him. *Vinko.*

Vinko was here! She wanted to scream out his name, but she could only stare. She had lost her voice.

Eva ran for the side of the barge and bent for the gangplank, but Moray intercepted her, using his vampire speed to outdistance her.

"Not so fast!" he snapped. He shoved her in the chest, sending her sailing through the air. She crashed onto the medallion and fell backward, hitting her head on the deck. Her skull filled with stars. Then everything went black.

"Help!" Joanna screamed.

Vinko sprinted for the barge as it chugged toward the mouth of the cave. He couldn't think about the dangerous current or the enraged vampire on the boat. All he could think about was saving Eva. He prayed Moray's brutal shove hadn't killed her and that she was merely unconscious.

At the last minute, Vinko leapt from the ledge and clawed his way through the air, every muscle in his body intent on reaching the moving target in front of him.

He landed just shy of his mark but grabbed the rail to keep from falling into the sea. His pulled himself up and over, bellowing with pain at having to use his injured hand.

As the barge tipped beneath Vinko's weight, Moray

roared, consumed by rage that another human was about to impede his progress. He stomped across the deck, his eyes like fire, but he wasn't quick enough to stop Vinko from clambering aboard. Moray lunged for him.

Vinko ducked to the side and vaulted aboard, scanning the vessel for something he could use as a weapon. He had no pods. Moray had taken them from him during his capture.

Moray caught himself on the railing and turned around. Then he raced back toward the tiller and stooped to pick up his abandoned pistol, but Joanna kicked it away. The gun spun across the gleaming deck toward Vinko. He scooped it up, while Joanna skittered past him to see to her sister.

Moray froze. Then he straightened to his full height and smirked, but the expression failed to coalesce into anything more than a crooked smile. Vinko averted his stare. Moray's wounded face was too grotesque to look at.

"Think that gun will stop me?" Moray taunted.

Vinko raised the pistol. "I shoot you through the heart, devil."

"Fat chance. And so what? A bullet won't kill me."

"Will stop you."

"Not for long."

"Long enough."

"Are you sure?" Moray took a step toward him. "Are you sure there are any rounds left? I don't think so."

Vinko didn't look at the gun. Moray wanted him to look, to catch him off guard.

"Stay back," Vinko said. He glanced to the side. In a few more seconds, the boat would motor out of the cave and into the sunlight.

"You die, Croatian!" Moray leapt through the air.

Vinko followed the line of Moray's trajectory and pulled the trigger. The blast knocked Moray backward. In horrified amazement, the vampire clutched his chest as he struggled to keep from falling. Blood bubbled through his fingers. Moray's pale vampire face turned even whiter as he staggered backward, in shock from the gaping wound in his heart.

"Me?" Vinko said, throwing Moray's own words back at him. "I never miss."

Then he dashed for the tiller and gave it a hard swing, using his armpit instead of his splinted hand. Moray hit the starboard rail. The boat swung around, exposing Moray to the shafts of light pouring into the cavern. His clothing started to steam. He bellowed and glared at Vinko with so much hatred burning in his eyes that Vinko's heart flopped in his chest.

If the sun didn't kill Moray, Vinko knew he was a dead man. The vampire would tear him to shreds.

"Damn you," Moray shouted. "Damn all of you to hell!" Then he turned and flung his legs over the railing. While his hair smoldered, he pushed off and dropped into the current. His head disappeared in the greenish-black water.

For a long moment, no one moved.

Then Joanna scampered up, her arms still tied against her torso. "Do you think he's dead? Does water kill vampires?"

"I do not know." For a moment, he stood with Joanna at the rail, waiting for Moray to bob to the surface. But the vampire never appeared.

Vinko untied the rope around Joanna's torso. "See to Eva. I will get this boat back."

Within minutes, Vinko had piloted the barge back into place. Vinko deftly secured the craft with lines. Then he scooped Eva into his arms and tromped across the gangplank.

"Tam," Eva muttered, her eyes still closed. "Tam."

"She must be delirious," Joanna put in. She hovered at his elbow, never taking her stare off her wounded sister.

"Was Tam here with you?" Vinko asked, thunderstruck.

"Yes, but he fell in trying to save Eva. He got sucked under."

"Did not swim?"

"No one in Londo knows how to swim."

With his heart breaking in two painful pieces, Vinko glanced over his shoulder at the swirling water of the cave.

"Vinko," Joanna put a hand on his forearm. "He's gone. I'm sorry."

"No. Not possible." Vinko's voice cracked. "Not Tam. Never."

"Tam," Eva moaned again.

Vinko was torn. Eva was in need of medical care, but he didn't have time to take her to safety. He had to look for the boy before it was too late. Frantic, Vinko glanced at the vampire doctor. He didn't fully trust the man. But the doctor had assisted the humans on more than one occasion.

Gabriel's behavior went against everything Vinko knew about vampires. And now here he was, the vampire Gabriel Stone, reading Vinko's thoughts and reaching out for the woman Vinko loved.

"Give her to me," Gabriel said. "Joanna and I will take Eva back to the house. I will see to her head injury."

Vinko paused, still not sure.

"Give her to me," Gabriel urged, holding out his hands.

"It's all right, Vinko," Joanna put in. "You can trust Gabriel."

Vinko frowned.

"We are not all monsters," Gabriel added.

Vinko sighed and relinquished Eva into the arms of the vampire doctor. It was the only choice he could make.

"I stay then," Vinko said. "Look for Tam."

Gabriel nodded and headed for the stairs.

"Wait," Joanna said, turning back.

38

"Shouldn't we stick together?" Joanna said. "We'd be better off."

"What do you mean?" Gabriel pivoted to face the water, still cradling an unconscious Eva in his arms.

"Moray's vampires might be waiting for us on the stairs. And if Vinko finds Tam, and he is still alive, he might need medical assistance."

"Joanna is right," Vinko said. "Come."

Vinko gestured the doctor forward. Gabriel tramped over the precipitous gangplank, seemingly more intent on Eva's condition than his own safety. He carried her to a cushioned bench inside the draped pavilion while Joanna hurried aboard.

Vinko untied the vessel and waited for Joanna to slide the plank back onto the deck. Then he piloted the barge away from the ledge and into the current.

"We find Tam," Vinko said over the rumble of the engine. "Look there, Joanna. I look this way."

"All right." Joanna grabbed the starboard rail and peered into the blackness of the cavern.

A dank breeze wafted through her hair as they motored deeper and deeper into the bowels of the cave. In the darkness, Joanna's vision shifted into vampire overdrive. Her supernatural self could now detect all life forms, from crabs and fish in the roiling water to the smallest spiders and beetles clinging to the damp rock walls. The sea creatures produced a light green glow. Vinko and Eva glowed pink. Gabriel was a beautiful celestial blue. For a moment she was distracted by her newfound visual powers. But only for a moment.

Joanna scanned the water, looking for a pink glow that might be Tam.

"Good Gottfried," she exclaimed.

"What do you see?" Vinko asked over his shoulder.

"Enormous fish. Bigger than a man. They are swimming all around us."

"Sharks," Vinko replied. "Was Tam injured when he fell in?"

"I don't think so."

"Shark smell the blood."

"There must be a dozen of them." Joanna leaned over the rail, desperate to locate Tam before the sharks did. The giant fish cruised back and forth, outlined by the halo of their auras as they circled the boat, as aware of the humans above them as Joanna was of them down below. Her heart thundered in her ears and fear ran up the backs of her legs. One false move and those fish would devour any one of them.

She spotted the guard's red coat floating by in the current. One of the sleeves was missing, displaying a ragged shoulder where the man's arm had been bitten off. She prayed she would not encounter a similar sight that had anything to do with the boy. To think of him being torn to pieces by sharks made her stomach turn over.

She held a fist to her mouth and took a deep breath. Her roiling stomach calmed down a bit, enough for her to keep searching.

"What is shape?" Vinko called. He let up on the throttle.

"What?" Joanna turned to follow his line of sight.

"I see something. There." Vinko pointed toward the mouth of the cave, where a triangle of rock rose out of the water like a giant tooth.

Vinko did not possess her vampire vision. But he might be able to spot shapes in silhouette against the light that poured into the cave.

Joanna scampered across the deck to stand beside him. She trained her vision on the rock face.

"Yes," she cried. "I see something. On the right."

"A body. Yes."

Joanna swallowed back a wave of fear. No light emanated from the lump. Perhaps it was the guard.

"Closer!" she urged, straining to see. The light burned her eyes, producing tears.

"Care required." Vinko guided the barge closer to the rock. "Not to crash. Tricky."

"Do your best." Joanna wiped away the tears and then shielded her eyes as they chugged forward. Sunlight pricked the edge of her hand and forearm.

"I think it's him," she gasped. "Hurry, Vinko."

Gabriel appeared at her elbow. "It *is* him. He's wedged in a crack."

Gabriel leaned over the railing so far that Joanna thought he might fall in. He swooped to snatch up the dark shape pinned in the rocks. Joanna grabbed Gabriel's coat in both hands, determined to keep him from plunging into the sea. The boat rose and fell with the surging current, making their recovery job difficult as well as dangerous. Gabriel's first two tries fell short of the mark.

"Closer," Gabriel shouted. He crawled over the railing and leaned out, holding on with one hand.

Vinko worked the rudder and throttle, expertly guiding the barge nearer to the body.

"All can do," he yelled over the engine.

Gabriel strained, stretching farther than Joanna thought possible. Only one booted foot and one gloved hand remained in contact with the barge.

This time, Gabriel got close enough to touch Tam. He clutched the boy's jacket and hung on as the barge bobbed and swayed. Joanna shot Vinko a pleading glance, asking for more navigational finesse. He set his jaw and worked the tiller, struggling to control the craft as wave upon wave buffeted the hull.

Gabriel growled, determined to lean even closer. He timed his efforts to coincide with the breathing of the sea. As the barge dipped after a large swell, Gabriel reached down.

"Got him!" he shouted. He grabbed Tam's left arm and pulled the boy free. Tam's body bumped across the rocks and then swung toward them like a heavy rag doll, with his feet dragging through the water, attracting the notice of the sharks. Green blobs sped toward him from three different angles.

Frantic to keep Tam from being torn to shreds, Joanna leaned over and grabbed his trousers, enough to pull his feet out of the water. Then they lugged him on board. Joanna laid him flat on his back as Gabriel clambered over the railing and dropped to the deck.

Joanna stared down at Tam, fearing the worst. He wasn't moving. Although he hadn't lost any of his limbs to the sharks, he looked as if he had drowned. There was no pink aura surrounding the boy. There was no color about him whatsoever.

His face was oddly white. His lips were gray and flaccid. His eyes were closed. She couldn't see him breathing.

"Is he dead?" Joanna fell to her knees beside Tam's body. "Is he dead, Gabriel?"

"He might be." Gabriel knelt beside her. "But I'll try to resuscitate him. Stand back."

Joanna scooted back and watched as Gabriel pressed down on Tam's breastbone. She had never seen a drowned person, let alone watched someone attempt to revive a drowning victim. But she had seen Gabriel switch into physician mode and administer medical care. Physician mode was his most natural way of being. And he was superb at his job. If anyone could save Tam, Gabriel could.

She watched him pump Tam's chest and then breathe into the boy's mouth. She knew how unusual the scene before her was. She was witnessing a vampire doing everything in his power to save the life of a human.

Joanna glanced up to discover Vinko watching Gabriel just as intently as she was. His handsome face was dark with concern and his lips were parted in confusion.

Both of them were aware that the vampire kneeling on the deck had cared enough for a human boy to risk his own life. That was Gabriel. An enigma. A black sheep. But above all, a beautiful being who steered by his own star.

Joanna could tell that Vinko recognized how special Gabriel was. Warmth poured over her. She was proud to be Gabriel's friend. Proud to be his mate. And lucky to have met him.

At that moment, Joanna knew she would love Gabriel Stone for as long as she lived.

"Tam!" Someone screeched behind her.

Joanna turned, surprised to see Eva staggering toward them and holding the side of her head.

"Eva!" Joanna jumped to her feet. She raced to her sister's side and propped her up to keep her from swooning. But Eva plowed forward.

"Tam!" Eva cried again. She stumbled to his side, just as the boy rolled over and vomited all over her boots. Eva didn't seem to notice. She fell to her knees.

"Oh, Tam!"

The boy coughed and sputtered. Gabriel edged back, giving him space.

Joanna watched in amazement as Eva gathered the boy into her arms and hugged him tightly, not seeming to care that his spittle and vomit would soil her dress.

"Tam!" Eva held him and closed her eyes as tears rolled down her face. "Oh, Tam!"

The boy's white hands clutched Eva's torso as he clung to her for dear life, coughing and shaking and fighting for breath.

Gabriel rose and touched Joanna's hand. "Let's get the boy into the pavilion and get him warm. There must be blankets somewhere on this boat. A first aid kit. Or something."

"I'll help you look," Joanna said, thankful for something to do.

She reached for Eva. "Come on, Eva. Let's get you two back to the pavilion."

Gabriel picked up the gasping boy while Joanna guided Eva back to the curtained area of the barge.

"We go now," Vinko announced. "You, devil," he nodded at Gabriel. "Seek shelter or die. We go to the open sea and the sunlight."

As Eva sank to the bench next to Tam, she heard a strange cracking sound above the rumble of the barge's steam engine. Startled, she looked over her shoulder. The sound came from the sea cave they had just chugged out of. She saw Vinko look back at the cavern as well.

"What was that?" Joanna said, holding the curtain to one side for a better view.

A second crack split the air. Then a rumble so deep, Eva felt it in her bones.

"Cave in!" Eva yelled. "Vinko, hurry!"

Vinko reached for a lever and yanked it downward. The barge leapt forward, beating through the waves while the gears screamed and the paddle wheels blurred with froth.

Charles had feared cave-ins. But had he envisioned a cave-in so large that it would destroy the entire facility? That was what was happening now. A collapsing void raced toward the processing plant, sucking down everything in its path.

Horrified, Eva watched the cliff fall in upon itself, as if it were exhausted from the countless centuries of holding back the sea. Earth and boulders tumbled into the sea, roaring like a thunderstorm. Then the stone walls of the prison crumpled and disappeared. A black line of water heaved out of the deep.

"Hold on!" Vinko cried. He pulled at another lever.

The barge plowed toward the open sea with a giant wave racing after them.

Eva's heart rose into her throat. If the surge overtook them, it would kill them all.

39

VINKO KNEW if he kept the barge in line with the surge, they might be able ride out the swell. But if he went off course by just a few degrees, the barge would be flipped and mauled by the giant wave.

He threw himself on the tiller, using his weight to keep the barge on course with the approaching tidal wave. Within seconds, the wave hit. The barge rose in the air, buoyed by the giant swell. Vinko's stomach rose with it in a sickening lurch. He heard Joanna cry out as she lost her balance. But she held on, gasping, as the barge paused for a moment and then barreled down the front of the wave, the prow pointing to the seabed, as if it would plunge into the depths.

Vinko grimaced, fighting the tiller, every muscle in his body straining to keep the vessel under control. For what seemed an eternity, the barge flew through the water, swept along by the swell, until the wave finally lost its urgency and fanned outward.

Vinko collapsed on the tiller, panting and spent. The

barge had been swept a mile off shore. But they had survived. He could rest for a moment.

"Vinko!" Eva staggered across the deck to him. "Are you all right?"

He nodded and swallowed.

"You saved our lives," Eva gasped.

"You are hurt, Eva. Your head…"

"I'm fine. I'll live." She shot him a tremulous smile. "*We'll* live."

"Good thing with cave-in," Vinko managed an exhausted wink. "No more Neal Moray. For sure. No one survive cave-in. Not man. Not vampire."

"Yes." She looked back at the ruined coastline. "No more Neal Moray."

———

VINKO ANCHORED the barge in the harbor, far from shore, to allow his exhausted passengers to sleep until late afternoon. The sun warmed his shoulders and head, reminding him of his homeland, and soon he drifted off to sleep as well, propped against the engine housing. He dreamed of his family and friends. Fresh produce from the kitchen garden. Olives and cheese. Swimming in the sea. Dancing. Laughing.

Something brought him back to consciousness. A noise? A knowing? He slowly awakened, still thinking of the laughter he'd heard in his dreams. Then the realization dawned on him that he hadn't laughed since coming to the Anglo Territories.

Such a place. The people here had no concept of the depth of the darkness they lived in. He felt sorry for them. But he was no longer sure what part he should play in saving them. He had learned enough about Londo to realize that what he had first assumed was a black and white situation—a simple scourge to eliminate—was far more complicated than he had ever dreamed.

Unsettled, he rubbed his eyes and looked up, and was shocked to see Gabriel Stone standing above him. The melting sun swam in a blood red sky behind the vampire, casting him in a towering silhouette. A chill spiked through Vinko. He had been caught in a vulnerable position by the very monster he had been sent to destroy.

Then the vampire did the inexplicable. He smiled and reached out a gloved hand.

Vinko stared at the man's glove. He had never touched a vampire. This might be some kind of trick. It would be madness to trust a creature of the night. But Vinko could sense that Gabriel meant him no harm. In fact, Gabriel had been nothing but helpful since he'd come to Port Pennwood. Even heroic. As far as vampire behavior went, his actions simply didn't add up.

Tormented with indecision, but not wishing to insult the creature that had saved Tam's life, Vinko extended his hand and allowed the vampire to pull him to his feet.

Vinko brushed off his clothing, stalling for time while he marshaled his racing thoughts. Should he trust or destroy? He didn't know what to make of Gabriel Stone and was reluctant to start a conversation with the creature while his head spun. What could he possibly say to a vampire? Certainly not small talk. He hoped he would be able to find enough words to express himself. He also hoped he'd come to a decision about what to do about the vampires of Londo City—and soon.

As if the vampire could read his mind, Gabriel asked, "So what is your plan for the immediate future?"

"I ask the same," Vinko countered. "Do you kill me now, devil? Is dusk."

A shadow of dismay flitted through the doctor's eyes. "You mock me."

"You are the vampire."

Gabriel's unwavering gaze pinned him in place. Shamed him. "And am I like all the other vampires you have known?"

"Well…" Vinko took a deep breath, looked out to sea, and then glanced back at the slender, auburn-haired man standing in front of him. "No." He sighed, frustrated by his limited knowledge of the Anglo language. "No."

"So you cannot judge us all as one."

"Maybe. But I see only you before me, devil."

"You came to trade with us."

"Yes."

"Or spy."

Vinko raised his chin.

"Or kill us." Gabriel crossed his arms over his chest. "Tell me the truth."

"I am the vampire hunter. Yes."

"I thought as much."

"You ask for it. Your kind come to my country. Feed on us." Vinko swept the air with one hand. "We are not like Londo. Like citizen cattle. We fight back."

Gabriel nodded but said nothing. There was nothing the doctor could say in the face of the truth. Vampires were killers. Vinko stepped forward and jabbed a finger at his chest.

"You come to Croatia. You kill my people. You pay."

Gabriel met the rude gesture with a cool, unwavering gaze. "And if we agree to stay away?"

"How can you promise this?" Vinko swept the air, indignant.

"My brother is the leader of Londo. He will listen to me."

Never once did Gabriel lose his patience. Never once did he raise his voice. Vinko surveyed the vampire's face, searching for signs of subterfuge and finding nothing but an honest, open expression. It was impossible to distrust the man. He radiated sincerity and goodwill. His vampire eyes were full of intelligence and kindness, far from the cruel gleam that Vinko had expected to see.

"If I go back," Vinko began, thinking aloud, "Without head of Silas Stone, I fail."

"If you go back with my brother's head, you will start a war. Is that what you really want?"

Vinko shot a glance at the vampire's serious eyes and then remembered to look away. The creature had the power to hypnotize. He must not forget that. Stone could be putting him under a spell even as they talked. He must remain on his guard.

"War is not the answer, Vinko. That is why the world is the way it is now. Because of war. Why keep repeating such madness?"

Vinko blinked and looked at the sea again while his thoughts churned. He heard Gabriel sigh behind him. Then Gabriel spoke, his voice softening.

"Because it is madness, Vinko. And you know it. I can tell."

Vinko recalled his lifetime of training to mistrust all creatures of the night. But this vampire was so human. If he closed his eyes, he would think he was talking to a normal human being. He never would have believed it possible before coming to Port Pennwood.

It was Vinko's turn to cross his arms over his chest. He kept his back turned and refused to give in to the thoughtful words of the doctor. No matter how much they made sense. Everything he had been taught, every hour of training he had undergone, would count for nothing if he accepted the doctor's philosophy. And yet, he was certain no other Croatian had encountered a vampire like Doctor Stone. What if there were more like him? What if vampires were not the monsters that legend made them out to be?

"We worked together to save Tam today," Gabriel put in. "We can work together to save the earth. You and I. Man and vampire."

"You speak impossible."

"I speak truth."

Vinko turned to level his gaze on the doctor, judging him, measuring him, but also seeing him as an individual for the very first time.

Something cracked inside Vinko. To think of Gabriel Stone as a person and not as a monster went against every tenet he believed in. He was so conflicted, he felt as if he would vomit. But as soon as the wave of nausea passed, he felt his chest open with an entirely new feeling. Hope.

Gabriel placed his hand on Vinko's shoulder in a friendly gesture. "I ask that you leave us, Mr. Sunara. Go back to Croatia." He released his hold. "Grant me time to change things. Let me find a way to exist together in peace. Man and vampire."

"Not possible."

"I believe it is possible. We don't have to kill each other to survive. With a little self-control, a vampire does not have to kill."

"Vampires are born to kill."

"Unfortunately, so is man."

Vinko stared at the doctor. The truth in Gabriel's words hit him hard. But with the blow came a decision—a choice he would not have believed he would ever make. He let out a frustrated breath.

"Oki doki, devil. I give you time. But no vampire come to Croatia."

"Agreed."

"Or I come to Londo City, with others."

"Agreed." Gabriel held out his right hand.

Vinko swallowed back a wave of loathing and shook the creature's hand. He was shocked to find the handshake felt as normal as any man's.

"Good," Gabriel said. "And now, take me ashore if you please. I will bring back food and then take care of the last of Moray's rabble horde."

Vinko nodded, still drowning in a whirlpool of worry and hope. But one thing he knew for certain. Gabriel was right. It would be safer to remain on the boat until morning.

Gabriel seemed to read his mind again. "In the morning, all will be clear for you to wait in the village until the next train arrives."

"What do you do?" Vinko asked. "Go back? With horse?"

"I will stay. Until a new commissioner arrives. The new prisoners will need to be fed. Reports filed about what happened here."

Vinko nodded and fired up the engine. Gabriel walked to the prow and stood in the breeze with his coattails flapping around his lean body and his gloved hands planted on the railing. Vinko tore his gaze off the enigmatic creature. He had never felt more conflicted about a being than he did about Gabriel. To let any vampire live was madness. Crazy.

But letting the doctor live was the right choice. In his heart he knew it. He just had to convince his mind. And his fellow Croatians.

Instead of torturing himself with thoughts of Gabriel,

Vinko raised his gaze to the cluster of buildings perched on the side of the hill.

Judging by the number of houses, Vinko guessed the village had once been home to a few hundred people. Fishermen and farmers, shopkeepers and clergy. Now only a handful of citizens remained to support the processing plant. He wondered if the citizens were hiding in their homes now, worried about what to do with all the chaos that had descended upon their small village. Maybe the citizens of the Anglo Territories were accustomed to hiding and not asking questions. He couldn't blame them.

Perhaps Gabriel Stone, pretending to be one of them, would allay their fears. Devil. Vinko sighed. What went on at Port Pennwood was no longer his concern.

As the sun plunged into the sea behind him, a glint of light caught Vinko's eye. At the top of the slope, light flashed on the weathervane of the commissioner's mansion and turned the windows to gold, reminding Vinko of the highlights of Eva's lovely hair.

Vinko let his gaze wander over the silhouette of the large stone structure. Once Eva had lived with another man in that grand house. He couldn't visualize it. It seemed impossible that Eva would have shared a bed with a man she didn't love. It just wasn't like her. But then again, she might have been forced to follow the rules of her Londo society. He guessed there were many rules and that her life had been difficult. Vinko thought of the way she had kissed him and sighed again.

If he had arrived in Port Pennwood just one week earlier when Eva's husband had been alive, he might never have met her. He was glad the timing had been in his favor. Whatever happened, wherever his life took him, he would never regret having met Eva Wilder.

Vinko studied the deserted village lanes as the barge

rumbled into the harbor. Leaving Port Pennwood would not be easy. He had made friends here. He had faced danger and death and had been forced to shift his world-view here. But most of all, he had tasted love here. He would never be the same because of this place. Part of his heart would remain in this tiny harbor forever.

He felt the weight of his own thoughts and shook his head at himself. This was the effect Londo could have on a person. Dark thoughts. Heavy thoughts.

No, such thoughts were not for him. He would shake off the gloom. He was a Croatian. But more importantly, he was a Sunara.

He took a deep breath and squared his shoulders. All would be well in the end. Things would work out. He had to believe that.

He concentrated on bringing the barge alongside the quay. Gabriel waited for the fenders to make contact with the old wooden pilings.

"I will be back with food," Gabriel called over his shoulder. Then he leaped onto the quay and waved. "Wait for me."

40

As THE BARGE rocked gently in the harbor, Eva wolfed down an evening meal of potatoes and fish. She was ravenous from the stressful last few days. Her head ached as a result of her fall, but other than that she had escaped Moray without serious injury. She knew she was lucky to be alive—and Vinko Sunara was the reason she *had* survived. She glanced at him and was surprised to find him studying Joanna, his eyes dark with concentration.

He felt her glance. With a flush, he broke off his stare, rose and excused himself. Eva watched him walk to the wheel. He fired up the engine.

A smacking noise brought Eva back to the present. Tam was licking his fingers, savoring the last morsel of his meal with gusto.

"Did you get enough?" Eva asked, glad to see him back to his normal, vibrant self.

Tam shrugged and raised his eyebrows.

"Here." Joanna held out the paper wrapping where most of her meal had gone untouched. "I have some left."

"Aren't you hungry?" Eva asked.

Joanna shook her head and turned to gaze at the village, avoiding her sister's stare.

"You should eat, Joanna. Something."

"Maybe later." Joanna shot her a pale smile.

Again Eva sensed that Joanna was not telling her everything. Something had happened. A gulf had formed between them. She could sense it, and she didn't like it. Maybe time and distance had created the gulf. But she suspected something human was the cause of their schism. Maybe she shouldn't have made all those comments about Gabriel. Maybe she shouldn't have pressed Joanna so hard.

"Gabriel will be all right," Eva ventured, touching Joanna's wrist, hoping to establish some kind of connection.

"I know." Joanna shot her another wan smile. "But I should have gone with him. He should have awakened me, told me he was going."

"He wanted to protect you, I imagine."

Joanna nodded and fell silent. Eva felt the gulf between them widen, and it frightened her.

"Joanna, what are you going to do?"

"What do you mean?"

"What are your plans? Are you going back to Londo with us?"

"Wait a minute," Tam said, his mouth full of food. He looked from Joanna back to Eva, his eyes bright with questions. "Who said anything about going back to Londo?"

Surprised, Eva turned to look at him. "But we have to."

"Not me. I can't."

"Why not?"

"My mother is dead. And she was the only link I had to rations and housing." He swallowed and balled up the paper. "No one knows I exist, Eva."

"I know you exist, Tam."

"Well, that won't get me an ID card, will it? I don't have a birth certificate, do I? I'm a nobody."

His words struck Eva to the core. She wrapped an arm around his bony shoulders and hugged him against her. For a moment, she was too choked with emotion to speak.

"You aren't a nobody to us," Joanna said, coming to her rescue just like in the old days. "You saved my life, Tam. I will never forget that for as long as I live." She reached out and squeezed his forearm. "I've never met a young man as brave as you. Never."

Eva felt Tam melt against her. Careful not to hurt his injured arm, she squeezed him tightly. She had longed to be loved and comforted when she was his age, but there had been no parent to hold her and tell her that everything was going to be all right.

"Everything is going to be all right, Tam," she murmured, speaking to the boy and her still-grieving young self. "You'll see."

She hugged him even more tightly. But as Eva held him, she wondered how she would broach the subject of Tam's parentage. She hadn't thought about how she would tell him the truth about his father. Or how he might take the news. She hadn't had time to think that far. Until now.

Her thoughts churned. She'd never had to take anyone's feelings into consideration before. But with Tam, she had to. She wanted to. Above all, she didn't want to break his heart, especially after he had just lost his mother. She could feel his warm breath on her neck and his skinny body pressed into her, all angles and energy.

Something inside her shifted and opened. Something pushed upward like one of Joanna's seedlings breaking free of the earth. She could feel something coming to life within her soul. It was as if Tam and her never-born son and her young self were intertwining and rising up from the shadows toward a glorious new beginning.

As the boy leaned against her, she knew the time had come to make an important decision. She was ready. She would wait to tell Tam everything, until they were both in a more stable place and more accustomed to each other. But for now, she was ready to take on a new way of life.

"I was hoping, Tam," she began. "That you would agree to come back to Londo with me. Live with us. Keep me company."

He pulled out of her grip to stare at her. "Do you want to go back?"

"No. But we have to."

"Why can't we stay here?"

"What would we do?"

"I don't know." Tam extricated himself. "We could fish or something. We could live in one of those empty houses. Fix it up."

"With what money?" Eva shook her head. "We have to be realistic, Tam."

"So you'll get a job? In Londo?" Joanna asked. "Really?"

"I won't have to. Charles left me a townhouse. And an allowance. As long as I go back."

"Ah." Joanna sighed. "That's all well and good if the Overseers don't take it away."

"I'm hoping Gabriel might intercede on my behalf if that happens."

"I'm sure he would."

"We can all live together there," Eva put in, glad to be able to offer Joanna something after all the sacrifices she had made over the years. "You, me and Tam. That is, if you want to, Tam."

"I'd rather stay here. I like it here."

"But it isn't possible."

"Your plan sounds doable," Joanna put in as Tam scowled down at the food perched on his knees. "Except for my part in it. I am a fugitive, Eva. I can't put you in danger by living with you."

"So what will you do?"

"I'll have to move around. At least until I'm sure the Overseers have forgotten about me. And now that Neal Moray is dead, that just might happen."

Eva nodded and gazed out at the open sea. The mention of Neal Moray cast a pall over her thoughts of the future. She and Tam would never truly be safe until a stake was driven through Moray's heart or his vampire body was turned to dust—and she saw it happen with her own two eyes.

"Do you think he's really dead?" Eva whispered.

"I have to believe he is. I choose to believe it." Joanna touched her wrist. "We can't live our lives in fear, right, Evie?"

Eva glanced at her sister. The old clear-sighted, positive-thinking Joanna was back. Her heart filled with love for her sibling. Eva grabbed her hand.

"Jo, I never want us to be apart again," Eva said. "Never. Promise me we will stick together."

"I promise, Evie. I promise."

"Me, too," Tam put in. He grabbed Eva's hand to make a human chain of the three of them. "You're never getting rid of me, Eva. We're a team."

"Oh, boy," Eva muttered and rolled her eyes. "I'm asking for trouble, aren't I?"

"Nothing but." He grinned.

Eva felt the barge pull away from the place they'd been anchored and realized with a pang that part of their team was missing. She glanced past Tam to the wheel where Vinko stood with his back to her.

She gazed at his tall, straight figure and wide, capable shoulders. Being kissed by Vinko Sunara had forever changed her perception of men. But she had matured enough to know that she must put his kiss away and relegate Vinko to her memory. Her future could never include him. She was from Londo, a widow who could never remarry. He was from Croatia, a vibrant bachelor with a full life ahead of him. No matter how much she longed for more days to spend with him, she knew their time together was at an end.

She rose.

"I'll be back," she said.

She ducked through the curtains of the pavilion and headed toward the wheel.

"Where are we headed?" Eva asked, coming to stand at Vinko's side. He didn't look at her. He seemed troubled. Or perhaps he was preoccupied with piloting the barge in the growing darkness.

"To small cove."

"You mean where the little shack is?"

"Yes. There." He tightened his grip on the wheel and clenched his jaw.

She studied the side of his face. "What's wrong, Vinko?"

"You speak of future."

"Yes."

He nodded but didn't look down at her. "Go to Londo. You and Tam."

"Yes. Are you still coming with us? Even with Gabriel knowing about you?"

"No. Devil doctor talk with me of truce. I return to my home. For now."

"Oh. When?"

"Soon. When ship come."

"When will that be?"

"I signal. They come. In morning. They wait. Close."

"Oh."

Even though Eva knew Vinko had planned to return to Croatia at some point, she wasn't prepared for the news that his departure was so imminent. Her heart twisted in her chest.

"I talk with you," Vinko added. "We walk. To top of cliff. I signal the boat of my father. We talk then. Oki-doki, Eva?"

His voice cracked. He glanced down at her, his eyes bereft of sparkle. She didn't like this dark side of Vinko. She wanted things to be different. Now that they had defeated Neal Moray, she wanted to bask in Vinko's warmth, his smile and his optimism. But something troubled him, and she knew she would have to wait to find out what it was until they could talk in private.

AFTER FILLING their pockets with Vinko's pods in case they encountered vampires during their trek, Eva and Vinko climbed the cliff path, using a lantern to guide them in the falling light.

Eva was reminded of the first day she had met Vinko, when she had asked him to climb up the cliff with her and break into the commissioner's house. That day seemed lifetimes ago. The woman she had been seemed even farther away.

She was glad.

Eva followed Vinko to a lookout point at the end of the path. For centuries, humans had walked to this spot to stare down at the crashing surf, watch for loved ones coming home or simply dream of what might exist outside the Anglo Territories.

Dreaming never fills your plate.

That's what she had been taught as a child. Still, she had come here many times, dreaming of what lay beyond the sea, never guessing that a stranger from the east would actually appear. But here he was.

Vinko lifted the lantern in front of his body and swung it back and forth, careful not to extinguish the light. Eva surveyed the sea but saw nothing but a black expanse and a faint sprinkle of stars. Wind blew her skirts around her knees and ankles, and tendrils of hair whipped across her face. She felt as if the wind might buffet her off the precipice. Without thinking twice, she reached for Vinko's free arm and clung to him with both hands.

He didn't react. He didn't even look at her. Instead, he swung the lantern again. This time a light on the horizon winked on and off.

"They see," Vinko announced, swinging the lantern a third time.

The light blinked twice in response.

Eva nodded. "So, they have been waiting for you all this time."

"Yes." Vinko lowered the lantern. "I come on Croatian ship. Follow vampires from Londo. Long journey."

"I thought you had sailed with the vampires."

"No. Too dangerous. Vampire kill me. Take my blood."

The truth suddenly dawned on her.

"Instead, you killed them, didn't you?"

It was Vinko's turn to nod. "Yes. When they come ashore. One by one."

"That's why I saw all that clothing in the surf."

"Yes." Vinko glanced down at her. "One of them tries

to kill me. But sun come out. The vampire leave me for dead on sand. Then you find me." He smiled for the first time. "Good day for me."

She was grateful for the smile. It was like having the old Vinko back. She tipped her head onto his bicep.

"That day seems like years ago."

She didn't want to walk back down the cliff just yet. It seemed natural to stand here like this with Vinko, linked to him and talking quietly. She didn't want to break the connection. Apparently, neither did he. He patted her hand and stood in companionable silence for a few moments.

Then she heard him sigh. "Much happens, Evie. This land. The people. The vampires. Not like Croatia."

"I would expect it is very different there."

"Yes. I am wanting the sunshine. The food of my home. And the sleep."

"I know. We haven't had much sleep since you arrived."

His body shifted. "I hear you talk to your sister. To Tam. You go back to Londo?"

"Yes. I have to."

"Why is this?"

At his question, Eva released her hold on him and rubbed her chilled arms. "Because of resources. And because I don't want to live far away from Joanna any more."

"You want this? Londo life?"

"I'm in no position to be picky." She stared at the sea. She could feel Vinko surveying the side of her face.

He took a step backward and touched her arm. "Come. Too cold. We go back. We talk."

41

By the time Eva and Vinko made it to the base of the cliff, night had completely fallen. Eva found it difficult to see the path, even with the lantern lighting the way. They scrambled down the final few feet of the path and onto the beach. Eva hurried along the familiar stretch of sand, stepping over the small stream that cut through the rocks and fanned out to meet the sea. Once or twice, she had drunk water from the bubbling stream, but tonight she didn't even stop to admire it. Her thoughts were focused on Vinko's departure and her future plans—and not on her old playground.

Vinko grabbed her wrist. "Wait," he said.

Surprised, she glanced over her shoulder at him.

"We talk here." He pulled her toward a jumble of driftwood at the base of the cliff. In the twilight, the logs glowed like a jumble of gray bones. "You and me. No one more."

"All right."

"I go tomorrow." He motioned for her to sit on one of the large gray logs. "Tonight we say everything. Last chance." He looked down at her, his face glinting in the flickering light of the lantern. "Truth, Eva. Tonight, only truth."

"All right. But just for the record, I've never lied to you, Vinko. I think you're the only person I have never lied to."

"Is good this, in way?"

"For me, yes." She was glad for the darkness that hid her blush. She wasn't proud of the girl she had been. But she was no longer that girl.

"Why lie before?"

"Because I was scared most of the time. All the time, really."

"Not now?"

"Not as much." She shot him a fleeting smile. "I'm working on growing a straighter spine."

He shot her a confused look.

"Being more true," she explained. "Completely true. Mostly to myself."

"Is good." He sat down beside her. "But now I must say one thing." He sighed and looked out at the sea, gathering his thoughts or thinking of words to express himself. He clenched his jaw. Eva watched him, wondering what troubled him so deeply. He had been preoccupied since the meal on the barge.

"I am not certain," he began. "How to say."

"Just say it, Vinko. I'm a big girl."

"You will not like."

"Just say it."

"First, the question."

She studied him, puzzled. "What?"

"Your sister. You see her many times in year? Or not?"

"Not. She had to leave Londo. She was accused of being a rioter and helping a criminal. My boyfriend. I told you about him. Aiden Bannister."

"Yes." Vinko nodded. "Where does your sister go then?"

"I don't know." Eva shrugged, wondering where he was headed with his interrogation. "I'm not really sure. I lost touch with her when I got married. I didn't see her for almost a year."

"But you and sister. Close?"

"Well…not so much at the end." Eva felt a flush creep up her neck. Their relationship had ended because of her immature behavior. But she didn't want to admit that to Vinko.

"And Gabriel Stone?"

"What about him?"

"Your sister know the vampire then?"

"Yes. We both did. We had no idea he was a vampire though. He used to visit us. Joanna mainly. And he treated burns that I had. Like a doctor. A regular doctor."

"They are lovers?"

Eva shot a glance at him. "Maybe. I don't know. Most likely they are. She didn't sleep in her bed last night. I do know that."

Vinko rubbed his jaw. "This is not the usual. Vampires enchant. But then they kill. Not make friend."

"That may be true, but Gabriel isn't like other vampires. He's…he's a…gentleman."

"Yes. Very strange, this vampire."

"And when I accused Gabriel of being a vampire, Joanna got really upset with me."

"Why?"

"Maybe because I'm not supposed to know about vampires in Londo. Maybe to protect me. Maybe to keep up the ruse. Maybe a lot of things. But she won't admit the truth to me, Vinko. Me, her own sister. It feels like she's lying to me for the first time in her life."

"So Joanna is good most of time?"

"The best. She would never lie unless she had a very good reason."

"Perhaps to protect," Vinko mused. "You and the doctor."

"But what makes me angry is the fact that she doesn't trust me enough to tell me the truth. We used to be partners. It was Jo and Evie against the world. But it's like she is turning her back on me now." Eva slumped. "Not that I don't deserve it."

"Why you say this?"

"I used to be a little bitch."

"You say this many time. I do not believe."

"Thanks, but Joanna knows the real me."

Vinko put his hand over hers. "I know the real Eva." He held her gaze until she couldn't stand it any longer. She jumped to her feet, too afraid to remain in contact with his warm hand. She ached to kiss him, to fling her arms around his strong neck and never let go. But she could not allow herself to touch him like that. It would be too self-indulgent—cruel to both of them. He was leaving. She was going back to her old life. To keep her sanity, she had to keep her distance.

She had to be an adult for once.

Vinko slid his hand back to rest next to his thigh. "Your sister. Not distrust of you, Eva. Love for the vampire. Make change to her."

Eva stared down at him. She hadn't thought of the situation in those terms. She had assumed Joanna's actions were a commentary on Eva's lack of character when, in fact, Joanna's motives might have nothing to do with Eva's shortcomings. Nothing at all. A huge weight lifted from Eva's shoulders.

Vinko continued with his questions. "Joanna will go to Londo?"

"That's what she says. She is tired of living alone, away from everyone. I know what she means. It will be so good to have family around me again."

"Not possible, maybe."

"What do you mean?"

Vinko took a deep breath. "I tell you something now, Eva. Something important. I tell you, but you stay and think. Oki doki? Not run."

She studied his face, wondering what he could possibly say that would induce her to run. The last thing she wanted was to waste her final hours with Vinko on silly dramatics like running. Running was what the old Eva would do. She turned to face him. "All right. What is it?"

"Tonight, you eat? I listen and watch. You, Tam, Joanna. When is dark, I see the line."

"Line? What line?"

"Small. Pink. Around your sister."

Shocked, Eva stepped back. "What?"

"Pink line. Not red. But vampire line."

Eva planted her fists on her hips. "You're telling me that you saw a vampire aura around Joanna? Impossible!"

"No mistake. Line is there."

"A pink one."

"Yes."

"So in your dealings with vampires, what would a pink line like that mean?"

"This I do not know." He shrugged. "Never do I see the pink line."

"So maybe it isn't a vampire line."

"Do not pretend, Eva." Vinko rose and took a step toward her. "Joanna is not the sister you think you know."

"No!" Eva turned away, clutching her upper arms, as if

to comfort the child that still lived inside her and had jumped back out at this stressful news.

"You say yourself she is not same. You feel it."

"But, like you said, because of Gabriel."

"Yes. Exactly, Eva."

Vinko stepped up behind her and gently cupped her shoulders. "She is not sister you think you know. The life in Londo? Not same old times."

Eva's throat clenched. She hung her head, glad for Vinko's support, but angry that he was forcing her to look more closely at a truth her heart already glimpsed on the horizon. Her head told her to be loyal to Joanna for once, to stay true to the course she had chosen, and one day she would be as stalwart as her sister. But her heart told her all was not right with her choice. What part of her should she listen to: heart or mind? Would they never be in accord?

"What are you saying?" she whispered.

"Be sure, Eva. Be sure of choice. You go to the dark place called Londo City for family. To be with the sister. But is not like old days now."

"You're saying that I'm wrong to go back?"

"Not wrong. But for you?" He squeezed the tops of her arms. "Londo? Think, Eva."

"I go to be near Joanna. It's my only choice."

"Is the other choice. Not Joanna choice. Eva choice."

"What are you talking about?"

"Croatia."

She whirled to face him, breaking his hold on her. "With you?"

"Yes. You and Tam."

She stared at him, her eyes burning. "So that's what this is about! You bastard!" Outraged, she shoved him in the chest. "You make up a story about my sister—the most heinous story imaginable—so I'll go to Croatia with you!"

"No story."

"You bastard!" She shouted. Spittle flew from her mouth. "You bastard!"

Before he could say anything more, she turned and dashed down the beach. She could hear him racing after her. She pressed into a run, intent on outdistancing him. Tears blurred her vision as she fled across the sand and into the surf. She grabbed her skirts and galloped through the waves, determined to get to the barge before Vinko could catch her and turn her head with his damnable words.

When would she learn? With her, men always had agendas. She would never listen to a man again.

Tam helped her clamber onto the barge. Once on deck, she scrambled to her feet, sopping wet from the knees down, and glad for the darkness that concealed her tears. She dashed them away with her fingertips and took a deep breath. She had never felt so betrayed. But she would rise above the violation. Never look at it. Never give it life again.

More composed now, she looked back at Vinko, just as the moon rode out of the clouds. He stood at the edge of the surf with waves lapping at his boots and his arms at his sides. He had stopped pursuing her. Good. She'd pilot the barge back to Port Pennwood and leave him to his schemes. The bastard could spend the night in the shack. And good riddance. Good riddance to him and all the lying bastards like him.

The Overseers' dogma came to her like a lightning bolt.

One look back, fall into a crack.

Truer dogma was never spoken.

JUST BEFORE DAWN, Eva was awakened by the sound of drapery hooks sliding upon a tent rail. She sat up with a gasp, still expecting Neal Moray to appear out of thin air and kill her. She was relieved to see Joanna ducking out of the tented pavilion.

"Joanna," Eva called lowly, so as not to wake Tam, who slept on the upholstered bench opposite her. She got to her feet, groggy and stiff.

Joanna looked over her shoulder but didn't say anything. She seemed annoyed that Eva had noticed her movements.

"Where are you going?"

"To find Gabriel."

"Now?" Eva stumbled toward her. "It's not safe. Wait until morning."

"I have to go now." Joanna dipped through the drapes.

Eva followed and padded across the deck to her sister's side. Joanna looked down at the water. Wind blew her brown hair away from her pale face, giving her a ghostly, otherworldly appearance. She stared down at the water in disgust, as if it were acid. Beyond Joanna, above the moor, dawn inched forward in a lilac glow.

Joanna shaded her eyes and glanced at the horizon and then looked back at her sister.

"Rethink how you left it with Vinko," she said. "Whatever he did to upset you, I'm sure he didn't mean it."

"Oh, he meant it."

A shaft of light filtered over the harbor and glinted off the surface of the calm water, enough to make Eva squint. Joanna winced and rubbed the back of her neck, as if something had stung her.

"Are you all right?" Eva reached for her hand.

"Yes. Just a crick in my neck." Joanna glanced over her shoulder at the approaching day. She seemed anxious, uncomfortable. She tried to pull out of Eva's grip, but Eva hung on, determined to disprove Vinko's theory about Joanna being a vampire.

If Joanna were a human being, sunlight wouldn't hurt her. If she were a vampire, she wouldn't be able to withstand the sunlight that would soon bathe the harbor. Joanna would have to dash back to the safety of the pavilion or seek the shadows at the base of the cliff.

The only way to get to the truth was to test her sister. She didn't like the idea. But Joanna's evasiveness had given her no alternative.

"Stay, Joanna. We can go out when it's light to make sure the Croatians actually leave."

"I can't." Joanna tugged at her hand. "Let me go, Eva."

"Why the rush?"

"I want to find Gabriel. Make sure he's all right. He's been gone for hours."

"A couple more won't hurt. Come on. Stay. Help me get this barge out of the harbor."

"You and Tam got it here just fine last night. You can very well take it back out. You don't need me for that."

Eva was surprised by the curtness of Joanna's words. Her sister was quickly losing patience. She watched Joanna closely. She was edgy and pale and kept glancing up at the sun rising above the cliff.

Eva's heart began to sink as the inevitable truth marched toward her, just like the sun.

"Eva." Joanna pulled at her hand again. "Let go of me. Right now."

Eva didn't comply with the request.

"Eva! Right now!"

Joanna's tone rose to that of an admonishing parent, a tone so familiar to Eva that she almost obeyed without a second thought. But then she caught herself. She wasn't a child to be admonished any longer. She held fast to Joanna's hand.

"You've changed, Joanna."

Joanna raked her with an annoyed glare. "So have you."

"Vinko told me you had, but I didn't believe him."

Joanna raised her chin. "What did he say about me?"

"That you aren't the same person you used to be."

"None of us are."

"That even if we both went back to Londo, it wouldn't be the same."

"He's right, Eva. We aren't the same women we were a year ago. Neither of us."

"He claims that Gabriel changed you. And he has, hasn't he. Really changed you. Tell me I'm wrong."

Joanna stopped pulling at her hand. The admonishing parent attitude seemed to drain out of her. She collapsed against the railing and looked down. Her shoulders slumped.

Eva stared at her in shock. In all the years she had known Joanna, she had never known her sister to be anything but formidable. Undaunted. She'd never seen her sister bow her head.

"Joanna?" Her voice cracked.

"Will you not let me go?" Joanna whispered.

"Not until you tell me the truth."

"Oh, so now you are interested in the truth." Joanna shook her head but still did not look at her.

"Please."

"Then you'll let me go?"

"Yes."

Joanna heaved a deep breath. "Very well. You deserve to know."

"I do." Eva stepped closer. "Yes, I do."

"You've come so far, Evie. And I am proud of you." Joanna straightened to look at her, her eyes full of love. "So proud."

Eva's heart swelled in her chest. Tears sprang to her eyes. She had never expected to hear such words from her much stronger sibling. Joanna's praise shocked her so thoroughly that she couldn't speak.

"And Vinko is right. Gabriel has changed me."

"How? What aren't you telling me?" Eva whispered, distraught.

Joanna tugged her hand again, and this time Eva released her. Desperate to get away, Joanna rushed to the railing and lifted her skirts.

"Joanna!"

Joanna paused, looked at her and then up at the glowing sky. Eva stepped closer, determined to learn the truth before Joanna bolted.

"Vinko said you are a vampire. I thought he was lying. But...was he?"

"I don't know." Joanna dropped her skirt and turned to face her. "All I know is that I'm changing. The sun burns me. I can see without glasses. I am stronger than you would ever dream. If you hadn't let my hand go, and I was desperate enough, I could have snapped your arm in two. Just like that."

Words fled Eva. Her lips parted in shock.

"I have to get away from the light, Eva. Now. Vinko is right. I am not the same. And you and I will never be the same. Not like we were."

She reached out and brushed back Eva's tangled hair, just as she had when they were younger. She gazed at Eva, all anger gone.

"I love you, Evie. But I belong with Gabriel. It is time we part ways."

"So you are a vampire."

"I don't know."

"Gabriel made you this way, didn't he?"

"Yes, but not how you think. It was a medical procedure. He saved my life, Eva. And I don't think even he knew what would happen."

"What did he do to you?"

"He gave me some of his immortal blood. Otherwise, I would have died."

"So he is a vampire."

"You know he is. And I did not have to tell you. I promised that I wouldn't."

"Oh, Joanna." Eva stared at her, arms at her sides. She ached to embrace her sister but wasn't sure if she should touch her now.

As usual, Joanna acted first. She moved forward and wrapped her arms around her younger sister.

"My dearest Eva. We will always be sisters. And I will always love you and want the best for you. But our paths lead in different directions now."

"But what about Londo? Gabriel leads a pretty normal life in Londo. So could we."

"You don't belong in Londo." Joanna eased back. "Look at you. So beautiful. Your hair so gold. Your cheeks so rosy. I barely recognized you when I got off the train." She stroked her cheek. "You were made for the sunshine and the sea. Don't you realize that?"

Eva shook her head. She was mute with grief for the loss she was already suffering.

"While I am made for moonlight and moor." Tenderly, Joanna brushed back the stray hair that blew across Eva's face. "You are light. I am dark. But we will always be sisters."

"No!" Eva whispered. Her heart was cracking in painful shards. "No!"

"Choose life, Eva. Go. Before it's too late."

"Without you?" Eva sobbed. "Where am I to go?" Tears streamed down her cheeks. "Where?"

"To the sun. To Croatia. To Vinko."

Joanna unclasped the pocket watch from the buttonhole of her vest. She held it out. "Take this. To remember our father and mother. To remember your homeland. And me. Wear it for me. And never forget me."

"I won't. Ever, Joanna." Eva blinked, her vision blurred by tears. She heard Joanna clearly but could only see her now as blobs of light and dark, as if her sister were changing form before her eyes—as if the old Joanna had already transitioned out of her life.

"Choose love, Eva," she heard Joanna say, "As I am choosing it."

EPILOGUE

THE NEXT MORNING, aboard the Mina

"CAPTAIN," a deckhand called down the hatch. "Woman requesting to come aboard, sir. And a kid."

Eva's heart skipped a beat as she saw Vinko emerge from below.

The sun poured over the sea, blinding her. All she could see was the outline of Vinko's broad shoulders and lean legs.

"Eva," he greeted. "Tam. Welcome aboard the Mina."

Tam beamed. "This is the finest ship I have ever seen!"

"And how many you see, Tam?"

The boy shrugged and grinned. "Can I look around?"

"Of course."

"Don't go far, Tam," Eva called after him.

"Eva." Vinko said again. "You surprise me, yes? Coming to visit the bastard Vinko."

"Vinko, I…" She broke off. "Is there somewhere private we can talk?"

"On ship?" He shrugged. "No."

What she wanted to say was meant only for Vinko. Frustrated, she frowned and glanced around, and then finally looked back at him. If there wasn't a secluded space to talk, so be it. She would give her speech in full view of the crew. She had gone over the words hundreds of times during the night, until they burned in her throat. "Vinko, I wanted to apologize for what I said last night."

"Bastard part?"

"Yes." She blinked, determined to continue. "You were right."

Vinko said nothing.

"About Joanna."

He nodded and crossed his arms, waiting for her to say her piece. His eyes were guarded, as if he half-expected her to fling accusations at him and run off again. She couldn't blame him.

"I said some awful things last night. I'm so sorry."

He nodded but kept silent and stared down at the planks of the deck. He wasn't going to make it easy for her. But she deserved it.

"Joanna agreed with you, Vinko. About going to Londo."

He glanced up, surprised. "She agree?"

"Yes, she said that she and I could live in Londo, but we would never be able to recreate the life we used to have. It would be futile, she said."

Vinko nodded.

"So, I..." Eva broke off and cast her gaze out to sea, searching for the courage to continue. Then she faced him, and straightened her spine. "So I was hoping...that your offer still stands."

"Offer?" His voice cracked. He flushed.

She glanced at him, hoping that he hadn't changed his

mind about her. "That you would take us to Croatia. Tam and me."

She paused and gazed up at him, her soul bared to view, as it never had before.

"Does it?" she whispered.

"What?"

"Still stand?"

"It will always stand." He fought down a cryptic smile, as if her choice of words amused him. "For you."

She smiled up at him, her mouth trembling and relief flooding her face. She hadn't been certain that he would be there for her.

"Do you doubt, Eva?" He grasped her shoulders and tilted his head to look deep in her eyes. "Me?"

"After the things I said to you? Yes, I did." She swallowed, contrite. "I wouldn't have blamed you, either."

"I am not boys you know from Londo."

"I know that."

"You can trust me. All days."

"Yes."

"I give you many reasons to trust. This is one." He cupped her face in his hands and drank in the sight of her.

Both of them were dirty, disheveled and exhausted from their adventure. But he didn't seem to care about any of that. He leaned down and pressed a gentle kiss on her lips, fusing her to him with the undeniable heat that flared between them.

She stood without moving, her face tipped up to him, savoring the public kiss without shame or reservation.

"But you trust Eva now, too," he added gently, not pulling away. "Important, this."

"Yes." She smiled. "I will from now on. I do."

"Not really need Vinko Sunara."

"What?" She pulled back.

"Not need." He smiled. "You live free. For you. For Eva. Not need man."

"Yes, but…"

"Is lesson of Port Pennwood." He brushed her bottom lip with the pad of his thumb. She ached for a second kiss. "You learn it. Good."

Her eyes clouded with confusion. "So what are you saying?"

"I am friend." He tipped his head, watching her. "Always to you, Eva Wilder. Not crutch."

"Friend?" Her voice cracked in dismay.

"Is your request."

"Yes, but…"

"If you want more kisses, you change rule." He raised his eyebrows. "Oki doki?"

"Oh!" She rolled her eyes and turned her back. "You *are* a bastard!"

He chuckled. He stepped up behind Eva and wrapped his arms around her. She took a deep, appreciative breath as his body molded against hers, fashioned to fit perfectly against her. Then he dipped his head to the small of her shoulder.

"Change rule?" he murmured. He kissed the base of her neck.

"I'll think about it," she teased.

"Then you are the bastard."

"I told you I was." She grinned and turned in his arms for a second kiss. When their mouths came together, the world around her vanished. All she was aware of was his warmth, his breath, his hands, and his powerful frame encompassing her.

When the kiss ended, he held her fast and looked down at her.

"When I come to your land, I expect to find vampire. Kill him."

She nodded, much more relaxed now, waiting for him to continue. He pulled her closer, cheek to cheek.

"But instead, my journey here?" He smiled into her hair. "My axe fall into honey."

"Your axe falls into what?"

"Honey. Is saying in Croatia." He kissed the tender flesh below her ear. "You will learn soon. About Croatia. About love."

"You love me?" she whispered, her heart rising into her throat.

"From first."

"Even when I was so awful to you?"

"Only with words. Never with eyes."

"I'm glad you could tell the difference."

"Yes. I tell you before. I know the real you." He smiled and pulled back to look down at her.

She could feel warmth and love streaming out of his eyes as he let his feelings flow unchecked this time.

"Before you know yourself, Eva Wilder."

Yes. She did know herself now. She was made of the same strong stuff as her sister. She always had been. But until a week ago, she had never possessed the confidence to test her own strength.

Port Pennwood had forced her to challenge herself over and over again, and she had endured. She felt like a newly forged sword after its first battle. She had come out of the fray, bloody and battered but still straight and true.

Because of the fight, she had formed a new opinion of herself and a confidence that fired her heart. She had earned the respect and love of her sister, Tam and Vinko. But more importantly, as Vinko had just said, she had earned the respect of her own self.

She no longer despised herself. What a strange feeling —and so exhilarating.

She was brand new. The past was behind her. She had lost her violin and her wind chime. But those things were no longer important. She had a new life ahead of her. And she would forge a meaningful future with the wonderful man she held in her arms.

A single gull flew over the ship, flapping until it reached a great height, and then soared out of sight on effortless wings. That was how her spirit felt. Lofty, soaring, and eager to explore new shores.

"No more rules, Vinko," she whispered in his ear. "Let's fly. Let's be free."

"Oki doki, Eva Wilder. Yes." He bent down for another kiss. "Best words I ever hear."

Later that night

THE DOOR OPENED and Gabriel looked up from the fire at Hannah Alexander's house. Ruby shut the door and leaned against it, sighing heavily. Her skirts were rumpled and her hair was disheveled. Gabriel had never seen the woman in such a state.

"Did Joanna make it back?" she puffed.

"Yes, she's resting upstairs."

"What a night." Ruby rolled her eyes. "Are we finally *done*?"

"I believe so," Gabriel said. "Any rabble hoard still standing will flee to Londo City."

"I am exhausted." The woman in purple heaved another sigh and smoothed back her hair. "That was some workout."

"And I appreciate it."

"Roman would have done the same thing. So I approve."

Gabriel bit back a smile. "I am honored that you approve."

She pulled away from the door. "Now can I have a bath? And some peace and quiet?"

"You may." Gabriel raked a glance over the harlot vampire. "But tell me. Why have you done all this? Helped Joanna? Helped me here at Port Pennwood?"

"A girl has to keep busy while Roman's in prison."

"Really?" He arched a brow.

"And I never liked that Moray character. Too cheeky."

"And you are not?"

"I might be cheeky. And a bit trashy." She raised her chin. "But I'm not cruel."

"True. So now that he's dead, what do you plan to do with yourself?"

"Smoke. Bath. Train. Londo." She counted off each word with a gloved finger. "In that order."

"And after that?"

"Oh, I don't know, doctor." She reached for the door-knob and then winked. "Live on the edge. As always. I'm sure something will come up to amuse me."

THE END

If you enjoyed PHOENIX,
please consider writing a review.

AUTHOR'S NOTE

The Londo Chronicles started out as a lark. I wanted to write a novella—something quick—just for fun after writing a really dark series, *The Forbidden Tarot*. So I wrote *The Marriage Machine*, which is a Steampunk story with a bit of romance thrown in. Little did I know that I would fall in love with the world I created and the people who live in it. The characters are all so real to me: Gabriel and Joanna, Silas and Eleanor, Eva and Vinko and Roman and...well, you are just going to have to wait to see who Roman ends up with.

I especially loved writing about Port Pennwood. I based descriptions of Port Pennwood on small villages I visited (and fell in love with) in Cornwall. A side of my family actually hails from Penzance, Cornwall, so the moors and coves really speak to my spirit.

In the third book of The Londo Chronicles, *Prodigy*, we go back to Londo City where a new character is introduced. You might be surprised to discover who she is!

If you'd like to read a few pages from *Prodigy*, you can find an excerpt following these author notes.

One caveat about the third book. If you happened to have read *Gabriel's Daughter* already, the third book will be familiar to you. I wrote *Gabriel's Daughter* as a standalone novel before I ever dreamed of creating a series. In *Gabriel's Daughter*, I kill off two people as part of the heroine's backstory. But now I can't allow two of my favorite characters to die. I like them too much! So *Gabriel's Daughter* has been rewritten to keep my characters safe.

If you have read *Gabriel's Daughter*, you may not need to buy *Prodigy*. Not much will have changed in the main story. Just the backstory and ending.

If that's confusing, please email ps@patriciasimp son.com for details and spoiler information.

MORE BOOKS

Whisper of Midnight

The Legacy

Raven in Amber

Lord of Forever

The Haunting of Brier Rose

Night Orchid

Black Panther Series | Lord of the Nile

Black Panther Series | Lost Goddess

Mystic Moon

Just Before Midnight

Jade

The Forbidden Tarot | The Dark Lord

The Forbidden Tarot | The Dark Horse

The Forbidden Tarot | The Last Oracle

Spellbound

Imposter Bride

Death in Amsterdam

The Londo Chronicles | Marriage Machine (Novella)

The Londo Chronicles | Apothecary

The Londo Chronicles | Phoenix

The Londo Chronicles | Prodigy

Visit Patricia Simpson's Website

www.patriciasimpson.com

EXCERPT | PRODIGY

Londo City, The Anglo Territories—2515

Angela Beach returned from work on Wednesday to see two men dragging Citizen Dunn out of her flat. *Citizen Dunn. Right.* The alias hadn't fooled her. She had recognized the hoyden Joanna Wilder the moment she'd seen her, pale and feverish, lugging a trunk into her flat. She also knew Joanna Wilder was wanted for crimes against the Overseers. And her. Gabriel Stone had turned away from Angela the day that woman had waltzed into their clinic.

And now, Joanna and a brat had moved in next door. She was most likely raising the bastard her sister had been carrying years ago, before the riot. Who knew where the real mother was. A family of sluts. That's what the Wilders were. Sluts.

Through the thin walls of the old townhouse, Angela had heard Joanna coughing all night. She was ill enough to be reported, taken away to the Central Compound and disposed of. What a stroke of luck that had been.

Angela hurried down the street. It was about time her

fortunes changed. Since Gabriel had fired her, the only job she could find was washing coal, filling a position vacated by the hoyden's sister, Eva. She hated every minute of the job. But even more, she hated being forced out of Gabriel Stone's world.

And who was to blame for her fall from grace?

Joanna Wilder.

The moment Angela had recognized the woman, she had turned her in—doing her civic duty, getting her own back and qualifying for a hefty reward in one strategic move. And today was payday.

She skittered across the cobblestones to Joanna's flat.

"Citizen!" she called. "It's Angela Beach."

A small man in a top hat ducked out of the flat. He held up a small dress. "You didn't tell us she had a kid."

For a moment, all Angela could do was gape at the agent's face. He had ugly pink scars on both sides of his mouth and blotches on his face and neck, where he had suffered other wounds that were still healing.

"Cat got your tongue, woman?"

"No, citizen, no. I'm sorry, what did you say?"

"I said, you never mentioned a kid."

"I thought the illness was enough. Is the child important?"

"Everything about a criminal is important."

Angela's heart skipped a beat. She didn't want to displease an agent of the Overseers. Her reward hung in the balance. Overseers used the slightest transgression to withhold food and favor. To ingratiate herself with the agent, she offered the only other tidbits of information she knew.

"She's probably at school, citizen. She looked old enough. She should be home any minute."

The agent peered down the street. "Well, that's good news." He glanced at Angela. "What's the kid's name?"

"I don't know. Verna or something. They just moved in."

"Hmm. Have you ever seen Gabriel Stone hanging around here?"

"The doctor?" Angela shook her head. "Of course not."

She would never betray Gabriel, even if she had seen him. Never. She loved him.

The short man shouted directions to his henchmen, ordering them to tie Joanna's hands and feet, take her to the coach and then drive the vehicle around the corner, out of sight. He ducked back into the apartment. Angela followed, worried that he was going to postpone her compensation.

"About the reward, citizen?"

The agent glanced down his broken nose at her. "What reward?"

"I was promised a reward for supplying information about the criminal."

He gave a curt laugh. "I don't handle rewards, citizen. Send an invoice to the Central Compound."

"But, citizen…"

"Out. You are interfering with a government operation." He held open the door and nodded at her to leave.

"But citizen!" she sputtered. "Might I have a receipt or something? To prove my claim?"

"I don't have time for that now." The agent slammed the door in her face.

For a moment, Angela stood on the stoop, mute with indignation. She raised her fist to pound on the door, but thought better of it and let her arm drop.

She knew if she sent an invoice, the paperwork would

be misplaced. She knew a reward would never arrive. That's just the way the Central Compound worked. She would have to be satisfied with the arrest of the hoyden, and leave it at that.

Next time, she would insist on credits up front. And when and if she ever saw the man with the scars again, she would refuse to tell him anything.

———

Eight-year-old Veronique Dunn paused at the corner of her block, immobilized by the warning sign on her doorstep. A chill shot down the backs of her legs as she stared at the Londo City flat she shared with her mother. A black scarf lay on the doorstep of her home.

The sign of trouble.

Her mother's stern voice echoed in her head. "If you see my scarf on the doorstep, Veronique, hide. Don't come back until the scarf is gone."

A gust of wind blew Veronique's dress against her legs. The October afternoon was cold and damp and had seeped into her bones during her long walk home from school. Her toes and fingers were blocks of ice. She had looked forward to a warm fire and cup of tea.

But now this scarf.

Veronique would never dream of disobeying her mother. She and her mother lived a nomadic life full of secrets and worry. From a very young age, she had been taught not to trust anyone, not to tell anyone where she lived or what her mother did for a living. She knew she had a father, but he worked on the northern borders, doing something her mother refused to talk about. Her mother put foul-smelling paste on her hair to dye it to a mousey brown, so she looked like every other girl in Londo City.

She hated that paste. And she hated looking ordinary. But her mother had insisted that she never draw attention to herself.

Worried and cold, Veronique ducked out of the street and ran into a nearby alley. Maybe if she waited a few minutes for the danger to pass, she could go home. All would be well. Her mother would not explain anything, as usual. But she would hug Veronique and tell her that she was so glad she was safe and that she was a good girl. The best. Her mother's hugs and praise were wonderful. All she needed.

She would have to wait for hugs and praise, though.

If Veronique and her mother been living in their old apartment, she would have gone to her friend Jane Ulrich's house to wait out the danger. But she and her mother had recently moved, and Veronique wasn't sure where Jane lived in relation to their new flat. It would be dark soon, and she could not take the chance of being found wandering the streets after curfew. Her mother would get in trouble if that happened.

Veronique would have to bide her time alone in this unfamiliar neighborhood until the danger passed or her mother whistled for her. Her mother's whistle could carry for blocks, and was an effective, anonymous method of communication.

After an hour, the scarf was still there. Rain began to fall. Veronique hurried back to the alley, found a pile of cardboard boxes and made a tiny enclosure to huddle in. She clutched her legs and sank her chin on her knees, waiting for her mother's whistle.

The whistle never came.

In the morning when she checked her street again, she saw the black scarf still there, like a dead crow lying on the doorstep. Fog rolled around Veronique's boots, as she stood at the end of her street, distraught.

"Mother, what has happened?" Veronique whispered. A sob caught in her throat. What if her mother had been taken away because of her illness? She had been sick for a week, barely able to get out of bed. People who got that sick often disappeared. Dread washed over Veronique. "What should I do, Mother?"

Cold and hungry and worried, Veronique trudged back to school. At least she would get a morning and midday meal there. Maybe her mother would come and get her at school. That had occurred a few times in the past, when they had moved to a new place without warning.

But after school, her mother was not waiting for her. And when Veronique returned to her new address, she saw the scarf still on the doorstep. A man in a greatcoat and top hat now stood at the door, tapping a cane in his hands and glaring up and down the street. He looked mean. And he was waiting for her. She could sense it.

Veronique's heart skipped a beat. She raced back to the alley and leaned against a brick building, trying not to cry. Her mother had always told her that crying never got a person anywhere. Thinking did.

She would force herself to think instead of succumbing to the panic flaring inside her.

It was clear that she would have to come back another time to search for her mother. The mean man would never let her into the flat. He might even abduct her. But she also knew that she couldn't face another freezing night in a cardboard box. Her only recourse was to try to find Jane's house. Jane would help her.

Veronique trotted down the alley and prayed she would find Jane's house before nightfall.

Visit Patricia Simpson's website
(https://patriciasimpson.com)
for purchase options.

www.ingramcontent.com/pod-product-compliance
Lightning Source LLC
Chambersburg PA
CBHW030932020726
47498CB00001B/214